THE BROKEN BILLIONAIRE

FRIENDS TO LOVERS

FRAZER FAMILY
BOOK THREE

ZOE DOD

Edited by
VICTORIA STRAW

MILKY DOWN PUBLISHING

Copyright © 2025 by Zoe Dod

All rights reserved.

No part of this book may be reproduced in any form or by any electronic or mechanical means, including information storage and retrieval systems, without written permission from the author, except for the use of brief quotations in a book review.

This is a work of fiction. Names, characters, places, incidents and dialogues are products of the author's imagination or are used fictitiously. Any resemblance to actual people, living or dead, or events is entirely coincidental.

The Broken Billionaire is written in British English.

ISBN ebook: 978-1-917413-04-6

ISBN paperback: 978-1-917413-05-3

Editor: Victoria Straw

Cover Design by ChristineCoverDesigns

❦ Formatted with Vellum

To Seema and Spike
Thank you for all the years of doggy love and cuddles. Run Free.
Forever in our hearts. Xxx

CHAPTER 1

ELIJAH

A wedding, its purpose—to celebrate the sanctity of marriage. For most, it's a joyous occasion where family and friends come together to celebrate the joining of a happy couple. In the case of my two brothers, Gabriel and now Caleb, that's true. They're both loved-up saps, devoted to their much better halves.

Their weddings are nothing like mine.

I focus on breathing in and out, my pulse roaring in my ears as I work to calm my racing heart.

I inhale, holding it for four, before exhaling softly, waiting for the pressure in my chest to ease.

I sit and grip the seat cushion next to me, observing my brother, Caleb. There's no trace of the gut-wrenching dread I experienced the night before my wedding. Instead, my younger brother is beaming, gushing about his up-and-coming nuptials. His twin and best friends share in his excitement.

Excitement that is palpable. His eyes are sparkling. He's practically dancing in his seat. If he checks his phone one more time, I think Gabriel's going to confiscate it. There are no thoughts of escape or concealment. It's clear to everyone he can't wait to make April his wife.

Caleb is happy. April is happy. Gabriel and his wife, Leah, are ecstatically happy.

The panic slowly subsides as I survey the room. Caleb is not me. Like Gabriel, he's marrying a woman he loves and who loves him completely. A woman who complements him in every way.

It's been years since I last saw my brother this at ease with himself.

Fuck!

I need some air.

I get up and head to the patio door, refusing to spoil my brother's celebration. Xander, one of Caleb's friends, calls over to me. I turn and offer a smile. The frown between his brows lets me know he's not buying it. I shake my head slightly, holding my breath and silently pleading he doesn't call me out. When he turns away, I exhale and continue my escape.

I step out onto the patio and look out over the manicured garden. One thing I can thank Darra for. But then I paid for an army of servants to help her. The house itself was a wedding gift from my parents. A four-bedroom detached stone cottage on the family estate. The seventeenth-century house still contains its oak beams and large fireplaces. The opposite of my apartment in the city. Which is made of glass, tiles, and stainless steel.

I sink onto one of the patio lounge chairs Lottie, my daughter, loves so much. Pleased, Caleb and April waited until summer before saying, 'I do'. Their initial plan was to have me sitting here freezing my balls off in mid-winter.

I inhale deeply, allowing the peace and tranquillity of The New Forest to sink in. This past eighteen months have been a roller coaster, and I'm tired. Tired of the speculation and questions, tired of work, tired of the endless battle between our divorce lawyers. Our marriage was nothing but a sham for years. One I tried and failed to protect Lottie and the rest of my family from.

Instead of protecting those I care about, I alienated and pushed them away. Now I have to fix it. I rest my forearms on my thighs and hang my head. The stretch in the back of my neck soothes the tension I'm carrying.

A bark of raucous laughter comes from behind me, followed by more cheers and chants. Caleb and his friends know how to party.

The door opens, and I look up, staring straight ahead.

"Hey," Gabriel says, appearing at my side. "Is everything all right?"

I turn to face my brother and hold up my glass.

"Just getting some air."

He tilts his head and pauses. His eyes miss nothing.

I turn away. It's impossible to hide anything from Gabriel.

I'm surprised when he lets it drop.

"Thank you for letting us use your house this evening. Caleb's attempts to see April would have been disastrous. It's bad enough with all the sappy text messages."

Smiling, I return my gaze to the garden.

Smiling is something I'm trying to do more these days.

"Glad it could be of use."

Since the divorce, the house has sat empty. After our marriage collapsed years earlier, I moved to London to be nearer my office. Darra stayed at the house with Lottie, and I visited on weekends. Darra liked the comfort and support of the staff I employed. But with everything finalised, living on my family's estate was not something Darra wanted to do.

"He's happy," I acknowledge.

"He is."

I feel Gabe's hand land on my shoulder.

He understands my life better than my other siblings and is privy to more than the others.

We fall into silence until Gabe speaks.

"When does Lottie leave for Italy?"

I take a long sip of my drink before exhaling.

"Two days. She'll spend most of the summer there. Darra has enlisted her in an art school that offers Italian lessons. She'll be back for Mum's birthday weekend."

"And you? What are you going to do while she's gone?"

"Work. We've got a new release due in a few weeks," I say.

Gabriel tuts. "Other than work? You can't spend the entire summer locked in your office. It's not healthy. Take it from a reformed workaholic."

"I know what you're trying to do, but I'm not going there," I say.

All loved up, and he thinks the rest of the world wants that, too. Both he and Caleb have done a complete one eighty on their feelings towards commitment and relationships. Where I'm concerned, I've been there and done that. Not to mention, once burned… Just the thought of getting involved with someone else is enough to bring me out in hives.

Gabriel doesn't let up.

"I'm not talking about getting serious with anyone. I'm just saying. It's been eight months since your divorce. You've barely been out with friends. Would it be so bad to socialise? Why don't you at least join us on boys' night?"

"I'll think about it," I say, my tone totally non-committal.

Gabriel huffs.

"Fine. I promise to seriously think about it," I concede. "But Lottie's happiness going forward is my number one priority. I'm not sacrificing that for anything or anyone. So much has changed for her. She needs stability."

The thought of meeting someone, giving up control.

Worse still, there being friction with Lottie. That's the last thing I need. Lottie has had enough to deal with, with her mother and me fighting constantly. I want to give her a peaceful environment. At least for the next couple of years.

"Thinking about it is enough for now," Gabriel says, squeezing my shoulder. "But you also have to think about your own happiness. You're not an island, Eli."

I drop my chin to my chest. "Maybe not, but I've certainly done a great job of isolating myself."

I know I've not been the easiest person to be around. There are a lot of bridges to rebuild. For years, I kept everyone at arm's length, thinking I was protecting them from my mistakes. Instead, all I caused was more heartache.

After years of being caught in a toxic marriage, where I lived each day under the threat of having my daughter ripped from my life. No, I don't ever want to open myself up to that kind of vulnerability again. But I took all that I had to because of my love for my daughter. Now that is over.

"The adoption is complete?" Gabriel asks, sensing I want to change the subject.

"Yes."

Darra can no longer threaten me with Lottie.

Not that she wants to. She received the vineyard in Tuscany as part of our divorce settlement, along with most of what I accrued over the years. I only asked that she stay away from my company and my art collection. My lawyer was horrified, but I got what I wanted most—Lottie.

Darra finally agreed to let me adopt our daughter. Although I think Lottie's insistence had more to do with it than mine. She's quite the little firecracker when she wants to be. It's also the reason she's spending the summer with her mother. To rebuild their relationship.

Gabriel clinks his glass against mine, making me turn my head. I'm surprised by his smile.

"Are you going to tell the others?" he asks.

It's been a bone of contention between us since Lottie arrived on his doorstep, having overheard Darra and me arguing. Not the way I wanted my thirteen-year-old at the time to find out I wasn't her biological father, that her mother had tricked me into marrying her while carrying another man's child.

"It's not important. I won't have Lottie suffering for her mother's indiscretions. I'm her father. That's all that matters."

Gabriel's reply is cut off as Quentin pops his head out of the door, making us both turn.

"Are you two coming back in? You're missing all the fun."

Gabriel responds, "Soon."

They exchange a look, before he turns and disappears back inside.

I sigh.

Of course, I'm the poor divorcé who has escaped from a disastrous marriage. Everyone knows it. My ex was not exactly discreet.

"Lottie's a great kid. She loves you. You're her dad, first and foremost. Nothing is going to change that. Divorcing Darra means you can now move forward with your life. Move on."

Running a hand through my hair, I sigh.

"I'm thirty-seven. I'm not sure what that looks like," I tell him truthfully.

In my heart, I know Lottie is happier that her mother and I are no longer at each other's throats. But I've remained trapped in a toxic cycle for so long that I'm numb.

"You need to be kind to yourself. Don't overthink things. We Frazers do that. It's a common trait."

I can't help the laugh that escapes. Since childhood, everyone has known Gabriel to analyse and re-analyse everything, looking for patterns. His ability with numbers is scary.

"All I'm saying is don't shut yourself off. I understand the need to protect yourself, but let those who love you back in. Lean on us the way we've leaned on you over the years. You might be the eldest, but as I said before, you're not an island. There is still time to reset and move on."

The door bursts open behind us. An identical face to the one in front of me appears.

"Why are you two skulking out here?" Caleb claps an arm around both our shoulders. "You appear excessively serious for the night before my wedding. You should be celebrating. Someone has finally tamed me."

Gabriel chuckles, and I smile. Caleb is right and more than a little tipsy. The beautiful April has tamed our playboy brother. His soulmate. She loves him as openly as he loves her. They complement each other, make the other better-stronger.

"Plus, I need your help. Those reprobates in there are not listening. I refuse to be hungover tomorrow. Tristan got out Uno. He's making up the drinking rules. I need you both back inside."

Gabriel shakes his head. "Grow a pair," he tuts at his brother.

I can't talk. I got plastered the night before my wedding. Drowning my sorrows, I think the word for it is.

"Go to the drinks cabinet," I tell him. "There's a bottle. It has a small red dot. Zero alcohol—tastes like shit, but if they test it, they won't know the difference. Use that bottle for your shots."

Caleb reaches up and pats my cheek. At six foot two, he's not small, but against my six foot six, I tower over my brothers.

"Big brother always looking out for us. What would we

do without you?" he says, his eyes shining with the amount of alcohol his friends have him drinking.

"Let's get back inside before your friends trash my house," I say, heading for the door.

Another cheer comes through the open door as we walk back inside and rejoin the festivities.

CHAPTER 2

PEN

Mum places a plate of food next to me.

"You need to eat. You've been working all day."

I continue to stare at my laptop, my brain whirling as it works through the figures in front of me. I hate going through the monthly reports. Give me code any day of the week.

"Thanks," I say, turning my head as I scoop a forkful of food into my mouth. I hate eating near my computer, but I need to get these finished.

"Oh, wow." I close my eyes and moan at the taste and texture as it explodes on my tongue. "This is delicious."

Mum chuckles as I open my eyes. I close my laptop and push it to one side, replacing it with the plate of beef stew.

"I don't know how you make it taste this good."

Mum pulls out a chair and sits next to me, picking up her own knife and fork.

"Years of practice. There's plenty more in the kitchen."

I take another mouthful, savouring the home-cooked food.

"Thank you," I say, suddenly realising how hungry I am.
When did I last eat?

"Don't thank me. It gives me something to do. I've never been one to sit around twiddling my thumbs," she says. "You've very kindly ensured I never have to lift another finger, so I shall continue to spend my time doing the things I enjoy. And cooking is one of them."

I chuckle. "That's why you volunteer at the local food bank on Wednesday and Friday, help at the children's hospice on Thursday and spend Monday and Tuesday organising games and events at the local old people's home."

"Idle hands and all that, and you can talk! How many charities are you currently supporting? You were teaching at the local secondary school, only a couple of weeks ago."

"Like mother, like daughter," I say, grinning.

This woman is my hero, my idol, my best friend. My deadbeat dad disappeared as soon as he saw a positive pregnancy test, leaving Mum, a sixteen-year-old, holding the baby. My grandparents helped out as much as they could, but they weren't wealthy, so Mum worked two jobs to support us. She gave up her own life to raise me. It's why, as soon as I made my fortune, I bought her a house. I pay all her bills, ensuring she never has to work or worry about anything again. At fifty-one, she looks ten years younger. Her skin is smooth, and her hair has kept its dark brown colour, with only a few stray grey hairs. She dated during my childhood, but being a single mum was difficult, so none of her relationships lasted. Not that she ever made me feel unwanted or unloved. The total opposite.

"When does Kris's flight get in?" she asks.

Kristophe Lansdown, my fiancé and soon-to-be husband. In three months, I'll be moving country and into the next phase of my life.

"His plane lands at six tomorrow morning. His driver will have him here by eight," I tell her.

Lucky for him, he can shower and get changed on the plane. The beauty of owning his own private jet.

"How long is he staying? You're meeting up with Kat this week, aren't you?"

"We were, but unfortunately, work calls. He'll be heading back straight after the wedding."

Silence descends, and I sit back.

"Spill," I say.

She sighs.

"I don't know. You both lead such busy lives. I'm surprised you have time for one another. He resides in the US. You live here—or at least until the wedding. What happens when you move there? I know you're setting up an office, but what about friends? Will Kris be taking time off to help you settle in? What happens when you have children?"

I bite down on my smile and take the hand she has resting on the table, giving it a gentle squeeze. She's always been my protector, my champion. Not to mention a total romantic.

"Don't worry, everything will be fine. I know a lot of Kris's friends and colleagues. I've met them over the years. Remember, we've been working together for a long time."

She drops her gaze, turning her hand under mine and wrapping her fingers around it.

"I know... I know. But working together and living together are two very different things." She holds up her hands in surrender. "I just worry. It's a mother's prerogative."

"You need to stop worrying about me. I'm thirty-five. Not exactly a spring chicken. I've spent my life..."

"I know—you've spent your life building up your business, and as your mother, I could not be prouder. But as your mother, I'm allowed to worry about you." She pauses, her eyes rising to mine. "I'm just concerned. This is all so quick. It's..." her voice trails off.

It's true. Kris and I went from friends to lovers overnight. But we're both decisive people. When we know what we want, we go for it.

I run my thumb over the back of her hand.

"It's not like he's a stranger. I've known him for years, both professionally and through the various charity events we've both attended. Please don't worry. I know what I'm doing."

Mum's brows furrow. "Do you?"

My career has eclipsed my social life. I've dated over the years, but before Kris, I had never found anyone who actually understood me. They either wanted more than I was willing to give, or it became clear my money was their driving force.

With Kris, he's man enough to have no issues with dating a powerful woman. He runs his own successful company and is wealthy in his own right. He's also ten years older than me, handsome, and, like me, ready to settle down. Our timing could not be more perfect.

"Don't get me wrong, Kris is a wonderful man."

"He is. And we're perfect together. We both want the same things in life, and he gets me. He's good to me, Mum."

Kris and I built our relationship on mutual trust and respect. As Mum said, we're extremely busy with our careers. We both have a lot of people relying on us. However, we want someone to come home to. Who understands the demands we're under and accepts them. Something I never thought I'd find.

"I just worry. You're giving up so much more than he is. You're moving halfway around the world. It's not like you've even spent that much time together, not really," she adds, her eyebrows drawing together.

I shrug. I understand her concern.

"One of us had to make the move and you know I've been wanting to set up an office in the US. As for spending time together. We will be doing more than enough of that going forward. We have a lot of common interests."

She tuts again, making me laugh.

"All those historical romances you read, Mum. The hero and heroine never live together before they get married. It's not like either of us has a shotgun to our heads."

She pats my hand and smiles, although it doesn't quite reach her eyes.

"Ignore me."

I squeeze her hand again.

I can't disagree with what she says. I *am* making the biggest move. Kris's life won't change as much as mine, but if we want to have a relationship, we can't do that on opposite sides of the globe. We have to make sacrifices.

Over the past two years, I've watched my friends fall in love with their other halves. Find *their person*. Gabriel met Leah, and their love developed from their friendship. Caleb and April. Theirs developed from passion and a mutual goal. Seeing them fall in love made me realise it's possible. With Kris, I can have that. For the first time, I have someone other than Mum supporting me. I'll be part of a team, a strong partnership.

Tomorrow, Caleb marries April. He was always so cynical, hid behind his playboy exterior. He's transformed his life. Settled down, both externally and internally. It's like April brings him a level of calm I've never seen before. It's the same when I look at her. Her prickly demeanour is gone. She flows now. Together, they light up a room.

I'm not comparing myself to Caleb or Gabriel. Kris and I share a stable and solid relationship. He'll make a fantastic father. He lost his first wife in his early twenties. I know he's dated since, but like me, his focus has been on work. It's why he's such a successful businessman.

"With Kris, what I see is what I get. I love that about him."

"I'm sorry, I shouldn't have said anything," she says.

I smile at her. "Yes, you should. If you can't say it to me, who can? I've always relied on you to call me out on my *shit*."

"Penelope Dawson, language!"

We both grin, but I can tell from the creases around her eyes she's concerned. When she catches me looking, she shrugs.

"You're my baby. I know I'm being silly and selfish. I'm going to miss you."

She sniffs.

I get up and envelop her in a hug.

"Don't be a silly goose," I say. "I'll always be your daughter, whatever. And you know Kris is renovating a cottage on his estate for you. It will be ready in a couple of months. Then you can join us if you want to, or visit."

She looks up at me.

Mum is just five foot five as opposed to my six foot. According to her I get my height from my dad.

"It's just a big move, and I've always wanted only the best for you. I know you've spent your life building up the business, and now you've achieved all you have, you're looking to settle down." She sighs again before adding. "I like Kris. You know I do."

She pats my cheeks as I step away.

I've dated plenty of men. Kris is the first to see me as an equal. He's never wanted to change me. Has always encouraged me to follow my dreams.

"I've kind of done the opposite to you. My biological clock is ticking. It's a good thing Kris and I met. It was fate. For me, it's kind of now or never. I don't want to be an old mum. Not when I've seen how awesome it is to have a young spritely one."

Mum laughs aloud at that.

"Spritely, I'm not so sure."

"I really don't want you to worry about me," I say truthfully.

"I can't help it. I'll always worry about you. You're my baby—all six feet of you, and you always will be."

We hug tightly.

God, I'm going to miss this woman when I leave.

CHAPTER 3

PEN

*E*veryone turns as the orchestra plays Handel's Eternal Source of Light Devine. Lois and Nick, April's half-siblings, followed by a grown-up-looking Lottie, step through the entrance of the marquee, their baskets filled with rose petals. All three are sporting the widest grins as they make their way forward, sprinkling petals as they go.

A gasp goes up as April appears, her arm linked through that of her foster father, Julian. I glance at Caleb. His eyes glisten as he watches her walk toward him. Their eyes meet and lock, and it's as if no one else exists.

The atmosphere is electric, as everyone holds their breath.

A lump forms in my throat as I watch the scene unfold. Kris's hand takes mine. I lower my gaze to our intertwined fingers, then back up to his face. I offer him a smile, dropping my head to his shoulder as I return my gaze to the happy couple. A weight settles in my chest.

April is glowing. Under her veil, her long, blond hair is half pinned up in tiny swirls against her head. Her makeup is minimal and flawless, her natural radiance and grace shining through. Her gown is simple yet classic. A princess line dress that hugs her dancer's curves. The intricate lace bodice overlay shimmers as she makes her way past us.

As she reaches him, Caleb steps forward. His face fills with wonderment and love. I'm not sure if they're aware of those around them, having once again got lost in each other. It's always the same when they're together. The constant touches, the silly grins, the yearning looks.

Lottie steps forward and reaches for April's bouquet. April jumps as if snapping back into the present, making everyone chuckle and Caleb grin. She turns and whispers something to Lottie, who nods, clutching the bouquet to her chest, before stepping back and sitting beside her dad.

Julian steps forward and places April's hand in Caleb's, and a pre-emptive cheer goes up, making them both smile.

Lottie whispers something to her dad, drawing my attention. Elijah looks down at her. My heart twinges when his arm comes up and around her shoulder, his love for his daughter shining through.

The vicar speaks.

April and Caleb exchange their vows. The loving couple at the front tumble over their words, their voices wavering as they're both overcome. By the time they're pronounced husband and wife, there isn't a dry eye in the house.

Caleb helps to lift April's veil, his hands moving to cradle her face, his thumbs wiping away her tears. Her hands clasp his wrists before she reaches up and brushes a tear from his cheek. They laugh as they stand lost in each other, leaving us, their guests, in no doubt of their love.

My stomach clenches at the sight, surprising me. It's not like I haven't seen these two around one another.

"You may now kiss the bride."

Caleb cradles April's face in his hands before drawing her

towards him. Their lips touch, and my stomach flips as their kiss deepens.

I break out in a hot flush. Is this what drives Mum to read her romance novels? Is this the love, passion, and soul-mates she always talks about? I turn my head to where she's sitting next to me, her cheeks damp. I smile and place my free hand over hers, giving it a squeeze. She turns her head and looks at me, her eyes glistening, before being drawn back to the happy couple. The marquee erupts in whoops and cheers. That's what happens when your guest list is made up of close friends and family.

By the time they break apart, smiles have replaced most tears. I doubt anyone watching questions their love for one another.

Kris hands me his handkerchief, which I accept, dabbing at the corner of each eye.

"Thanks," I say, smiling at him. "I think I got something in my eye."

"Love does that to people," he says, smiling across at me. "It was an emotional ceremony. Caleb is a lucky man."

I wonder, for the first time, if his wedding to his first wife, Annie, was like this. Full of love and excitement for the future. A future that was ripped from them both.

"He is," I say, squeezing his hand. "He's spent a long time looking for his person, and I'm so happy he's finally found her."

"You're going to miss them," Kris says.

I smile at him.

"I will, but it's not like I'm leaving the planet. I'll be travelling back and forth with work. We can catch up then."

We stand up, and I slide my arm through his, stepping into his side.

An excited voice comes from nearby. "Aunty Pen, Kris!"

We turn to face an eager Lottie walking towards us.

"What do you think?" she says, stopping in front of us and giving us a twirl, showing off her dress and new shoes.

"You look beautiful and so grown up. I almost didn't recognise you," I say, earning myself a grin.

I can't believe she'll be turning fifteen in a few months. Gone is the little girl, replaced by a beautiful young woman. A sense of sadness descends as I know once I move, I'll no longer be her first port of call as I have been over the years.

How time flies.

I pull her in for a hug.

"How is my favourite goddaughter?" I ask, shaking off my melancholy. "Are you all set for your trip to Italy?"

Lottie laughs. "I'm currently your only goddaughter. And I'm good." She rolls her eyes. "Dad has had me check everything twenty times to ensure I haven't forgotten anything."

"That's what Dads are for," I tell her.

"I better go. Dad and Granny need my help. Granny has given us all a list of jobs to do," she says before turning tail and leaving us as quickly as she appeared.

My eyes drift to Elijah, who is deep in conversation with his mother.

"She's a lovely girl," Kris says.

"She is. She's had a tough time with her parents' divorce. But she's coming through it," I say, watching as she joins Elijah, his arm snaking around her shoulders.

"She's got an amazing network of people around her," Kris says, his eyes following mine.

I watch Lottie's face light up as Franny says something to her.

"That she does."

I move towards the exit, feeling the need to get some air, the marquee becoming claustrophobic.

"Let's get a drink," I say, taking Kris's hand and leading him toward the house and the fully stocked bar.

We step inside and find Caleb and April surrounded by their friends.

"Pen," April calls over as we walk in.

I smile at her as we change direction.

She steps forward, and I pull her in for a hug.

"Congratulations. You look beautiful," I say before holding her away from me and taking in her gown. "You look like a princess, as Lottie would say."

"She did when we were getting ready." April chuckles. "I can't believe we got through our vows. I don't think I've ever felt so nervous."

I squeeze her arm. "There wasn't a dry eye in the place," I tell her, making Caleb chuckle. His arm slides around her waist, her body curving into his.

"Including us," Caleb admits, laughing. "Not long now. This will be you two in a few months," he adds, shaking Kris's hand. "Pleased you could make it, Kris."

"I wouldn't have missed it," Kris replies. "It was a beautiful ceremony."

Caleb and April look at one another. If this was a cartoon, little birds and love hearts would float around them right about now.

We step away as more guests move forward to congratulate them.

"A drink?" Kris asks.

"Please," I say before we make our way towards Gabriel, Leah, and little Callum.

CHAPTER 4

ELIJAH

As the evening festivities slow down, I make my escape. Lottie has joined April's students in our old games room, where Mum's hired a projector and gaming equipment after we moved our old gaming machines to the community centre next door to April's dance studio.

I make my way to the pool. I long to shed my suit, dive into the warm water, and swim until I've relieved the stress of the day. But today isn't about me, and the last thing my mother needs is drunk guests taking a dip.

I drop onto one of the sun loungers positioned around the side and stare into the blue-lit water. I've spent countless hours at this pool since learning to swim. It's always been my safe place.

When my hobby and love for the water became an obsessive goal to make the Olympic swimming team, I was driven by an unshakeable force to be the best. I swam every morning and every night, weight trained, ate a specific diet, and had the best coaches. I trained for years, only to have it end with a snap.

My hand goes to my ankle, rubbing the now almost invisible scar through my trouser leg.

A snap it truly was. It happened during my final year of university. It was January, and I was cycling to the pool early one morning. I hit a patch of black ice and lost control of my bike. I hit the kerb and came off, breaking my ankle. Surgery, followed by months of physiotherapy, meant I missed out on team selection. When I finally did make it back into the water, I knew I'd never regain the form I once had. With that and finding out about Darra's pregnancy, I refocused my attention. I concentrated on my finals and building a future for myself and my new family rather than trying to reclaim a lost dream. Frazer Cyber Security went from being an idea to a company whose growth over the past fifteen years has surpassed my wildest dreams.

There's a movement to my right.

"Hi," the last voice I expect to hear says. "Are you shirking your duties, Mr Frazer?"

I look up, my heart racing.

"All duties complete. I've officially signed off for the evening."

A flush of adrenalin shoots through my body at the sound of Pen's voice.

"Impressive. I would have assumed Franny would have run you ragged until the last guest left," Pen says.

She's the only person who gets away with calling my mother, Francesca Frazer, Franny. And Mum won't hear a word against it.

"I could ask, what you're doing out here?"

"Reminiscing," she says, stepping closer. "Why are you skulking in the dark on your own?"

"Who says I'm skulking?"

"Sat in the dark, by an empty pool, no one else around in the middle of a party?"

She has a point.

"Getting some fresh air?"

"The marquee is outside, and they've taken the sides off. Plenty of fresh air over there."

The laughter and music from the DJ reaches us, and Pen raises an eyebrow.

"Fine. I admit—I'm hiding."

Pen drops herself onto the sunbed next to mine, putting her feet up.

"Do you want me to go?"

I turn and cock my own eyebrow as she makes herself comfortable.

When her gaze meets mine, she smirks.

"Depends," I hear myself say.

"On what?"

"Are you going to sit and offer me platitudes about my divorce or how I'll meet someone else? I'm still young, with my whole life ahead of me?"

Pen sits back against the raised back and shrugs.

I grumble, and Pen chuckles again. The sound light against my tension.

"I wasn't intending to," she says. "So you're out here hiding from the divorce sympathisers?"

"Honestly, if someone else gives me *that look* or offers me their sympathies," I say.

"They mean well, and this *is* a wedding. Everyone is all about *the love*," Pen says, her fingers making inverted speech marks in the air. Not that she will believe it. She was never a fan of platitudes. It was one of the reasons we got on so well. She was a straight talker, said it how she saw it.

"No shit," I say, making her laugh.

"You know what I mean. *Love is in the air,*" she sings badly while batting her eyelashes.

I laugh. The sound surprising me.

It's been a long time since I sat with Pen, and we laughed. Truly laughed. She always had a way of making the world seem lighter.

Another thing my marriage took from me. My best friend.

"You do know it's only going to get worse?" she says, leaning forward.

"What do you mean?"

"You are now the only single Frazer male left. All those social climbers your brothers have been fighting off—"

"Will be sorely disappointed. That is one path I never intend to tread again," I say, running a hand down my face.

The mere thought of committing myself to someone ever again, giving them that sort of power over me, makes me want to break out in a cold sweat. I turn my head sideways and groan.

Pen shakes her head. "Never say never."

"I can. I've been there, done that, and got the t-shirt, Lottie is my priority now," I say. "I thought you were going to make me feel better, not wind me up."

"Just pointing it out. You got away with it the first time around, unlike poor Gabriel and Caleb."

I did. Darra was the perfect shield. The *society* mothers and their *husband hunting* daughters left me alone. But the last laugh was on me. I ended up married to the biggest social climber of them all.

And now here I am, divorced.

As Pen pointed out, it's going to be free season on my ass. I grimace at the thought.

I turn back to face the water, my elbows resting on my knees.

"I forgot how much of a know-it-all you are."

She leans forward and pats my shoulder, withdrawing her hand almost instantly.

I turn my head again.

"What are you really doing out here?"

She purses her lips, biting the skin where her lip ring used to be.

"Taking a break," she says, and I incline my head.

Pen huffs. "From all the *congratulations, let me see your ring, to how are your wedding plans going.*"

It's my turn to chuckle, my eyes drop to the enormous rock Pen is sporting on her engagement finger.

"It is a wedding, after all," I parrot.

"Touché," she says.

"No Kristophe?" I ask.

She shakes her head. "He's inside talking to *The Boys.*"

"I wish I could go for a swim," I say suddenly.

"Nothing changes. There are a lot of memories tied up with this pool."

We both turn and face the water.

We spent every summer around this pool. It was in the time *before*, a time when responsibility was nothing but a word, and laughter filled the air. My friends and I returned here every holiday. Zach and Jaxson were on the university swim team with me and would help me train in the holidays. Darra, my girlfriend, and some of her friends would tag along, and eventually, I convinced Pen to join us. I was different then, sociable. Focused on making the Olympic team. I had my whole life ahead of me.

"We had fun during those summers."

"Including you and Jax teaching me to swim after I nearly drowned," she says.

My breath catches at the memory. I'll never forget that day. No one knew Pen couldn't swim. No one but Kat, and she'd gone inside. We were messing around, childish horseplay, when Darra pushed Pen into the deep end. We all thought she was messing around. It was only when Kat returned and plunged in, pulling a half-drowned Pen from the water, we uncovered the truth. My sister ripped us all a new one that day, and her ongoing friendship with Pen was formed.

"The guys and I swore, by the end of the summer, you'd be swimming."

"And I was. You were all very bossy if I recall, but great teachers. If not for you, I wouldn't have swum off the Great Barrier Reef or been surfing in California."

My heart swells. "You always were one to make the most of something."

After my initial panic, I'd been so angry with Pen. Water safety was my number one rule. It was ingrained in me from childhood.

"I still can't believe you didn't tell any of us you couldn't swim."

I watch her shrug but don't miss the twitch of her lip.

"Really? A little hard to admit when you're surrounded by the university's team of elite swimmers. *Oh guys, by the way, I can't swim.*" She chuckles again, the sound filling the air. "And it wasn't a case of not being able to swim. I could manage the basic strokes. I learned those at school. I just needed to be where I could put my feet down."

This is nothing new. I quizzed her about it after the event. With her mum always working and money tight, there'd been no after-school swimming lessons for Pen. It was the first time I realised how privileged I was and why it became our mission to ensure Pen could confidently swim by the end of the summer.

"If I remember. It was the perfect trade-off. I helped you with your coding, and you taught me to swim. A win-win."

My chest aches as memories of our time together. She shuffles forward, making herself level with me, her feet now on the floor.

"I can't believe that was sixteen years ago," she says wistfully. "We were all so young and carefree."

"Life is very different now," I mumble.

Silence descends as we stare at the water.

"The wedding was beautiful," Pen says eventually.

"Very different to mine, you mean," I say.

I sense Pen turning her head towards me.

"That's not what I was going to say."

I turn my head to face her, our eyes locking. "But it's true."

"I'm sorry it didn't work out between you and Darra," Pen says.

"Are you?"

She pauses as if weighing up her answer. She sighs. "No."

It's my turn to chuckle. "Always brutally honest."

Pen shrugs. "I didn't like the way she treated people. You most of all, but it wasn't my business. She gave you Lottie, and she's the best of both of you."

My heart warms at her words, but my chest constricts. Would she say that if she knew the truth? Pen's love for my daughter, her goddaughter is renowned. She's stepped in over the years and supported her, been like a second mother when Darra was too wrapped up in herself.

I shudder to think what would have happened if Pen had been in the country the day Lottie overheard Darra and me. It would have been Pen who Lottie ran to, and that would have been more serious than Gabriel and Leah.

"Good to know," I say.

"So what next?" Pen asks. "You've clearly dismissed hooking up with any of the *social climbers*. What are your plans while Lottie's away?"

"The usual," I admit. "Run my company. We have a release going out. I may take Gabriel up on his offer to attend boys' night."

"Ah, the infamous *boys' nights*. You should. They're fun, and it will get you out. I'm going to miss the girls' night equivalent."

I know from Leah and April that Pen is part of their girl squad.

"How are your wedding plans coming along?"

Pen groans.

"Sorry."

She sighs. "I can't believe it's been seven years since we last chatted like this."

We both turn our heads and face the water. The blue light dances on the surface.

"After Dad's funeral," I say.

Pen came to my office. She, Mum, and Dad had been close. Dad's death hit her hard. She'd bought a bottle of my dad's favourite whisky and two glasses. We talked all afternoon, reminiscing over time gone by. Finally raising a glass to the man he was. We celebrated my father's life that afternoon, but then it was back to usual the next time we met—pleasantries.

"I said it then, and I'll say it now. Thank you for all you've done for Lottie over the years. She's going to miss you. I'm sorry Darra stopped me from taking her out of school for your wedding."

Pen sighs. "Don't thank me. Every moment spent with her is a blessing. I appreciate being in her life. As it stands, I should have checked before the save-the-date cards went out."

There's a small pause, and I feel a hand touch my arm, squeezing before it disappears.

"Don't be too hard on yourself, Elijah. You always were your own worst critic. That drive of yours *to be the best*. You've done an amazing job. Lottie is a wonderful young woman."

"And you always were my biggest cheerleader," I say before I can stop the words.

There is another pause as Pen stands.

Shit!

"I better go back in," Pen says. "Kris will wonder where I've disappeared to."

A sudden pressure builds in my chest, and I draw in a breath.

"Are you coming?"

"I think I'll hang out here for a bit longer."

Pen comes to stand in front of me.

"Take care of yourself," she says, as I find myself looking up at her.

We were the perfect team. Her partnership inspired me to excel. My natural competitive streak taking over. I was determined she wouldn't beat me, but she always did.

"I'll leave you in peace."

She smiles down at me.

This Pen is so different from the initial Penelope Dawson I brought home that first weekend. Gone is the harsh white and black makeup and a face full of metal piercings. Now she is polished. Her makeup is flawless, her hair styled in dark waves. Her charity shop buys have been replaced with designer chic that shows off her toned and tanned physique. And gone is her prickly, defensive demeanour. In its place is a woman quick to laugh and happy to help those she cares for.

"Take care of yourself, and good luck with the wedding plans. Kris is a lucky man," I say, knowing I mean every word.

My chest constricts.

Pen, out of everyone I know, deserves to be happy. She's worked harder and given more back to society and everyone around her than anyone I've ever met.

"Thank you. Take care of you, big man," she says, giving a small smile. "This has been…nice."

I chuckle at her choice of word.

"Nice is a biscuit," I say, smiling back. "You better get back."

She nods before turning and walking away.

I watch her disappear into the gardens and out of view.

My heart sinks as my once best friend walks away—again.

I rest my forearms on my knees and stare into the water. Fate intervened between Pen and me. I should be happy for her, but the pain in my chest refuses to subside. Out of everyone I know, she deserves to find true happiness. If Kristophe Lansdown can give her what she wants, then I wish them well.

I press the heel of my palm into the muscle of my chest and rub as I stare at the water.

"This is where you've got to," another voice from the past states.

I look up and smile.

"I needed a break," I admit.

Jaxson drops himself onto the sun lounger next to mine.

"Wanting to jump in the pool and swim away the stress of the day?" he asks.

"If only," I say.

"Was that Pen I just saw leaving?" Jax asks.

"It was," I say with a sigh.

"A long day?"

"Don't you know it."

Jax leans over and squeezes my shoulder. He's one of the few people who understands the stress of today. He was by my side throughout my wedding to Darra.

"Caleb and April, aren't you and Darra," he says. "You can take comfort in that. April is very much in love with your brother. Not to mention he's completely besotted with her."

I can hear the amusement in his voice. I know he was there when Caleb first met April in New York. My brother confided in him about *the girl who got away*. He and Caleb have been business associates and friends for many years. Jax, having built up a successful architectural business specialising in energy efficiency, and Caleb, Frazer Development. Together they've transformed large portions of the capital.

I turn my head to face my old friend.

"I know, and I'm happy for them. Both my baby brothers have found great partners."

"And you? What next?" Jax asks.

"Now I concentrate on Lottie. She's suffered enough with all mine and Darra's fighting. It's time I put her first."

"Remember, her dad being happy will make Lottie happy," he says, his tone tinged with a hint of sadness.

I look back at the water.

If only I knew what that looked like.

"I'm sorry," I say. "I'm sorry I shut you out." I run a hand through my hair. "I've been saying that a lot recently."

Jax turns his head to face me, so I move mine to look at him. We exchange a look, mirroring a moment long past.

"Hey, I'm here now. And what's fifteen years between genuine friends?" he adds, smiling widely.

I chuckle.

"Only you," I tell him, shaking my head.

"No," he says. "Every one of us is here whenever you're ready."

I choke back the lump forming in my throat.

"How about we grab dinner, catch up? I'm not heading back to the US for a month," Jax says.

I smile, the pressure in my chest easing.

"I'd like that."

CHAPTER 5

PEN

I smile as Kat, makes her way towards our table. She turns and says something to the maitre d', who stops in their tracks.

I stand up as she reaches the table, pulling her in for a hug.

"It's good to see you," I say, even though it's only been a week since I saw her at Caleb and April's wedding. Work has kept us apart a lot recently.

"You too. The wedding was crazy. I forget how many aunts, uncles, and cousins we have." She rolls her eyes, making me chuckle. "Mum was determined to keep us all busy. *No time for idle gossip.* Lunch today, however, is fair game."

I laugh as we take our seats. Kat's eyes sparkle with mischief as she takes her napkin and places it on her lap.

"Did Kris make it back to the US okay?"

I nod. I'd called Kat to let her know Kris would not be joining us. "He did. He's disappointed that he missed our lunch and apologises."

"The joy of being engaged to a businessperson. Man or

woman, we are first and foremost married to our professions."

She understands that better than anyone. Like me, her social/personal life has taken a back seat to her business. Although I plan for this to change once Kris and I get married and start a family.

Kat's a businesswoman in charge of the family's international hotel chain. There's never a off day. Unlike Mum and some of my other friends, Kris's work commitment doesn't faze her.

Kathryn Frazer and I have been friends for over fifteen years. Our friendship grew over the summers I spent at the Frazer's home but was cemented when she pulled me half-drowned from their swimming pool. Her then dating and living with one of Elijah and my uni friends, Zach, sealed the deal.

"Did you speak to Zach at the wedding?" I ask, knowing how much she was dreading seeing him.

It may be nearly three years since they split, but it was an awkward breakup. He proposed, getting down on one knee, and announced he wanted them to start a family. Kat freaked. She later told me she didn't want to, at least not with him. Nothing like realising you don't love the person you've been living with for the past seven years.

Kat inclines her head. "It was strange. Five years of on-again, off-again dating, followed by seven years living together—still, I question it all. I can't explain it. It was nice seeing him. He looks well, but there was nothing. No pang of regret."

"And you were worried there would be?"

"I suppose so... My mind held a vague, fleeting idea, wondering if I'd been too hasty in turning down his proposal. I'm not getting any younger."

I can understand her position. It's one I've found myself

in. We've spent so many years concentrating on building up our businesses that our private lives have taken a back seat.

"It wasn't right. You said so yourself. It wouldn't have been fair to either of you."

"I know. It's just. Starting over. It's been nearly three years. I don't have time to socialise, to meet anyone. I just worry it's going to get dusty up here on this shelf."

"Hey, the right person will come along. Look at me," I say, winking across at her. "You just have to be receptive when he does."

Kat groans. "Easier said than done. You know that. At least Kris and you have a lot in common. You know he's not after your money, he loves and respects you. The last time I went on a date, I almost asked him if he wanted to take measurements. Who had the bigger dick?"

"Sounds like he *was* a dick," I say, laughing as she pulls a face.

"And your wedding plans? How are they going?"

"Everything is coming together. Kris's mum is doing the majority of the heavy lifting."

Kat's eyebrows draw together. "And you're okay with that?"

I chuckle. "More than okay. She knows the venue, the florist, has organised the guest list, seating arrangements. She's in her element. Who am I to step on her toes?"

"If you say so. It's just not like you or any bride to relinquish *all* control."

Kat is wearing a similar expression to the one Mum wore when I told her.

I shrug. "I'm getting in practice," I say. "Preparing for a time when I have to loosen my hold on the reins."

Kat doesn't look convinced, but she lets it slide.

"And your dress?"

"I had my final fitting this morning. It will be ready for

me to collect next week before I head over to visit Kris. I'm looking at potential office space."

"So everything is full speed ahead?"

"It certainly is."

It's going to be hard setting up and working out of a new office. The London office is my home base. I know all the staff and have an amazing team. I'm going to miss them.

But marriage is about compromise.

If the truth be told, I've handed the plans over to Kris's mum because she knows the lion's share of the guests. My wedding party is pretty small. I'm not having any bridesmaids and Mum is giving me away. Darra did not want Lottie pulled out of school, so without my goddaughter as a bridesmaid, I decided to forgo any, especially when she only made the announcement after my save-the-date cards had been sent out.

Lottie was devastated, but I told her it was her mother's prerogative. That she could come and stay with Kris and me the following summer.

"Well, you'll be pleased to hear your hen weekend is all organised," Kat says, grinning.

I shudder. "I hate to think what you've planned," I admit.

Especially after the hen parties we threw for Leah and April.

"Revenge is sweet, according to April and Leah," Kat says, and I groan.

Our waitress appears and takes our order.

"A bottle of Champagne. We're celebrating," Kat tells her.

She scurries off.

I raise an eyebrow, and Kat wrinkles her nose.

"To our last lunch... without pre-planning. Another couple of weeks, we'll be scheduling our lunches to coincide with you or me flying across the Atlantic. Today, I'm making the most of spending time with my friend. But we're also celebrating your future. I'm happy for you. May all your dreams come true, as Mum would say."

"Thank you."

An ache forms in my chest at her words. Our friendship has drifted, as all do when you allow work to get in the way, but we have started to reconnect in recent years. Firstly through Leah and Gabriel and then through April and Caleb.

"As long as you're happy, Kris has my vote. And if he doesn't, then I'll come and kick his ass."

I laugh. Professionally, Kat projects an icy demeanour known throughout the industry and media. However, she has a warm and protective side with friends and family. A Frazer trait. Like me, Kat is a successful woman at the top of her game, under pressure, fighting against the establishment and coming out on top. We both know and understand each other.

"Don't worry, he treats me like a princess, and it's time I settled down. I've focused exclusively on work for too long. Now I want to play for a bit," I say, shooting her a wink.

Kat sighs. "I know. I just wish you weren't moving so far away. It feels like we've only just reconnected."

"Me too. But I'll be back regularly, and you're always flying across the pond. We probably won't notice the difference."

Our Champagne arrives, and the waitress serves it before placing it in a cooler and taking our food order. When we're alone, Kat looks up.

"Did you speak to Eli?"

I shoot her a sad smile. "I did, briefly. He seemed—"

I stop, struggling to find the right words. Our relationship is merely cordial these days.

"Lost?" Kat says.

I nod.

"I hope he can mend his spirit now Darra is out of his life.

Release his burden of guilt. I have to be honest, her departure has made me very happy."

Never a truer word spoken.

Despite what I said by the pool, everyone has spent years knowing that he was trapped in a toxic and loveless marriage, but the more anyone tried to help, the more he withdrew.

"I'll never understand why he didn't divorce her years ago. The woman is toxic," Kat says.

"I know," I say, knowing exactly how toxic she could be.

In the early years, my frustrations stemmed from my inability to help him, but I had no right to speak out. I'd failed him too, so who was I to judge?

"All we can do is support him, show the stubborn fool he's not alone," Kat says.

I hear the sadness in her voice, and it pulls at something in my chest. Something I suppressed a long time ago.

Kat looks up, her face brightening.

"Anyway, I didn't bring you here to discuss my brother."

She grabs her glass and holds it up. I follow suit as we clink them together.

"To celebrate or commiserate. You leaving for fresher pastures. May this move and your marriage bring you every happiness. If anyone deserves it, it's you, Penelope Dawson."

My breath catches, and I choke back the tears that threaten.

"*Shit*, I told myself I wouldn't get emotional," Kat says, getting up and pulling me in for a hug and squeezing me tight. "Don't be a stranger."

"Never."

CHAPTER 6

ELIJAH

"Are you eating properly?"

Lottie stares over the video conference.

"Of course, I'm eating," I say, forcing a smile.

"Just checking. You look stressed."

Shit, that's because I am.

Not that I can tell Lottie that. The last thing I need is my soon-to-be fifteen-year-old worrying about me.

"I'm fine. I promise I'm eating," I say, trying to crack a smile. "Who's the parent here? You look decidedly relaxed. You must be enjoying your course."

"I am," she says, grinning from ear to ear. "I have so much to tell you and show you when I get back. You're going to love some of the techniques my teacher is showing me."

"I can't wait," I tell her honestly.

She looks over her shoulder and then back at the screen.

"I have to go. Breaks over. I love you, Dad."

"Love you too, angel. Take care of yourself."

"Will do. Bye."

Lottie disconnects, and I sink back into my chair.

I miss every hair on her head. This is the longest we've

been apart since the day she was born. From the moment I held her in my arms, I was a goner.

I pinch the bridge of my nose before returning my gaze to the data on my screen. Stomach acid hits the back of my throat, and I run to the private bathroom off my office and empty what's left of my breakfast into the toilet pan.

I stare at my reflection in the mirror over the sink.

"Shit! Shit! Shit!"

Returning to my desk, I stare at the log on my screen, my throat tightening as a heaviness settles in my chest and stomach.

Fuck!

Not a glitch.

Fuck!

My login has been compromised, and someone has tried to cover it up!

Pages and pages of code changes!

I scroll through the backup file I have downloaded from the server.

Fuck!

I pick up my phone and dial, weighing up the pros and cons of what I'm about to do.

"Todd, can you pop in?" I say, trying to keep my voice calm.

"Right away."

Within five minutes, there's a knock at my door and Todd, my head of technology and second in command, appears.

"What do you need?" he asks, his voice decidedly chipper.

"The latest release…"

His shoulders tense, making me pause and rethink my next statement.

Todd's been with me from the beginning. He was on my university course and is an exceptional coder. He's unusually outgoing for our field, this has proved helpful over the years, especially during our initial meetings with investors and clients. And then later with staff.

I force a smile, a line of sweat breaking out along my spine. "I wanted an update on the latest changes. Where are we with testing?"

A frown mars his brow. "Did you not receive the latest report? I sent it to you this morning."

Shit, he had.

Breathe! Smile!

"I wanted to check if there was anything I was missing," I add quickly.

His shoulders relax, although his frown remains.

"No issues. Everything is going according to plan," he says, smiling. "Phew, I thought you were going to tell me you needed additional functionality."

The words, *whose plan?* shoots into my mind, but I stomp down on them as another wave of heartburn stabs through my chest.

Could Todd be involved?

"That's great," I say, forcing another smile.

Todd's frown deepens, and he steps further into the room.

"Is everything okay? You seem…"

"I'm fine," I say, almost through gritted teeth.

What could be wrong?

An unknown person has compromised my login and made hundreds of code changes in my name, some of which are already live. Worse case scenario, my reputation is ruined, I lose the company, fifteen years of devotion, gone in the blink of an eye.

How the fuck, does *The Cyber Guy* tell his clients his software and company have been compromised right under his nose, and he's only just noticed?

My vision narrows as my stomach roils violently.

"I'm popping out for an hour," I say, standing up.

Todd's eyebrows rise slightly.

"Okay," he says, rubbing his chin, his eyes narrowing.

"Are you sure everything's okay?" he asks again.

No! I want to shout. Instead, I take a deep breath.

"Yes. Why?"

He shrugs. "I don't know. You seem a little....distracted."

I square my shoulders, tightening my muscles.

Todd's my friend, although that might be pushing it. A close acquaintance. I don't let people get close to me, not anymore.

He takes in my expression and holds up a hand. He offers me an encouraging smile.

"Elijah, please don't take this the wrong way, but as your friend and colleague. You've been through a lot recently. You need a break. Why don't you take a holiday after this release goes live? Get away somewhere hot."

I look away, no longer able to hold Todd's gaze. Instead, I stare at my desk.

Get away? After this release, there'll be nothing left.

I say nothing.

What can I say?

I press my lips together as I try to stop the tic in my jaw. I need to get out of here before I say or do something I can't take back.

Todd continues, oblivious to my churning stomach.

"You've been working too hard. Since Lottie went to visit her mum in Italy, you've been here every weekend with the developers. I have to say something. It's not healthy, you're going to burn out."

Keep cool, Elijah. He means well.

Instead of ripping his head off as I may have done a year ago, I surprise myself by saying, "Thank you, Todd. I'll think about it."

Todd's genuine smile surprises me.

"I'm popping out," I say again.

Todd's grin widens. "Not a problem. I won't keep you."

I give him a curt nod, and he turns to leave.

It can't be Todd.

However, with a significant client release launching early next week. I need to know what's going on, and I'm not sure who I can trust with what I've just uncovered. I should call a board meeting, but—I dismiss the thought as soon as it enters my head. What the hell do I tell them?

I download a copy of the files I was reviewing before he came in, sliding the memory stick into my pocket. I make my way across the city to my brother's office in the financial district. Gabriel is the sensible one. Maybe he can tell me I'm overreacting.

CHAPTER 7

PEN

I sit across the table from Kris's mother, Cybil Lansdown, and his younger sister, Freya. Kris has once again abandoned me for a work meeting, leaving me to deal with our wedding plans and his mother.

"As for bridesmaids—"

"I've already told you I'm not having any. I shall walk down the aisle with my mother, and that's it." When it became clear Lottie couldn't make it, I decided I would forgo bridesmaids.

Cybil looks over her glasses and tuts.

"The photographs won't look right without bridesmaids. I've asked Kris's cousins' children to step in. It's fine. I've seen to their dress fittings and they'll match the flowers."

I grit my teeth as my heart rate picks up, a bubbling forming in my chest. I draw in a breath and try to form a smile.

"Thank you, but again, my answer is still no. I will not be having bridesmaids."

Freya takes a sip of her drink to hide her smirk. She's

twenty-five years younger than Kris. *A welcome mistake* is how she's described in their family.

I bite my lip against the retort I want to make. Kris is a wonderful man, but his mother needs a hobby other than sticking her nose into her children's business. Poor Freya can't blow her nose without running it past her mother first.

"I'm afraid Cybil, this is one area I won't be backing down on."

"We shall see. I'll speak to Kris."

"You can speak to Kris, but at the end of the day, he'll back me up."

Or at least he damn well better.

If his mother hadn't jumped the gun and sent out the save-the-date notices, we wouldn't be in this predicament.

She harrumphs, and Freya lets out a little cough. I look over as she winks. There may be hope for her yet.

"I think Pen's right. If she doesn't want bridesmaids, why would she want some children she's met once to walk down the aisle with her. I know I wouldn't."

Cybil shoots her daughter a look that tells her to shut up.

Freya simply shrugs and shoots me a wink. I like Kris's baby sister a lot. At twenty-one, she's young and has lived a sheltered life. Her upbringing is the complete opposite of my own. Something tells me she's waiting for her moment.

"As I said, I'll speak to Kris. This just isn't right."

She busies herself with the file she's created containing all the wedding plans.

What started out as a project deemed to allow her to *get to know my soon-to-be daughter-in-law* saw me sidelined and her take over all the plans. Living on the other side of the Atlantic Ocean has meant she's made the lion's share of decisions. But there are some things I will put my foot down on. If not, I'll be opening myself up to a whole host of issues when Kris and I start a family of our own.

Lunch drags until I make my escape, lying about an appointment to see potential office space. Cybil tuts again. To her, I should be giving up my career when I marry Kris, staying at home and making his life comfortable. The way Annie, his first wife, did. I've been told over and over again how she was there and supported him through the early years of his business until she and their unborn child were ripped from him in such a tragic way.

I've explained to Cybil that I'm not Annie, but it seems like, in Kris's mother's eyes, I need to live up to a ghost.

On my way home, I visit designer stores, collecting a few additional items for our honeymoon. Kris and I are taking his yacht, somewhere neither one of us can be contacted for a whole week. Not that I believe that for a moment. Kris is more of a workaholic than I am, and that's saying something. But I'm hoping the time away will be good for us. From the moment Kris proposed, everything snowballed. I'm hoping this will allow us time to… connect.

Kris's driver drops me back at the house and I find Kris exiting the kitchen, phone pressed to his ear.

He smiles across at me.

"I've got to go. Pen just got home." There's a pause. "Nine AM is fine. Call my secretary and have her put it in the diary."

He ends the call and pulls me into his arms, dropping a kiss on my lips.

"Sorry about running out on you earlier. I hope Mom behaved herself."

"I take it she's called you?" I say.

He raises an eyebrow and smiles. "Of course, and I told her *whatever Pen wants is what I'm going with.*"

"Ouch," I say, wrapping my arms around his neck. "She was positive you'd take her side."

"That's her problem, not yours or mine. I'm sorry if she

was pushy. I don't think she ever thought I'd get married again. She's just excited."

I don't burst his bubble. His mother is a control freak. She can't control her son, so she's trying the next best thing. To try to control me.

"We have dinner tonight with the Duffys," Kris says.

I groan. "I thought we were having a quiet one. We haven't stopped since I flew in last week. I'm jet-lagged."

"Duffy is looking to invest. I can't exactly turn him down when he tells me he wants to meet my fiancée. It's not like you're living here. You fly over and leave again."

I unwind my arms and step back.

"It's not like you've spent much time in the UK with me either," I say, trying to keep a lid on my rising temper.

I press my thumbs into my temples, the pressure of the day and jet lag catching up with me.

"That's not fair. I don't have offices in the UK. You're looking to set up here. Me staying in the UK is wasted time."

"So getting to know my friends and family is wasted time. Good to know."

Kris steps back and looks at me.

"What's biting at your ass?"

"Sorry. As I said before. I'm tired. I was looking forward to a quiet night cuddled up on the sofa. Just the two of us."

I rub a hand down my face and draw in a breath. When I raise my eyes to his, I force a smile.

"It's been non-stop since I landed, and it was a busy week before I left. I'm trying to get everything ready for my move. It will be a while before the US office is up and running. I need to make sure I dot all the i's and cross all the t's before the wedding."

Kris pulls me against him, and I go willingly, resting my forehead against his shoulder.

"If I could get us out of tonight, I would, but—"

"Don't worry about me. I'll go and have a lie down now. That way, I'll be refreshed for this evening."

"Want some company?"

I bite my tongue and force another smile.

"If you do that, then I won't be refreshed for tonight's dinner," I say, pulling myself out of his arms.

Kris nods. "I'll wake you up at six," he says. "We're due there at seven-thirty."

I turn and head towards the stairs.

"Pen," he says, and I turn. "We'll make it work."

I nod, but the hollow feeling in the pit of my stomach makes me wonder whether Mum was right. I am giving up a lot more than Kris to make this marriage work.

CHAPTER 8

ELIJAH

"Amanda," I say, approaching Gabriel's PA.

She looks up and smiles. "Elijah, how lovely to see you!"

"Is Gabe free?"

I glance over at my brother's closed door, the ride over having strained me to my limit.

I turn back. A frown has appeared between her brows.

"Is he expecting you?" she asks.

My brother's calendar has appeared on her screen. Super efficient, as always.

"No," I tell her, running a hand through my hair as I try hard not to snap at her. "I was passing and wondered if he was free."

Her shoulders relax, and her smile widens.

"Not a problem. I'll let him know you're here."

"Don't bother him if he's busy," I say, staring at his closed door, questioning why the hell I'm here in the first place.

Gabriel has an open-door policy. He told me that he likes to see what his team is doing and vice versa. The fact I've turned up and his door is closed. Is that the universe trying to tell me something?

"He's never too busy for family," Amanda says.

She picks up her phone and presses a few buttons.

"Gabriel, Elijah is here to see you," she says.

I can't hear his reply, but Amanda smiles before putting down the phone.

"Go straight in," she says before adding. "Can I get you something to drink?"

My brother's office serves the best coffee in the city. With my frayed nerves, I'm not sure coffee is the best option, but what the hell. This day can't get any worse.

"I'll have a coffee, please," I say with a forced smile.

"Usual?" she asks before motioning for me to go in.

I nod, making my way to Gabriel's door.

I open the door and step inside.

My youngest brother looks up from his desk and waves me in, his phone pressed to his ear.

"Give him a big kiss from me," he says. "I love you too. See you later."

A smile tilts his lips at whatever is being said on the other end of the phone.

"Yeah, I will. Bye."

He replaces the handset and sits back.

"This is a surprise," he says, motioning to the chair in front of him. "Leah says hi and sends her love."

"Same back, and to that gorgeous little nephew of mine," I say, dropping into the seat opposite and letting out a deep breath.

Gabriel scowls, inclining his head.

"Leah wants you and Lottie to come around for dinner. She has apparently promised Lottie more Callum time."

"As soon as she's back from Italy," I say.

"I'll hold you to that, but I'm also waiting for you to turn up at boys' night. Don't think I've forgotten."

I go to stand, making Gabriel sit forward and rest his hands on the desk.

"Okay. Not a social call. What's wrong?"

I get up and begin pacing.

I pause and pinch the bridge of my nose before setting off again.

"Okay. You're going to wear a path into my carpet, want to tell me what's got you so riled up?" Gabriel asks.

I turn, folding my arms over my chest. I tilt my head back and stare at the ceiling, my brain whirling as I try to work out what I'm doing here and what I want to say.

Gabriel gets up and moves around his desk, perching on the edge.

"Take a deep breath."

I stare my brother in the eye.

"I think someone is trying to destroy my company. Or me, or both."

Gabriel tilts his head and crosses his arms over his chest.

"I think you need to sit down and start at the beginning."

I update Gabriel on my findings. The compromised login, hundreds, maybe thousands of code changes I haven't made but are logged against my name. The deleted code change emails.

"And you're sure it's not innocent?"

I shake my head. My heart rate finally slows as I unburden my findings.

"The changes don't make any sense. A lot of them seem pointless like they're hiding something else. Others are definitely calling other pieces of code. I just don't know what they're doing. They are hidden amongst the rest."

"Have you notified the board? Spoken to Todd?"

I run a hand down my face.

"I'll take that as a no. Elijah, you need to let the board know. Protect yourself."

"With what?" I snap. "The fact the CEO's login has been compromised? That our cyber security company is about to become a laughingstock of the world as it becomes known as *the cyber company that got infiltrated*. If this gets out, it will destroy us. Mine and the company's reputation will be worth nothing. The more people who know, the more vulnerable we are. I need to try to get to the bottom of this before I bring anyone else in."

"And Todd?"

I sigh and drop my elbows to my knees, my eyes on the floor.

"I don't know."

"Elijah, something like this, you can't keep it from the board for long. It will look like you're trying to cover something up."

"Someone is trying to set me up, Gabe. I need to know who and why."

"Can't you pull the release, make up an excuse?"

"Not without one hell of a good reason! This is the company's reputation at stake. We have never had to delay or pull a release."

"I hate to point out the obvious, but if you don't, you'll be finished anyway if this gets out."

"Thanks for stating the fucking obvious. However, if I pull the release, I'll tip my hand. I may never get to the bottom of this. What if the damage is already out there, and they're just waiting? I know some of these changes are live. I can see from the dates. I need to know what they do."

"Have you called Pen?"

My eyes clash with Gabriel's.

"Why the hell would I call Pen?"

My muscles tighten, and my heartbeat echoes in my ears.

"I don't know? Maybe because she's the best coder we know. Was going to be your business partner, until she wasn't."

"Are you kidding me?" I stare at Gabriel open-mouthed. "Have you forgotten she's engaged to my biggest competitor—Kristophe Lansdown would love this."

"All I'm saying is, if you aren't going to let anyone in the company know what's going on, then you need help from somewhere. All I'm saying is Pen—"

"Don't," I say, holding up a hand. "I'm not calling Pen."

Gabriel opens his mouth but shuts it again, clearly weighing up his next words.

"Don't be an idiot, Eli. It's not just your reputation at stake," he says calmly in a typical Gabriel manner. "If you're correct and espionage is afoot, then the whole Frazer brand could be damaged. The fallout will affect us all. Are you willing to take that gamble?"

I rub my chest, the pressure causing heartburn, my face burning under his scrutiny.

"I don't know why I bothered coming here," I say defensively. "I should be in the office trying to work out what this bastard has done," I say.

"But you aren't. You're here because you know I'm talking sense."

I stand up and move away from the chair.

"Twelve hours," Gabriel says. "Then I'm contacting Pen."

I stare at my brother and realise he's serious.

"You'll be ruining me," I say quietly.

"No, I'll probably be saving your stubborn ass," he says.

My throat tightens, as I move to the door, spots appearing in front of my eyes. I want to forbid him, but I can't seem to form the words.

I pull open the door and come face-to-face Amanda who has two coffees in her hand.

I move past her.

"I've got to go," I say, making my way towards the elevator.

Fuck!

CHAPTER 9

PEN

The phone rings, and I groan, wrapping my pillow around my head. The Duffy's soiree lasted a lot longer than I hoped. Not that they aren't a lovely couple, but making polite conversation with complete strangers when you're already tired is exhausting.

"What the hell?" I mutter as the ringing continues.

It feels like I've only just shut my eyes.

I pat around in the dark feeling for my mobile.

"Who's calling me this early?

"You need to put your phone on *do not disturb*," Kris grumbles next to me.

"I have," I say, finally scooping up the offending object. "Only my *favourites* override that," I tell him, sliding out of bed and pulling on my dressing gown.

Cursing the *favourite* who may soon find themselves removed if this call is not life or death.

I glance down and spot Gabriel's name on the screen.

Why the hell is he calling me?

Out of everyone, he's aware I'm in the US and in a different time zone. He also has enough *bloody* clocks on his walls both at home and in his office to know it's only five AM.

Exiting the bedroom, I make my way downstairs just as the ringing stops. When it begins again, I slide the screen to answer.

"This better be urgent," I grunt at one of my closest friends. "Do you know what time it is?"

"Of course, it's five AM," he says in his matter-of-fact Gabriel tone. I bite my lip to stop myself from smirking.

So Gabriel.

"I've waited until now. I was expecting you to be up. You've always been an early riser."

I groan. "I'm jet-lagged, Gabriel. Ever heard of it?"

"Still? You've been there a week. Your UK office is open."

"And I'm in the US. Yes, to jet lag, wedding planning, and late nights socialising. I'm on holiday!" I say.

The man is a machine. I don't know how Leah copes with him. I think he sleeps even less than I do.

I hear someone in the background, and Gabriel lets out a harrumph.

"Okay, fine…I'm sorry for waking you. I'll wait until later next time."

"Happy now?" I hear him mutter, Leah's voice barely audible in the background.

"Hi, Leah," I say into the phone.

"Hi," echoes from somewhere in the background.

Oh, how this man has changed.

"Now I'm up. Want to tell me what's so urgent it can't wait?"

I know it has to be something important for Gabriel to even pick up the phone.

"Are you alone?"

I pull up sharply, my eyes darting back upstairs.

"Do I need to be?"

"I'd prefer it if you were, for what I'm about to tell you."

I make my way towards the empty kitchen and step inside, closing the door behind me.

"I'm on my own. Kris is still in bed," I say. "I'm downstairs."

I make my way across the enormous kitchen and flick on Kris's state-of-the-art coffee machine. It rivals Gabriel's, and I'm tempted to send him a photograph, but refrain. Maybe later.

I step back as the machine begins to bubble and hiss.

"It's okay, you can tell me whatever you need to," I say.

Gabriel knows I hold a secure phone. I test for bugs and taps regularly. A force of habit. I work in a competitive industry. Industrial espionage is common. And then there's my other line of work.

"Elijah's in trouble."

My heart stops beating at his brother's name.

"What do you mean? Clarify, in trouble," I whisper. "Has Darra? Is Lottie okay?"

They're the connections my brain makes whenever I hear his name.

"Darra and Lottie are fine, or at least I think they are. They're not why I'm calling." Gabriel sighs, surprising me. "This is business related."

I pause, wracking my brain to determine what could be wrong with Elijah's business and why Gabriel would call me about it. He runs one of the largest cyber security firms in the world. His reputation for perfection is flawless.

I make my coffee as Gabriel gives me the rundown.

"Let me get this straight," I say. "Elijah accidentally opened an email that should have automatically deleted. It shows he's made code changes, he hasn't made? Hundreds, maybe thousands of changes?"

"The long and the short—Yes."

I sink back onto one of the kitchen stools, glad of my earpiece so I can cradle my coffee.

"What does Todd say?" I ask.

Todd's been with Elijah almost from the beginning. Was a friend to both of us at uni. He assumed my role when I stepped aside.

"He hasn't asked him," Gabriel admits.

Oh crap! Why the hell wouldn't Elijah talk to Todd?

"Does he think Todd's involved?"

"He doesn't know. In all honesty Pen, he doesn't know much. When I saw him earlier, he was in a spiral. It's one of those catch-twenty-two situations. He doesn't know what these changes signify. He came directly here this morning. Typical Elijah, he wants to get to the bottom of it before he involves anyone else."

My brain scrambles, making links and connections, as it always does in a crisis.

"Hasn't he got a massive roll-out next week? Has he pulled it?"

I haven't heard anything, but then I'm away from the office.

"No, he won't. Not yet, at least."

Elijah's firewall is impenetrable, or almost impenetrable. I never say anything is one hundred per cent, especially with the right skill set.

A thought crosses my mind.

"Does Elijah know you're calling me?"

Silence descends.

"I'll take that as a no."

"I gave him twelve hours to sort out his shit."

"If he came in this morning, that's not twelve hours."

"Semantics. It will be twelve hours or more before you're in a position to actually help him."

"He didn't forbid you from calling me?"

"Even Elijah knows he can't do this on his own. This

could ruin him, Pen. His company is all he has left. Darra took him to the cleaners during their divorce."

I squeeze my temple points, using my thumb and middle finger, before leaning forward and resting my elbows on the kitchen work surface.

I take a deep breath, already knowing the answer but wanting to hear him say it.

"Why are you calling me, Gabe?"

A sigh comes over the phone. "You know I wouldn't ask you."

"But you're going to, anyway," I add.

"You're the best at what you do," Gabriel says.

"Stroking my ego? You must be desperate."

"I say it as it is, you know that better than anyone," he says.

I roll my shoulders to ease the tension that's building up.

"Why do you believe if I return to the UK, he will want or accept my help?"

"It's not what he wants, Pen. It's what he needs. This is your forte. You were his best friend. He trusts you."

"*Were* being the operative word. That was a lifetime ago," I tell Gabriel honestly.

"That kind of friendship doesn't disappear. I know it was difficult between you when he was married to Darra. It was for all of us. But this is bad."

I inhale and hold my breath before releasing it slowly. My mind wanders back to the man I saw by the pool on the night of Caleb and April's wedding. There were flashes of my old friend.

"If you won't do it for Eli, do it for me. I'm worried about him."

His words are like a punch to the gut. Everything about Elijah Frazer affects me. It always has. From the moment we met, or as I uncovered years later. Bought his way to being my partner.

"Low blow, buddy."

But he's right. I'm being obtuse. I would never turn my back on any of the Frazer family. I owe them too much, love them all too much. If someone hurts one of them, they also hurt me.

"I'll be there as soon as I can," I say, hearing a noise behind me. "Look, I've got to go. I'll call you and let you know what time my plane gets in."

I hang up before Gabriel can say anything else.

Kris opens the kitchen door and steps inside, his hair dishevelled from sleep.

"Hey, sorry I woke you," I say, walking towards him.

He smiles at me, inclining his head.

"Who was it?"

"Gabriel. I need to fly home."

"What about Freya's birthday party this weekend?"

I drop my head forward onto his shoulder.

"Something's come up. I can't ignore it."

"So Gabriel calls, and you jump and leave. What about our wedding plans? Not to mention the full list of engagements we have this week."

I lift my head and scowl.

"You're really going to call me out on wedding plans when you went back to work yesterday and left me to deal with your mother?"

"That's not fair."

"No, it's not. This is supposed to be *our* wedding. So far, your mother has done the lion's share of the decision-making."

"I thought you'd want the help. It's not like you can arrange a wedding from thousands of miles away."

"Help, yes, but she's taken over. This is her wedding, not

mine. We could have been married in the UK. Then I could have organised it."

I move back until I'm leaning against the kitchen island, crossing my arms over my chest.

"You know that wasn't practical with all my relatives."

I pinch the bridge of my nose and squeeze. Not wanting to rehash the same old argument again.

Kris places a finger under my chin and tilts my face up towards his.

"You want to help Gabriel?"

I nod. "They're my family."

"What about me? Aren't I about to become your family?"

"You are. But I owe them everything. More than you can ever understand."

Kris looks at me, an expression I can't quite decipher crossing his face. He drops his gaze and gives me a sad smile.

"I'll tell the pilot to prepare my jet. It will be faster than trying to get on a commercial flight."

"Thank you."

I lean forward and press my lips to his.

I move past, only to have him grab my hand. He interlinks our fingers, his eyes dropping to them before rising to mine.

"This is a big move for you, Pen. Be certain."

"I am. This is an emergency."

He raises our joined hands to his lips.

He lets go of my hand and ushers me towards the door.

"Go. Do what you need to do."

Heeding his instructions, I head toward the enormous spiral staircase. I hear Kris move into the kitchen, his voice echoing as he makes a call to his pilot. I know he'll also be making us both a coffee. This man has many lovable qualities.

I drag my overnight bag out. I don't need to bring clothes. I have a separate wardrobe at home. My belongings won't be shipped until after the wedding when I move here permanently. Not that I need much. Kris's home offers everything a woman or man could ever want. It sits on acres of manicured lands, a twelve-bedroom mansion. Modern in style but with old-fashioned touches, like the winding staircase. On-site housing accommodates the key staff. Kris is preparing a house for my mother, should she decide to join us.

Kris was born into wealth. His family made their fortune by importing and exporting tobacco, sugar, and rum after emigrating from Scandinavia to America in the eighteen hundreds. But Kris has taken his personal wealth to a whole new level.

We've talked about keeping my home as our UK base. It will make travelling with children much easier than staying in hotels. However, the wedding is only a couple of months away, and we still have so much to do, so we've put off that decision for now.

Kris appears in the doorway. Two steaming coffee mugs in hand.

"You're a lifesaver," I say, moving to sit on the edge of the bed. It takes three cups of coffee to kick-start my day.

"Any idea when you'll be back?"

He drops down next to me.

I turn my head to stare at him.

"I'm not sure. Gabriel didn't say much, only that my skills were needed."

He smiles and squeezes my knee.

"Ah, my little hacker."

I nudge him with my shoulder.

"No, my superior coding skills, actually," I say, my tone full of sass.

If only he knew how close to the mark his nickname is.

"I hope they appreciate you," he says.

"They do."

I know that for sure.

He wraps an arm around my shoulder, and I sink into his side as he kisses my temple.

"I look forward to getting to know them properly when we finally get married."

"I do, too," I tell him truthfully.

Elijah and Kris are competitors, know each other only as business associates. As for the rest of the Frazers, Kris met Kat, and I introduced him to Gabriel and Caleb at a couple of charity events we all attended. If I'm honest, our busy lives have kept us apart.

"I'm sorry to abandon you. I know it's your sister's birthday this weekend," I say. "I'll send her a note and an additional gift."

"Pen, stop worrying. Freya will understand. She has me, her brother, remember. She's grown up knowing work commitments trump most things."

"That's not something to be proud of," I tell him. "Things are going to have to change when we have children."

His eyes soften at my words. "I agree. When our children arrive, I promise to take my foot off the gas. As their mother, you'll need to do the same. No more gallivanting backwards and forwards to the UK."

My hackles rise, but I stamp down on my annoyance. It's not like I don't want children. I do, more than anything. I've spent my entire adult life working, but now, I'm ready to slow down.

"What will you tell your mother? We're supposed to go over the final wedding plans."

"Let me worry about my mother. Knowing her, and as you said before, she has everything under control. It's a formality. Stop worrying."

I grimace, and he smiles.

"I promise to put an end to bridesmaid talk," he adds.

"Thank you."

Typical Kris. He doesn't care what anyone else thinks. We're getting married in two months, he tells me to have faith in the process and the hired managers. I admit, where his mother is concerned, I should have no concerns. Maybe her being in control is a good thing, especially now.

"Remember, you're marrying me, not my mother, father, or sister," he says.

"Damn, there I was hoping—Freya—"

"Get out of here!" he says, laughing.

"I'll be back as soon as I can," I tell him, standing up and handing him my now empty coffee mug.

I lean forward and drop a chaste kiss on his lips.

CHAPTER 10

PEN

Mason, Caleb's driver, is waiting for me when my plane lands. Trust Gabriel to get things organised.

I called him on my way to the airport to give him my flight details. I told Kris to remain at home and that I'd see him soon, but he insisted on his driver taking me. During the flight, I arranged a bouquet for Freya and the silver ring I saw her eyeing up in the store the last time we went shopping. This is my apology.

"Ms Penelope," Mason says, opening the door for me. "It's good to see you."

I return his smile. Mason's driven Caleb for years. He's family. With Caleb and April on their extended honeymoon, he's working for Gabriel and Leah.

"You too, Mason."

"Gabriel suggested I take you straight to his office," Mason says as he closes the door before climbing into the driver's seat.

"Change of plans," I say. "Can you take me straight to Elijah's office?"

I was thinking about it on the way over. If what Elijah fears is true, then we need to understand it as quickly as possible.

Mason's eyes meet mine in the rear-view mirror.

"As you wish."

I pull out my phone and fire off a secure message.

A reply comes back almost immediately, making my shoulders relax.

Next, I send a message to Gabriel.

ME

I'm going to head straight to Eli's office.

My phone rings, and I answer it.

"Are you sure? I can act as interference," he says.

I laugh.

"I don't need you to run interference. I spent years dealing with your grumpy brother."

"That was a long time ago."

I flinch at his words.

"He's going to know who contacted you," he says unnecessarily.

"He will. But you warned him. Has he called you? Told you it's resolved?"

"No."

"Then he knows I'm coming. He'll also know you did it from a place of love and concern. This is how your family supports each other."

"It's why you're part of that family."

My heart warms at his words, as it always does.

"I am. And I value that bond. Don't worry about Elijah. I've got this."

"Thank you, Pen, I know it's difficult," he says. "Was Kris okay with you coming back? I know you're busy with the wedding."

"Kris is very understanding. He knows what you all mean to me."

Gabriel remains silent. He's not one to comment on other people's affairs of the heart. He never has been.

"Tell me again what you know," I say, changing the subject.

By the time we finish our call, Mason is pulling up outside Elijah's office.

He retrieves my bag and hands it to me.

"Call me if you need a lift," Mason says.

"Thank you."

I leave Mason and walk towards Elijah's office. The foyer is double height with glass elevators running up the inside and a lot of tile and stainless steel. It screams futuristic with its clean cut and technology stereotype.

"Good morning. Welcome to Frazer Cyber Security," the receptionist says, looking up and pausing. "Oh, Ms Dawson. It's lovely to see you. Is Mr Frazer or Mr Saunders expecting you?"

I smile at Lynda. She's worked in the main reception for years. I may create computer games for a living, but I also design computer components and hardware, and they are one of my clients. Few people know I was here at its inception. It was me, not Todd, who helped create the company's business plan with Elijah. That the company was originally named Frazer Dawson Cyber Security.

"I was in town and thought I'd pop in, see if Mr Frazer is available," I say, giving her an extra bright smile.

"That's wonderful. I'll message Jules and let her know you're on your way up."

Lynda gives me a visitor's pass and buzzes me through the security gate. The glass elevator rises, moving me high above reception. My eyes scan my surroundings, checking for a visible security breach, and they come up empty. When it finally pings, I step out and walk towards Jules, Elijah's PA.

Jules gets up and moves around her desk, pulling me in for a welcoming hug.

"I thought you were moving to the US?" she says, looking up at me, gripping my forearms.

"After the wedding," I say with a smile. "I was this side of town and thought I'd see if Elijah was free."

Jules grimaces. "He's in there, but he's cancelled all appointments for today. He told me he doesn't want to be disturbed."

I rest a hand on her shoulder and give her a wink.

"And when has that ever stopped me? Can you get us some coffee? I'll pop in and see him."

"On your head, be it," she says with no malice. "Don't say I didn't warn you."

I know I'm the only one outside the direct family Jules would say this to. She's loyal to Elijah, almost to a fault. But as a known friend of the Frazer family, as well as a client and supplier, I get added bonus points.

"Penelope," her voice takes on a more serious note. "I haven't seen him like this. Not since his divorce. Not since Darra and Lottie's accident all those years ago."

I give her shoulder a squeeze before letting it go.

"You get the coffee. Let me deal with Elijah."

She nods, her expression sad. She cares about him.

I move towards his door. Knocking once and opening it.

"Jules, I told you I didn't want to be disturbed."

"I sent her to get coffee," I say, stepping through the door and closing it behind me.

His head shoots up as I enter.

"Pen? What the hell are you doing here?"

"Is that how you greet an old friend?" I say, moving

further into his office and dropping into the chair opposite his desk.

"Pen, I don't mean to be rude, but I really don't have time for this," he says, turning back to his screen.

His face flushed, his brow wrinkled. He looks like shit.

"Well, make time," I say, watching his scowl deepen. "I'm here to take you out to lunch."

Elijah drops back in his chair with what sounds like a frustrated growl. The stress lines around his eyes are deep. He's aged in the past four weeks since I last saw him.

"Now really isn't a good time," he says through gritted teeth before running a hand down his face.

"I personally think now is the perfect time," I say, leaning forward, resting my hands on my knees. "Gabriel called me."

Elijah sits up and groans, pinching the bridge of his nose.

"My bloody brother called you?"

"Yes, he did. Thought it would be a good idea if I took you to lunch since I flew in from the US this morning."

"He had no right."

"Is that what you think? Get your head out of your ass, Eli. You may be the eldest Frazer sibling, but you're not an island."

I'm shocked as I watch Elijah drop back in his chair, his head tilting back as he stares at the ceiling. I know he's counting to ten.

"I—"

Elijah stops as a knock sounds at the door.

Jules enters carrying two steaming mugs of coffee.

"Thanks Jules," I say as she places them down on Elijah's desk.

"Is there anything else I can get you?" she asks.

Her gaze turns to a very dishevelled Elijah, a frown appearing between her brows.

"That will be all, Jules. Thank you," Elijah says, his voice full of the exhaustion that is showing on his face.

"Thanks, Jules." I grip her arm and squeeze as she passes, shooting her a look that lets her know I've got this. She inclines her head. "I'll contact you if we need anything, but we're going to grab some lunch."

She smiles, shooting me a look of gratitude, before leaving.

When the door closes, Elijah sits up.

"We are not going to lunch."

I reach into my bag and pull a business card out. Pushing it across the table.

Elijah's eyes drop to the card, his brows furrowing as he reads what is written on the back.

"Back down, tiger. I'm here to help," I say truthfully.

Elijah runs a hand through his hair, highlighting the fact he needs a haircut. It's the longest I've seen it since our university days.

Elijah opens his mouth to speak, but I hold up a hand, stopping him.

"Let's get out of here," I say, standing up and retrieving the card from his desk, slipping it back into my pocket.

Elijah goes to open his mouth again, but I shake my head.

A frown mars Elijah's brow, but he remains silent. His head inclines slightly as he stares at me as if trying to work out my angle.

"Lunch," I say.

"I see getting engaged hasn't affected your bossy attitude," Elijah says, reminding me of how he would pull faces when I organised our group work at uni. "I hope Kris knows what he's letting himself in for."

I chuckle. "He sure does," I say, winking, earning myself another scowl. "Now, let's go."

CHAPTER 11

ELIJAH

Don't argue. Do what I say.

The note written on Pen's business card.

What the fuck?

Despite my better judgement, and because I'm getting nowhere fast, I do exactly what she says and follow Pen out of my office.

One thing's for sure, I'm going to kill my brother when I get my hands on him.

What the hell does Gabe think he's doing?

I went to him in confidence, and the first thing he does is blab to Pen. Pen who happens to be engaged and about to marry my biggest competitor. Was he not listening when I uttered those words.

I know he threatened to call her, but he certainly didn't wait twelve hours. If he had, she wouldn't be here yet.

I follow her to the elevator in silence. It's taken a while to get here. Too many of my staff wanting to say '*Hello*', and '*Congratulations*'. You'd think she was *bloody* royalty.

While I'm waiting, I pull out my phone and fire my brother a message.

> **ME:**
> What the hell, Gabe

Three dots appear.

> **GABRIEL:**
> You're welcome.

> **ME:**
> I told you in confidence. Told you I didn't want Pen involved.

> **GABRIEL:**
> I warned you. And Pen is family. I wouldn't share it with anyone else.

> **ME:**
> No, she's not.

Although I know I'm lying. Pen is an honorary member of the Frazer family, and my parents and siblings all but adopted her years ago.

> **GABRIEL:**
> Not in your eyes, maybe, but to the rest of us.

> **GABRIEL:**
> Don't be an arse. Be grateful. Pen has your back.

I sigh and stuff my phone back into my pocket.

The elevator arrives, and we step inside. Luckily, it's empty.

"Gabriel tell you to stop being a grumpy bastard and accept my help?" Pen asks.

I look up and find her watching me.

I grunt. "You think you're so clever?"

She turns and faces forward, but I don't miss her grin. "That's because I am. My IQ is—"

"I know. You reminded me every day at university. You're also a smart arse."

"And don't you know it? Smart arse meets grumpy bastard. I wonder who's going to win?"

Before I can say anything more, the elevator pings, the doors opening onto a busy reception.

I ignore her. I know she's trying to needle me, snap me out of my funk. She used to use the same tactic when we were at uni together, especially after I broke my ankle.

I hold out my arm, motioning for Pen to lead the way. She smiles over her shoulder, and I can practically hear her words.

"Always the gentleman."

She steps ahead without argument, giving me time to take in her appearance. She's wearing blue designer jeans that hug her tight ass. An off-the-shoulder light jumper exposes her tanned shoulder. Her hair is scooped up in a messy bun, knotted at the base of her long neck. Her shoulders are back as she carries herself with an air of confidence. For someone who's just flown in, she looks surprisingly refreshed. She's one hundred per cent the powerful and assertive businesswoman. Although her underlying sassy attitude hasn't changed, or at least where I'm concerned. Despite all the stress of the past couple of days, I realise I like that.

CHAPTER 12

ELIJAH

We leave my building in silence, heading out into the sunshine and busy lunchtime rush. I look over at the woman next to me.

What the hell is she doing here?

I know from my siblings she's been finalising her wedding plans, had flown to the US last week. Not that I've been keeping tabs on her.

I curse Gabriel under my breath.

Who the hell does he think he is?

In fairness, I've no one to blame but myself. In an effort to rebuild bridges and reconnect, I was the one who confided in him, shared what was going on. What did I expect the most rational of my siblings to do? Sit around on his hands? He warned me. I just didn't think he'd follow through.

His friendship with Pen is solid. She was the first person to bring him out of his shell. It's recently emerged that Gabe, like Pen, is a gamer. As is Leah. Something else they all have in common.

It shouldn't have surprised me. When I first brought Pen home, Gabriel found a kindred spirit, both intellectually brilliant and outside societal norms. She talked to him, got him building his own computer at thirteen, challenged him.

Pen takes off down a different street, and I turn to follow her.

"Care to tell me what that note was all about and why we couldn't talk in my office?" I ask, calling after her.

Pen stops and looks at me. Her eyes scan our surroundings. I want to roll my eyes but refrain.

"Not here. Wait until we get to the restaurant. And for god's sake, take that damn scowl off your face. You're meeting a friend for lunch, not facing a firing squad."

I open my mouth, but before I can say anything, she pushes me into an alleyway and reaches into her pocket. She presses me against the wall, her hand in the centre of my chest. An unexpected warmth radiates through my shirt, where her hand rests.

I stare at Pen as she pulls out a handheld device and switches it on.

"From what Gabriel said, you suspect espionage."

"It seems like my brother dearest has said quite a lot."

Pen looks up, her dark brown eyes locking on mine.

Fuck she's serious.

I remain silent, wondering if I'm about to be pranked by a TV reality show.

"Elijah, concentrate," she says.

"On what?" I ask.

The heaviness that has sat in my stomach and chest for the past two days returns with a vengeance.

"I don't have time for this. I need to work, not play spy in whatever your latest fantasy game is."

"This is far from a game. It's also not outside the realm of possibility that your office is bugged. Listening devices and cameras are a real thing."

I drop my head back and stare at the sky, counting to ten.

This is the help Gabriel sent me? Conspiracy Theory 101?

When she moves the device around, my patience snaps.

"What the hell is that thing?" I ask, motioning to the flashing device in her hand.

She looks up and rolls her eyes. "It runs interference. If anyone has bugged you. They're getting a nice lot of static right now."

I run a hand through my hair and sigh. "Are you being serious?"

Pen raises her eyebrows and shoots me one of her looks. One that tells me I'm the naïve one here. I'd laugh if I wasn't so stressed.

"Fine, I'll play along."

I roll my shoulders, hoping to relieve the tension that's building up. At this rate, I'm going to be suffering from a major headache.

"In all honesty, I don't know what I suspect. When I saw Gabriel, I was in shock. The more I investigate—yes, there are discrepancies. Someone or someones have definitely been messing with code using my login, and the changes are outside our project's scope. I was attempting to decipher the purpose of those changes when you interrupted."

"Did you get anywhere? Find anything conclusive?"

I shake my head, happy to be back on a more realistic train of discussion.

"All the changes are time-stamped with my login, therefore easy enough to track. If you want to class that as a positive."

I look once more at the flashing device in Pen's hand.

"You really believe someone may have bugged my office?" I shake my head. "There's no way, security is tight."

Pen crosses her arms over her chest and waits.

Her note, cryptic conversation about lunch. The way she spirited me out of there before we even drank our coffee.

Shit!

"I agree." She sighs. "But we can't discount anything and we won't know until it's been swept. The problem is, if there's a camera, then doing so, may just tip them off. They may have bugged your office to gather information. See what you know."

I run a hand down my face, my jaw clenching. I replay yesterday's conversations. Did I give the game away? Tip their hand?

What? Am I really jumping on board with Pen's conspiracy delusion?

Pen squeezes my arm, capturing my attention.

"Don't panic." She goes into her bag and pulls out a watch. "Put this on. When you get back to your office, walk around. If it vibrates against your skin, then it's found something." My face must give away my disbelief because Pen shrugs. "This is a precaution. I'm sure I'm being overcautious," she says, but something in her tone tells me she doesn't believe she is.

I shake my head and pinch my arm, hoping I'll wake up.

Nope, shit, looks like this is real.

Since Caleb's wedding, Pen has haunted my dreams, but this one is exceptionally bizarre. Pen barging into my office waving spy gadgets at me, is new-level crazy even by my standards. I really am losing the plot. Maybe Todd is right. I do need a break.

"The gaming community is highly competitive. As a company, we run sweeps regularly," she adds, patting my arm before dropping her hand.

As if that explains everything.

I pinch the bridge of my nose to stem the growing headache. My mind is all over the place, having suffered a sleepless night. I'm not sure I can deal with Pen and her *conspiracy theories* on top of everything else right now.

I step around Pen and make my way back onto the main street. Needing to put some distance between us. Pen appears next to me, putting the device back into her pocket, still activated.

"Let's grab some lunch," she suggests. "I take it you forgot to eat breakfast this morning?"

My stomach growls in response, and Pen chuckles. I sometimes forget how well she knew me. Although my forgetting to eat in those days was rare.

"Come on, I know a great place."

I follow her to one of the nearby restaurants. Pen snags us a corner booth in an American Diner replica.

"Missing American cuisine already?" I ask drily, only to be rewarded with a grin.

Pen knows I'm not a burger and chips kind of guy. Years of training at Olympic level, I'm cautious about what I put into my body, carefully balancing my diet.

"No." Pen laughs, her eyes locking on my face, sparkling as she takes in what is no doubt a scowl. "This place serves the best shrimp in London," she says, handing me the menu. "See for yourself."

I take the menu. She's right. The food here looks good.

It's not long before the waitress comes and takes our order. I copy Pen. She knows I have a weakness for shrimp and seafood. Especially as my daily workout means I need to consume a vast quantity of protein.

Shrimp improves my mood, and right now, I could do with a mood enhancer.

We remain silent until the waitress is out of sight.

"It's okay, we can talk freely." She pats her pocket.

Ah, her cloaking device.

"Pen. I don't know what you think you can do, but I've reviewed a large portion of the code changes. There's nothing obvious. I've also checked. The firewall and main security code appear untouched."

Pen shakes her head as our waitress delivers our drink.

"The code changes have to do something. Or someone has gone to a lot of trouble for nothing," she says, eyes losing focus, a habitual response to deep thought.

"As I said before, I was investigating when you arrived."

"So you said. You also said you hadn't got very far. Two heads are better than one. That's the reason I'm here."

One look at her expression tells me I will not win this battle. I have to admit, Pen is one of the best coders I know, or at least she was. If anyone can decipher the additional code, it will be her.

"Shouldn't you be planning your wedding, attending a dress fitting?"

Pen scowls. "For your information, I was. Until someone called and said I was needed."

I'm being an ungrateful jerk. I can do with her help, I'm not getting very far by myself and time is running out.

"Fine, you can look."

I sigh.

Pen grins. "I was going to, with or without your permission," she says, just as our food arrives. "I didn't travel all this way for nothing."

I grunt, making her chuckle. Damn woman, why is she so perky? I think I preferred the moody Pen of old. It's like we've done a bloody role reversal.

We finish our lunch in relative silence. I have to admit, Pen is right, the food is good, and I was hungry.

While Pen excuses herself to go to the restroom, I settle the bill, much to her disgust.

"Look, as you pointed out. You've flown all the way over here to help me."

"But you didn't ask me to."

"No, but you did it anyway. The least I can do is buy lunch."

"Well, thank you."

Despite our differing upbringings, Pen always insisted on self-reliance and financial independence. I still remember our late-night arguments over me buying us takeaway when she wouldn't leave the lab to eat.

As we make our way back to the office, Pen stops me, turning me to face her. At six feet, she is one of the few women I don't have to crick my neck to talk to.

"We cannot do this in your office. My presence is going to raise questions."

I fold my arms over my chest.

"I'm not giving you access to my server, Pen. That's like opening the door."

"It's not, I promise you. Trust me on this."

"Why?"

Pen's expression falls. "Will you trust me if you find a bug in your office?"

"How can I be sure you didn't place it during your earlier visit?"

"Because you saw me the whole time. My chair was the only place for planting it. That's why I didn't move around. I had a feeling you might be suspicious."

We stare at each other. *Am I suspicious?* When did our relationship become so distant? When did I start looking at friends and question their integrity? My life has gone to shit.

"You're engaged to my biggest competitor," I say, trying to defend myself. "You could spy for him or be planting something."

"That's true," she says, surprising me when she doesn't protest. "I can also turn around and walk away now if you want me to. But Elijah, I could never hurt your family. Ever. Kris is my fiancé, yes. But Kat is one of my closest friends, and Gabriel is my silent partner. Your mum is like a second mother, and your father—"

Her voice catches. The death of my father devastated Pen as much as it devastated the rest of us.

I know what she says is true. My entire family loves Pen. Sometimes, I wonder whether they love her more than me. But then, there hasn't been much to love in recent years.

"Okay, if I find anything, I'll think about it."

Pen nods her affirmation at my words.

"I'll leave you here. If the watch vibrates, do not show any emotion. If they've planted a camera, you don't want them to know you're onto them."

A crowd of people walks past us.

"How about dinner at my place? I know Mum would love to see you."

I frown. Pen opens her eyes wide, clearly hoping I catch on. Will Louise be there? It's been a while since I saw Pen's mum.

I roll mine and say with a hint of sarcasm, "That sounds great. Lottie is with Darra. I'd appreciate some company."

Pen bites her lip to hide her smirk at my lack of enthusiasm.

"Great," she repeats, her smile wide. "I'll get out of your hair," she says, moving towards me.

She wraps her hand around my neck and pulls me forward. Her breath against my ear, doing strange things to my heart rate.

"Here," she says as I feel her hand move to my pocket, pushing something inside. I freeze as a shot of desire shoots straight to my cock.

What the...fuck!

Pressing a chaste kiss to my cheek, oblivious to my state, she whispers, "Plug that into your computer. It will check for malware." She steps back and smiles, declaring, "I'll see you later at mine. Oh, and can you bring my case? I left it in your office." She turns and heads towards the kerb, raising her hand to hail a taxi before I can say anything else.

My hand goes to my cheek, where her lips have imprinted on my skin. I stare into space, wondering what the hell is going on in my life, willing my body to calm down. This is Pen. Pen's engaged, soon to be wed. Not someone who should be on my radar. She was my friend, is here to help. It's clearly been too long since I spent any time with the opposite sex.

I push my hand into my pocket and pull out two items. A memory stick and a gate fob.

It looks like it's dinner at Pen's.

I make my way back upstairs and wander around the room. The watch on my wrist vibrates as I move past my bookcase and again near the sofa in the corner.

Shit! I'm becoming as paranoid as Pen.

I sit at my desk, staring at the place I discovered the bugs. I hope she has a plan. My mind is presently stuck on the spin cycle. What the hell is going on? Turning to my computer I plug in the memory stick before hitting the prompt that appears. I sit back and watch as a program runs, checking for whatever... when it finally pings, I shudder. My own fucking laptop camera has been spying on me. I slam it shut and run and hand down my face before remembering what Pen said.

I need to remain unaware.

My stomach churns, and my lunch threatens to make a reappearance. I take some deep breaths before reopening my computer and the file I was looking at before Pen inserted herself into my morning. It's going to be a long afternoon.

CHAPTER 13

PEN

"Hi, Mum," I call as I let myself in through the front door.

Her head appears out of the kitchen with an enormous grin, her arms wide as she walks towards me.

"Just couldn't stay away," she adds, pulling me in for a hug, although I can't miss the shimmer of concern in her eyes. "I've just stocked your fridge. Milk and fresh fruit."

"Thank you. I'd be lost without you," I say hugging her back tightly.

"How are the wedding plans going?"

"Fine," I tell her. "Kris's mum has everything in hand."

Mum's lips purse, but she keeps her counsel. It's not like we haven't discussed this a number of times in the past few months.

"I was surprised you came back so soon," she says changing the subject.

She understands my career takes priority, always has.

I shrug, not wanting to go into too many details.

"You work too hard. You're supposed to be on holiday, spending time with your fiancé," she says, tutting. "I expect things to change when you move to the US and start living with Kris. What does he say?"

I tilt my head. "He gets it more than most. He's worse than me."

I don't mention he's been working flat out since I arrived last week and that even our evenings have been taken up meeting friends and clients.

She lets out a sigh and shakes her head. "You're as bad as one another. It's going to have to change when you have a family."

Having a family has become my dream. Kris and I have discussed it. Once we're married and I've settled in, we'll start trying straight away.

"I'm not complaining. It may only be a week since you left, but it's been quiet around here."

I roll my eyes as she wraps an arm around my waist and leads me into the kitchen. I've missed her and the flow of normality.

"Are you going into the office?"

"No, I'll be working from home," I say, unable to meet her gaze.

A frown appears between her brows. "Pen, what's going on? Why have you cut your stay short? Is everything okay?"

I sigh. Mum is too smart for her own good. Nothing keeps me out of the office. It's my safe place.

I sigh. "Elijah is coming over later. We have some work to do."

"Elijah? As in Elijah Frazer?"

Her eyebrows almost hit her hairline.

"One and the same. Do I know any other Elijahs?" I say, trying to make light of his visit.

She huffs, making me smile. "Since when have you and Elijah become such bosom buddies?"

I shrug. She has a point. As I pointed out to him at the

wedding, it has been seven years since we sat down and actually talked.

She turns her gaze on me, her hands going to her hips.

"I don't want to interfere, but is that wise? You're about to marry another man. Elijah Frazer is newly single. What if the press catches wind of it? Does Kris know?"

I hold up my hands, slowing her tirade of questions.

"Firstly, Elijah needs my help with something. Secondly, there's no reason for the press to suspect anything. As far as they're concerned, I'm in the US."

My mind wanders back to Elijah and our public lunch after I visited his office.

I'll cross that bridge when I come to it.

"Kris knows why I'm back. I don't have any secrets from him."

Although he thinks I've come back to help Gabriel, not Elijah. Not that I lied. It was Gabriel asking for my help.

"Just be careful. You don't need a scandal following you down the aisle. I know Elijah was your close friend at uni, but that was over fifteen years ago. You don't owe him anything. Not if it could jeopardise your future happiness and not for some sense of misplaced loyalty. I know you're close friends with his siblings…"

"As I said, Kris knows I'm here. Elijah and I will be working from the house, so there will be no scandal."

There's a deafening silence.

"Except the man in question is now single."

I stare at Mum, realising for the first time she knew my feelings for Elijah were more than I ever admitted. It's easier to keep unrequited love to yourself than face the embarrassment of others knowing, including those closest to you. Especially when the man in question marries and has a child with someone else.

I think back to that time. I was a wreck when Elijah

married Darra and I had no right to be. We were close friends, but we never dated. We were partners, an unstoppable team. Everyone said so. He was the good-looking, popular guy friend on who I, the misfit, developed a crush. I even managed to convince myself his feelings mirrored my own.

Ha, how wrong could a person be?

I fell in love with catastrophic consequences. Within a couple of months, he married someone else after swearing he was all about work and making something of himself. His marriage and impending fatherhood triggered a series of unfortunate events in my life that threatened to destroy my future until his father, Robert, came to my rescue.

But Mum knows none of this.

There's a deafening silence.

"It's none of my business," she says after a while, but I can tell from her expression she wants to say more.

I open my mouth.

"None of my business," she says again, holding up her hands.

I want to growl at her. I recognise her disapproving tone. I grew up with it.

"I'm helping him with something work-related," I continue.

She shrugs, grabbing a cloth and wiping the already clean kitchen side, her eyes not meeting mine.

"Stop—I know you don't approve, but—"

The emotion in her tone surprises me. "He needs to leave you alone."

"It's not like that. Gabriel contacted me. Elijah was furious when he found out."

"Gabriel should know better."

Her eyes finally clash with mine. I'm shocked by the anger I see there.

"Hey," I say, stepping forward and gripping her upper arms. "What's going on? I thought you liked Elijah?"

Her eyes moisten, and she shakes her head.

"I do. I like him a lot. It's nothing. Forget I said anything. It's just me being a protective mother bear."

She laughs, but the sound is hollow.

"Talk to me. Tell me what you mean."

"You've finally moved on, settled down. I know what I said before, but I know Elijah Frazer broke your heart, and now you're finally, *fifteen* years later, opening your heart to someone else, and he or his brother has you flying back across the water to do his bidding."

"It's not like that. Elijah isn't the reason I've stayed single. Is that what you think?"

At least he's not the only reason.

My other job made it impossible to invest time in a relationship. Finding such a man, one not intimidated by my success or secrets, has been another difficulty.

Mum shrugs again, and I tilt my head, making her look at me.

"I promise. There's nothing between Elijah and me. Until Caleb and April's wedding, we've barely spoken since Robert's death. I really am only here to help him, and then I'll be returning to Kris and continuing with our wedding plans. Nothing is going to derail that."

"Okay," Mum says, cupping my cheek. "I just worry. A mother's prerogative."

I tilt my head into her hand. "I wouldn't have it any other way."

"Well, I'll leave you to get sorted. I'm only next door if you need me."

"We'll be working," I repeat.

She looks sceptical. Her problem, not mine.

I need to get ready. Elijah and I have work to do.

CHAPTER 14

ELIJAH

I pull up at the enormous wooden gates shielding Pen's driveway from the outside world. A combination of high fences and laurel hedges surrounds her land. It's clear she values her privacy as much as my family does.

I pick up the gate fob from the centre console and watch as the gates swing open.

Hitting the accelerator, I drive up the tree-lined driveway towards the impressive house at the end.

I pull up at the base of her front steps, only to find Pen waiting for me.

She moves to the driver's window, pointing to the side of the house.

"Park it in the garage," she says.

I move in the direction she tells me, towards the enormous door linked to the side of the house.

Her home is spectacular. According to my siblings, she bought a derelict manor house and meticulously restored it over the years. The front is the original brick, with large sash windows and a central doorway at the top of wide stone steps. According to Caleb, Jaxson Lockwood, our friend and top-class architect, has created a masterpiece at the back of the house.

I've not been here, but I've seen the pictures. Caleb raves about its design, the developer in him going into overdrive. The back of the house overlooks the rest of the property, which comprises woodland and grassland. I remember Kat telling our mother, Pen saw the view and immediately put in an offer. Fire had destroyed the main property, leaving a burnt-out shell, so she and her mum moved into one of the smaller cottages on the grounds until the renovations were complete.

I manoeuvre my Range Rover Autobiography SV next to a sleek Porsche.

The garage door closes quietly behind me.

Pen emerges from a side door as I climb out.

"Canary yellow Porsche? You surprise me?"

Pen grins. "Why? Jealous?"

She clearly remembers the time I went to test drive a two-seater sports car and how my six-foot-six frame got stuck behind the wheel. The salesperson nearly had a coronary, thinking they might have to dismantle the steering column.

"I'll stick to cars I can actually get in and out of," I say.

"It goes well with black," she says, smiling, her eyes moving lovingly to her car before returning to mine. "Welcome to my home. If you want to follow me."

She turns on her heels and walks back through the same door before I can say anything.

I catch up with her in an extensive hallway. A wooden staircase leads up to a mezzanine landing, with rooms leading off. I can make out additional corridors. Downstairs, the doors are all open, offering glimpses into bright rooms. As someone who appreciates light, especially natural light, this is stunning.

But critiquing Pen's home or choice of car is not why I'm here.

"Pen. I haven't got time to strategise. The release goes live in five days."

I almost called her and cancelled, but after the watch vibrated and her program picked up on the malware, I decided against it.

Who the hell wants to bug my office?

More importantly, who got access to do it? My offices are supposed to be watertight. Vigorous checks are performed on all my staff. We have some of the world's largest industries as clients, and they have to know they can trust us.

Pen leads me into the house. When I walk through the doorway, a buzzer goes off.

"You've got to be kidding me," Pen says, holding up a hand.

She places a finger to her lips. She pulls out her scanner again and runs it over my body, like security at the airport.

It beeps when it passes over my pocket, and I pull out my phone.

Pen takes it off me.

"It's a tracker," I tell her. "All Frazers have them. My father made us have them installed in case of kidnapping."

Pen's shoulders sag.

"Of course. I'm just a little paranoid, especially after today. I take it you found bugs? I get the impression you wouldn't be here if you hadn't."

"I'm confused about why someone would bug my office."

And how they got in past security.

The thought has made me sick to my stomach.

"That's the simple part. They want to know what you know. Want to stay one step ahead of you. It could be a competitor and has nothing to do with the code changes you've uncovered. They may have been planted years ago. But we can't take that risk."

She takes my phone and places it in a metal box.

"What are you doing?"

"I'm not prepared to risk that someone has compromised it."

"But what if Lottie needs to call me?"

Pen sighs and takes my phone back out. She holds it up to my face, unlocking it. Her fingers move at incredible speed before she drops it back into the box, closing the lid.

"It will now redirect any calls to a secondary phone downstairs."

"Downstairs?"

"Yes, downstairs. Follow me. We have work to do."

No nonsense. Pen is at work. It takes me back to when we first worked together at uni.

CHAPTER 15

ELIJAH

EIGHTEEN AND A HALF YEARS AGO

"*You've got to be kidding me, Professor Dunn?*"

"*What is it now, Miss Dawson?*"

"*Elijah Frazer, really? Why would you partner me and him together?*"

I stand in the doorway and listen to her complain as our names are called. As usual, I'm a couple of minutes late as swim practice overran.

"*Oh god, they've paired you with Goth Girl?*" *Darra's voice appears beside me.* "*I feel for you.*"

"*What are you doing here, Darra?*" *I ask, not expecting to see her until later.*

Her hand snakes up over my chest. I take it in mine to stop its progress. There's a time and a place, but not outside lecture halls. She doesn't take the hint, instead pressing herself against me, wrapping her arms around my waist.

"*I missed you this morning,*" *she purrs.*

"I had training, you know that."

"Well, you can make it up to me later. I woke up feeling horny, and you weren't there." She pulls my head down, placing her lips against my ear. "I had to use my toys, but it's simply not the same. I'm still wet and incredibly frustrated," she whispers, making my body harden at the thought.

Darra is the perfect girlfriend. She's sexy, intelligent, and knows what she wants in life. She also isn't afraid to go after it. Her family is wealthy, although not in the traditional sense. They're what is called, in our circles, new money. Her father having made his fortune rather than inherited it. With Darra, I find I can be myself. She understands what it means to grow up in the limelight, and the expectations I have on me. She's supportive of my swimming aspirations and of my plans for the future. She never puts pressure on me or asks for more than I'm willing to give.

"I'll make it up to you later, gorgeous, I promise. Right now, I really have to attend this lecture."

My words earn me a dazzling smile.

"It's a good thing I caught you then," she says. "I just wanted to say good morning. I was passing on my way to my lecture when I saw you."

She flexes her manicured nails against my skin, igniting memories of them pressed into my shoulders last night as she came hard around my cock. I shift awkwardly as she smirks, knowing exactly what she's done to me.

"Morning, gorgeous." I drop a kiss on her nose and give her a smile. "Look, I really have to talk to my partner," I say, only to have her laugh.

"Oh, please! Not that freak," Darra says, looking over her shoulder towards the woman I need to win over, who is currently shooting daggers in our direction.

Penelope Dawson's eyes have turned towards us, and I watch her roll them as she takes in Darra and me. Darra has now wrapped herself around me like a snake.

My eyes lock with Penelope's, and something passes over them.

"What did you say?" *I ask, my voice hardening.*

Darra freezes, her gaze returning to mine. She flashes me a dazzling smile as she flips her hair over one shoulder.

"I said it would be a shame not to speak to her, clear the air," *she replies, not missing a beat.*

I frown.

"I will," *I say, watching Darra's eyes harden just a fraction before they sparkle up at me once more.*

"Oh, I forgot," *she says, her arms snaking up and around my neck, pulling my face towards hers.*

Our lips touch, and I return her kiss. When she pulls away, she bats her eyelashes dramatically and giggles.

"See you later, sexy."

It's my turn to grin as I watch her walk off, hips swaying.

"You most certainly will," *I say before turning and walking into the classroom.*

I pass one table.

"You're one lucky bastard, Frazer," *one of my peers says, whose name I can't recall.*

His gaze remains fixed on the doorway, where I stood moments ago alongside Darra.

I shake my head and shrug.

Damn, I miss what Professor Dunn said when telling Penelope why he paired us together, although I soon get my answer.

"It's okay, Prof, I'll partner Elijah, if Dawson doesn't want him," *another member of the class says as I make my way into the room towards Penelope.*

When I locate the voice, she grins at me, flipping her hair.

"I'm also happy to partner him," *several of the other guys add.*

God, the Frazer name can be a real pain in the ass. If I was Joe Blogs, no one would want to partner me.

"I'm happy, thanks," *I say, although the look Penelope is shooting me tells me she doesn't share my sentiment.*

I finally arrive in the far corner where Penelope is sitting. We've shared a number of classes in our first semester but have had little interaction. The look she shoots me tells me I should keep my distance. Until recently, my life worked. However, my last grade was different. I've stretched myself too thin, and I need a partner with a strong work ethic. Will get down to business, not wanting to know the ins and outs of my family or social life. Penelope Dawson gives me no inkling she'd be interested in what my favourite grilled sandwich is, or my favourite washing powder. No, Penelope Dawson is dedicated to her work, and that's what I need.

"Hi," I say, positioning myself on the chair beside her.

She shoots me a sideways look that would kill me if looks could genuinely kill.

"I think we seem to have got off on the wrong track," I say, keeping my voice low, not wanting to create an even bigger scene than has already occurred.

"Um, no. I don't think we have," Penelope says, staring at her book, ignoring me.

"Look, I've clearly offended you. Whatever it is, I'd like to apologise."

My dad raised me to be a diplomat. Whatever rod has positioned itself up Penelope Dawson's back passage. I can't fix it unless I know what it is.

Professor Dunn takes that moment to begin talking about the assignment, so we have to stop talking. The hostility resonating from my partner is almost palpable. It's only at the end, when she gets up to leave, I snag her arm.

"Wait," I say as the rest of the group file out of the room. Several glancing our way.

Her eyes drop to where I'm holding her, and I release it.

"Sorry," I say, running a hand through my hair.

Could this morning get any worse?

"If you find working with me difficult, I'll request Professor Dunn reassign you."

Penelope shakes her head and lets out a dry laugh, exposing her tongue piercing.

"Exactly my point."

Her eyes lock on mine. I'm shocked at their dark brown colour, surrounded by thick black lashes. Her makeup does little to hide them. If anything, it accentuates them. It's then I realise Penelope is tall. Not as tall as me, but taller than the average girl. She's closer to Jaxson's height.

She folds her arms over her chest. It's rare for me to be around a woman I don't have to look down on, especially when she's only six inches shorter than me.

"I ask, and I'm told I have to live with it. You ask, and I'll be reassigned. Some of us are here to work, Mr Frazer. I need this degree. I don't need to be carrying people who're only here for the experience."

I almost take a step back at the venom in her tone.

"I see you and your friends partying. You rock into class half asleep..."

My annoyance rises. How dare she? She doesn't know me. She's slinging mud when she has no idea.

"Get your facts straight," *I hiss.* "As for rocking up to class half asleep. That's not the case. I'm at the pool every morning at five AM, training. I swim at a national level and I'm hoping to qualify for the Olympic team in two years. Believe me, that lifestyle excludes partying and drinking."

I pinch the bridge of my nose, wondering why the hell I'm standing here explaining myself.

Then I remember.

I need her.

"Look, I may appear half asleep, but one hundred lengths in a hot chlorinated environment has its effect."

I watch as the woman in front of me shrinks and realise I don't like it.

"Oh," *she says.*

"Yes. Oh," I say, letting the silence between us stretch. "But I can promise you. I'm here to work."

"Fine. But I will not carry your sorry ass. If we're partners, then it's an even share," she says suddenly, making me want to smile.

"Deal," I say, holding out a hand. "I wouldn't want it any other way," I tell her truthfully.

She looks at my outstretched palm and shakes her head.

"Fine. Write your initial thoughts on the assignment, and we can discuss it in our next class," she says, picking up her laptop.

"Why wait?" I ask. "Two days, and we can get ahead. I hate putting things off."

She looks at me and inclines her head. A small smile playing at the edge of her mouth.

"Done."

She returns her laptop to the table and holds out her hand.

I raise an eyebrow until I realise she wants my phone. I hand it over to her after I unlock it. She tuts but says nothing. Instead, she inputs her number and saves it, handing it back to me.

"Tomorrow morning. Meet me in the library, first period. Message me when you're ready."

"I will."

I watch as she scoops up her laptop and leaves without a backward glance.

I'll need to thank Professor Dunn. I wasn't sure he'd do it when I approached him about who I wanted to be partnered with. Penelope Dawson is the top student, and I want to work with the best. I haven't got the time or inclination to be fawned over, not for work. The downside of my last name and all that entails. Miss Dawson gave the impression she finds me less than appealing, which I should find irking. She's an individual both in her style and her approach to life. Her makeup and extensive piercings give the impression she's not as confident as she wants everyone to believe, but that's not my issue. All I'm interested in is if we can work together and I can stay on track. I don't need to be her friend.

I need to get my grades up, and Penelope Dawson is going to help me do that.

CHAPTER 16

PEN

*E*lijah follows me into my library. Something I installed when I renovated. I blame my mother. She brought me up on Beauty and the Beast. I didn't have a *beast* to provide me with all the books I wanted.

As an independent woman of means, I bought my own.

He stops behind me. His eyes take in the expanse of shelves covering every wall, floor to ceiling.

"Impressive," he says, running a finger over the spines of some of the more traditional hardback books I searched high and low to acquire. My library is an eclectic mix of old and new, from classical to modern, spicy contemporary. There's a whole paranormal fantasy section too. Although that's further away from the door.

"Every old house needs a library," I say.

Mine is based on the one at his parents' house. Every summer I visited, I flicked through the books. Franny lent me multiple titles over the years. Part of this collection comes from her. After I completed the renovation, she came to visit. Her housewarming gift, five hundred books to begin my collection. She also introduced me to her principal supplier, who I now have on speed dial.

Computer Nerd and *Bookworm* were my names growing up. As a child, I lost myself in stories. As an adult, I lost myself in code.

How have I made my fortune?

By combining the two things I love the most and writing first-class computer games that sell the entire world over.

I leave Elijah and move further into the room.

I pull an attached ornament on one bookshelf forward, exposing a hidden doorway.

"Very spy novel," Elijah says over my shoulder, making me jump.

I didn't sense his approach.

"Similar to a library. Every old house needs a secret passage," I say, my heart pounding as I turn my head to look at him, our faces inches apart. "And you can talk."

His eyes sparkle. It's not like Elijah isn't used to secret passages. Secret passages litter his family home. Doorways hidden in the walls or behind wooden panels. Years ago, the servants used them to silently move from place to place without bothering the lord and lady of the house. Gabriel told me they used them to torment one another growing up. Looking back, poor Franny and Robert must have had their hands full.

I step forward, putting some space between us.

"I admit, Jaxson outdid himself with this one."

Elijah grunts.

"Come on."

I gesture towards a flight of stairs leading down into the basement.

"Are you leading me down there to kill me?" he asks.

"Don't tempt me," I say, suddenly wanting to put some space between us. "I could murder you, take over your company, rule the world. Although, quite honestly, I've got better things to do with my time."

Elijah's chuckle echoes around the enclosed space, causing my stomach to contract, but I ignore it.

I lead us down the brightly lit staircase into my sanctuary. The closer we get, the more the gentle hum of my equipment sinks in. My shoulders relax, and the knot coiling in my stomach releases. This is my safe space. My creative sanctuary, a refuge from worldly chaos.

"I'm amazed. I don't have to duck," Elijah says, taking in the additional ceiling height.

I remain silent, not wanting to admit even to myself why I asked Jaxson to make the ceiling height taller. Then, it was about fitting in all my computers, but now seeing him here, in my space, I realise I was kidding myself. I've always dreamed about showing Elijah the *real* me.

I plaster a smile on my face and turn towards him as we reach another doorway.

"Jaxson," I say. "I told him I didn't want to watch my head the whole time, so he designed the space to be above normal head height, unlike most basements."

I input my code into the security pad and wait for the door to slide open, wanting to change the subject.

Elijah steps up behind me, his body too close for comfort.

"You take your security seriously."

"I've had to," I say, stepping further into the room, cutting off any more questions, and putting some well-needed space between us.

Inside, lights flash and twinkle, welcoming me home.

Elijah steps into the room behind me, exhaling loudly.

"Welcome, Pen," Tiffany, my AI system, says, her voice coming from my speakers.

"Thank you, Tiff," I reply. "This is Elijah Frazer. He'll be working with us. Please ensure he has access to everything he needs."

"Certainly, Pen. Welcome, Elijah," Tiffany says.

Elijah looks at me, and I shrug.

"Tiffany is company. She's great for bouncing ideas off. Don't knock what you haven't tried."

Elijah holds his hands up but doesn't look convinced.

"What happened to Daphne?"

Oh crap, I forgot he knew about Daphne.

"Tiffany is an upgrade."

"So Daphne was tossed aside for the latest model? Not like you," Elijah says, raising a brow.

"It was a little more complicated than that and not something we need to get into now."

I'm thankful when he lets it drop.

I move towards the back wall and the bank of monitors and computers I have set up. A seating area, TV, and full kitchen are at the far end of the room.

"This is—"

I turn and smile at the man now standing next to me.

"Only a handful of people know this place exists. I'd like to keep it that way," I say.

Not even Kris knows about my room. There's been no need to tell him.

He nods and takes in our surroundings.

"This is quite the home setup," he tells me, moving around me, taking in the different screens. "I considered Gabriel and Leah's place advanced."

He stops and stares at me when I burst out laughing.

"Gabriel wanted to base it on this place. Not that he needs all I have. Your baby brother is a tech nerd like me."

Elijah chuckles, taking me by surprise.

"So he is one of the few?"

"That he is," I say.

When he's finished looking around, I direct him to the sofa and take a seat opposite.

"So why are we here?" he asks.

"We can't work at your office. My presence will raise too many questions. We don't want to tip off whoever is behind this, and I can't be seen with you. I'm a soon-to-be-married woman to your main competitor, and as you are now a single man..."

I leave the rest of the statement hanging.

His lips purse, but he remains silent.

I have my suspicions that this is bigger than either of us is aware. I've sent out feelers to my contacts, but I can't tell Elijah that. I've just got out of this business. I don't want to expose myself to *the life* anymore.

"Whoever is involved may be the one who planted the bugs. If I'm seen to be there, we may cause them to change course. The element of surprise is going to be our greatest advantage. At least until we know what we're facing."

"We're facing?"

I raise an eyebrow.

"Yes, *we're*. I'm involved in this now. I was the moment Gabriel called me."

"You don't have to be," Elijah says.

"Are you telling me you don't need or want my help?"

Our eyes clash, and Elijah pauses. I can see his brain whirring, wondering if he should tell me to mind my own business, stay out of his business. Maybe I should have. It's not like we're friends anymore. Not in the true sense of the word. Acquaintances at best.

That ship sailed a long time ago. The day I made a promise, circumstances forced me to abandon our business venture and, as Elijah saw it, our friendship.

Elijah runs a hand down his face, squeezing his mouth as he studies me over his hand.

When he finally let's go, he exhales.

"You're one of the best coders I know. If anyone can help uncover what's going on, it will be you."

I nod, surprised when he continues.

"We used to be an unstoppable team. Am I stupid enough to cut my nose off to spite my face? No chance. I have clients to consider, their businesses, and my employees. Whatever is going on, I need to understand it, and fast. If that means working with you again, accepting your help…" He pauses, his eyes still locked on mine. "I'd appreciate your help, Pen."

No gloating or sarcastic comment springs to mind. Instead, a wave of sadness envelopes me. If only things had turned out differently.

If only, a pointless statement.

Elijah looks at me as if waiting for me to add something. When we were students, I would have teased him endlessly, but life and our experiences have transformed us both. We're different people than we were back then.

Instead, I nod and rise to my feet, making my way back over to the monitors.

Elijah moves to stand next to me.

"I understand your presence in the office might raise questions, but what can we do from here? We need access."

I turn my head to look up at him. His closeness sets me on edge.

"Pen, what's going on?"

I jump at his words.

"Sorry, I was miles away," I say, earning myself a harrumph.

Pulling up my chair, I sit down, motioning for Elijah to do the same.

"We don't want anyone to know you've uncovered their plot," I say, my fingers flying over the keyboard in front of me. "Whatever it is. Someone removed the change files from the main backup and meticulously deleted or redirected all email notifications for your login. There must be a backup for them to reinstall at a later date if they want to set you up. If it's there, we'll find it."

Elijah's fingers drum on the desk, his tell that his brain is up and running as he processes all the information he has to date. Sorting, trying to make connections.

"Your program found malware on my computer. They've been watching me through my own fucking camera."

"It looks like we're not dealing with an amateur. Whoever it is means business."

Elijah grips the back of his neck.

"There's a secondary backup. It's where I got the data download."

I smile. "I taught you well."

His lips twitch. "Only a handful of people know about the secondary backup."

"We can't discount them. If that was deleted too, then we'd be able to narrow our list of suspects."

"We don't even know what the code changes do," he tells me. "I've looked. They all seem innocuous, scattered with no pattern."

"That's why there are so many changes. That's what they want you to believe. A mass of small, pointless code changes hiding the dangerous changes among them. It's what I would do. It's why there are so many. If we didn't know about the bugs and camera, this would definitely tell me we're not dealing with an amateur. This is someone who knows how to cover their tracks and go undetected. They want it to look like you were tinkering to anyone who notices your changes. Who'd challenge the boss over minor code tweaks?"

His eyebrows fold inward, and his nose wrinkles as my words sink in.

"I'd hope my coders would call me out on it," he says before pausing as my words sink in.

"Shit!" He spins to face me. "What do you mean? *It's what I would do.*"

I press my lips together. Things that have remained hidden are unravelling. I made a promise, one I cannot break.

"If I were to sabotage a system. I'd bury it in a mound of harmless changes. Make it near on impossible to find."

I spin to face my screens, unable to answer the unspoken questions I see on his face.

"That's not what you said."

I ignore his pressing and continue what I'm doing.

"Fine," he huffs. "But this release goes live in a matter of days. There are thousands of lines of code changes. There's no way we can uncover what they've done. If I delay, the consequences..."

"Get it into your head. You're going to have to delay the release. What we're doing here is damage control. Giving you the facts to go to the board with. For your information, there's no way Todd is involved. I'd bet my mother's life on it. As for working out what's going on. They're not me."

I crack my fingers and flex.

"Let's get to work," I say.

"What do you mean? We can't do anything from here. We won't be able to get through the firewall."

"Oh, ye of little faith," I say, turning to face him. "I'm already in. What do you think I've been doing all afternoon? Painting my nails?"

CHAPTER 17

ELIJAH

"You can't be," I tell her, folding my arms over my chest.

She points to one of the screens in front of her, and I see her logged onto a system, my bloody system.

I freeze.

What the fuck! This is not good.

As if sensing my rising panic, Pen looks over her shoulder.

"Don't worry. I'll fix it. Believe me, it wasn't easy. It took me over four hours. I only broke through just before you arrived." Pen says before returning her attention to the screen.

"Pen," I say, my voice elevating in both pitch and volume.

Pen stops and pivots to face me. Her eyes take in my expression and soften.

She reaches forward and grips my forearm.

"I have mad skills and the equipment to do this. I'm not trying to show you up or your company. When I leave I'll make sure even I can't get in."

I shoot her a look, and she shrugs.

"Remember, I helped to design the original code."

"That was over fifteen years ago. Not much is the same," I huff, sinking down into the chair next to her. "Stop trying to make me feel better. You just hacked your way past a firewall I state can't be hacked. Of course, I'm going to be pissed."

"Fine, be pissed, but can you park it for the next few hours? We need to solve one problem at a time, and I think identifying what this mystery code and person are up to probably trumps your damaged ego."

"It's got nothing to do with my ego."

Pen turns her head and rolls her eyes.

"As I said before, it's taken me hours to get in. We need to do what we are here to do, and then we can fix your exposure. Believe me, it wasn't easy to find, and I nearly called to tell you we were going to have to sneak into the office."

I don't respond. Instead, I let her return her attention to the screens in front of us.

I watch as Pen's fingers fly over the keyboard.

Memories of late nights spent coding, of celebrating problems solved.

She lets out a little grunt, her brows furrowed.

I know I'm being petty, but the fact is she broke through my firewall, a firewall I've prided myself on, and sold as being hacker-proof. If Pen can get through, then who is to say someone else can't? They clearly have. Someone has changed my code. I'm still struggling to believe it could be anyone on the inside.

Who is this woman? I'm not sure I recognise her anymore.

I sit and watch her work, and for the first time in months, I feel energised. Her confidence is galling, but then it always was. I want to know more about her, and my curiosity has been awakened.

She picks up her necklace and captures it between her

lips, sliding her pendant back and forward. She sucks it into her mouth when she needs two hands.

Shit, I am staring!

I turn to one of the three screens in front of me and start scrolling through the logs I brought with me on a flash drive.

"What have you looked for?" Pen asks, her eyes never leaving the screen.

"I scrolled through. Some of the code is dead, dummy code. Goes nowhere and does nothing. There are definitely some lines that call to other code. It was taking me time to track them down and link them."

"Do you have an example?"

I pull up one of the lines of code I identified.

She looks across and begins tapping away again.

If she has knowledge of how this was carried out, maybe she can help identify the pattern.

"I'm writing a program to filter and group the changes. See if there are any patterns or links."

Her fingers continue to type as she speaks.

"When did you last make actual code changes?" she asks.

I pinch the bridge of my nose. "About five years ago."

Pen stops. I sense her gaze on me.

"What?" I ask, looking up.

"I'm surprised. You always loved coding."

I shrug.

But my stomach tightens in defensiveness. It's true what Pen says. I loved coding when she and I were in the lab together. She made me want to be better, challenged me. It was always that way with us. She filled that competitive streak I have. After our initial spat, our partnership took off. I was determined to prove to her she was wrong about me. I wasn't some lazy, rich kid. Even though it meant I was working double time in the beginning.

It was why, when my Olympic dream ended, I hadn't felt

like my world had come crashing down. She had given me another focus, something else to fall back on. By the time we reached our final year, I wanted Pen by my side. Wanted her as my business partner. We had big plans for the future until one day she walked away.

"I did. I do. However, being CEO, the paperwork and the politics have taken precedence. I admit I'm a little rusty. My day-to-day job is more about the management." I stare at her. "Are you telling me you're still coding?"

Pen turns and looks at me, grinning.

"Nothing would stop me coding. It's why my company hasn't expanded to the size of yours. I'm a control freak—you should remember that."

Her eyes sparkle with amusement, and the feeling is almost electrical when our eyes meet. I find myself smiling in response.

"You were. I assumed you let go of the reins a little."

She lets out a deep sigh.

"It's something I'm going to have to learn to do. Especially when Kris and I have children. I can't keep up my current rate of work, lifestyle, and raise a family. It wouldn't be fair."

My heart stops as her words sink in. For a moment, I'd got lost in the moment. Forgot Pen is about to get married, and of course, she's thinking of having children with Kris. Pressure builds in my chest, and bile burns the back of my throat.

"You want children?" The words sound stupid as soon as they leave my mouth.

"You sound surprised." Pen's gaze softens as it moves to mine. "I guess it's catching. Gabriel and Leah have Callum. You and Darra have Lottie, not to mention some of my other friends. They've all settled down and are starting families. In striving to build my business, I've put that part of my life on hold. Let my personal life slide." She shrugs and lets out a sigh. "I'm not getting any younger. As a woman, I'm unfortunately bound by my biological clock, and I don't want to be too old to enjoy a child or children. Like your mum, I'd prefer not to have them raised by a team of nannies."

I get it, however much it irks me. Pen's the same age as my sister Kat. A year older than Leah. It's the exact reason Leah and Gabriel got together.

"None of us are getting any younger," I admit.

Some days, I wonder where the time has gone. I was twenty-three when I married Darra. Lottie arrived a few months later. Finding myself married with a child, I smothered my own wants and dreams. Shut out the rest of the world, concentrating instead on building a future for my new wife and daughter.

Pen finally hits return and leans back, stretching out her back, her spine making a satisfying crack.

"What now?" I say when she gets up and moves away.

"Now we wait for my program to run and for Tiffany to collate the parameters I have set her."

I sit back and stare at her.

"Who are you, and what have you done with Penelope Dawson?"

Pen chuckles, the sound making my stomach flutter.

"I've always had mad skills. You're simply unaware of half of them." She shrugs, not expanding, but there is no missing the sass in her tone. "Look, the program is going to take a while. Let's get some dinner ordered in. I can't work on an empty stomach."

That's a lie. I used to remind Pen to eat all the time. Because she was so focused on her work, she forgot that her body and brain needed fuel. Her near collapse after a gruelling night prompted me to begin ordering takeaway for late nights.

"But don't we need to wait until Tiffany does her thing?"

Pen taps her smartwatch. "She'll notify me as soon as it's complete."

"Now you're just trying to pacify me," I grumble.

"Am I that obvious?"

"Yes."

"Or maybe I've simply learned to take better care of myself," she says.

My chest aches. It's true. Fifteen years is a long time. We're no longer those two carefree young adults. Now, we both run multi-million-pound empires.

"Come on," she says, moving towards the door. "I'm starving. There's nothing we can do here. Let's order a takeaway."

I stand up. I should be annoyed. I've stood here watching her, an outsider break through my company firewall and rummage through my code. But watching Pen at work has stolen my breath. Her skills are off the charts. As a fellow programmer, I can appreciate that. If I'm honest, I'm not sure what I'd do without her. I realise I trust Pen. My brothers and sister trust her, so instead of bitching and moaning, I take her lead and follow her back upstairs. Yet I know, the hollow feeling in the pit of my stomach is more than simple hunger.

CHAPTER 18

PEN

The walls of my sanctuary are closing in, and I need to get out.

Why the hell am I talking to Elijah about my wish to start a family?

We aren't close, haven't been for years. But talking to him now. It's like the years have melted away. A wave of sadness washes over me.

Elijah says nothing. He rises and follows me back up the stairs.

FIFTEEN YEARS AGO

"Penelope Dawson?"

I stare at the two men standing in the doorway to my room.

Fuck!

"Can I help you?" I ask, trying to hold my voice steady.

"Are you Penelope Dawson?"

The taller of the two asks again.

I nod my head but hold his gaze.

"Can I help you?" I repeat.

Don't show any fear, play dumb. They've got nothing on you.

He and his partner hold up ID badges, which I step forward and look at.

Police.

Shit!

Act cool.

I wrinkle my forehead as if confused.

"You need to come with us, Miss Dawson."

"May I ask why?" I say, my heartbeat pounding in my ears.

"We will explain everything down at the station."

I sift through my memories.

What did I miss?

I move towards my desk.

"Please stay where you are, Miss Dawson," the shorter of the two says.

"I'm just going to grab my phone," I say, shooting him a smile over my shoulder.

"We'd rather you didn't."

I stop in my tracks.

"I'd like to know what I'm being detained about?" I say, turning to face them.

Isn't that what an innocent person would ask? I know it will be better for me not to provoke these two men, at least until I know.

"They've traced an illegal hack to this address," the shorter of the two says, earning him a look from his colleague. "We're here to take you in for questioning and seize all the equipment."

"Do you have a warrant? You can't just take a person's things. This is my personal property. I know my rights."

Or at least those I've watched on police shows.

One of the men reaches into his pocket and pulls out some papers.

I raise an eyebrow.

"I'm not the only person who lives at this address."

"And your housemates will also be questioned."

Although the look he's sending me and my equipment lets me know he thinks that's a waste of their time.

I route it through that many places. Did I mess up?

The two men continue to stare at me.

This is like something out of a bad cop show. This is my life. Have I been careless? I know the rules...I wrote them. Stay alert, be observant. Most of all, be meticulous when covering your tracks. Fuck and double fuck!

I draw myself up and take a deep breath.

Damn it! I've worked all afternoon on my dissertation. But what the hell?

"Daphne," I say to the room.

"Initiate shutdown protocol nine, one, seven, six, nine, six."

"Initiating shutdown protocol nine," an AI voice comes through my speakers.

I hold up my hands in surrender and drop to my knees as I've seen the crooks do in the movies. The two men in front of me move at speed, one coming for me, the other heading for my computer. Although he'll be too late. Daphne's program has wiped my hard drive and any evidence they would have hoped to have found.

He hits a few keys to try to stop what he knows is happening, but once the protocol starts, nothing and no one can stop it. It's how I designed it. I may only be twenty-one, but I've been doing this a long time, and I'm good.

He turns to stare at me, but I shrug as his partner pulls my hands behind my back and secures them with handcuffs.

"Penelope Dawson, you are under arrest for unlawfully breaking into the systems of Redbourne Pharmaceuticals. You do not have to say anything, but it may harm your defence if you don't say anything when questioned..."

He continues on and on, and I nod when he asks if I have understood.

His partner makes a call.

"Get the IT guys in here. We need to bag up the electronics."

They can bag up whatever they like. They won't find a scrap of evidence. Not here at least, but I've been careless, which is not like me. I'm usually paranoid about security and ensuring I leave no trail. But then my mind was elsewhere, which is not surprising. It's not every day your best friend announces he's marrying his pregnant girlfriend and shatters your heart into a billion pieces. I should have known better.

* * *

THE ROOM *I'm placed in is stark.*

I sit back and take in my surroundings. Plain walls, a battered table, and a few chairs. A camera sits high on the wall, a light flashing, letting me know it's recording my every move.

I've spoken to enough hackers online to know the drill. It's a misconception that we're loners. We're a very close-knit community. At least, the ethical ones are. I stay away from the dark web as much as possible.

The rules of engagement with police. I know staying quiet is my best option. Being tripped up is everyone's downfall, as in all the good detective shows. The criminal can't help but mess up their story, and then the police have them. And I love a good detective show. I also like the silence of being in my head. I rerun the night in question, replaying every move, keystroke. What did I miss? One benefit of having a photographic memory is I can at least recall what I did. Then it hits me.

Fuck!

I can't have been that careless.

Shit!

I led them straight to my door. A trickle of sweat runs down my spine. I need to get my story straight and fast. Convince the men and women I know are coming to question me that I've been busy working on my dissertation for weeks and weeks, end of story.

The door opens, and I look up. I draw in a deep breath as the last person I expect to see enters.

"That will be all, officer."

The door shuts behind him and two minutes later, the light on the camera blinks off.

"Penelope Dawson, what have you done?"

My chest tightens, and my face, neck, and ears feel impossibly hot.

Robert Frazer pulls out a chair and takes a seat opposite me. The man, like his son, is a giant. The only person to rival Elijah on the height front. His presence is imposing.

I drop my gaze to the table in front of me, drawing circles with my nails on the surface.

Undeterred, Robert continues.

"You're in deep trouble, young lady. Hacking into Redbourne Pharmaceuticals. What on earth possessed you?"

My eyes flick to the camera, which is still off.

As if sensing my unease, Robert sits back.

"It's okay, we're alone."

"How?"

"How did I know you were here?" *he asks.*

"Yes. I haven't made any calls."

"No. I'm friends with a lot of important people. When the Police Commissioner saw your name, he called me."

I choke on the air I've just drawn in.

"The Police Commissioner?" *I stutter.*

I lift my gaze to meet his. I've spent the past four summers at this man's house. Built computers with his younger son, become close friends with his oldest daughter. I'm working on a business plan to set up a company with his eldest son.

Elijah!

"Does Elijah know?" *I ask, my stomach sinking.*

My best friend has enough on his plate. He's still recovering from his broken ankle, and then with Darra announcing she's pregnant.

"No, he doesn't know, and I suggest you keep it that way. With everything that's going on, he doesn't need to worry about you, too."

I drop my gaze once more, not being able to stand up to Frazer senior's scrutiny.

I sigh, my stomach sinking, pressure building behind my eyes. I've let him down. A man I look up to, who's welcomed me into his home.

"I was trying to prove or disprove the information in the press," *I say quietly.*

Redbourne is being hounded for unethical and illegal practices. I worked for them during my placement year. They seemed legitimate, but I needed to know. It was on a whim, and that has clearly been my downfall. I never go in unprepared. It usually takes weeks of preparation, but that night was a one-off. Elijah had just told me about Darra.

"And? What did you find?"

"They're clean from what I can see," *I tell him honestly.* "If I could hedge my bets, it's one of their competitors trying to libel them in the press."

Robert sits back and stares at me, his gaze searching.

"How long, Pen? How long have you been hacking?"

My fingers go back to playing with the scratches on the table. I suck my lip ring into my mouth.

"Since I was about sixteen. Initially, it was laptops of teachers, then different devices, platforms, servers."

"Why?"

"Why not?"

He raises an eyebrow, his expression almost identical to Elijah's.

I draw in a breath.

"It's a challenge. Like overcoming a technical problem, you work around obstacles others have put in your way. It takes all *your creative strategising...and then there's the thrill of not getting caught,"* I admit. *"Although it looks like I messed up in that department right now."*

I flatten my hands against the table and look straight at his eyes. So familiar, yet older and wiser.

"I do nothing with it—the information I gain. I usually send a message letting the company know they have a weakness in their system and tell them how to fix it. Stop others going where I've been." I shrug. *"I do it for the thrill. Me against the machine. It tests my skills and knowledge. The ultimate puzzle to solve."*

"They've been hunting you for a while," he says, making me sit up, my fingers stilling.

"Who?"

"Some people I know."

I watch Robert run a hand through his hair, a movement so similar to my best friend.

"Fuck," I say before slamming a hand over my mouth. *"I'm in trouble, aren't I?"*

Robert looks at me, a small smile on his mouth. He drops his head.

"I can't stop what is going to happen next. I've tried," he says, a sadness in his voice.

"Am I going to prison?"

My blood runs cold. Shit what will I say to Mum. She'll be so disappointed in me. After everything she's done, sacrificed.

"You're in deep trouble. I'm not going to lie to you."

"There are some people here who want to talk to you," he says quietly. *"Have you heard of ethical hackers?"*

I nod. It's what I'd class myself as. I'm certainly not an unethical hacker. I don't abuse anyone with my skills. It's more of the thrill of the experience, beating the system, or in the case of Redbourne, righting a potential wrong.

"There's an agency that employs ethical hackers."

It's my turn to sit up.

"What sort of agency? You mean a government agency?"

He nods.

"Your skill set could be very useful to them." He pinches his neck. *"This is not what I wanted for you, but there's only so much sway I have, and you, young lady, have developed quite the reputation."* He sighs. *"This is the best I can offer. If not, it's prison time, Pen. Your good deeds mean they can link you to several other hacks."*

"I destroyed all the evidence."

"You may have done, but they'll hound you. These people are powerful and relentless. You'll never work in the computer industry, do what you dream of doing. It's join them, or they'll destroy any chance you have at building a secure future for you and your mother."

"But Elijah and I are setting up our own company. I don't need to be employed by anyone."

He shakes his head, his expression in that one second letting me know how seriously I've messed up. My stomach knots, and I drop my head onto the table as I realise exactly what my getting caught means.

"There will be no business, no contracts. They'll see to that. Your and Elijah's business venture will be over before it even begins."

I bang my forehead on the desk in front of me before sitting up and sinking back into my chair. The walls of the room close in around me. Elijah and I have worked for months and months on our business plan, produced a prototype of the security system we can offer. My skills have been useful in its development, not that Elijah understands or knows. He just knows my programming skills are off the charts.

"What do they want?" I whisper.

Robert leans forward and squeezes my hand before getting up and moving to the door, allowing two people to enter.

"It's probably better if I let them explain."

I drop back into my chair and watch as a man and a woman, both in dark suits, enter.

Shit just got real, and I know whatever they offer, I'm going to have to accept. I can't go to prison. I can't do that to Mum. Not after everything she's given up for me.

"Miss Dawson, let us introduce ourselves. I'm The Seamstress," the woman says, taking a seat opposite me. "This is Rooster."

Welcome to my new future.

CHAPTER 19

PEN

I lead us upstairs in silence. My head spinning. It's been years since we've been in close proximity, just the two of us, and it's messing with my equilibrium.

We enter the kitchen. My pride and joy. It sits along the back of the house, overlooking my landscaped gardens and the woodland and fields beyond. I love entertaining here. It's my happy place, and baking has always been my stress reliever, so when I designed this space, I wanted airy. A place to sing and dance freely, somewhere to *let go*. The opposite to my work sanctuary.

The kitchen itself is modern, with sleek units and hidden draws. The surfaces are granite and reflect the cleverly positioned lighting. It's minimalist, apart from my necessities, which include my coffee machine and toasted sandwich maker. A girl has her favourites.

Elijah walks up to my sandwich maker and turns to face me.

"You can take the woman out of the uni, but you can't take the student out of the woman."

"What? I can't like toasted sandwiches because I earn millions a year?"

"Of course you can. It just surprises me."

"I haven't changed that much," I say, suddenly defensive.

"Don't kid yourself. Everyone changes as they get older. It's called growing up and being responsible. You might like to think you're still the same carefree Pen you were, but it's impossible when you have responsibilities to staff and clients. Look at the house you live in. A far cry from the two-bedroom apartment you lived in with your mum with the broken tap and cracked sink."

"I don't think you can say I was carefree at university," I say, raising an eyebrow. "I had a stick rammed up my backside and a chip the size of Greater London on my shoulder."

Elijah chuckles but doesn't deny it. He can't because he knows it's true.

"I may not be scratching a living, or living pay cheque to pay cheque. True. But I still enjoy the same things. Tuna melts, or a ham and cheddar cheese toastie are still my favourites."

He wrinkles his nose, and it's my turn to laugh. He always was anally retentive about what he put in his body.

"You're just a food snob. But don't worry. I'm going to order us a takeaway. I won't offend your tastebuds."

He says nothing, instead he walks around the space.

"Kat said this space is amazing," Elijah says, moving to the wall of windows that look out over the lit garden. "The light must be incredible during the day.

I'm surprised at his words.

"It is," I reply, unashamed to admit. "I had reflective windows installed to offer additional privacy, but with an unhindered view out. After drones became a thing, I didn't want anyone able to spy on me."

Call me paranoid, but such is life. My privacy and the

safety of my friends and family are my number one priority. I love my home, but I'm not so naïve to think my wealth doesn't make me a target for the gutter press. Salacious gossip sells.

"It must be hard to up sticks and leave. You've put a lot of work into this place," Elijah says, facing me.

I shrug, although my stomach rolls each time I think about leaving, but I shake it off. I'm moving to start a new life.

"One of us had to compromise. It's easier for me to upend my life than for Kris," I say.

Elijah remains silent, his eyes focused on the garden.

I move to one drawer and pull out a pile of my favourite takeaway menus. Moving towards Elijah, I hold them up.

"Any preference?"

When we were students and working late, we often had a takeaway delivered at Elijah's request, although he always ordered the plain and boring, healthy versions of dishes. When I was in the zone, I was happy to ignore my stomach. However, he always needed refuelling and always ordered enough to feed an army. At the time, he was swimming over a hundred laps a day, and he was weight training with additional cardio.

I would complain, as I hated anyone eating near my keyboard. The thought of the germs alone gave me the ick. It still does. That's why my office provides a first-class, subsidised canteen, and we encourage all staff to take breaks for meals instead of eating at their desks.

"I'm happy with whatever you fancy," Elijah says.

"Really?" I say, unable to hide the hint of sarcasm.

Elijah always had a preference.

"Don't sound like that," he says, turning to face me. I don't miss the glint in his eyes. "You'd think I was fussy or something."

"You bloody well were. You always influenced what we ate. I know it's been fifteen years, but I can't imagine you've changed that much. Old habits and all that."

His face falls and I realise I've hit a nerve.

"Fine, how about Chinese?" I say, not wanting to go there.

Knowing it's what he always chose.

"I'd prefer Indian," he says.

I shake my head, and he shrugs. Indian was always my preference. Is he trying to be thoughtful?

"Indian it is," I say, not wanting to argue. "Here, take a look."

Elijah takes the menu out of my hand, and I keep our fingers from touching. I don't need this added complication. I'm already too aware of his presence.

He shoots me his order. I open my phone and access the app my company developed. It's installed in all of Caleb's new developments, connecting the residents with local businesses, encouraging a symbiotic relationship. It's done wonders for building communities, giving the smaller, independent businesses the same reach as many of the franchises have.

I input our order and hit send.

"Forty minutes," I say, gesturing for Elijah to take a seat on one of the sofas. "Can I get you anything to drink? Wine, beer?"

I know I won't be drinking. I need to keep my wits about me. I need to stay on my guard. I'm sure alcohol and Elijah would not be a good combination.

"A beer," Elijah says as I move to my wine fridge, grabbing a bottle and using the bottle opener to pop the top.

"Glass?" I ask as he shakes his head.

Still the same. Elijah always preferred swigging from the bottle. Said it lacked flavour in a glass.

I grab myself a juice and move to join him, taking the seat opposite.

I hand him the bottle.

"Any more ideas about who could be behind this?"

He rests his forearms on his thighs, cradling the bottle in his hands.

Something passes over his face.

I wait.

"I've been wracking my brains and come up empty. As a company, we pay over the odds, and our staff are all vetted." He looks up, his eyes locking with mine. "If you've got in, is it possible someone else has hacked in?"

I shake my head. "I doubt it," I tell him truthfully. "I searched for evidence of an external hit. Nothing. They are also using your login. That seems personal."

"So, you still think it's an inside job?" His expression hardens. "It's driving me crazy trying to think who is walking past me every day, wanting to put a proverbial dagger in my back."

His jaw clenches, the tendons on his neck standing out. A thick vein pulses on his forehead as it always did when he was stressed. I don't think I've seen Elijah look so stressed since Darra announced her pregnancy.

I move my head, capturing his attention and holding his gaze.

"It's okay. We'll figure out what they've done, and then we'll find out who is responsible. We'll get them and stop them."

"I believe you. My question, however, is how? How do we track the perpetrator?"

"We'll set a trap and see who springs it," I tell him.

There's so much he doesn't know. Darra wasn't solely responsible for driving a wedge between us. I single-handedly achieved that through my own sheer stupidity and ego.

"Clearly," he says drily. "Just like that."

A shot of adrenalin shoots through my system as he pauses, as if weighing up his next words.

"This isn't a standard setup, Pen, even for you. I'm not stupid."

My pounding heartbeat steps up a notch.

"How would you know?"

We stare at each other, our eyes locked, waiting for the other to give.

The gate chimes.

Saved by the buzzer.

I move to the intercom and buzz the delivery driver through.

I grab my purse from the side, but Elijah holds out a wad of cash.

"This far out, I take it you give the driver a generous tip?"

I nod and accept his cash.

Why not? I'm doing him a favour.

I move to the door and open it.

"Hey, Ms P," Jeremy, the local delivery driver, says.

He unzips his bag and holds out a large paper bag containing our takeaway.

"Evening, Jeremy. Thank you. How are your studies going?"

"Great, especially after you explained that coding tip. I got eighty-nine per cent on my project."

His smile lights up his face.

"I'm pleased it helped. Remember to send your CV to the office for our summer internship program," I remind him.

"Already done," he says, and I make a note to ensure the enrolment team keeps an eye out for it.

I hand him his tip, and his eyes widen.

"That's too much," he tells me, shaking his head while trying to hand it back.

"My guest has donated to your college fund," I tell him with a smile. "And believe me, he can afford it."

Jeremy smiles and stuffs the money into his pocket.

"Thank you," he says.

"Keep up the good work," I say as he climbs onto his motorbike.

"Will do. Take care, Ms P."

"You too, Jeremy."

I watch as he heads back down the driveway. The gates open, and I check on the camera to ensure nobody enters as he leaves. We don't need any uninvited photographers waiting in the bushes. I wait until they close before returning to the kitchen. I inhale deeply before I enter, the smell of the food making my mouth water. I didn't realise how hungry I was until now.

"He sounds like a nice kid," Elijah says, having clearly listened in on my conversation with Jeremy.

"He is. He works hard and has a lot of potential. His mum and dad run the post office in town. I overheard her telling one of her friends he was struggling with his assignment. His teacher was off on sick leave, and the supply teacher wasn't an expert. Since it was not something that could be taught by reading a textbook, I stepped in and took their classes for a couple of weeks. I have my police check from working with the foundation, so it was easy enough."

"That was kind of you."

I smile. "You forget, I was *that* child once upon a time. They're good kids, all of them. But Jeremy is a natural if given the right support and encouragement."

"Well, if he doesn't enjoy gaming, send him in my direction."

I laugh. "Are you trying to poach my potential staff, Mr Frazer?"

My heart stills when Elijah grins back, the sight making

me draw in a breath. It's been a long time since I last saw him smile like that.

I hold up our dinner and it is then I notice Elijah set the table while I was gone.

I move across the room and begin unloading the containers. We've over-ordered, but then we always did. Elijah always had a voracious appetite. But that was a long time ago. He's enormous now. Years of working out have made his shoulders broader and his legs and biceps wider, although his waist is still trim. I doubt there's an ounce of fat on him. His physique has always been impressive; summers spent by his parent's pool proved that.

I stop my thoughts from going any further. I will not think about him naked! I'm about to marry another man.

I turn away and grab two plates from the cupboard before taking a seat opposite.

Silence descends as we both tuck into the food.

"Have you spoken to Kat recently?" Elijah asks.

"We were due to meet in New York, but I'll see how things go here," I tell him.

He nods, and we continue eating, each lost in our own thoughts.

When we're done, he helps me clear away the leftovers and puts the plates in the dishwasher. Robert and Franny ensured their children pulled their weight, even though their house had an army of staff. No billionaire brats. According to his parents, the staff were there, not for picking up toys, but so Franny could raise her children when Robert was away. Their stately home was too large for one person, and Franny refused to employ a team of nannies. When I asked her about it, she replied, "I wanted children. They are my and Robert's responsibilities. The men and women they become will be due to the values and lessons we bestow on them, not a stranger." When I stared at her wide-eyed, she rubbed my arm. "I am blessed, Pen. My husband has money, which means I can raise my children myself. Not everyone has that luxury, but I do, and I'm making the most of it."

She knew my situation and how hard my mother worked to keep a roof over our heads, but I appreciated her sentiment. Mum didn't have that luxury, even though I know she would have loved it. But lack of resources meant she had to work. My grandparents and the after-school club cared for me in her absence, and it was fine for me. But I could also appreciate Franny's philosophy and loved that she was always around when I stayed at the Frazers during our university breaks. And I'll give her kudos. Her dedication to her family has paid off. Every one of her children has gone on to make something of themselves.

When we've finished, I look over at Elijah, who is leaning against my kitchen side.

"What now?" he asks.

As if on cue, my watch chimes.

"Well, time to see what Tiffany has uncovered."

"And then?"

"We make sense of the code changes and set a trap."

CHAPTER 20

ELIJAH

We make our way back down into her cave. Despite the food I've just eaten there's an empty feeling in the pit of my stomach, and my imagination is running riot with *what-ifs*.

Pen walks ahead, her shoulders back as she carries herself with new confidence in her poise. It's not new. It's only I wasn't there to see it grow. Her jean-covered hips sway from side to side, and my eyes lock onto the movement, distracting me. Her jumper hugs her breasts and small waist. Gone are the sloppy oversized sweatshirts and long skirts of old, that hid her body. The new Pen carries an air of confidence. One I'm finding myself increasingly drawn to.

A heaviness enters my body at the realisation. I've enjoyed our talks. I didn't realise how much I've missed her and them until now. Someone willing to call me out on my shit, someone who knows me...knew me. Suddenly, I want to uncover everything my onetime friend has done. Is she happy? Has she achieved everything she wants to? I know she wants a family, but the rest of her life? She was always a goal person. Would drive me nuts with her lists of long, medium, and short-term goals. Does she still have those? Have they changed?

My senses are telling me there's more to Pen than she's letting on, and I wonder if my brother and sister know. I want to press her and uncover all I can, but I know I lost the right years ago. The day she walked away from our business venture and accepted a scholarship from my parents, our relationship went into free-fall, one it never recovered from.

I blame myself. After my accident, Pen was there for me, supporting me, lifting my spirits. We became close. Then Darra announced she was pregnant, and my life seemed to spiral. I'd always been in control. My swimming had my future planned out. Suddenly, I was on a merry-go-round, and there was no getting off. I could have walked away from Darra, but that wasn't how I was raised. Darra and our unborn child were my responsibility. I wasn't going to tarnish the family name by walking away. I made my bed, and I had to lie in it.

The main problem was that Darra was jealous of everyone. My friends and my family. Once she had a ring on her finger, she changed. Gone was the easy going woman I dated. In her place was a new Darra, who flipped between tears and screaming. In order to keep the peace, I backed away from those who triggered her, not wanting to cause her or our unborn child additional stress.

And now, Pen and I are not the same people, even if she does still love toasted sandwiches and coding. She's no longer the prickly woman I met at university, and I'm no longer the carefree bachelor I was. It's almost like our roles and personalities have reversed. Pen now being the relaxed, easy-going one, while I'm the one with a rod stuck up my backside, sniping and barking at those around me, shutting people out and holding them at arm's length. Learning about Darra's betrayal isolated me further from everyone I cared about. Her ultimatum kept me trapped in a toxic situation with no escape. The strain of being with someone I despised broke something inside me.

I shake my head, glad Pen can't see me.

I watch as she walks ahead.

I wonder what I've done to earn myself such a friend? Instead of chastising me for being a grumpy ass and telling me to go to hell, she dropped everything to come to my aid. Or has she? Is she doing this for me or my siblings and her love for them?

"Right, let's see what we have," Pen says, snapping me out of my melancholy as we re-enter her *she-cave*. She drops into her chair, sliding it into place in front of her keyboard, her attention focused on the task at hand.

I grab a chair and draw up alongside her. Her proximity and scent do strange things to my chest.

She taps away, her fingers like lightning across the keyboard. When she said she keeps a hand in, she meant it.

I don't want to interrupt her. I recognise the intensity of her expression. I know my time will come. I just need to trust the process.

Lines disappear. Whatever parameters she's entering are removing changes from our search.

"Interesting," she says, biting her lip, a habit of old when she used to chew on her lip ring. She scoops up her necklace and once again places it between her lips.

Her fingers move again at high speed. Her head tilts as she stares at the screen. Her finger comes up to tap her lip and move her chain, sliding it back and forth. My eyes locked on the movement.

She opens another set of files on another screen. The speed at which they open draws my attention. My eyes flash between the screens. Whatever she's doing, I'm struggling to keep up. At uni, I would have made her slow down, ask her to explain. But she's in the zone, and I have a deadline.

The thought takes me by surprise.

I trust Pen completely.

Trust her to identify what whoever broke into my system has done. Know if anyone can uncover it, it will be her.

We sit there for hours. Pen directing me, and me following. Surprised at how quickly my skills return.

"Like riding a bike," Pen says, grinning when I let out a whoop, having achieved what I need to.

I make us both coffee, and keep her hydrated with water and isotonic drinks. I even raid her fridge and make her a cheese toastie.

I wait while she and Tiffany process and break down the changes in patterns.

"What the *fuck*!" Pen says suddenly. "You sneaky bastard."

I jump at her outburst, stopping myself from throwing my coffee across the desk.

Her head is now moving between the screens as she double-checks her findings.

"Look," she says, pointing to several rows of code over several screens. "We've got you, you bastard," she mutters. She slips into the code itself and I scan alongside her, but find myself unable to keep up. She shifts backwards and forwards through the various changes.

"Clever," she mutters.

My heart races. I'm dying to know what she's found, but don't want to disturb her. I berate myself for letting go of this particular skill set. A time existed when I might have kept pace with Pen or at least attempted it. Now—no chance.

I've had my head bitten off and spat out in the past for interrupting her when she's on a roll, so I stay silent.

Eventually, she sits back, grabs the large bottle of water I have placed within reach, and unscrews the top. She closes her eyes as she takes a deep swallow, her throat bobbing as she drinks her fill.

My mouth dries as I watch the motion, picking up my bottle and drinking half in one go. Get a grip, Elijah!

"So?" I ask, feeling pretty redundant, when she finally puts her bottle down and turns to face me.

Her grin tells me she's happy, and the heavy weight I've been carrying around in my chest for the past couple of days lifts a little.

"They're good," she says, sounding proud, which makes me frown. "But I'm better," she adds.

"Pen," I caution, nearing my limit.

She grins like a Cheshire Cat.

"Oh, don't be a grouch. Let me enjoy this moment. It's four AM, and I've been going solidly since dinner."

Guilt hits me. She's correct. But I'm being framed, and I need to uncover the culprit, their motives, and their method.

As if taking pity on me, Pen sits back in her chair, swirling to face me.

"They've embedded code to break through your firewall undetected." When I frown, she adds, "Someone from the inside has set up a backdoor, but not one simply anyone can use."

My heart hammers at her words.

"But it's not just my firewall, is it?"

"No," she tells me truthfully. "It's not actually written into your code. It's embedded. Which is good. It will be easier to remove."

I run a hand through my hair. "Which clients are affected?"

"All of them," she tells me gently. "But it looks as if each has its own unique ID written in. Someone can open pathways in or sell the ability to the highest bidder."

I stare at her. She cracked the code in hours despite its complexity.

"A cyber attack?"

"Maybe," she says, her intense gaze locking with mine. "Or they want to ruin you. If the threat becomes public knowledge. You'd be finished."

It's my turn to drop back in my chair. I run a hand down my face and stop to stare at her.

Pen continues. "They're going to blackmail you, your clients, or sell the information to the highest bidder."

"Fuck," I say. "Imagine what that means. Companies could access their competitors' systems potentially undetected, steal plans, mess with financials. What about these code changes?"

She pulls a file across from one of her other screens so it appears in front of her. She scrolls until she finds what she's looking for.

"Shit!"

A furrow forms between her brows, her eyes dart to mine, her pupils wide.

She turns to a second bank of computers, pulling forward a second keyboard.

Her fingers dance over the keys, yet an icy chill washes over me as I realise Pen's location. She's on The Dark Web.

"Pen?"

"There is a lot you don't know about me, Elijah. Just let me do my job."

I open my mouth and shut it again. *Job?*

Her hands fly once more over the keys and I watch as she communicates with someone. My heart sinks further as I watch the back of the woman I've just had rummaging around in my company's system converse with people on the dark web.

Pen picks up a phone I hadn't spotted.

"It's *The Tailor*," she says.

I can't make out the words on the other end, but I freeze as Pen looks at me. Her gaze locking on mine.

"It's a chance I'm willing to take."

She sighs and pinches the bridge of her nose.

"I understand, but we don't really have a choice…Yes, I'll deal with the consequences… Fine, just check out what I'm about to send you." I go to open my mouth, but she holds up a hand. "And do it fast."

She swivels in her chair and puts down the phone before returning her attention to me.

"Who was that?" I ask.

"No one of importance to you," she says, not quite meeting my gaze.

"Pen, don't bullshit me. You notified a third party? We're talking about my company?"

"Fine." She inhales, and I wonder if she's trying to figure out what she can get away with telling me.

Instead, she surprises me with, "My handler."

Her tone, neutral.

"What do you mean, *your handler?*" I say, my body temperature rising at her words.

I scan the room, hoping to find answers, half-expecting someone to emerge from the shadows and reveal it's all a sick prank. A stitch-up.

"Long story and not one I'm prepared to go into right now. Maybe never," she says, her voice suddenly sounding tired. "We need them. You need them. Some of these code changes are live, installed at your client sites. Next week's release will add the finishing code and allow all the other changes to be activated."

"What the hell are you talking about?"

She turns to me, her face a hardened mask. An expression I don't recognise.

"Look at the date stamp, Elijah." She points at the list of changes. "This latest code change unlocks the door."

CHAPTER 21

PEN

I watch as my words sink in. The colour leeches from Elijah's face. I reach over, and his eyes move to where my hand grips his. A warmth spreads where our skin touches and I swallow past the constriction blocking my throat.

His gaze meets mine.

"It's okay, we can fix this," I say, wanting, no needing to pull us back into a place we both understand.

"Pen, if the code changes are out there. All my clients are vulnerable."

He withdraws his hand, running it through his hair.

I miss our connection, but I'm also relieved. We don't need any complications. We're in a charged environment, with our emotions running high.

"Do you trust me?" I ask.

Elijah's eyes lock on mine, the steely determination I recognise from the past appearing, making me smile.

"There he is," I say.

"What's the plan?" he asks before adding. "I take it you *do* have a plan?"

"Oh, ye of little faith," I say. "As I mentioned, this person's good at covering their tracks. Their coding skills aren't shabby either," I tell him.

I don't say I recognise the signature. That would not be wise at the moment.

"Don't do that," he says. "It sounds like you admire what they've done."

I look across but drop my gaze at his expression.

"Sorry. I don't agree with what they're doing, but it is hard not to appreciate their skill. This is pretty ingenious."

"Can we fix it?"

I raise an eyebrow.

"Let me guess. You appreciate their skills, but you're better," he says.

It's a statement rather than a question.

When I say nothing, Elijah smirks and shakes his head.

"Glad to see your modesty hasn't diminished over the years."

"They're good, but I *am* better. I've cracked it, haven't I?" I say.

He looks at me, and I can see the questions swirling around.

"Don't ask," I say. "I don't have time to go into it now."

"I trust you, Pen. I always have."

My stomach contracts at his words. The pain of what was and what could have been coming to the forefront. I move my hand to where his is now resting on the table and squeeze.

"Good, because I'm going to need you and your rusty coding skills in a little while."

He nods, turning his hand over and interlinking our fingers, returning the pressure.

It's my turn to look at him.

"Thank you," he says, his eyes softening, lighting up under my steady gaze.

"You're welcome."

I break our gaze and return my hand to the keyboard. I need to concentrate, not lose myself in the gaze of Elijah Frazer. I allowed myself to do that once before, and it nearly broke me.

As if sensing the change in my demeanour, Elijah stands up.

"I'll make us a fresh coffee and raid your cupboards for some snacks. I need to recharge. It's going to be a long morning."

Needing to put some distance between us, I say, "Go and grab a shower, freshen up. When we're done here, you're going to need to go into the office. Appear as if nothing's wrong. We cannot risk alerting *the mole* that you're onto them. Not if we want to catch them in the act."

"Can we?"

CHAPTER 22

ELIJAH

Pen offers a sly smile.

"There's nothing more enticing than a game of cat and mouse. Especially if you're the cat. I know exactly what trap to set."

"You appear to be enjoying this way too much," I grumble.

"No," she says, her tone becoming more serious. "But I enjoy taking down the bad guys."

Something in the way she says it makes me wonder if she's had years of practice at bringing them down.

I stare at her, but she gives nothing away.

I shake my head. "I know. No questions. But you will explain it to me when all this is over?"

She nods, but somehow, I'm not sure I'm going to be given the whole truth. Pen has changed, there's a definite edge to her now.

She returns her gaze to the screens, making it clear this conversation is over—for now.

I leave the room and lean against the wall. Dropping my head back, I stare at the ceiling. I'm not sure what I'd have done if Gabriel hadn't called Pen. I'm rusty. I wouldn't be able to do what she's done in the current timeframe.

I always knew she was good. It's why I bought my way into her life. Paid to become her partner all those years ago, not that she or anyone other than myself and Prof Dunn know that. It was the best money I ever invested.

I inhale deeply. Her scent is everywhere, invading my senses, getting into my head. The same way it did at university. I resisted her for years. I knew back then Pen was dangerous to me. When she was around, I could forget all about my responsibilities of keeping up expectations. I was able to be myself. Then I split from Darra that Christmas and broke my ankle a month later. Pen was there, helping me pick up the pieces, never asking more than I could give, and supporting me as I recovered from my broken dreams. That was when I fell in love with her, my best friend, but before I could act, fate stepped in.

FIFTEEN YEARS AGO

"So today is the day you're finally going to ask Pen out?"

I can't keep the grin from my face as I turn to my best friend.

"I am."

He claps me on the back.

"About time, man."

"I know. I just hope..." I stop, not sure I want to vocalise my fears out loud. "It's going to be more than a little embarrassing if she doesn't feel the same."

"Believe me, she does, I'd bet money on it," Jaxson says, squeezing my shoulder. "And, just so you know. You two will look great together."

I want to laugh. When we first met one another, nothing could have been further from the truth. We were polar opposites. But over time, Penelope Dawson has definitely thawed in her feelings towards me. She's become one of my best friends. She challenges me. Makes me feel alive. Around her, I strive to be a better version of myself. Not what I've programmed myself to be, as I try to keep up with expectations of being the eldest Frazer son. Pen is not what you would call a typical woman my parents or society would expect me to date. However, my parents love Pen, my whole family does. She's special.

"But what if I ruin our friendship? Have misread the signs."

"Stop panicking. You already know each other's likes and dislikes. You've been friends for nearly four years. Plus, she's got drive. She's crazy-mad intelligent, not to mention industrious. May have a more competitive streak than you, and that's saying something. You and she are the perfect pair. Your family adores her. She's also not hung up on the Frazer name. Shall I go on?"

I laugh. "No, I think that's enough of her virtues."

"Pen will never try to hold you back."

I grimace at his words, knowing full well who he's talking about. Darra, my ex-girlfriend.

I raise an eyebrow, making Jax grin.

"And you haven't been able to keep your eyes off Pen since we got back this term. You've been panting after her."

I give him a playful shove but know he's not wrong. I'm not sure when my feelings for Pen changed, but they have. She's all I can think about.

My phone rings.

I stare at the screen and groan.

"What does she want?" *Jax says, staring down at the offending piece of tech.*

"I don't know, but it's about the tenth time she's tried to call me today. It's like she knows I'm about to ask Pen out."

To say Darra has issues with Pen is an understatement. If she knew what I was about to do...but then, even before her demands of a marriage proposal, I was growing tired of all Darra's sniping. Her possessive tendencies were taking their toll.

"Ignore her. You and she have been over for months. You don't owe her anything," Jax says when I frown. "Look, I hate to say it. I know she was your girlfriend, but she's pushy and not in a good way. Treated you like a possession. She's never going to let you simply walk away, at least not without a fight. Stand firm, my friend."

I shake my head. I can't deny what he's saying.

I've been so focused on my Olympic goal, Pen, my business plan and finals. I missed the signs. I simply stared at her when she announced at Christmas that her parents were coming to see us after New Year and that I should think about talking to her dad about my proposal. I initially thought she was joking, but the look on her face told me she wasn't. The conversation that followed was hard. Explaining to the person you have dated casually in your eyes for four years, that you don't love them in that way.

Darra hadn't cried. She laughed. Asked me what love had to do with it. Told me we'd be the perfect power couple. How we would be unstoppable.

Staying together after that was impossible. I explained I would never marry someone I didn't love and broke up with her. Cutting off all contact until today.

Jax turns me to face him, gripping my shoulders and looking up at me. He doesn't know what Darra said to me that day.

"You were straight with her from the beginning. Yes, you dated, and in all honesty, for longer than most would have put up with her. Eli, you were very clear about where your priorities lie and that being in a serious relationship, aka marriage, was not one of them. She knows of your plans and aspirations. It's all we talked about every bloody holiday. We all did. Whether she's willing to admit it. You never made her any long-term promises."

I flinch. I know he's right.

The phone rings off, and I breathe a sigh of relief until it starts up again almost immediately.

"For fuck's sake."

I answer the phone with a growl.

"Darra," I say, offering no niceties.

"About time," she snaps, followed by a sniff.

"Can I ask why you feel the need to blow up my phone?"

"I need to see you," she says.

"We have nothing to say. I made myself very clear. I'm sorry you misunderstood, but nothing has changed."

"Everything has changed," she says cryptically.

Shit, has she found out I'm going to ask Pen out? I shoot a look at Jax, but he shrugs. He's the only person I've confided in, and I know he's watertight.

Darra sighs. "Look, Elijah, I really need to see you."

I press my thumb and forefinger into my eye sockets.

Darra has never been one to surrender. I need to make sure she stops whatever she's doing.

"Fine," I say after a moment. "I'll meet you in the coffee shop."

"No," she says. "It will be better if you come here."

"I'm not coming to your house, Darra."

"I can't say what I have to say in a public place. I need to see you, Eli. You owe me that much."

"I—"

Darra sighs again. "Bring your sidekick if you must."

I turn to Jax, and he shrugs.

"We'll be there in ten minutes."

I disconnect, wondering what the hell's going on. Glad Jax is going to be with me. I don't want any further misunderstandings.

"What the hell does she want?"

Jaxson is not a member of the Darra fan club. He thinks she's a user and social climber, irrespective of her father's wealth. Not surprising when she treats everyone she considers beneath her with contempt. Something my friend admitted to me after Darra and I split. As Jax comes from a middle-class family, she's dismissed him on more than one occasion, and as for Pen...I wish she'd told me some things Darra had done. When I broached it with Darra, she shrugged and made a joke of it, telling me they needed to toughen up. Life is hard.

"I don't know. Let's get this over with."

We arrive at Darra's apartment. Her parents have put her up in a luxury three-bedroom penthouse. She is no longer a student, having graduated at the end of last year, and she's working as a personal assistant to one of her father's friends.

I knock on the door and wait.

Darra opens it, her hair dishevelled, her makeup smudged, not her usual immaculate appearance.

"Darra?" I question.

"Come in," she says, stepping back from the door and holding her arm out toward the living area.

I limp my way inside. It's been almost two months since my accident, and although my leg is out of plaster, it's still healing. We make our way inside. Her parents have furnished the apartment to a high standard. Nothing is too good for Daddy's little girl.

Jax drops himself down on the sofa, but I remain standing. I want to get out of here as soon as possible.

"How are you?" Darra asks, her eyes going to the boot supporting my ankle.

"I won't be making this year's Olympic trials if that's what you're asking," I say.

"I'm sorry, Eli," she says, her eyes filling with what looks like genuine concern.

"It is what it is. My fault," I say.

Something my therapist has been helping me work on.

"Can I get you a drink?" Darra asks, always the perfect hostess.

"No thanks," I say. "Just tell me what you want, and we'll get out of your hair."

Darra stares up at me, her eyes filling.

Shit!

I hate tears.

She's used them a lot in the past six months. They seem to be her number one manipulation tactic in public, I'm beginning to realise.

"I'm...I'm pregnant."

I stare at her.

"Did you hear me, Eli? I said I'm pregnant."

"I heard you."

"It's yours," she says, her hands going to her flat stomach.

"Impossible. We've always been careful. We've also only been together once since Christmas."

She tilts her head and raises an eyebrow.

"No form of contraceptive is one hundred per cent reliable, and do I need to tell you, it only takes once?"

I think back to the night in question. It was the night before she'd dropped her parental engagement bombshell. We'd all drank too much to celebrate the New Year. Everyone stayed over at my parents' house, and Darra came to my room. Fifteen hours later, our relationship was over.

Fuck.

I sink down onto the sofa, my head spinning.

This can't be happening.

Jax remains silent next to me.

"What are you going to do?" *I ask.*

Ultimately, it's Darra's body. It's her choice.

"I'm having our child," *she says firmly.* "We're having this baby."

I squeeze my eyes closed as spots dance across my vision. My lungs constrict as I struggle to take in enough oxygen.

This can't be happening.

"How does he know it's his?" *Jax says, the venom in his voice unmistakable.*

"You bastard," *Darra says, her eyes filling.* "I know you hate me, Jax, but that's low, even for you. I'm just over two months pregnant. Do the maths, dumbass!"

"It's mine," *I tell him.*

"Oh hell," he hisses.

Oh, hell, indeed.

"Now you have to marry me, Elijah. If you don't, I'll make sure I go to every newspaper in the country and disparage your name. The Frazer name will be mud by the time Dad and I are done."

The look in her eye lets me know she's telling the truth. I may have the Frazer name and money behind me, but reputation is everything, and Darra will be out for blood. I can't let her destroy my family.

"Okay. I'll marry you. Once it's been proved the baby is mine."

"Elijah," Jax says. "You don't have to do this."

I turn sadly to my friend. "Yes, I do."

"Fine," Darra says. "I'll get a DNA test done and prove the baby is yours. I'll need a sample."

"Fine. Tell me when and where, and I'll do it."

If the baby turns out to be mine, there's no way on this planet I'll leave a child of mine to be raised by this manipulative bitch, even if it does mean giving up my own freedom to secure theirs.

CHAPTER 23

ELIJAH

I make my way upstairs, happy to put some distance between us. Memories of what was and could have been are coming thick and fast. Pen never knew I was going to ask her out. I called her up and cancelled our night out, choosing instead to get blind drunk with Jax and Zach.

I retrace my steps and grab my and Pen's bags from the car. Pleased now I had the foresight to bring a change of clothes and my wash-bag before I left the office.

I head upstairs and enter a bedroom. I realise my mistake instantly. This is Pen's room. I leave her case by the door and step inside.

A large four-poster bed sits in the middle of the back wall. A chaise longue positioned in the window. Because the bedroom is at the back of the house, one of its walls is entirely glass, like the kitchen it has spectacular views overlooking the picturesque landscape. I see the sun rising and realise Pen's bed is perfectly positioned to enjoy the view.

I know I should leave, but I can't. Instead, I make my way through the room towards another door. Opening it, I enter

Pen's en-suite. A claw foot bath sits in front of another all-glass window. My mind pictures Pen lying back amongst bubbles, her hair wet, her hands running over her body, taking in the view.

I turn away.

Fuck! I need to get a grip.

Pen is about to be married, and I am concentrating solely on Lottie for the foreseeable future. I've no right fantasising about Pen naked in the bath. We hardly talk these days—but being with her tonight. It feels like the past fifteen years have melted away. I felt it at the wedding, and tonight has cemented those feelings. We've fallen back into our old patterns and I realise I've missed it, missed her.

I shake myself and turn towards a large walk-in shower. I recognise Jax's design. My brother Caleb's is the same. I should find another bathroom.

I spot a set of folded, clean towels in the corner and grab one. The smell of washing powder, a scent familiar to Pen, wafts out.

I strip in record time, my cock aching.

I grab my body wash from my bag. The thought of walking around smelling like Pen for the day is a little more than my mind and body can take right now. It's been a long time since I was with a woman I cared about. Not that I've been a saint. I've been careful about the women I've hooked up with. Darra and I have both been discrete over the years, or at least I have. After the truth came out about Lottie, I couldn't touch her, didn't want to. Too many lies, so much deceit. I could barely stand to be in the same room as her. I walled off my heart to protect my daughter. I knew Darra would not think twice about preventing me from seeing Lottie, it was her only bargaining chip left, so she maximised it, and that threat was not something I could risk. The thought of never seeing my daughter again was enough to keep my libido in check.

I stand under the thundering spray and close my eyes. I run my hands over my body, washing off the stress of the day and night. When my hand grazes my rock-hard cock, I bite my lip to suppress the groan that rises in my throat.

The flat of my hand hits the tiled wall, and I drop my head as I count to ten.

My cock throbs, begging for attention.

Wanking off in Pen's shower, an engaged woman, my friend will not happen. I have more respect for her than that.

I squeeze my eyes closed and feel for the shower controls.

My muscles clench as I switch the setting from hot to ice bath cold. The sting of the spray stealing my breath, the icy shards, calming my raging libido.

I stand under the spray until my skin is red and tingling from the onslaught.

I flip the switch and turn off the jet, drawing in a deep, cleansing breath as I reach for the towel I collected. Drying off, I pull on a fresh set of jeans, a t-shirt, and a jumper, my standard office attire. Time to re-face the music.

When I make my way back downstairs, I hear a noise coming from the kitchen.

CHAPTER 24

PEN

With Elijah out of the way, I throw myself into double-checking my findings. Whoever did this knows what they're doing. They've covered their tracks brilliantly. I'm not wrong. I recognise the code. What I don't understand is why? If it's who I suspect, we're supposed to be on the same side. Does The Seamstress know? Is she in on it?

Fuck!

Who could have imagined that being out of the game would be this complicated?

I park my thoughts, and instead, I create a file containing all the changes that will need to be backed out. By the time I'm done, my head is about to explode with what-ifs. I need to get out of my *she-cave*. The walls have become restricting, and my sanctuary has begun to feel more like a prison.

I make my way up to the kitchen and stare out over the garden. The rising sun appears over the trees in the background. I went upstairs and saw my suitcase before hearing Elijah in my bathroom, so I made a hasty retreat. Seeing him naked is not something I need in my memory banks. Tonight has already ignited a whole pile of memories and feelings I thought were long buried.

We're very different people now, and I'm about to marry a wonderful man.

I turn sharply as Elijah enters the kitchen, instantly wishing I hadn't. He's fresh out of the shower, my shower, looking refreshed, his hair damp, his clothes new.

The jumper he's wearing stretches across his broad chest. I know his jeans will hug his ass if he was to turn around. My mouth dries, and I take another swig of coffee.

"How was your shower?" I choke.

"Great," he says. "I used yours. Hope you don't mind. I thought, rather than dirty another room."

The back of my neck grows hot, and a fluttery sensation of a thousand butterflies setting flight in my stomach hits.

"No-no problem." I stumble over the words. "Did you find everything you needed?"

"I had a change of clothes and my wash bag in the car. I used the folded towel. I put it on your wash basket. I also popped your case by the door."

"Perfect. Thank you."

My mind wanders to the all-nighters we would pull at mine before our exams. Elijah would often use my shower then, too. He left his body wash and shampoo for ease, claiming mine were too girlie. I used to steal small amounts every night before I went to bed. I had no shame then, his toiletries were high end, and I loved the smell. It was comforting.

I bite my lip and notice Elijah's eyes lock on the movement.

I turn away as the pressure builds between my legs. I take another drag on my coffee cup, only to find it empty.

Shit.

You're an engaged woman, Penelope Dawson. You're just frus-

trated. You and Kris were too tired with all the running around last week. Soon, that won't be a problem.

"Coffee?" I ask, moving across the kitchen, needing a distraction. "I know I could certainly do with another one."

"That would be great," Elijah says, pulling out a stool at the kitchen island.

Fantastic! It appears we've moved on from talking business to that awkward morning after speech. Only this one is without the orgasms.

What!?!

"Did you get what you wanted done?" Elijah asks.

I exhale, flicking my eyes to the ceiling.

Thank you. Back to something I can control.

I nod. "And I have an idea how to catch whoever is responsible," I add.

A slow, sexy smile spreads over Elijah's face, and my heart pounds in my chest.

Stop.

"I'm going to send Gabriel a very large case of wine as a thank you for calling you," he says. "What can I do for you?"

I swallow hard.

"Nothing. Catching the bastard will be reward enough."

That, and getting back on with my life.

Lusting after an old friend is not okay. I boxed up my feelings for Elijah Frazer years ago. I cannot let old emotions resurface and derail my current life, especially when I'm weeks away from marrying someone else and fulfilling my heart's desire.

Unrequited love sucks!

My best friend. That's all Elijah ever was. It's not his fault I fell in love with him while we were at university, and I wasn't the only woman to do so. His charisma and charm made him irresistible. He just didn't know it, or was so used to it, it no longer registered. To him, work or swimming was his priority. Plus, he had a beautiful girlfriend on his arm, not someone I could compete with. Never even thought to try. At least not until they split up. Then there was a speck of hope until there wasn't. His beautiful ex-girlfriend, announced she was pregnant, and he married her. No surprise there. Elijah would always do the right thing.

He told me after Christmas, they were over, then he had his accident. Next he was engaged to beautiful, put-together Darra, who came from the right breeding stock, unlike me, with my charity shop clothing, heavy makeup, piercings, and single-parent family.

I slam down on the pity party taking place in my head. I refuse to let these unwelcome feelings of inadequacy resurface.

I'm going to blame my overactive libido. On the fact, it's five AM, and our banter and close proximity have reignited memories I've suppressed over the years.

They aren't real.

We scarcely know one another now.

I've read articles stating it's not unusual for brides-to-be to get cold feet, especially when marriage is going to involve a monumental change in their lives. And mine most certainly is. I'm upending my life and switching continents.

I move to the warming draw and pull out the plate of scrambled eggs and toast I prepared while he was in the shower. I slide it across the island to where Elijah is sitting, along with a steaming mug of coffee.

"This looks amazing," Elijah says, looking up and smiling.

I drag my eyes away from his lips. "You're welcome. I thought you might want something before we get started again."

He looks a lot more relaxed. Now he's washed some of the tension off.

"So, what's the plan now?"

I take a seat next to him as he attacks the food with enthusiasm.

"We wait. Set the trap I've devised and wait for whoever is responsible to trigger it. Or we trigger it and see who pops up."

I can't keep the smugness out of my voice. This is my favourite part, bringing the bad guy to justice. This will be extra satisfying as they've gone after my friend. A bad move on their part.

"I promise, this person or persons will not get away with it."

I've been in charge of several sting operations in the past. I know what I'm doing when it comes to catching Elijah's mole. Not that I can tell Elijah that. But secrets have been in my life for as long as I can remember.

We finish up, and Elijah once again clears away the mess while I grab a quick shower.

Knowing he's been in this room, stood naked where I'm now standing.

The air smells of his body wash and shampoo.

I pick up the towel he has folded on the wash basket next to the sink. Before I can stop myself, I raise it to my nose and inhale deeply.

No!

I throw it into the far corner before turning and resting my forehead against the cool glass of the shower.

It's okay

If everything goes to plan tomorrow, you'll be back on a plane and heading back to your new life. Elijah Frazer will be back in his box.

I shower before screwing my wet hair up into a messy bun and pulling on a fresh set of clothes. I give myself a quick once over in the mirror to ensure I don't have mascara running down my face. I'm not redoing my makeup. Once Elijah is gone, I shall head to bed.

I find Elijah downstairs, scrolling through the code changes.

"I can't believe you deciphered this," he says, turning towards me.

My chest swells at his praise.

"Code and coding are my hyper-focus. You know that. I could sit for hours—experimenting with code. That's why writing computer games is perfect for me. It's the management, and organisational part of running a company that's always been the hardest. But then I have an awesome team for that."

Danika, who is my right-hand woman, has been a godsend. She ensures I don't get lost in the cyber world and forget to eat or speak to clients. She's my version of Gabriel's Leah, only without the sex.

"Right, let's do this."

Elijah moves closer as I explain my plan. We go backwards and forwards as we come up with a solution that will work with his code and fit into company policy. We don't want to trigger the wrong person.

For the next three hours, we work together to perfect it. I write, and he tests. The code I'm amending was changed before this release, so no one should be looking at it. It's the recent changes, and they are harmless on their own. Layering is a clever method of attack.

When I'm done, we both sit back.

"Now you go into the office and act as if nothing is wrong," I say, turning to Elijah, whose enormous frame has sunk into his chair.

It's then I notice the stress lines around his mouth.

"What's wrong?" I ask.

"It's nothing, just my ankle. Sitting for any length of time causes it to ache."

"Still?"

"It only aches when I've been sitting for hours. Blood flow or something."

I push back my chair and tap my knee.

"Put it up here," I say, scowling when he stares at me blankly.

"Give me your damn leg. You can't go into the office hobbling or drive, for that matter."

I watch as he lifts his leg, placing it on my knee.

"Damn, you've got a heavy ass leg," I grunt letting his foot rest on the chair between my legs.

My cheeks warm, but I rub my forehead with the back of my hand.

I roll up the bottom of his jeans and pull down his sock. The surgery scar has faded to a fine white line over the years. Who would have thought coming off your bike could destroy a career?

I move my hands to the aching muscles and knead where I feel the tightness.

Elijah flinches under my fingers.

"Sorry," I say as I knead a particularly tight spot.

I look up to find Elijah watching me, his eyes shadowed.

"You're good at this," he says, almost with a groan.

I continue my ministrations, ignoring the feel of his skin under my hands and the throbbing ache between my thighs.

This is me helping a friend in pain.

I focus on the task at hand, tuning out the distractions his close proximity brings.

When my body can't take anymore, I pull up his sock and unroll his jeans. Patting the top of the material.

"How's that?" I say, hoping I don't sound as breathless as I feel.

I keep my eyes averted from Elijah and spin back towards the desk when he removes his foot.

"Amazing, thank you. You have magic hands," he says, his voice a little strained.

I look at the clock on the screen and breathe a sigh of relief. Our time is up. It's close to nine AM.

"Hopefully, you'll be able to walk on it now," I say. "You need to get going, or someone might wonder where you are."

"It's okay. I messaged Jules. If anyone asks, I have a doctor's appointment and then I'm popping in to see Gabriel on my way to work. Since it's something I do regularly."

"That's good," I say, not wanting to turn towards him.

"Pen." He pauses. "Is everything all right?"

I turn and flash him my brightest smile. "Everything's fine. I'm crashing. It's been a long night. The adrenalin is wearing off."

"Understandable."

Elijah stands, and I follow suit.

"Thank you. For everything, Pen."

"The testers shouldn't pick up on anything."

"There's a code freeze in place. Whoever is responsible shouldn't be able to make any more changes now."

"Don't be so sure. It's why they're using your login. You and Todd are the only two people who can grant permission. However, if anyone makes changes or tries to log in using your or Todd's login, we will catch them." He raises an eyebrow, and I grin. "I made a few minor changes while you made that last coffee. I altered their automatic delete. It now deletes to a specific folder on your computer, one that only you have access to. If they login or try to make any more changes, we won't have to hunt. It will show up there."

"You're sure?"

He looks sceptical, and I harrumph.

"Really?" I say, eventually. "After everything?"

"Okay, I trust you," he says with a smirk. "But I want to thank you."

"No need. You can owe me one." When he frowns, I roll my eyes. "Not really," I say, pushing his shoulder. "It's what friends are for."

Elijah drops his head, a strange look appearing on his face. When he lifts his eyes to mine, his expression is drawn. "But then, I haven't been a very good friend over the past few years."

Our gazes lock, and I let my lips tilt.

"Maybe we've both let our friendship slide. Life getting in the way and all that."

He nods his head slowly. A furrow appears between his brow.

We both know it's too late now. I'm marrying another man and moving across the world. That ship has sailed, quite literally.

He steps forward and takes my shoulders in his hands before planting a kiss on my cheek. I freeze, the warmth of his lips against my skin sending jolts of electricity to my core, my body waking up. Before I can think or do anything, he moves back.

"You truly are a remarkable woman, Penelope Dawson," he says.

I incline my head, wrapping my arms around my waist,

"Don't you forget it, Elijah Frazer. Now get out of here. I need to get some sleep."

We go upstairs and to the garage, where his car is parked.

Elijah grabs my hand and squeezes. "I mean it, Pen. If there is anything you need, ever, just let me know."

I look up into his eyes, shades of the young Elijah shining through.

"I will," I say, although know I never will.

He squeezes my fingers once more, and I miss the sensation when he withdraws his hand and gets into the car. I open the garage door using the keypad on the wall and lean against it as he reverses out.

My mum appears at his window and knocks, smiling in at him.

Elijah stops the car getting out, sweeping my mother into a bear hug, swinging her around.

"Now, Elijah Frazer, what are you doing sneaking out of my engaged daughter's house at this early hour?"

I move to the entrance of the garage and laugh as Elijah's cheeks turn red at my mother's scrutiny.

"We were working," he splutters, shooting me a panicked look, which has me doubling over even further. His eyes dart to mine as my mother's twinkle with mischief.

"It's okay, Elijah. She knew we were working on a project. She's pulling your leg."

His shoulders relax.

Elijah's respect for the older generation was drummed into him, although my mother is not technically that much older.

"I'm only teasing," she says, giving him another squeeze.

"That's okay then," Elijah says, shooting me a look that would render me unconscious.

Mum has always liked to tease.

"Mum, Elijah needs to go to work," I tell her.

"No problem. Just don't be a stranger," she says, patting his enormous chest before stepping back. "See you soon."

I watch as he stoops and drops a kiss on my mother's cheek.

"You too, Mrs D," he says, making her growl as he grins. "Two can play at that game."

"Get to work," she says, smiling. "I need my daughter to make me a coffee. Her machine is better than mine."

A total lie since I bought her an identical model.

Elijah is still smiling when he gets back into his car. Mum comes to stand next to me, and we watch him leave.

When he's out of sight, she turns to me, her eyes questioning. "And?"

"We were working."

She grunts as she walks past me and into my house.

"Come in," I say under my breath before rolling my eyes and following her. It'll be a while before I get any sleep.

CHAPTER 25

ELIJAH

Adrenalin courses through my body as I enter my office, priming my muscles despite my lack of sleep. I look to the bookshelf where the watch Pen gave me buzzed.

Fuck.

It's something when you can't even feel safe in your own environment.

My nerves are stretched raw from stress and now a lack of sleep.

Everyone I passed on my way here, anyone who acknowledged me, I wondered.

Is it you? Are you the one who sold me out?

My mind is racing.

Whoever it is, I've been working alongside them for months, maybe even years. It could even be one of my founding members.

Fuck! This is messing with my head. I still need to speak to Todd and the board.

I move towards my desk and drop into my chair. It lets out a loud creak in protest and I drop my head back, closing my eyes.

A knock on my door has me jumping upright.

"Yes," I shout, my voice sharper than usual.

The door opens, and Jules enters.

"Are you ready for our weekly meeting?" She pauses. "Or we can reschedule?"

I look at my calendar.

It's our meeting to plan up the following week. I like to be organised, always have done. I may not have control over everything in my life, but within the office, I like to run a tight ship.

"No, it's fine. Come in, take a seat."

A frown mars Jule's brow, but she says nothing.

Pen's words echo through my mind.

"It's important you keep up appearances. You don't want to tip off the mole by changing your routine. At the moment, we have the upper hand."

I smile, but it's impossible to miss the look of concern she shoots me. She's worked for me for years. Is used to my mood changes and is likely more attuned to them than most. I need to give the woman a pay rise!

In true Jules style, she refrains from calling me out on whatever she's picking up on.

"Sorry, I had a late night," I say, wanting to offer some excuse for my less than friendly behaviour.

She smiles, her shoulders relaxing.

"Say no more."

The smile she gives me tells me she thinks I was up late *having fun.* If only she knew.

"Let's get started," I say.

We run through the minutes and tasks from last week. We close off completed tasks and reset outstanding ones.

I dictate a couple of memos I want to be sent out and pray I have thrown off whoever is listening.

It seems absurd and a little disconcerting knowing there's someone out there listening to us. Taking their own notes.

Jules asks her usual questions, and we discuss next week's planned meetings. When she finally leaves, I sit back. My concentration is shot. I'm getting too old to burn the candle at both ends. Knowing someone is out to get me, take down my company. When Darra finally left, I thought life would become less complicated. I could pick up the pieces of my shattered existence. Live again, but no, instead, I'm now dealing with this.

By midday, I'm done.

I get up and grab my coat.

Opening my door, I head to Jules' desk.

"I'm heading out."

She looks up and grins.

"It must have been a good night."

I groan. "I wish. I spent the night tossing and turning."

Realising I don't want her to get the wrong impression.

"She'll be fine, you know. A summer in Italy will be amazing. She'll come back with all these stories."

I take a moment to realise Jules has equated my sleepless night with Lottie being away. I breathe a sigh of relief.

"I know. It's just hard. This is the longest she's been away. The apartment feels very empty."

At least, if anyone is listening in, this sounds genuine. It's true I am worried about Lottie, but I know she's having a great time. Her calls and messages are saying as much. It's also important she spends time with her mother. I may not be Darra's biggest fan, but Lottie is her daughter, and it's important they forge their own relationship.

Jules shoots me a sympathetic look.

"Take the time to enjoy yourself. Meet up with friends."

I nod, not wanting to point out that fifteen years of

prioritising Frazer Cyber Security, alongside alienating my friends to conceal my secret, has left me with few remaining.

I smile. "Maybe I'll do that. I'll be back in an hour. I just need to get some fresh air."

I get out my phone and dial Lottie's number.

"Hey, Dad," Lottie says.

"Hey sunshine, how are you?" I ask.

Jules looks across and mouths.

"Take as long as you need. If there's an emergency, I'll let you know." She shoos me away with her hand and a warm smile. "Go."

I return her smile and head for the elevator, continuing my conversation with Lottie, my phone pressed to my ear.

"Elijah."

I turn at the sound of my name.

Todd is walking towards me.

"Hey, sweetheart, I've got to go. Enjoy your class this afternoon...love you too."

I turn to face Todd, my heart thumping.

Is it Todd?

He's been with me since the beginning. Could he be the saboteur?

"I'm just heading out," I say, holding the elevator door. I try to force my shoulders to relax as he joins me.

"Did you see my memo? Testing is complete. We're good to go. The teams are in place for this weekend, ready for the first rollout."

We never let everything roll out at once. Too dangerous if there does happen to be an issue. Easier to only have to back out a couple of sites, not everyone.

"Great news," I say, trying to add an influx of enthusiasm.

I have to trust Pen and the code we changed last night. That it will hold up to whatever this person has planned, that we haven't missed anything. Not knowing their target is killing me.

Is it a particular client? Or is it me and my firm they want to bring to its knees? Hold me to ransom.

"You look knackered," he says, turning to face me. "You been burning the midnight oil more than usual? We're not getting any younger."

He chuckles to himself.

"Didn't sleep great," I tell him. "Lottie is away with Darra."

I use Jules' excuse as it fits the narrative.

"Ah, I'm sorry, man. It must be difficult. Divorce and children are never easy. Seems to be the hardest on the guy as well. Custody going to the mum most of the time."

I stare at his hand as he grips my shoulder and squeezes.

Oh fuck, now I've got people feeling sorry for me.

Not what I want going around the office.

"No, it's more the silence. Lottie lives with me full time now, and her mum has moved to Italy," I tell him.

He grins. "Ah, teenagers. Noise and money pits. Mine cost a fortune. Always wanting the latest gadget and don't mention the school fees."

He grins and rolls his eyes.

My spine stiffens.

Is that what this is? Someone selling me out for money?

I pinch the bridge of my nose, trying to stem the headache forming behind my eyes.

The elevator reaches the lobby, and I step out. Todd claps me on the back.

"Get some rest. Things here will be fine without you."

"Thanks, Todd. I appreciate it," I say, almost through gritted teeth.

Little does he know, or maybe he does. Things haven't been running without me. My divorce from Darra took my concentration and look at what's happened. My company is one of the few things I have left, having given Darra everything else in order to ensure Lottie's adoption.

I make my way onto the street. It's warm, the summer sun reflecting off the surrounding office buildings, trapping the heat at street level. I hail a taxi, too tired to walk to Gabriel's office. I need to see him. Thank him for arranging Pen, but also give him a brotherly bollocking for overstepping. In all honesty, the second point I'll let go. I'm not sure what I'd have done without her. Although her skills have raised more questions than answers. I wonder if Gabe knows more about Pen's life. The thought bothers me more than it should.

The taxi pulls up outside, and I climb out, making my way into his reception.

The main lobby calls up and announces my arrival. Amanda, his PA, is waiting for me by the elevator when it opens.

"It's a busy day today," she says, and I shoot her a questioning look, making her smile. "Leah is here with little Callum, and Ms Dawson has just arrived. They're all in Gabriel's office if you would like to join them."

My heart thunders at the mention of Pen's name. I need to speak to Gabe, not face the one person who has invaded my thoughts all morning. I realise it's not only the company that has taken my focus but the woman I sat beside all night. A woman who's driven me insane from the moment I met her over eighteen years ago. A woman who's always been just out of reach and is now moving even further away.

It's not how I always saw us. At one point, there had been hope, but fate had other plans for us then, and it seems like now. She will forever be *the one who got away*.

Kristophe is a lucky man.

Amanda bustles me forward and knocks on Gabriel's door, opening it before I can stop her.

"Gabriel, your brother is here," she says, pushing the door

wider so Gabriel and the other occupants of the room can see me.

I take in the scene in front of me. Gabriel is sitting smiling at his wife while Pen is grinning on her hands and knees. Her ass is in the air as she operates the plastic figure, dancing on the carpet in front of her while my nephew shrieks with laughter. Her boots are missing. Instead, her brightly coloured socks stand out against her black trousers. Who knew?

It's at that moment Callum looks up.

"Unc Lij," he squeals, clambering up and stumbling towards me. He staggers, and I scoop him up into my arms, swinging him into the air. I grin as he squishes my cheeks in his tiny hands.

"Hey, scamp, how are you?" I ask him, my exhaustion suddenly gone.

"Good," he says. "Throw," he adds, and I shake my head.

He loves me throwing him in the air and catching him. I'm his giant uncle.

"Not inside, buddy, no head banging, or Daddy and Mummy will be cross with me."

His bottom lip pops out, and he looks over my shoulder.

"Where Ottie?"

"Lottie is with her mum today."

His little shoulders sag, but he shifts his focus and grins.

"'Kay," he says before turning around in my arms and pointing. "Ant Pen here."

My eyes meet Pen's over my nephew's head. She's shifted position to sit cross-legged on the carpet. She's surrounded by a barrage of stuffed and plastic toys.

"I can see," I say, unable to keep the mirth from my tone.

Pen looks disgustingly refreshed seeing, like me, she had no sleep last night.

"Morning sunshine," she says. "Come to join the fun?"

Gabriel groans, and Leah chuckles.

"This is my workplace," he grumbles. "Caleb's away. Now I get my big brother instead."

"I can leave," I say, turning towards the door, Callum still in my arms.

A resounding *no* goes up from Leah and Pen, followed by laughter.

"I'll get more coffee," Amanda says, reaching up and tickling Callum, making him squirm before she leaves.

"Juice pees," he says.

"Of course, young man."

"Enclosed cups," Gabriel calls after her.

Gabriel won't have open mugs of coffee or tea around Callum, not after he nearly pulled one onto himself when he first started walking.

"Come in and sit down," Leah says, pointing to the sofa near where Pen is sitting.

I close the door and put the now squirming Callum back onto the floor. He returns to Pen, who opens her arms and has him fall into them.

She tickles him until he's squealing with delight.

"More," he says breathlessly when she stops.

"Enough, Callum, let poor Pen come up for air."

Pen cuddles him close to her chest, and he rests his head against her shoulder. The sight does strange things to me. I think back to how she was with Lottie. Not that I got to appreciate it very often. We made her Lottie's godmother, along with Jaxson and Zach as godfathers. Or should I say, my father insisted, even though we were barely talking at that point. He must have had foresight into what an amazing godmother she would be. She's always been there for Lottie, still is. Day trips and homework. Nothing is or has been too much trouble for my daughter, but with me, she always made sure I was absent.

"Getting ready for your own?" Leah says as Callum snuggles deeper into Pen's shoulder.

He's clearly exhausted himself and is beginning to fall asleep listening to Pen's heartbeat.

She looks across and smiles.

"I can only hope," she says, her gaze wistful.

My heart gives a kick at the thought of Pen's stomach growing round with Lansdown's child.

"Not long until the wedding," Leah says, grinning. "How are the preparations going?"

I want nothing more than to tell my sister-in-law to stop, but one look at Gabriel, and I swallow my retort.

"I can't believe it's only two months. It's been mad. Although Kris's mum has taken over and coordinated everything with the wedding planner. She knows the move is crazy enough. But Kris and I didn't want to wait."

I wonder if I hear an underlying current in her voice. No. It's that her words are like an arrow to the chest.

I look up to find Gabriel staring at me.

I decide to change the subject.

"I didn't expect to find you here. I would have assumed you'd be catching up on some sleep."

Leah eyes dart between us.

Pen laughs.

"After you left, Mum came in and began drinking coffee. I made the mistake of joining her. She would not leave easily."

Gabriel knows what's going on. He knows why she's here. I'm not sure how much he's told Leah.

Pen, as if sensing Leah's confusion.

"That thing Gabe was talking about. I was helping Eli. It took all night."

"Ahh," Leah says, a small smirk appearing on her lips.

I shoot her a look, and she raises an eyebrow. It seems I no longer intimidate my sister-in-law, not that I'm convinced I ever did, nor did I ever want to. That she's forgiven my surly ass shows what an amazing human being she is and why my brother fell so madly in love with her. She's a forgiving soul, and I was a complete asshole. Luckily, we've put that behind us. We both love Gabe and want the best for him.

"How did it go?" Gabe asks.

"Good," Pen says, not adding anymore.

She shoots me a look. Surely, she doesn't think that someone has bugged Gabriel's office, too.

She shrugs as if answering my unspoken question.

"It's safe. I checked this morning when Pen called," Gabe says.

I should know my brother, Mr Gadget, would have a tool.

"Good. I taught you well," Pen says, grinning. "We plugged the leak, let's say."

Gabriel nods, his eyes flashing to mine.

"And?"

"I do not know," I say, shaking my head. He wants to know if I've worked out who's behind this and why.

"*Shit*," Gabriel says.

"Gabe!" Leah chastises, sending him a dirty look before flipping her eyes to their son, who is now sleeping peacefully against Pen's chest.

My eyes catch sight of them together, and it does another flip.

Pen looks down at the sleeping tot in her arms, and a look I've never seen passes over her face. It's wistful…peaceful. Her arms tighten before her eyes raise to mine. Our gazes lock before I drag mine away, turning towards my brother.

"I've got someone working on it," she says, surprising me.

My gaze flies to hers, and the look she shoots me tells me not to dig any deeper, so I comply. More because my brain and body are in turmoil than for any other reason.

"I'm going to go," I say, standing up just as Amanda returns with our drinks. I hold open the door as she places the cups on Gabriel's desk.

"I need to get a couple of hours shut-eye. I can't think straight."

"Try having a child. I've been running on empty for months," Gabriel says, earning himself a playful slap from Leah.

"Get some rest," Leah says. "It's time I got this little man home, anyway. But coffee first. I miss your coffee-making skills."

She shoots Amanda a grateful smile as she passes through the door.

Stooping, she scoops the sleeping Callum out of Pen's arms. While Pen sets about collecting the toys from Gabriel's floor.

"Not bunny," Leah says, at the teddy with big floppy ears that Lottie chose for Callum when he was born.

Pen smiles and holds him out as Leah places a still sleeping Callum in his buggy.

Only handing the worn teddy over once Leah straightens.

"Thank you."

I bend down and help Pen clear up the carnage Callum has made.

"I'll see you later," I say when we have returned Gabriel's office back to the professional place of work it has always been.

"I'll walk you out," Gabriel says, diving out of his chair, joining me at the door before I can say anything.

"Bye, ladies," I say, exiting the room.

We walk away in silence.

"Are you okay?" my younger brother asks.

"Not really," I tell him truthfully.

I'm working on letting my family back into my life. For

too many years, I've shut them out, thinking I was protecting them from my disastrous relationship. What I've learned is I fooled no one. Instead, I caused them more worry and strife. Something I'm struggling with, and my therapist is helping me with. That feeling of being isolated, unable to connect with people meaningfully. Thinking things would never improve or that there was no escape. How I made my bed, and now I must lie in it.

"Pen is the best at what she does," he tells me, and I wonder if Gabe knows more about Pen's mysterious past than I do. I know the two are close.

"Gabe?"

He shakes his head, his eyes locking on mine.

"If you want details, you talk to Pen."

The look on his face tells me I will not win this battle.

"That's because I'm a genius," he says, his lips twitching at my unasked question.

I groan.

"Don't forget it's boys' night next week. If this is resolved. We expect you there. No excuses."

Another battle I don't think I'll win.

CHAPTER 26

ELIJAH

FIFTEEN YEARS AGO

One look at Pen, and I know it's not good news.

"Where the hell have you been?" I snap.

I know I shouldn't, but I've been worried. Pen has been gone a week. Disappeared, no note, no nothing. Even her mum couldn't tell me where she was, only that she needed time away.

Her computer was missing, and she had vanished.

"Good to see you too," she says, slumping down on the sofa opposite me.

"Is that all you've got to say for yourself?"

I find my chest tightening as I stare at her.

Something is off. She still has her gothic makeup and her black clothes, but I'm sensing something—I just can't place it.

When she shrugs, my temper rises.

"Pen, you missed the meeting with our backers."

She breaks eye contact, and I stop, my heart rate picking up. Pen's gaze won't meet mine, and my stomach sinks.

"About that."

"Pen, what the hell is going on?"

There's a long pause.

"Whatever it is," I say. "We can work it out."

Although the sinking feeling in my chest tells me maybe we can't. Things have been a little awkward since I told Pen Darra was pregnant. A wall of silence hit me that day, too.

"I can't do this," she says eventually.

"What do you mean, you can't do this?"

She looks up, her eyes finally meeting mine. The pain in their depths steals my breath. I go to open my mouth but stop at the look passing over her face. One I don't recognise.

"I can't go into business with you."

I drop back on the sofa and stare at her.

"What do you mean?"

She shrugs. "Exactly what I just said. I'm not going into business with you. I can't."

I sit forward, my forearms resting on my thighs.

"Can't or won't?"

She sighs, a sound I rarely hear from Pen.

"It's not what I want. Frazer Dawson Cyber Security is your dream, not mine. I want to create and design computer games."

"I don't understand. You designed the initial software." I try hard to understand what the hell I'm hearing. "Cyber tech is your baby. The software you've designed is off the scale in terms of what it can do. We're set to make a fortune. Even the backers I met with yesterday said as much."

She shrugs again.

"This is not about money," she says, although her voice is flat.

"Then what the hell is it about?" I say, my voice beginning to rise. What the hell is wrong with her? This is not Pen, or at least not the Pen I know and I....

Fuck, I can't let my mind go there.

"Look. I've done a lot of thinking. This will not work. Us working together. You need to focus on Darra and the baby—"

"Is that what this is about? Because?"

"No, yes, partly." She sighs. "This is also about me. I've realised this isn't my dream. I don't want to lose myself."

I shake my head. I sense there's more to it. Maybe it's unfair to push. It's my fault, after all. If I wasn't marrying Darra, having a child with her... but I can't lose Pen, not now.

"Pen—"

"No Elijah. The software, the business plan, it's yours."

"But."

"I applied for a scholarship and got it. I'm going to follow my dreams of creating computer games."

"Where?"

I know this has always been her dream. It came up one night, but I thought she'd put it to one side, was going to do it as a side project.

"The Frazer Foundation," she says, her gaze now planted on the floor in front of her.

My heart sinks.

Not Pen.

"Is that what all this was about?"

Her eyes rise and clash with mine. A flash of fire and anger burst out. There she is, the Pen I recognise.

"Is that what you think? I've done all this just to get a foot in the door with your parents?"

"What else should I think?"

"Well, piss off, Elijah. Have you forgotten your parents have only just set up the foundation? I've been your friend for four years."

She gets up and storms towards the door.

"Pen." I watch her hand grasp the handle as she pauses. Her chin drops to her chest.

"I have to do this," she says quietly. "I'll help with the code if you need me, but Todd and Theo, they know what they're doing. I'd recommend approaching one or both of them to work with you."

"I don't want Todd and Theo. We're a team, you and me," I hear myself say.

She's been my rock, pushed me to be better, made me more. She's been the light in my fucked up world over the past few months, ever since Darra told me, ever since I broke my ankle.

She turns, her expression hollow.

"You need to let me go," she says quietly before turning and leaving the room.

"But what if I can't?" I tell the space she's vacated.

CHAPTER 27

PEN

*L*eah's gaze is locked on me as Gabriel and Elijah leave the room.

I turn to her, and when she raises an eyebrow in my direction, I smile.

"Is that all I'm going to get?" she asks.

I shrug and busy myself with the last of the toys, ignoring her question. When I'm done, I pick up the coffee Amanda brought in.

"Delicious," I say, closing my eyes and letting the taste explode across my tongue.

Leah lets out an unladylike *harrumph*, something she's picked up from her husband, and I chuckle.

"Have it your way," Leah says good-naturedly before I open one eye and look at her grinning. "Shall we get out of here?"

She pushes the still-sleeping Callum towards the door.

"Absolutely," I say, jumping up and following, placing my empty coffee cup on the desk.

It's been too long since we've chatted.

I couldn't believe my luck when, ten minutes after I

arrived at Gabriel's office, Leah turned up with Callum. One of my favourite little humans. I was on the floor in seconds, shoes off so as not to catch little fingers as we crawled around.

Seeing Gabriel with his wife and son warms my heart. I never thought I'd see the day. He had a toy pile stored in his office and was happy to have them strewn all over the floor. I wonder if Kris will be the same?

A fluttery feeling began deep in my belly when the door opened behind me. My pounding heart revealed his identity before he uttered a word.

Should I be surprised?

I know Gabriel called me after Elijah spoke to him, but Elijah has held himself back from his family for so long. What is surprising to me is my body's response to the man who I've tried to distance myself from for years. Why is it that when I'm finally moving on, old feelings are being dragged back to the surface?

This is my problem, and I need to get a grip. I'll be leaving soon, going back to Kris and my future.

One thing is for sure. It's good to see Elijah finally reaching out and reconnecting, mending the bridges and relationships his marriage broke. Whatever happened between him and Darra left its scars. His focus was always on his swimming and then his business, but when we first met, he was never closed off. He was sociable, family-oriented. The Frazer household was a hub where we all gathered. We still do, but instead of him being at the heart, he's been skirting around the edges, looking in for far too many years. Hopefully, this is the start of change.

I didn't miss Elijah's smirk when he took in my wacky socks. It was a joke at uni. He would always buy me the brightest, garish pair of socks he could find. He told me, even if he couldn't see them inside my boots, they would brighten up my goth look. I resisted until I couldn't. Now, it's a habit. I loved black in those days, and it was not only my clothes but my hair, my nails, my eye makeup. I look back at pictures and scare even myself.

I still wear a lot of black, but I've toned down my makeup and hair. Running a multi-million-pound empire does that to someone. I have removed most of my piercings. My nose, eyebrow, and lip rings, as well as my tongue stud. I still sport a belly button bar and have multiple hoops and studs in each ear.

"So, what's going on with Elijah?" Leah says as soon as we hit the street.

I move alongside her as we navigate our way through the crowds.

"I was helping him with something," I tell her.

"All night?"

She stops, causing the surrounding people to swear and step around her.

I grab her arm to get her moving again, apologising to those Londoners cursing us.

"It was a big something," I say.

It's only when the words leave my mouth that I realise what I said. I turn to Leah, whose face crumples with laughter. Shaking my head, I manoeuvre us into a nearby coffee shop. I will need more caffeine if I'm going to be quizzed.

"Sorry," she chokes out as she tries to get her laughter under control.

"Hilarious," I say drily.

"Oh, come on, it was a little bit funny. I *am* married to a Frazer," she says, waggling her eyebrows.

My cheeks heat.

"I wouldn't know," I say, feeling more flustered than I should.

Leah coughs, choking on the air she has inhaled. I slap her on the back with a tut.

Leah and I have become firm friends since she started dating and married Gabriel. I liked her from the get-go. She's smart, funny and put the society bitches in their place. I can still see their faces, and Gabriel's. I don't think I've ever seen my friend go so red. But the way he looked at Leah, how he looks at her now. It's like he could devour her, and she him. When they're in the same room, it's as if the air will combust.

We grab a seat in the corner where there's space for the pushchair. A waitress comes over to take our order. Once she's left, Leah turns.

"I saw the way Elijah looked at you. Are you telling me nothing happened?"

"I am. Nothing happened. We worked all night, reminisced about the past. But I hate to disappoint your romantic streak. You're seeing things where there is nothing."

Leah scowls at me.

"If it's nothing. Why did he look like he'd swallowed a wasp when I mentioned your wedding?"

My heartbeat picks up at her words.

"You're imagining it. Weddings aren't exactly Elijah's favourite topic. The man's wedding was a train wreck. Darra's parents overwhelmed him, parading him around like a prize bull. A society and celebrity who's who. It was awful. Believe me."

It was before Leah's time, but I'll never forget my friend's face when I found him hiding in the bathroom.

I give myself a shake. That happened ages ago. A lot has changed since then for both of us.

Leah snaps her fingers in front of my face.

"Earth to Pen," she says as I refocus on her. "I'm not blind. It was more than that. He couldn't take his eyes off you, and when I mentioned Kris, I swear he went green around the gills."

"Don't," I say.

"Why not?"

Leah grips my forearm, stopping me in my tracks.

"Because you're marrying Kris?"

When I say nothing, Leah continues.

"Why are you marrying Kris?" she says, her fingers gripping my arm tighter.

I frown down at her hand.

"Leah," I warn.

"No Pen. You're my friend. I'm worried about you."

"You don't need to worry about me. I'm fine."

Leah groans at my words.

"Fine? Really?"

I grimace at her tone.

"Do you love him? Do you love Kris?"

Her eyes lock on mine, and I know she's not going to let this go.

"Of course, I love him," I tell her.

She pauses and inclines her head, staring at me. I squirm under the intensity of her gaze.

"Okay, let me phrase that slightly differently. Are you *in love* with him?"

I shoot her a warning look. I love Leah, but right now, I want to get up and walk away. She's overstepping. I love the man he is, the way he treats people. But when I look at her and Gabriel, Caleb and April, do we have that same intense kind of love? No. But that does not mean it's not there.

As if sensing my frustration, she holds up her hand.

"Please, hear me out. Let me say my piece, and I promise I won't say another word."

I nod in affirmation and sit back.

Our waitress arrives with our order. Leah pauses until she's gone.

"Before Gabriel, I nearly married someone I thought I was in love with." Her eyes glaze as she sinks into the memory. "I mistook love for my desperate need to settle down and get married, start a family. Thought time was running out. Luckily for me, fate stepped in, and I was forced to change direction, reevaluate. It was the best thing that ever happened. Look at where I am now."

We both glance down at her sleeping angel.

I sigh. "I'm not you."

Fate has already stepped in. It stepped in fifteen years ago when the man I fell in love with married someone else.

I pinch the bridge of my nose.

Leah pulls my hand away.

"I'm sorry, Pen. I spoke out of line. It's just you and Kris were so sudden. You barely mentioned him, and then, after a couple of months of dating, you're marrying him."

Her eyes widen as the words leave her mouth, and it's then I realise where her mind has gone. She and Gabriel fell head over heels for each other.

I smile at her.

"We're not you and Gabriel," I tell her truthfully. "And you're not wrong. I have let my career rule my life. Kris and I want the same things. We both want a family, someone who understands us. So it's true, we may not be the love affair of the century. But then again, until I saw you and Gabe and April and Caleb, I was sceptical true love existed."

Leah's eyes swim with unshed tears.

"I'm sorry. I shouldn't have said anything."

I smile and squeeze her hand, knowing it comes from a good place.

"No, you're concerned for a friend. I appreciate it. But please don't worry. I'm happy. This is what I want."

I haven't known Leah for long, and it's scary how perceptive she is. How perceptive everyone seems to be.

What they don't understand is Kris and I *get* one another. We want the same things.

"Like you said. I've hit *that* age. My career has meant I've put my personal life on hold. I want to rectify that before it's too late."

I look down at the little boy sleeping in his pushchair, his thumb tucked between his lips. My chest constricts as I think back to how he fell asleep in my arms. How holding his tiny body felt as he nestled into me. I want that more than I realise.

Kris and I are compatible in so many ways. *Do I love him?* I care for him deeply. *Am I in love with him?* No. But I'm not kidding myself that he's in love with me. We trust and respect each other and what the other has achieved. I'm proud to stand by his side. He never makes me feel less, instead he encourages me. It may not be what Gabriel and Leah have, or what Caleb has found with April. But then that kind of love is rare and could have been missed as much as grasped. Kris and I are new to this. Maybe we just need time. Look at Leah and Gabe. They were under each other's noses for eight years before they finally got together.

"I'm sorry, I'm out of line," Leah says.

I lean forward and pull her in for a hug.

"If friends can't speak their minds, then I don't know who can. Never be afraid to tell me what you think," I tell her truthfully.

She hugs me back.

"I'm going to miss you," she says. "We all are."

My heart constricts at her words. I'm going to miss them all, too. The past week in the US proved that. Was that why I jumped at the chance to come back here, help Elijah?

"Nah, you won't," I say, needing to deflect. "You have

Stella and Nat, and Kat and Harper. April now as well. You'll have forgotten me in a heartbeat."

Leah pulls back and stares at me, her eyes wide.

"Is that what you think? You, my lovely lady, are very much mistaken. No one can replace you. There is only one Penelope Dawson."

Her eyes glisten as she pulls back, taking her drink in her hands.

"Thank you," I say, her words meaning more than I can express.

Old hangups die hard, and as an outcast, being accepted is something I still find challenging.

"I promise not to be a stranger."

We finish our drinks, and I pay the bill before Leah can say anything.

"I better get this little man home before he wakes up."

We walk back onto the street, and I see Mason pulling up at the kerb. Before Mason can get out, I help her unclip the seat of the buggy that also doubles as a car seat. Mason is out and holding open the door in the blink of an eye.

"Hi, Mason," I say, leaning into the car and strapping Callum's seat in while Leah helps Mason with the rest of the bags and buggy frame.

Leah climbs in, and Mason moves back to the door.

"Do you need a lift?" he asks.

I smile. "No, thank you. I have some jobs to do."

He smiles and closes the door. I bend down and wave through the window before turning away.

I have something to do, and there's no time like the present.

CHAPTER 28

ELIJAH

I stumble into my apartment, barely able to put one foot in front of the other. How did my life become so complicated? I can't shake thoughts of Pen or that she's hiding something major from me.

What the hell, and who is her handler?

It pisses me off my brother knows more than he's letting on, but then he always was watertight. It's why I wasn't afraid when he found out about Lottie. Then again, he could simply be yanking my chain where Pen's concerned. It's hard to tell these days.

I sink down onto the sofa and drop my head back against the cushion, closing my eyes. I thought taking the initiative and splitting from Darra was going to be my biggest move. How wrong could I have been?

It's dark when I open my eyes. The incessant ringing of my intercom forces me awake.

I run a hand over my face, rubbing my eyelids to get them to function.

"Lights on," I say sleepily, activating the in-house system I installed a while back.

I get up and make my way across to the wall.

"Yes," I snap, pressing the intercom button.

"About time." Pen's voice fills the surrounding space, my stomach clenching at the sound. "I was wondering if you weren't in, but I hacked your phone's tracker, and it said you were here."

"I was asleep," I grouch, hitting the accept button to open the door. "What the hell were you doing hacking my phone, and how on earth did you get up to this floor?"

She sweeps past me and into the space behind me, shooting me one of her *don't be ridiculous* looks as she goes. I know for a fact she's not on my accepted visitors list. She sometimes visits Lottie, but I would have been consulted before her name was added. It's never been necessary. Yes, we've worked on projects together. Her hardware designs are some of the best on the market, but she comes with her designers to the office for meetings with Todd, myself, and the team. However, she's never here and never alone.

"Well?" I ask, turning to face her, only to find she's moved further into the apartment.

I shut and lock the door before following her.

"Pen?" I say, finding her by the window, staring out over the city.

"Quite the view you have here, although I'm surprised you moved from Hampshire. You always loved the greenery."

I move to stand next to her.

"I do, but then needs must. It's easier to live here," I say as if that explains everything.

Pen turns to me.

I sigh. "Darra was there. It *was* easier to live here."

Pen shakes her head as she stares at me.

"What the hell went wrong?" she asks.

I'm not going there, especially with her.

Only Gabriel and Leah know the truth.

"You didn't answer my question," I say, trying to distract her.

"You first," she says.

"No way. I asked first."

Pen pulls a face.

"My contact came back. I have a list of names I want to run past you. As for the other. Hacking is my thing if you haven't realised by now, and getting up here was child's play."

I'm instantly awake.

"A list of names?"

I ignore the rest of her statement, which I'll focus on later.

"You must have been in a deep sleep," she mutters. "Keep up."

I take the list she has in her hand, my eyes scanning over it.

"What are these names?"

"These are employees with unusually large transactions in their accounts or those of family members."

I grab a pen and move to the table.

Five names are present.

The first three I can disregard immediately.

"Won the lottery."

"Are you serious?" Pen asks. "That could be a ruse."

"No, he had his face splashed all over the papers. His wife has run off with the gardener and is trying to take half of his winnings."

"You're not serious?" Pen's face is a picture.

I smirk. "Not entirely. She didn't run off with the gardener, but she has left him and is fighting for half. It's a genuine win. The press and news stations were hanging around for weeks, wanting his story. I had to ban them from the building as a security risk."

Oh, the irony!

"Okay, not him. What about the others?"

I look at the second name on the list.

"His wife received an inheritance. He's retiring once this release has gone live. Didn't want to leave me short."

"Could be fake."

"No, his father-in-law was a duke. Owned some stately home in Scotland. His wife hated her old man, but she's an only child. Their children inherited the title, but they appointed her as caretaker until they come of age."

"Next…"

"Another inheritance."

"You're sure?"

"Positive."

Pen takes a deep breath. "Okay, that leaves the last two."

I recognise the names, but they're not people I've worked with directly.

I grab my laptop and pull up their personal files. Stopping when Pen adds a layer of anonymity to stop my search flagging up.

Who is this woman?

I take a seat, and she leans in next to me. My body hardens as the scent of her perfume invades my senses. She wears the same scent she did at uni. The light floral scent clashed in the past with her exterior look, but it suits her now.

"James Buchanon. He's a number cruncher. Good at his job. I don't know where his money has come from, but his history is in numbers, not programming. There's a chance he's let someone else in, I suppose, but looking at this file. I doubt it."

"We won't discount anyone. What about Peter Levon?"

I pull up Peter's file the way Pen showed me.

I recognise the face as soon as it appears.

"He works under Todd. Is a bit of a loner. Can be gobby but normally keeps himself to himself."

"Someone sent his money to an offshore account," Pen admits.

I turn to stare at her. "And you didn't think to mention that at the beginning?"

She raises an eyebrow. "Leading the witness. It was better you gave me your opinion on each of the names without me influencing you."

I can see her logic, but I don't like the idea of being played.

"He's also our number one suspect."

I wonder who the *our* are, but let it ride. Instead, I think back to Peter and what I know about him.

"I can't believe he has the skills to do this. While a coder, he's only mediocre, at best, from what I understand. He's someone Todd has on his radar for letting go. He held off because the guy is going through a hard time. His wife ran off with his brother."

Pen turns to face me.

I run a hand through my hair as the contents of Todd's memo comes to the forefront.

"His wife was taking him to the cleaners in their divorce. Threatening to withhold access to the kids," I say.

I remember the memo because it brought home memories of Darra's threats.

Pen shakes her head. "Outsiders look for the weakest link. If someone found out about his divorce, then it's possible they made him an offer that was too good to refuse. He may have seen it as the only way out. Someone has paid him a large sum of money. This is bigger than Peter. Organised. I'd say Peter is a puppet. Someone paid him to add code or enable someone else to do it. I'd guess someone bigger is pulling the strings."

I can't fault her logic. I just wish Peter had come to one of us.

Who am I kidding?

I've never been a warm and fuzzy boss. Too locked in my own soap opera of a life.

"What happens next?"

Pen straightens, her shoulder brushing mine, my muscles contracting at the contact. She should not be having this effect on me.

"Now we flush him out and hope whoever is behind this exposes themselves in the process."

Pen pulls out her phone.

"It's *The Tailor*," she says. "As we thought. It looks like Peter Levon is our guy. Proceed with caution. The trap is ready to be sprung."

I turn and drop my ass on the table, watching Pen as she talks to the mysterious person on the other end of the phone.

She ends the call, and we stand and wait. Her phone rings again ten minutes later.

She turns to face me.

"They have eyes on him. He's leaving the building."

Her eyes lock on mine as she listens to whatever the person is saying on the other end of the phone.

"Great," she says. "I'll leave it with you."

She disconnects the call and sinks into the chair next to me, looking up at where I'm perched.

"They're going to let him move away from the office and close in. See what his next move is. I activated the protocol I inserted last night. It let him know we are onto him. If he's working with someone else, he may try to contact them. Whatever happens, they will pull him in for questioning."

I fold my arms over my chest and stare at the woman before me.

"Okay Pen. Now, will you tell me what the hell is going on?"

CHAPTER 29

PEN

I sit back and look up at the man I've known and distanced myself from for so long.

After leaving Leah, I made my way to my handler. I needed clearance to do what I'm about to do. It's a risk, but it's one I'm pretty sure is a safe bet.

"Pen, what the hell is going on?"

I cross my legs and sit back.

"Tell me what you *think* is going on."

He looks at me strangely.

"Will you tell me the truth?"

I nod. "As much as I can," I say.

"You've already proven your hacker skills. Do you work for the government, or are you a private contractor?"

His face screws up at the latter. He always was ethical.

I smile.

"I *worked* for the government," I admit. "I retired, although I probably now owe them a huge favour or three."

Elijah sucks in a breath, and I smile.

"Don't worry, that's on me. Personally, what we uncovered may win me brownie points with the powers that be. If the threat is as large as I think it is, the damage we've prevented is exponential. This would have left businesses vulnerable and affected the stock market. They may be owing me."

Elijah crosses his arms over his enormous chest and scowls.

"I'm being serious."

"So am I." I sigh. "I've worked for the government for the past fourteen years. Give or take a few months. Fifteen if you count the training they sent me on."

Elijah's eyes widen as he takes in my words.

"I don't—"

I offer him a small smile.

"No, I don't suppose you would." I get up and put some distance between us before turning to face him. "I got myself into a bit of bother in our final year. Wasn't as careful as I should have been."

A wrinkle appears between his eyebrows.

"What do you mean?"

"I'm a hacker." I fold my arms over my chest, mirroring his stance. "Always was, or at least I was, from the moment I began coding."

His frown deepens, and I laugh.

"Why do you think I was so good at writing the code for Frazer Dawson Cyber Security, uncovering loopholes?"

Understanding crosses his face.

"When I hit eighteen, I decided to use my skills to build a life for myself and Mum. University was me cleaning up my act, learning to use my skills, shall we say, more productively?"

I stop.

"If you cleaned up your act, what changed?"

Shit! I can't say *it was you breaking my heart that caused me to relapse.*

I have no one other than myself to blame for my carelessness.

I sigh.

"I hacked into places for *shits and giggles*. The challenge," I say, skirting around his question. "I'd tag wherever I went, leave a calling card. I never took anything or did any damage. It was the thrill of the experience."

"Like gaming."

I screw up my face in a lopsided grin.

"Exactly. Gaming is the perfect substitute. That's why my games are so popular. I design levels the gamer needs to break into the same way a hacker would. They test the best minds." I smirk. "Drives Gabriel mad."

"Okay, but I seem to be missing something."

I shrug. "This one particular hack, I was careless, and I got caught. Didn't hide myself or cover my tracks well enough."

"When, how?"

I move back to my chair and sit down, resting my elbows on my knees and placing my chin on my clasped hands.

"Just after you got married."

"What the hell, Pen?"

Elijah jumps up and starts pacing. "Why is this the first I'm hearing about it?"

"You were kind of busy if you remember."

"That's not an excuse," he tells me, his nostrils flaring. His arms sweeping. "You were my friend. I might have been able to help. Dad might have been able to."

I ignore his words. Robert helped me, but that's not something Elijah will ever hear from my lips.

"Calm down," I say.

He stops, glaring in my direction. I incline my head.

"I couldn't tell you. They made me an offer. Either join a

government team and work for them pro bono. Or go to prison. The choice was a no-brainer."

Elijah pushes off the table and paces, a variety of emotions flitting over his face.

Eventually, he stops and spins towards me.

"What did you do for the government? I take it, it is *our* government?"

I laugh, earning myself another scowl.

"Now, what I did... that's something I can't tell you. That would land me in jail and you in a whole heap of trouble. As for the other. Yes, it was our government."

"I don't understand."

"You don't need to. It is what it is," I tell him truthfully.

There's more, but I have made other promises I will never break.

"Now you owe them again? Because of me?"

"Maybe? Maybe not. I'm a pretty good negotiator. I'm also a powerful businesswoman in my own right these days."

Elijah drops into the chair next to me, and I straighten up.

He takes my hand in his. His eyes lock with mine, his thumb tracing circles over the back of my hand.

"I'm so sorry, Pen. I'm sorry I wasn't there for you."

I turn my hand over, interlinking our fingers.

"You have nothing to be sorry for. It was my own stupidity and ego that got me caught. I made myself a promise when I got into uni that my hacking days were behind me. I broke a promise to myself. Was too cocky. I have no one but myself to blame."

The intensity of his gaze has me looking down at our hands.

"Somehow, I still think there's more to this."

Elijah always could read me. Explains my intense infatuation. I could be myself, and he accepted that wacky side of me.

"Don't read into it," I say, going to pull my hand away but finding it held fast. "It is what it is. Fate takes us down certain pathways. Some of our choosing, others not. You know that better than anyone. Sometimes, we must simply play the hand we've been dealt."

We both fall silent, our eyes moving to where our hands are joined.

"Pen." Elijah's voice comes out strained.

"Don't," I tell him, pulling back and flattening my hand on my leg, pressing my fingers into the material.

"But—"

"No."

My phone rings again, and I get up and move away.

"Tailor."

"He's in custody," is the only reply I get. "Bring Mr Frazer."

I turn to stare at Elijah.

"We need to go."

CHAPTER 30

PEN

*E*lijah drives us to the police station where they're holding Peter Levon. We're greeted by plain-clothed officers who lead us into the maze of corridors before taking us into a debriefing room.

"Has he said anything?" Elijah asks, taking a seat.

"No, he's requested a lawyer, who is currently on his way."

"Do we know the name of the lawyer?" I ask, my suspicious mind running.

The lawyer he has chosen may be the key to who is behind this.

The officer passes over a piece of paper with the name on it. It's not anyone I recognise, but then again, it doesn't surprise me. I'll need to investigate potential connections. The law firm is small, but it doesn't mean it doesn't have a parent company lurking in the background.

Another officer enters.

"Evening, Mr Frazer. I'm Detective Ross. Sorry to have called you in so late, but we felt it important because of the severity of the claims you've made."

Elijah stands and shakes the hand of the man who entered.

"Are you ready to give your statement, Mr Frazer?"

"I am."

Detective Ross looks over at me, and I nod. Time to make myself scarce.

"I'll have a colleague take your statement as well, Ms Dawson."

I smile, getting up and following his colleague to the door.

"I'll see you later," I say to Elijah.

We exit, and I follow the female officer down the corridor to another door.

She holds it open for me to enter before closing it behind me.

"You really can't stay away, can you?" a voice I recognise comes from deep inside the room.

"You know me," I say, stepping forward with a grin. "It's good to see you. I missed you before I left."

"How's the move gone? Are you settling in?"

"You know, still surrounded by boxes, but baby steps. I was only there for a week before I came back."

"Wedding plans? How was Kristophe when you left?"

"What's this? Twenty questions," I ask, dropping into the chair opposite.

"Small talk?"

I laugh. "You and small talk? Kristophe was fine. He understands me."

"I'm glad."

We sit in an awkward silence.

"What next?" I ask finally.

There's only one reason The Seamstress is here.

She smiles. "Nothing."

I incline my head. "Nothing?"

"You're retired. That hasn't changed. They sent me to thank you. You foiled a plot that could have had a serious impact on businesses and the government. But then you know that."

I nod. "I added safeguards."

A small smile plays on her lips.

"I expected nothing less. You always were the best."

"Am the best," I say.

"Are the best," she agrees. "How is Elijah doing?"

"Frustrated, confused, as we all are. Unable to see the bigger picture."

"The Frazers are under attack. This is likely to be just the beginning."

I think back to the number of plots I uncovered that stopped after Robert's death. My heart lurches at the memory.

"And we're still no closer to discovering who is pulling the strings?"

"No. Whoever did it is covering their tracks well."

"You got my statement?" I ask. I finished it while Elijah showered. "I recognised the code patterns. Know Needle is involved."

"You need to leave us to do our jobs."

"These are my friends," I tell her.

"You're retired. Enjoy it. Go back to the US, make beautiful babies with Mr Lansdown. We've got this. I promise."

I hate that she's shutting me out, but what more can I do? I can't force her to share what she knows.

"Can I ask you to keep me updated? I'm also available if you need me."

A look of shock passes over the face of the woman sitting opposite me.

"You're out," she says.

"These are my friends, and I owe Robert. If you need my skills, I'll be there."

The Seamstress nods.

I stand up and turn to leave. Pausing as I reach the door.

"I want Robert's killer brought to justice."

"We all do. But until we have more evidence, it remains a tragic accident. We don't need any added complications, Tailor. Is that understood?"

I nod. "It's okay. I wouldn't do that to them. Knowing myself is torture enough."

The words catch in my throat. The secret I've held from those I love for seven years.

"I'm glad we understand one another. No good will come of it," she says. "Go back to the US settle down. Live your life. I promise to call if we need you."

I place my hand on the door handle.

My thoughts flash to Elijah, to Gabriel, Caleb, Kat, and even to Harper.

They got to Robert, and now they may come after his family.

"I mean it. If you need me. I'm available."

"I heard you. Now go."

With that, I leave the room, making my way back to where Elijah is still giving his statement. I grab myself a coffee from the vending machine and hiss at the bitter taste as I wait for him to finish.

CHAPTER 31

ELIJAH

I'm still filled with a sense of unease as Pen, and I re-enter my apartment. It's gone midnight. For the fact I've only had a couple of hours of sleep in the past forty-eight hours, I feel remarkably awake.

"A drink?" I ask, making my way to the kitchen.

"Please," Pen says, following behind.

"Do you think he's going to crack?" I say, motioning to my vast array of drink choices.

Pen points to a juice mix favoured by Lottie. Being the dad of a teenager, the house is well stocked. It's often a conveyor belt of teens running in and out. My daughter, at fourteen, is growing up fast.

I pour myself a whiskey, grabbing some ice from the freezer.

I hand Pen her drink and follow her into the living room, both taking a seat on opposite sofas. I've spent a lot of time touching her in the past few days, and my body is getting used to her presence. It wants more, but she's not here for that. She's come to help, and before I can blink, she'll be gone again. This time for good.

"There's something off about this whole thing. Peter's not a mastermind, and we know he received payment from someone. From what I've read in his file and after you called Todd, the coding was too advanced. Whoever wrote that code knew what they were doing."

Pen presses her fingers into her eyes.

"There's something..." she sighs, taking a sip of her drink.

It's then I notice how tired she looks.

It's my turn to lean forward.

"Pen, you've flown in and been on the go constantly ever since you arrived. When did you last sleep?"

She gives me one of her side smiles, although it doesn't quite reach her eyes.

"I slept on Kris's plane. The bed is surprisingly comfortable, but it's never the same."

She closes her eyes and drops back against the sofa.

I smart at the fact she slept in a bed owned by Kristophe Lansdown, even though I know I have no right. She's engaged to the man. She does a lot more than sleep in his bed. Nausea hits at the thought. Every time Pen has dated over the years, it's left me with a sick feeling in the pit of my stomach. Not that I deserve anything else. She was never mine. I still remember the time she lost her virginity. The guy was hanging around for months. He'd been a complete nerd, and to this day, I don't know what Pen saw in him. When she finally did the deed, he let the entire campus know he popped her cherry. Jaxson, Zach, and I made him regret that move. Pen was ours. In between sobs, he told us it was a dare, but he would not give up the person who dared him. Pen laughed it off, but I saw the pain in her eyes. Trust was not something she readily gave, and the fact he abused hers.

I made my choice. Duty to the family above everything else. I gave up any right to Penelope Dawson years ago. She deserves every happiness, and I should be excited for her.

She works tirelessly for others. Mum adores her and all she does for the Frazer Foundation. As their fledgling recipient, she's shown her gratitude over and over. Offering internships, scholarships. Not to mention the vast amount she personally donates to fund future projects. She's their poster girl, their big success story. Mum and Dad couldn't have been more proud if she was their own daughter.

"Shit, I'm surprised you can string two sentences together," I say, standing up. "You can crash here tonight. It's not like I don't have the room."

Pen remains silent, and it's only when I look more closely I realise she's fallen asleep. Not just dozing, either. She's sound asleep. Soft little snores escape.

I smile at the memory of finding her passed out on the table in one of the computer labs after she pulled an all-night session. She'd made the same noises then. She was so mad when she woke to find me sitting next to her, continuing our project.

I move towards her. Her head is at a strange angle, and I know when she wakes up, she's going to have a dreadful neck ache.

I grab one of the throws Lottie likes to snuggle under when she's watching TV, but throw it back down. Pen deserves a comfortable night's rest, and my expensive, handcrafted sofa is not going to offer her that.

Leaving her, I head upstairs and open the door to one of my many spare rooms. Chrissy, my housekeeper, has them all aired and laundered. I pull back the covers on the freshly made bed before making my way back downstairs. Pen hasn't moved, although I can't stop the smile at the tiny snorts she's giving off.

She always was a great sleeper. When she went to sleep, nothing would wake her. It was like she hit a brick wall and needed time for her brain to recover.

Looking down, my heart clenches as I stare at my once best friend. I lost her once before, and now I'm losing her again. Before I can think, I stoop and scoop her into my arms. Pen is not small, although she's all height and long limbs.

She lets out a grunt of protest before snuggling into my chest, her head resting on my shoulder, her breath teasing the skin on my neck.

I bite my lip to suppress a groan at the feel of her in my arms

I carry her up the stairs, manoeuvring her through the door before lowering her onto the bed.

Her arms snake around my neck, and she lets out a little moan as I go to pull away.

I freeze, with my hands going to where she's locked hers behind my head. She's surprisingly strong. She pulls my face towards her, and I close my eyes, letting her scent wash over me.

She's sound asleep, but her body is calling to mine. She arches up towards me, trying to pull me closer. Before I can stop her, her lips find mine. Her tongue snakes out and dances along the seam of my mouth, asking for entry. My lips soften, and I groan, deepening the kiss before I come to my senses.

I squeeze my eyes closed and resist. Pulling her hands from behind my head, I stare down only to find she's still sound asleep. She groans in protest, but I place her hands down and pat them. Noticing once again the garish socks she's wearing.

As always, Pen removed her shoes when she entered the apartment. She's been no different. Her mum has a no-shoes in the house policy. I think because she worked such long hours, she didn't have time to clean the floors as often as she would have needed to or liked. They may not have had much money, but Ms D always kept an immaculate home.

Pen rolls onto her side with a moan. The sound shoots straight to my cock, and I harden like a teenager.

I lean over and pull the duvet up to cover her, ignoring the increasing pressure between my legs.

She lets out another moan, and I pause.

As I stare at the sleeping woman, my chest constricts.

I pull back sharply as I begin to lower my head towards hers.

What the hell am I doing?

I need to go. Pen is probably leaving in the morning, and I have to prepare for Lottie's return.

I move away, taking one final glance at her sleeping form, as I switch off the light before closing the door behind me with a gentle click.

I enter my room and seal myself in.

Shit. Pen.

I've spent years suppressing my feelings for her. Kept my distance. Now all those feelings are back, and I can do nothing about them. She's no longer free. I have commitments. I'm a selfish prick. She came all this way to help me and what do I want? To sink myself between her thighs and make love to her until she's screaming my name and coming hard around my cock.

Never going to happen, Elijah!

I drop onto the bed and lie back, staring at the ceiling.

I'm an idiot.

Who am I kidding? My feelings for Pen have never changed. They never had a chance to. They were always there, only I suppressed them. It's why I've struggled. I could never simply switch off what I felt.

Yes, I married Darra. She was having my child. The moment she announced her pregnancy, my fate was sealed.

But I never loved her, never had. The whole time we were dating, she was a convenience. She was quite happy to admit she never loved me either. She and her father wanted to form an alliance. Create a power couple, and I was what her father wanted.

My friendship with Pen was collateral damage. I look back now and realise one reason I distanced myself from my family, my friends, was because to have been around her would have been unfair to everyone. I would not have been strong enough to resist her. When she refused to go into business with me after university, I used it as an excuse to push her away despite what we planned. At the time, I blamed her, but I refused to be the reason she lost loved ones, even if it meant isolating myself from my own family.

My brain fires up. I wrack my brain.

Pen was positive about our business for months after Darra announced her pregnancy. Even after we got married. Or did I imagine that, want it to be true? I know what Jaxson said, but did Pen have feelings for me? We'd got close in the months after Christmas, but was it more than a close friendship? I suppose I'll never know, as we never got the chance to find out.

The unfulfilled sexual tension between us, or at least on my part. Pen withdrew, put up a professional wall.

I sit up and swing my legs off the bed.

If they arrested Pen for hacking. There's no way she would have been able to set up a cyber security firm. If it had come out, it would have ruined us both, and she would have known that.

I grab my phone.

"Elijah, it's late."

"Hi, Mum."

"What is it? Is Lottie okay?"

"She's fine. I spoke to her earlier. She's loving the art school. Her Italian is improving too."

There's a pause.

"Mum, did you know?"

"Know what Elijah. I know many things, but I still sadly lack the ability to mind read."

Her tone is dry, although I can hear the amusement in her voice. I could also dispute her ability to mind-read. I swear she has read mine more than once.

"Did you know they arrested Pen for hacking?"

"Ah. The lovely Penelope Dawson. How is she?"

"Mum."

She chuckles.

"Of course, we knew. Why do you think we set up the Frazer Foundation? It was the only way we could help her. That woman is proud and always has been. She would not accept our help any other way."

"But."

"She made a mistake." Mum's tone takes on a serious tone. "But your father and I would not let her ruin her future."

"Do you know about—"

"Shhh," she hisses down the phone, giving me all the information I need.

"She didn't abandon you, but you two remaining together would have been a disaster."

Mum always was far too perceptive, and she loved Pen. Although she tried her best with Darra, Darra never wanted that kind of relationship and kept my mother, father, and siblings at arm's length.

"I heard there's been trouble."

"It's under control."

"I'm here if you need me."

"Thanks, Mum."

"I love you, Elijah. We all do. You don't need to shut us out."

There's nothing I can say. I've spent years trying to protect them from my mistakes, but I know I hurt them.

"Night," I say

"Goodnight, my darling."

The line goes dead. My mother is a dark horse. She's like an onion. You peel aside one layer only to uncover another layer.

I lie back down.

Pen didn't abandon me. She had no choice.

Fuck.

All these years, I blamed her for leaving me, abandoning our company. Distanced myself from my own family as they wouldn't let her go. They said she deserved better.

Damn you, Pen, why weren't you just honest with me?

But in my heart, I know why.

That single tear, all those years ago, when she found me hiding in the bathroom at my wedding. When she held me while I quietly fell apart before telling me to suck it up and get back out there.

I fucked up.

Tomorrow, I will put her back on Kris's plane and send her home.

I'm not going to fuck up her life again.

CHAPTER 32

PEN

I wake up in unfamiliar surroundings. The scent of laundry detergent lets me know exactly where I am. It's the same as it always was. He's a man of habit.

Before I open my eyes, I reach sideways, letting out a sigh of relief when I don't come into contact with a body. My dreams were vivid. Strong lips, a teasing tongue. My dream last night of being held in powerful arms, which I've desired for so long, has left me wet and wanting, and it has to stop. This is not what I need, not what I want. Being around him is bad for my mental health.

I have a fiancé, we are happy.

I have my future planned.

I will not send that into free fall over a man who's never looked at me the way I look at him, whatever people like Leah and Kat and Gabriel say. Their opinions are biased. There was a moment when I thought... but I was wrong. There was always Darra.

Who spends fifteen years pining after a man they never had, have never even kissed?

I throw back the covers and clamber out of bed. I make

my way into the attached bathroom. Stripping out of my clothes, I step into the enormous walk-in shower.

I let the hot water and shower jets wash away the grime of the police station and the stress of the past forty-eight hours. It may not be my company under attack, but when someone I care about is being made a target, I'll fight tooth and nail to help them. I heed the warning of The Seamstress. Something is coming, and I need to be ready.

As I leave the bathroom, there's a knock on the door.

"Come in," I say.

"Morning, Ms Dawson."

"Chrissy," I say grinning. "It's good to see you."

I've met Chrissy on a number of occasions when I've collected Lottie or delivered her home. My relationship as Lottie's godmother is screwed up. But I'll forever be grateful to Darra for allowing me to be part of her daughter's life. I'm not sure why she agreed. It may have been because she wanted a babysitter initially, but for me, having no siblings allowed me to direct some love her way. It's also meant we've developed a strong bond over the years. One I cultivated when it became clear her mother and father's marriage was in trouble. She'd done nothing to deserve being caught in the middle.

"Elijah sent up some fresh clothes for you."

"Thank you. A fresh set is very welcome."

She grins at me.

"I'll leave you to it."

"Thank you again. Do you know where Elijah is?"

"Last time I saw him, he was heading to his gym."

"Thanks."

Chrissy leaves, and I open the bag of clothes Elijah sent up. I look at the sizes. Smooth, Mr Frazer, realising he's guessed my size perfectly. I pull out the black jeans, laughing as a pair of brightly coloured socks drop onto the floor at my feet. I dip my hand back into the bag and pull out a jade jumper. I bite my lip. One way to get me into colour, Eli. The wool is soft, and I rub it against my cheek. I look in the bag, my mouth dropping open. Inside is a matching set of bra and panties, the lacy, satin scraps the same colour as the jumper.

My heart does a flip.

I know Elijah didn't realistically choose these. He can't have done. But I imagine his face. What would he think if I paraded into his gym wearing only them?

Stop!

I pull on my new clothes, ignoring the sensitivity of my nipples against the satin of the bra, and the panties resting against my fiery core.

I find a new toothbrush in the bathroom and clean my teeth before making my way downstairs. The apartment is immense, covering two floors. It's bigger than most houses.

I head to the gym. Lottie gave me a tour on one of my visits.

I enter the room and freeze.

Loud music pumps through the speakers, hiding my presence despite the door closing behind me with a click. Elijah is in front. His back glistens in the light as he pulls himself up in a perfect chin-up. His muscles contract and relax beneath his skin. Growing up swimming made him lean and muscular. Age and gym work have filled him out further. His biceps bulge under the assault as he lifts himself up and down. His body is an art form, perfectly sculpted. I stand and watch in fascination.

Eventually, he drops to the ground with a grunt, stretching out the muscles, before grabbing a towel from the bench next to him.

It's then he notices me.

His eyes give me the once over before a slow smile appears as he takes in my appearance.

"Did you sleep well?"

"Like a top," I say, moving further into the room. "That's a very comfortable bed you have in your spare room."

I refrain from licking my lips at the sight of his exposed and ripped chest.

Down girl.

He moves to the bench.

"Did you?"

"Did I what?"

"Sleep well."

"Not really," he says.

Something flashes through his eyes, but I ignore it.

"Not surprising, everything considered," I say

He grunts as he picks up his t-shirt and pulls it on.

My gaze fixates on his abs until they're finally covered. A hot flush overtakes me, and I move to the water fountain and get us some water.

"Thank you," Elijah says, taking a cup from my outstretched hand.

Our fingers brush. I hold myself steady, not wanting to jump at his touch and throw water all over the floor or him.

"I just wanted to say thank you for letting me stay last night," I say. "My work here is done, so I'm about to head home before I go to the airport. Kris has the plane ready and waiting."

A shadow passes over his face, but he corrects himself and smiles.

"Thank you for all your help. If there's ever anything I can do to help in the future, you only need to ask, and it's done."

I smile.

"Thank you, but hopefully, my life is going to become boring and mundane in the near future."

I look up, and our eyes lock. Elijah's softening.

"Good luck, Pen, I hope you have everything you wish for."

"You too," I say, my heart sinking. "Will I see you at the wedding?"

He purses his lips and shakes his head.

"I don't think—with Lottie."

I hold up my hand, stopping him.

"It's fine," I say, even if my heart feels like it's being ripped from my chest.

He doesn't say any more, instead grabbing the towel and wiping his face. When he removes it, he says, "I'll let you know if Peter gives up any information."

I nod.

Before I can stop myself, I step forward, pressing my lips to his cheek, holding them there for several seconds. I close my eyes briefly before pulling back.

"Take care of yourself," I say.

His hands move, gripping my upper arms. He drops his head, resting his forehead against mine, his own eyes closing for a moment before he reopens them, holding my gaze.

"Goodbye, Pen. Take care of yourself," he says, pulling back.

I bite my lip and grip his damp forearms, squeezing them once before I turn and leave the room.

"Be happy, my beautiful friend. Time and fate never were on our side."

His whispered words reach my ears, and I freeze as the door clicks shut behind me.

I drop my chin to my chest and inhale deeply. "Goodbye. I hope you find the happiness you deserve, too." I whisper back, before kicking myself into motion. It's time to go.

CHAPTER 33

PEN

Mum pulls me in for a hug, and I go willingly.

"I'll see you in a few weeks," she says, squeezing me tightly. This is just what I need.

"You will, then it will be full steam ahead," I say.

She pulls back and cups my face.

"Just be happy," she tells me.

"I will. I promise."

Knowing eyes stare back at me. It's eery how perceptive she is. The years when it was only the two of us, have formed a bond stronger than most.

She hasn't mentioned Elijah this morning, instead, she's gone full steam ahead in getting me back to the US and Kris.

"I love you," I say, moving towards the car as Mason holds the door open. Gabriel having sent him to pick me up.

"I love you too."

Mason shuts the door, and I hear mum say something to him.

When he gets into the driver's seat, he turns to face me.

"Do you need to stop off anywhere, or is it straight to the airport?" he asks.

"Airport. The plane should be ready to go by the time we get there."

He nods in confirmation and starts the engine.

I contacted Kris this morning. He managed everything despite the early hour. He's heading to his sister's birthday party at some fancy resort a couple of hours away. By the time I get back, I'll be ready to crash, so I told him I'd see him on Sunday when he gets back.

My phone rings, and I pick up.

"Gabriel?"

"I just wanted to say *thank you* before you left."

"No thanks needed. You guys are my family. I should be thanking you for sending Mason to drive me to the airport."

There's a chuckle.

"As you said, no thanks needed. It was the least I could do." There's a pause. "Well, that's all. We'll see you in a couple of months for the wedding."

"That you will," I say, trying to inject some enthusiasm into my words.

I'm tired, and leaving home and Mum is always hard. I know all I need is to get back to Kris, and everything will be fine. Once I'm back with him, these feelings of uncertainty will disappear, I'm sure of it.

"Take care, Gabe, and give your wife and son an enormous hug from me."

"See you, Pen, safe travels."

Gabriel cuts off, and I stare out of the window. It's not long before we're turning into the airport. Mason oversees my check-in before driving me out to the plane, which is ready and waiting.

"Thank you, Mason," I say, offering him my hand.

"You're welcome. Take care of yourself."

"You too."

I make my way to the foot of the steps where Kris's crew is on hand to welcome me onboard.

"Afternoon, Ms Dawson."

"Afternoon."

I make my way into the cabin and settle at the table, pulling out my laptop.

I logon, and answer the host of emails that are waiting for me, only stopping to stare out of the window as we taxi down the runway. My heart sinks as we speed up. My mouth is dry, my chest tight. I grip the seat as I'm overcome with the sudden need to get off, as though I've forgotten something important. I suck in air and close my eyes, pinching the bridge of my nose. I inhale for four then exhale for four, continuing the process until the wheels of the plane leave the ground and London is far behind me.

CHAPTER 34

ELIJAH

Bad news travels fast.

Peter Levon's arrest hit the newspapers within days, and I've spent the past couple of weeks firefighting. The morning after the arrest I called a board meeting, updating them on what had gone down. They weren't impressed I'd withheld the information from them, but when I explained the necessity of keeping it quiet, they backed down.

"So what happens now?" Gabriel asks.

He finally managed to convince me to join them at boys' night. I must say, it's been fun. With Lottie in Italy for a few more weeks, I needed a distraction.

"We've postponed the new release to retest everything Pen, and I did and for client reassurance."

"What's the fallout been?"

I run a hand through my hair, looking at my brother.

"Some clients have left, which was inevitable. Others have decided, better the devil you know. There's been no lasting damage, or at least that's what the company's PR team is telling us. Being open and transparent appears to have gone a long way in calming the media storm."

I wonder if Pen and whoever her *handler* is have smoothed the way.

I still shudder whenever I think of what could have happened had I not come across that email.

It was as if fate had stepped in.

"How did Todd take it?"

"He was furious," I say, remembering how he'd slammed into my office and tore strips off me for not confiding in him. "He eventually simmered down when I explained about the bugs in my office. He then had the entire office building swept as a precaution. It's good to know my office is once again a safe space."

Although one which is now filled with memories of Pen sat in it.

As if reading my mind...

"Have you heard from Pen since she left?"

I shake my head. She's been radio silent since she returned to the US. Peter hasn't given anyone up, so there's been no reason to contact her. I told her I wasn't going to her wedding, using Lottie as an excuse. To her, however, it must have seemed like I wasn't willing to support her in her happiest hour.

I don't deserve someone like her in my life.

Gabriel looks at me, and I shrug.

"I'm seeing my therapist again," I admit. "I think it's time I sort out my shit for Lottie."

I need a clean break to continue with my plans of devoting my time to my company and Lottie, helping her heal.

"That's great," he says. "But Eli, it's not just for Lottie. It's also for you."

Gabe is right. I need to do this for myself as much as for

Lottie. I realised once Pen had left, that she has moved on from the past, has planned a new life. I take my hat off to her. Commend her. She's given me hope. So much so that I called my therapist and scheduled a meeting the following day. I intend to take them more seriously, move forward. I'm currently damaged goods with a lot of baggage, it's up to me to sort through it. He helped me once before when I broke my ankle, and he's helping me get my head together now, be a better man.

My biggest problem isn't one I can share with Gabriel or anyone else. I see Pen everywhere, wherever I turn there are memories of her. In my apartment, my office. It's like her scent has become a permanent fixture sent to haunt me. I even slept in the spare room after she left, although Christie had already changed the sheets.

Fate is screwing with me. She was my friend for years, and I messed that up. I fell for her but could do nothing about it. I'm falling for her again, but she's out of my reach and can never be mine.

Somehow I know Pen will always be *the one who got away.*

"Are you guys going to come and play cards, or are you going to mope all night in the kitchen?" Xander says, sticking his head through the door.

"We're coming. I need to whip your ass after last month," Gabriel says. Apparently, Xander managed to beat Gabriel, which is nearly unheard of.

"Bring it on," Xander says, moving to the fridge and grabbing another box of beers.

We make our way back into the living area, where the rest of the guys are waiting. Caleb is still away, but it hasn't stopped the rest of them.

"Come on, Elijah, you're dealing," Quentin says, holding out the pack of cards. "I'm expecting a great hand."

It's late by the time I head back to my apartment. It was a

great night. Gabriel was right. I felt human hanging around with my brother's friends. I laughed. Not something I've done all that much. At least not before Pen arrived.

I head upstairs and hit the keypad on the door. It unlocks with a pop, and I enter my studio. The specialist light comes on immediately. The large windows are dark as they look out over the night sky. The smell of oil paint and turps assaults my senses, my body instantly releasing some of the tension it's been storing, settling the nerves that have been stretched taut, first by Levon and then by Pen leaving.

I move towards my easel, pulling off the dust sheet. It's been a couple of months since I was last in here. The divorce, work, Lottie going to stay with her mother. I lost my mojo for a moment. It took my therapist reminding me, it's time to set aside some time for me.

I stare at the half-finished painting before lifting the canvas from the easel and placing it against the wall. That's not what I'm feeling at the moment. I grab a blank, pre-stretched canvas from the pile and gather my tools.

I close my eyes, allowing my mind to focus on the blank canvas in front of me. A picture forms, and I want to groan.

Why?

But I don't fight it. Instead, I let the moment take me. Inhale, exhale, I allow the painting to take shape. When I open them again, I begin underpainting, allowing the bigger picture to take on a form.

FIFTEEN YEARS AGO

"Penelope is here to see you," Mum says, coming into the room, followed closely by Pen.

"Hi," I say, sitting up, my extended leg making the process a little difficult.

"I'll grab you some refreshments. Juice, Pen?"

"That would be amazing, Mrs F," Pen says, making me smirk.

She's the only one who can get away with calling Mum Franny or Mrs F. Mum loves it.

When she's gone, Pen steps closer.

"How are you doing?" she asks.

"I'm okay," I lie.

Pen pulls a face, and I grin.

"Okay, in that I'm bored out of my ever-loving mind," I tell her truthfully, patting the sofa beside me.

Pen takes a seat.

"What did the specialist say?"

"That the operation was a success. The pins will hold the ankle bone in place, and with physio, I should be back in the water within six months."

Pen's hand comes out and squeezes my forearm.

"I'm sorry," she says

"For what? I'm the idiot who misjudged the kerb and came off his bike."

I expected to be devastated when they initially told me the prognosis, but instead, I felt nothing. Years of training gone in an instant. I'll miss the trials for the Olympics, that dream has ended. But then, life has taken a different turn, one I'm excited about. Pen and I have almost completed our business plan for Frazer Dawson Cyber Security so life is far from over.

"Here, I brought you something," Pen says, handing me a gift bag. "A little something to stop you moping around."

I pull a box out of the bag and stare at it.

"What the hell is this?"

Pen laughs.

"Paint by numbers."

I look at her like she's lost her mind.

"What the—"

Pen shrugs.

"You've been moping around since you broke your ankle. You've

done all your assignments in record time. You hate reading. Our business plan is almost complete. I thought this might be something you could do while sitting. It doesn't involve any brainpower and is actually good for your mental health, according to the woman in the shop. And god only knows, you could do with some help in that department."

She jumps out of the way as I lob a cushion in her direction.

I look down at the set in my hand.

What the fuck! I'm a swimmer and a computer programmer, not an artist.

Pen raises an eyebrow. A look of disdain must be written all over my face.

"The box contains everything you need. The picture, the paint, the brushes. Remove that look from your face. If you don't like it, then give it to Harper or throw it away. But don't knock it until you've tried it. Who knows, maybe there's a budding artist hidden inside that enormous exterior of yours."

I realise I've hurt her feelings. She's only trying to help. It's true. I've been like a bear with a sore head since my accident. Not because of what it means but more because I'm like a caged animal, unable to do anything for myself, confined to the sofa or my bed.

"Fine—I'm sorry. Thank you. It was kind of you to think of me."

I grimace, and Pen laughs, her laughter lightening my mood.

"Don't poo-poo what you haven't tried. It might surprise you."

I nod, unconvinced, as Pen sits down on the sofa by my feet.

I wince as the movement jars my ankle.

"Oh shit, sorry." Pen's face wrinkles when she realises what she's done.

"Please don't apologise. I'm going stir-crazy sat here. Mum is on the warpath. Doctor said rest, and that to her means I can't move. I feel like I've got ants crawling all over me. I need to move that badly."

Pen inclines her head in sympathy.

"Try the painting. It might surprise you."

"I will. It can't be any worse than this," I say, motioning to my current place of rest.

* * *

Pen never found out how that one paint-by-numbers set opened my mind to another world. I spoke to my therapist about it, who recommended art therapy when he realised how enjoyable I found it. Art therapy then turned into a hobby. I look at the number of completed canvases. It may be a trifle more than a hobby.

I stare at the outline composition that now covers the canvas. I love this part, where big sweeping shapes form what will become something. I grab my cloth and begin rubbing out and smudging the paint. My brush and cloth move over the canvas, and before I know it, a picture is taking shape.

By the time I leave my studio and lock the door, I feel calmer, more myself. That was one thing Pen got right. Art is good for my mental health. The room I chose for my art studio floods with light during the day, and I had specialist lighting installed for nighttime painting. It is, and always has been my sanctuary, like Gabriel has his tech man-cave.

My private room, somewhere only Lottie knows about.

Darra never lived here, and to Lottie, it's always been Dad's room, somewhere we paint together. Lottie joins me, and it's been our time, our thing to do together. My heart clenches. I miss her. She messages every day, but it's not the same. My protective instincts are in overdrive. She may be almost fifteen, but that makes it worse. She's growing up before my eyes, and my fear grows that one day soon, she'll no longer need or want me as her dad anymore. She'll realise I'm broken.

CHAPTER 35

PEN

It's been two weeks, and instead of feeling settled, I'm finding myself more and more restless. I've not contacted Elijah, although I've kept myself abreast through online UK newspapers and news outlets. He looks tired, but then who wouldn't be?

I've blamed my unease on pre-wedding nerves, but somewhere deep in my gut, I know it's more than that.

I bash the cushion on the sofa next to me and let out a growl of frustration.

"Hey, what did the cushion do to you?"

I jump, my heart rate picking up.

"*Shit.* Kris, you scared me. I wasn't expecting you home," I say, looking up and forcing a smile at the man lounging in the doorway.

He inclines his head and looks at me, his eyes softening, as they always do.

"Want to talk about it?"

"Nothing to talk about," I say, shooting him another smile while busying myself with the real estate options I have in front of me.

"Then come here," he says, stepping into the room.

I take a deep breath, my chest tightening before I stand and make my way across the room. I stop before him, and he stares at me.

His hand comes up and cups my cheek, his thumb brushing my skin.

"Talk to me," he says. "You always have before."

I look up at him, trying to stay neutral, but my eyes must reflect the devastation crushing my chest because he pulls me into his arms. I go willingly, resting my head against his shoulder. Kris has become a close friend, but where my head is currently, I can't confide in him.

"Did something happen in London? Something you haven't told me?"

I pull back and stare at the man who, in a month and a half, will become my husband.

I shake my head. "No," I tell him truthfully.

He knows now it was Elijah I was helping and not Gabriel. Although I explained to him, it was Gabriel who asked.

"Ah. But you still love him, don't you?"

I drop my forehead to his chest, his hands going to my shoulders, his fingers flexing, soothing the tight muscles.

Kris knows all about my past with Elijah, or lack of it. He knows about my unrequited love for a man that was never, and could never be mine. It's amazing what you'll admit when playing truth or dare after a few drinks. It was before we got together so he knows everything. Why I've been single all these years. My shattered hopes and dreams.

"We reminisced. It brought back a lot of memories."

He runs a soothing hand up and down my back.

"He's single now," Kris says. "Maybe—"

"No, he has Lottie. He's made it clear she's his number one priority."

"He can raise his daughter and be in a relationship," Kris says.

"Maybe if he felt that way about me. Our relationship has always been platonic on his part. It was me who fell for a man outside my league. To him, I'm a close friend. Nothing more."

Kris lets out a bark of laughter.

"Is that what you think? Elijah Frazer is out of your league? Take it from me, Penelope Dawson. You could not be further from the truth. That man has it bad, and, if anything, you're out of *his* league, and he knows it."

I pull back and grip Kris's forearms.

"No. Stop. I know what you're trying to do." I pull away, but he holds on to me. "I won't let you."

He inclines his head and stares at me. "You really have no idea, do you?" he says. "Pen, the way Elijah looked when he saw us together at Caleb and April's wedding. I can promise you he was jealous. He's not as immune as you think he is. He can't even bring himself to come to our wedding."

I shake my head. "You're mistaken. He has to look after Lottie, especially as the rest of his family are coming."

My thoughts return to Leah's words, to Kat's. To the words Elijah muttered when he thought I was out of hearing. *Could he want me?*

Kris takes hold of my hand and leads me to the sofa.

"Pen. You're Penelope Dawson, a self-made millionaire. You're a genius with a workforce who would walk through fire and ice for you. Half the men in the world would give their right arm to date you. Why do you find it so hard to believe Elijah Frazer is any different?"

"Only half the men?" I quirk an eyebrow, not understanding why Kris is telling me all this.

"Okay, maybe three-quarters. What I'm saying is. You're beautiful, intelligent, and witty, but for some reason, when it comes to Elijah, you seem to have a block. He turns you back into the woman you were before. The one you showed me pictures of. The one who wore a mask of metal and face paint."

I rest my forearms on my thighs. My hands still clasped in Kris's.

"I'm not sure where you're going with this. Why are we even talking about Elijah Frazer? He doesn't matter. I'm marrying you in six weeks. We're starting a new life together, putting the past behind us. We both agreed."

I look up, and his expression breaks my heart.

He purses his lips.

"Pen, I would love to marry you for all the reasons I just stated." He sighs. "But I don't think I'm the man for you."

I sit up and spin on the sofa, releasing his hands and capturing his face.

"You are. You're the first person to understand me, accept me for who I am."

My stomach drops as he takes my hands in his and draws them down into his lap.

"I'd say that's not true." He inclines his head. "There's another man who understands you. A man who accepted you long before I did. Only fate stepped in and pulled you apart."

His words echo the ones Elijah said, about time and fate never being on our side.

"Pen, listen to me. You can't walk away, not if you have a chance at true happiness. True love." He gives me a sad sigh. "You tried to ignore what you saw at Caleb and April's wedding, but you can't. Not when you've felt it yourself."

I shake my head from side to side.

"Can you?" he says. "We are perfect in so many ways, and I do love you, Pen. But I'm not, and I don't think I ever will be the love of your life."

"You're wrong," I say, but the words sound hollow even to my ears.

"Am I?" he says. "Pen, I need you to listen to me."

He waits until my eyes meet his. His shape blurs as reality takes hold.

"When I lost Annie, I lost the love of my life. But I wouldn't change a moment of the time I spent with her for all the heartache and pain. That kind of love is rare."

"I'm sorry," I say.

"Don't be. But one thing I know is I can't deprive you of that same love, that feeling of completeness. Not if you can have it too."

"But how many times do I have to tell you? Eli sees me as his friend. He *doesn't* love *me*."

My voice rises with despair and desperation.

This can't be happening.

"Are you sure about that?"

I pause.

"Did your heart race when you were together? Did he find reasons to touch you? Hold your hand?"

"We were working," I say, but my mind recounts every memory of Elijah touching me, albeit to pass a coffee or to offer comfort. That last morning when he told me he wasn't coming to the wedding, the look in his eyes.

Could it be true?

No, stop! I have my life planned out, damn it. *I'm not going to do this to myself again.*

"You're wrong," I say, more firmly this time.

"If you don't have feelings for Elijah and truly believe he doesn't love you, that you don't love him. Come to bed. Let me make love to you," Kris says, holding out his hand.

My muscles tense, and my chest tightens. I inhale a shuddering breath.

Kris surprises me, taking my head in his hands once more.

"Look at me."

My eyes drop to my knees.

"Pen, look at me," he says more firmly.

I raise my eyes slowly, unsure what I'll see there.

"You love him, Pen. You can't ignore that, even if you want to. I won't marry someone who's so clearly in love with another man." He shakes his head, his expression hardening.

"But... I..." I fumble over the words. This is not what I was expecting. Shouldn't he be screaming and shouting. As if sensing where my thoughts have gone, Kris smiles.

"Not when you haven't explored whether that love is a real possibility," he says. "Tell me part of you doesn't want to try?"

I flinch at his words but know he's right.

Fuck, this can't be happening.

This is not what I want. To spiral back into the days when Elijah Frazer was my sun and moon. Kris is stable. I know where I stand with him. He's safe. We have a future planned. I have my future planned.

"We can make it work. You and me," I say. "We have the wedding booked. We can't just call it off."

He gives me a brotherly, patient look. One I have come to recognise so well.

"We probably could make it work, until that nagging doubt in the back of your head has you questioning everything." He draws back, and I open my mouth to speak. He holds up a hand and I close it again. "You'll wander if you made the right choice? Then after this conversation there will be the - What-if?" He lets out a deep sigh. "You talk about fate. Have you thought maybe fate sent you back? Wanted to show you there's still a spark between you. That you need to go back and see what it means?"

Kris's eyes lock with mine, and I see the determination in his.

"No," I say, shaking my head frantically, as pressure builds in my chest, threatening to smother me.

Kris sits back, folding his arms over his chest, a vein throbbing in his forehead.

"Pen, you haven't let me near you since you came back. It's been one excuse after another. Our relationship will not work if you can't bring yourself to be with me."

"I'm sorry."

I let out a sob. For the first time, realising what he says is true. I have pushed him away every time he's approached me. Guilt wracks my mind.

He rests his forearms on his thighs, taking one of my hands in his. His thumb rubbing soothing circles on the back of my hand.

"Don't be sorry, beautiful lady. Loving someone is a gift. I loved Annie. Know that feeling. I care deeply about you, Pen. I want what's best for you, and if Elijah Frazer is that man, then you need to at least try."

I press my lips to Kris's, silencing him.

But it contains no passion, feels more like a goodbye.

"What did I do to deserve such an amazing friend?"

It's then I realise. That's what he is, all he will ever be — my friend.

"Friendship goes two ways. Because of you, I now believe moving on is possible after losing Annie, something I never thought I could do. You're a special person, Penelope Dawson. You've gone after everything you wanted in this life, so why stop now? It's time you go after the one person you desire. Find out if he feels the same way."

I bite my lip, missing the feeling of the metal between my teeth.

Is he right?

Elijah always accepted me, goth girl, or not.

"What if you're wrong?"

My insecurities rearing their head.

"I promise you. I'm not."

He takes my hand in his, linking our fingers.

"But if I am, I'll still be here, and Elijah Frazer is even more of an idiot than I thought."

I can't prevent the single tear that escapes and tracks its way down my cheek.

Kris catches it.

"I'll get them to prepare the jet. It's time for you to go home."

Home—a surprising warmth spreads through my chest at that one word.

I shake my head.

"No, I'll book a flight. I can't take your jet."

"Pen, let me do this for you. You *are* and always will be my friend. It's what friends do."

He pulls me into his arms, and I relax against him, absorbing his strength. I hold on, letting his belief eat away at my self-doubt. I'm not sure how long we stay there, but the comfort of a friend when you're in need. There's nothing like it.

CHAPTER 36

ELIJAH

"Have you spoken to Pen?" Gabriel asks.

"What do you mean, spoken to Pen?" a beautifully tanned Caleb asks. "Why would he speak to Pen? Isn't she in the US with Kris, preparing for her big day?"

I shoot Gabriel a warning look.

"Hang on. What did I miss?" Caleb asks, his gaze flipping back and forth between us.

"Nothing important," I say. "We're out talking about your awesome honeymoon."

"Oh, no, you don't. No deflecting, big bro. What did I miss?"

The look Caleb sends me tells me he's serious.

"We've put up with silence for fifteen years. You promised, after your divorce, no more secrets." He turns to his twin. "Gabriel, if mean and moody here won't tell me what's going on. It's up to you, brother."

Gabriel looks at me and raises an eyebrow. Rebuilding relationships is what I'm doing, I remind myself. It's why I'm now letting myself be interrogated by my younger brothers.

"Fine," I say, running a hand through my hair and down

my face. "While you were away, someone tried to sabotage my new release. Not only sabotage but leave all my clients vulnerable to industrial espionage. I uncovered the plot by accident, and Gabriel contacted Pen. She came and helped me rectify the problem."

When I look up, Caleb is staring at me wide-eyed.

"And this is the first I'm hearing about this because?"

I shake my head. "Because, little brother. You were on your honeymoon, and Pen resolved it within a couple of days."

"So, the news articles I was about to question you on? The ones that I've been reading since we landed?"

"True, but limited. It could have been a lot worse had it not been for Pen," I admit, closing my eyes briefly.

The weight in my chest since Pen left has not lifted. The time we spent together reopened old wounds.

"How was Pen?" Caleb asks, his eyes never leaving my face.

"Good. Getting ready for her wedding. Only six weeks now," I say, trying to add some enthusiasm to my tone. Wanting, no, needing desperately for my brother to shut up and move on. It's been bad enough with Gabriel and Leah dropping her name at every opportunity. Even little Callum misses *Ant Pen*.

The last thing I need to think about is Pen, who is back in Kris's arms, preparing for her wedding. Not when it hurts this much.

I sense Gabriel's eyes on me. He's been very quiet, too quiet. Assessing me.

"When are you flying out for the wedding?" Caleb asks, his eyes once again flipping between us.

"The Thursday before," he says, but his eyes never leave mine.

"Elijah?"

I move my gaze from Gabriel to Caleb.

"I'm not going," I tell him, holding his gaze.

Caleb quirks a brow.

"Not going?"

"No—Not going. Pen is aware. We spoke about it. Someone needs to stay with Lottie."

Caleb crosses his arms over his chest and leans back in his chair.

"You're not going to Pen's wedding?" He stares at me wide-eyed, like I've lost my mind. "What the fuck, Elijah? After everything."

Caleb glares at me. It is the same look I got from Gabriel when I told him. Only then it was Leah, who stepped in and broke us apart before my little brother could do anything.

"Look, I can't," I tell him quietly, holding my voice steady.

I don't expect them to understand. I'm not one hundred per cent sure I do.

"Why can't you?" Caleb's voice deflates as if he's giving up on me. "She was your best friend. I'm sure Lottie could stay with one of her friends' parents."

Bloody hell, drop it.

I hate talking about feelings. My counsellor explained that as the eldest, I've spent years trying to protect my siblings, my parents, from my mistakes, from the world itself. But in doing so, I've buried my own wants and needs deep inside. Pen is one of them.

"Because I want her to be happy," I tell him truthfully after a moment.

A furrow appears between both of my brother's brows. If it wasn't for Caleb's tan, I would struggle to tell them apart.

A dawning crosses Caleb's face.

"You're in love with her."

Gabriel harrumphs at his twin.

"For goodness sake. Newsflash, he's always been in love with her."

I grab my beer, placing the bottle to my mouth. Swigging it down.

"Have you told her?" Caleb asks.

As if it's just that simple.

I drop the bottle away from my mouth and stare at him.

"Why the bloody hell would I want to do that? She's about to marry someone else, get everything she desires. I know I can be a dick, but I'm not that big of one."

Caleb's eyes narrow, and he compresses his lips.

"Oh, I don't know. Because she's been in love with you, for like forever!"

"She's marrying another man," I snap, really not needing to hear this bullshit.

"Only because she fucking gave up waiting!" He smacks his forehead with his palm. "And here I was, thinking I was the emotionally stunted one." Gabriel's sharp tone has both our heads spinning to face him. "You really are dense for someone who's supposed to be intelligent."

My head spins, and my skin tingles with discomfort.

"Elijah, Pen has spent years watching you from the sidelines. She's been there whenever you needed her. She helped raise your daughter when you and Darra were too consumed by anger. She pushed aside her wants and dreams and threw herself into her business. But she's a woman. Seeing her with Callum, with Lottie. She wants that for herself. Is it so surprising she looked for it? Pen has always been someone to take charge, go after what she wants. She's no different from Leah in that respect."

I think back to the number of times Lottie told me Aunty Pen had taken her somewhere or helped her with her homework.

It's my turn to quirk my brow.

"If she always goes after what she wants, then why, brother dearest, has she never said anything to me? Told me how she feels?"

They both groan, and it's Caleb who slaps his forehead this time.

I begin to wonder if I really have been that blind and stupid.

CHAPTER 37

PEN

"Penelope Dawson, open this door and let me in."

There is another bang on the door, followed by incessant ringing as someone holds their finger on the bell.

I throw open my front door.

"Bloody hell, Kat, I was downstairs."

"What? In the cellar?" she says, brushing past me and into the house.

"I was checking something out," I say vaguely. "Why don't you come in?"

Kat turns and winks at me.

"I will," she says, continuing her journey towards my kitchen. "Now, where's that coffee machine Gabriel bought you?"

She makes her way across the kitchen and sets the coffee machine going.

"You and your brothers are coffee addicts," I tell her, grabbing two mugs out of the cupboard.

She turns and grins.

"And you're not? I think we should totally blame Gabriel.

He set us all on this path. Even Harper now agrees with us, though she always preferred tea, like our father."

My heart pinches at the mention of Robert. We still feel his loss all these years on. His advice and support stretched beyond his family. I owed that man a lot. I owe Franny a lot.

"How is H?" I ask.

Kat smiles. Harper is eleven years younger than she is, but over recent years, the gap has closed.

"She's loving her university course. It's as if it was made for her. She's also enjoying the anonymity." She nods, her eyes glowing. "I think she likes not being a Frazer for once. Enrolling under our mother's maiden name was pure genius. She's toned down her makeup and returned her hair to its natural colour. Even I nearly didn't recognise her when she turned up on my doorstep. I'm pleased for her. This is what she needs."

Harper took Robert's death incredibly hard. She was only seventeen when he died in a car accident. He was on his way to pick her up. Since her father's death, she's been hiding behind a mask, something I recognise. I'm pleased to hear she's finally moving on.

"I agree," I say. "Good for Harper."

"Now we have got that out of the way. How are you doing?"

Kat moves closer, her eyes lock onto mine, her eyebrows drawn together.

I sigh and bite my top lip to halt the quivering.

I lead her into a room off the kitchen. It's a small sitting room with a large television and the world's comfiest sofa.

Tissues and chocolate wrappers litter the coffee table and floor.

"That good, huh?" Kat says, taking in the scene.

Moving up behind me, she squeezes my shoulder.

"I had a marathon movie fest. All the saddest, most

depressing love stories I could muster," I admit. "I've cried a lot and eaten my weight in chocolate and ice cream."

"You should have called me to join you," she says, spinning me around, her hands on my upper arms, squeezing. "I would have come."

"I know," I say, giving her a watery smile. "However, it was something I needed to do out of sight."

Kat, out of everyone I know, understands that concept. As successful businesswomen who've fought to be at the top of our game, we do not want to show weakness. At least not in public. Even sometimes to our friends and family.

"Fair enough. But I'm here now."

She grabs the bin from the corner near the door and begins scraping all the rubbish into it.

We work in silence, removing all evidence of my mini meltdown.

After I flew home, I barricaded myself in the house for a few days, telling Mum I needed some space. As she was already due to visit my grandparents, I told her she needed to go. She reluctantly agreed, but I know Kat is here because Mum called her. Mum will have given me time, but not enough to wallow completely before she called in the cavalry.

I smile. As a mum, she's always known what I need.

"Now you've eaten all that chocolate and ice cream and cried yourself a river. How are you feeling?"

"Like I need a workout."

Kat grins at me.

"Good thing I packed my running gear. Let's go. The weather is perfect."

I look outside. The sky is overcast, but it's not cold.

"Let's do this."

Kat heads to her usual bedroom to get changed before we head out.

We run the first couple of miles in silence.

"Is it completely over? You and Kris," Kat asks.

I nod.

The pressure in my chest has eased over the past couple of days, along with the nausea I felt at the thought of all I've lost.

"How are you? I mean, really?"

I turn my head to look at my bestie.

"Surprisingly. I feel okay," I say. "Yes, I've grieved because it's over. But if I'm honest, it's hard to explain. You know me, Kat. My life to date has been all about work. This was supposed to be a new chapter. I planned to change. For Kris and I to get married, start a family. Now—"

I pause, not knowing how to put my feelings into words.

"What about Kris?"

I smile.

"He's called me every day. Checked in. He's always been my friend first and will remain that way. He made me face a lot of things."

"What do you mean?"

"Kris is my friend, and as a friend, I love him dearly. On paper, he's perfect. We both wanted the same things, someone who understood us, a family. We were lonely and for a while, we filled that gap for one another. But when he pointed out that was not the right answer—" I sigh. "I realised he was right. We were both settling."

I stop and bend forward, trying to catch my breath. I stand and look up at the sky. Kat stops next to me.

"I can't explain it. Now some time has passed, it's almost a relief. Coming back here was like a weight lifting off my shoulders. I didn't realise how much I would miss home until I moved over there." I let out a laugh. "Who would have thought Penelope Dawson was a home bod?"

Kat inclines her head, and I chuckle.

"Okay, maybe you would. But it was when Gabriel called me. I would have jumped at any excuse to get on a plane and come home." I run a hand down my face. "I think Kris saw that too."

Kat looks at me. She knows about my past.

"What next?"

"I get on with my life," I say truthfully. "I spent the weekend planning out a new game. It's more intricate than anything I've created before. The team are going to want to *part* kill me, *part* kiss me, when I go through it with them."

Kat laughs. "No keeping a good woman down."

I grin. "You should know. What about you?"

She sets off down the road, looking over her shoulder.

"The hotel in the Maldives has hit a few snags. Nothing I can't resolve, but I'm going to need to head out there if the onsite team can't sort it out."

"Worse places to go," I tell her as we turn the corner and head back to the house.

After we've showered, I throw us some lunch together. My staff are still off, although all have jumped at the chance to come back when I invited them. I'm not supposed to be here, so I gave them an extended paid holiday. They all return next week. In the meantime. I'm in charge of my own destiny.

"Does Elijah know you're back?" Kat asks, resting her hip against the kitchen island, a bottle of isotonic water in her hand.

"No. Neither does Gabriel nor Caleb and I'd like to keep it that way. At least for now."

Kat turns her head to the side.

"Can I ask why? Did something happen between you and my brother?"

"No," I tell her truthfully.

"But—"

"No buts. We're friends." I pause. "Hopefully, we can be friends again. The past fifteen years have been messy, but we did quite a lot of talking while I was helping him. Cleared the air. He's mending. I don't want him to think my engagement ending is his fault."

"But it is—indirectly."

I shake my head, and Kat sighs.

"Friends? Is that really all you want?"

I raise an eyebrow. She knows better than to go there.

"All I'm saying is—you're both single. The chemistry has been sizzling between you for years. Don't you think you should at least explore its possibilities?"

Not Kat as well.

It's bad enough with Leah and Kris. Kris has asked me every day if I've spoken to Elijah. I made him swear he wouldn't call him.

"Don't say that. It's not appropriate."

Kat grips both my shoulders.

"We both know if Darra hadn't got pregnant, you and Elijah…"

I shake my head. "No, we wouldn't. Elijah didn't see me like that. I was one of the boys, his partner," I whisper. "That was a lifetime ago. We're no longer the same people."

"You need to speak to him. Let him know you're back. See what happens. You don't need to tell him anything else. Not unless you want to. My big brother might surprise you."

My chest aches at the thought of seeing Elijah again. I don't tell her how many times I've picked up the phone and put it down again.

"It won't help."

"Why not?"

"Because—"

"Because what?"

"Because if he doesn't want me. I don't know what I'll do."

Kat pulls me into her arms.

"But at least you'll know once and for all. This time, you're both free. Maybe it's your time."

"And if it's not?"

"Then we work on a plan Z."

CHAPTER 38

ELIJAH

There's a knock on my office door.

"Come in," I say, looking up as Todd pops his head in.

"Hi," he says, stepping into the room. "Got a moment?"

"Of course. What can I do for you?"

"Well, I wanted to give you the good news. The final release has gone live with no issues on any site."

I drop back in my chair and smile. The tension I've been holding finally releasing.

Todd smiles back. "I also wanted to let you know the new procedures you recommended are also being installed this week. They should stop anything like this from ever happening again."

I get up and move around my desk, holding out a hand.

"Thank you, Todd, for everything."

He stares at my hand and grins.

"Don't thank me. You're the one smart enough to realise something was amiss." His smile drops. "If you hadn't."

He doesn't need to say anymore.

"Look I'm sorry I didn't trust you with what I found. I was in a bad place," I admit.

Todd inclines his head.

"I'll admit it hurt, but I also get it. I'm not sure what I'd have done in your place."

My mind wanders back to the woman who helped resolve the issues. What's she doing now? The procedures Todd is implementing are one's Pen, and I devised. She wanted to ensure what happened could never happen again. At least not easily. Random rotating security methods would mean someone would be constantly having to update their process to override current procedures, and it's now something we're looking to incorporate into future client rollouts.

"Thank you anyway. It's not something I say enough."

"You're welcome, but working here... It's more than I ever dreamed of when we left university. It's been a pleasure."

"It's been quite the ride."

Todd's glass is always half full. He's a positive influence around the office. I wonder if Pen realised that when she recommended him, how much of an impact he would have.

"The guys on the team are going out for a drink this evening. Would you like to join us?"

His words surprise me.

Do I?

It's been years since I attended team drinks. Usually, I send my credit card to pick up the tab.

"That would be great. Send me the details."

Todd's mouth opens slightly before he slams it shut, his grin widening.

"I'll get straight on it," he says, making his way to the door.

I make my way back around my desk, my mind wandering to Pen. I made the right decision by not attending her wedding. I can't physically sit there and watch her say, 'I do.' It's selfish, but I have to think about my own mental health.

Out of sight, out of mind.

I can continue on as if nothing has changed, as I have done for many years.

Pen deserves every happiness. I'm glad one of us has finally found it.

I spin back around and face my computer, opening my email.

I send a congratulations message to all the teams and a more personalised one to each of the major players. They've all gone above and beyond over the past few weeks.

I spend the rest of the day throwing myself into work. Development meetings with team leads and answering client's emails and phone calls. By the time six o'clock comes and Jules knocks on the door, I've distracted myself for most of the day.

"Come in," I say.

"I hear you're joining us for drinks this evening."

"I thought I'd make an appearance."

"Excellent. The team will love it."

"Are you telling me I should have been making more of an effort?"

"I'm not telling you anything, but it will be a popular move."

I shake my head as I get up.

"Only you would get away with pointing that out," I tell her.

"Exactly, and that's why I'm telling you now."

I smile, and she shoots me an incredulous look.

"Who are you, and what have you done with Elijah Frazer?"

"Okay, okay," I say, grabbing my jacket. "I've not been that bad."

"No, you haven't. But Elijah, it's good to see you looking more relaxed."

We move to the elevator in silence. I realise then, I *am* more relaxed. Since my divorce, an enormous weight has been lifted from my shoulders. I'm no longer trapped. I can do what I want. Within reason. Maybe I need to think about that.

The pub is bustling. Todd has rented the whole place, which is filled with faces I recognise. Sales team, human resources, developers, testers. It appears that most of the company has turned out.

"The man of the hour," Todd says, coming up and handing me a beer.

I take it and chink the top of my bottle to his.

A cheer goes up, and I smile.

"Speech," someone shouts.

I move further into the room. Todd on my heels.

I hold up a hand.

"I'd like to thank each one of you for the work you've put in. Not only on this project, but on making Frazer Cyber Security what it is today. The company is nothing without you. The past few weeks have been stressful for everyone concerned. I appreciate every person here who has worked tirelessly to ensure our clients were safe. Thank you."

I hold up my bottle and I'm joined by the rest of the staff.

I spend the next few hours mingling, talking to members of staff I've passed in the corridors but never spoken to.

I relax, letting the old me rise to the surface. The one who, at university, was surrounded by people and who enjoyed social situations. A man who could be himself.

"You being here," Todd says close to my side. "It's made a huge difference to the staff."

I turn to him.

"I've enjoyed it," I say truthfully. "Let me know when they're happening. I'll try to put in an appearance."

Todd nods and smiles.

"I'll hold you to that."

It's then I realise Todd has been carrying this side of my business. His sunny disposition, with his fair but firm business manner has kept the staff happy. Every team member tonight has sung his praises.

I look around and smile as a thought begins to formulate.

CHAPTER 39

ELIJAH

I make my way outside, where Lawrence, one of the company drivers, is waiting.

My phone beeps, signalling a news item.

"Home, sir?"

"Please, Lawrence."

I sit back and unlock the screen, my eyes widening as I read the headline.

Penelope Dawson and Kristophe Lansdown call off their engagement.

I scan the article, but it offers no further information, only that they've asked for privacy at this time.

What the hell?

It's a month until their wedding.

What the hell happened?

I pick up the phone and dial Pen's number.

There's no answer.

I try again, only this time, it goes straight to voicemail.

Fuck.

My heart is racing as I pick up the phone and dial Kat's number.

"Hello, big brother," Kat says, not sounding at all surprised I'm calling her.

"You know?"

"Of course, I know. Pen's one of my closest friends."

"She was my best friend first," I hear myself say.

Kat harrumphs. "How old are you? Before you answer that, may I point out you blew that friendship when you got your girlfriend pregnant and pushed her and everyone else you loved away," Kat snaps.

I ignore her. This isn't the first time we've had this argument.

"What happened, Kat?" I say, lowering my tone. "When I last spoke to Pen, she was all in. The whole nine yards— marriage, kids, settling down."

My chest constricts, and I pause as I try to draw breath into my lungs.

"You need to ask Pen," she says, her tone dropping.

"She's not taking my calls," I admit.

"You find out the same day everyone else does and call her, expecting her to simply pick up? Have you thought she might be busy, not want to speak to anyone?" Kat sighs. "Have you even tried to speak to her since she saved your ass?"

I stop. "I picked up the phone several times, but…" I say, realising how ridiculous I sound.

Of course, Pen doesn't have to answer my calls. Why would she?

There's a pregnant pause.

"I've fucked up," I say.

"Don't you dare hold a self-pity party! All I'm saying is Pen might have a reason for not answering. Think," she says. "You, of all people, should understand that. Did you answer your phone when news of your divorce broke? Like hell did you."

"I threw it in a drawer with silence mode on."

"Exactly."

I know she's right. But it hurts to know I've lost my place in Pen's inner circle. My siblings and mother now hold those positions.

"Are you okay?" I ask, realising Kat is behaving very out of character.

My sister is a straight talker but not usually this snappy.

I hear Kat inhale.

"Sorry. It's been a long day. Shit is going down in one of our hotels. Actually, multiple hotels, and I've spent all day firefighting. That and like you, I'm worried about Pen."

"I'm sorry, Kat," I say, realising what a selfish prick I've been. "Is there anything I can do?" I ask.

My sister works even harder than I do, and that's saying something. We're both driven by that same internal force to succeed. As the oldest siblings, we've taken our parents' work ethic to heart. Not that our younger siblings haven't, but in recent years, they've gained the perfect work-life balance.

"No, I've got this."

And I know she does.

"Just remember I'm here if you ever need me."

"Thank you." Kat pauses. "Elijah. If you speak to Pen. Don't push her. She's been back a few weeks. She's trying to get back on her feet."

"She's what?"

"Oh shit."

I can imagine Kat pressing her temples, wishing she'd stayed quiet.

"Look, she wanted to keep it quiet. They both did."

"The man must be an idiot," I hiss under my breath.

My sister lets out a frustrated grunt.

"Typical! How do you know it wasn't Pen who walked away? Why do you assume it was Kris?"

Hope blossoms in my chest, and my heart rate picks up.

"I didn't." I run a hand down my face. "It's not that. It's just when we were talking she had everything planned out. Her entire future was mapped out in a way only Pen does." I pause. My heart sinks. For Pen to have changed her mind, and that quickly, something must have happened.

"Is she okay? Damn it, Kat. Please."

A sense of dread overwhelms me.

Kat sighs again.

"I just want to know she's okay."

"Why? Why do you want to know if she's okay?" Kat presses.

I run a hand through my hair.

"She was my friend. I care about her. If she's hurting—"

"Pen has a lot of friends who are there for her."

Kat's words make me smart.

"I know she does," I mumble.

"So why do you care?" Kat presses.

"Because I do."

"Not good enough," my sister's voice snaps me out of my funk. "God, Elijah, for once, get out of your head."

I drop back against the seat and watch the city go by.

"Why are you snapping at me?"

"Because...I want to know why you care. Say the first thing that comes to mind."

I stare down at my phone and frown.

"You're sounding like my therapist," I tell her.

There's a pause.

"You're speaking to him again?"

"Yes."

"Good. Now tell me, why do you care?"

I close my eyes and rest my head back against the seat. My hand comes up and rubs the centre of my chest.

"Because it hurts to know she's hurting."

There's silence on the other end of the phone.

"She's at her house," Kat says. "And Elijah. Don't fuck it up this time."

"I won't," I say, although the line has already gone dead.

I lean forward and press the intercom, giving me access to the driver.

"Change of plans," I say, giving him Pen's address.

We leave the city and head south. Pen lives close to our family home. She fell in love with the area after spending her holidays with us, and as soon as she could, she bought her and her mum a home nearby, moving out of the city while I moved in.

We approach the gate. Last time, I had a fob to let myself in. I dial Pen's number again, but still no reply.

I dial the only other number I can think of. This time, I get a response.

"Elijah Frazer. It's late."

"Hi, Louise, I just found out."

"Ahh, my daughter's been holding out on you." There's a pregnant pause. "Why are you calling?"

I look up and stare out the window at the gate, realising how impulsive I've been.

"I'm outside the gates," I admit.

"I know. I can see you on the camera. Pen transferred the tech to my house when she moved to the US. She hasn't taken it back yet," she explains. "More the question is why are you outside her gates?"

Everyone wants to know why?

"I need to know she's okay."

"She's not," Louise says bluntly, all amusement gone from her tone.

"Let me in to see her," I say. "Please, Louise."

There's another pause.

"If she doesn't want to see you, promise me you'll leave without a fuss."

"I promise."

I hear a buzz, and the line goes dead. The gate opens.

Lawrence pulls up outside the garage, out of the line of sight of the gates. The driveway might be long, but the paparazzi and their telescopic lenses... The last thing she'll want is pictures of me arriving after dark.

I didn't see anyone, but you never can be too careful. With any luck, they still think she's in the US.

"Do you want me to wait, sir?"

"No, Lawrence, you can head off."

If Pen doesn't want me here, I'll call a taxi.

He turns the car around and heads back down the driveway.

I inhale and make my way to the front door, ringing the bell. Its chime echoes through the enormous wooden door.

When there is no answer, I ring again and again. Louise said she's here.

Is she choosing to ignore me?

The door opens to a flushed-looking Pen.

"Hold your horses," she says, not looking up, her phone pressed to her ear.

"That should be it," she says into the receiver.

There's a pause as she listens to whatever the other person is saying.

Her features soften.

"It was the least I could do. Let me know if there are any issues."

She finally looks up, her body tensing as her eyes lock on mine.

"Elijah." The words are out of her mouth, surprise crossing her face.

Her attention is drawn back to her phone, to whoever is on the other end of the line.

"Sorry...Yes...Elijah is here." There's another pause. "Look, I have to go. I'll call you later, Kris. But everything seems to be secure."

Whatever he says to her has my stomach hardening at the look on her face.

"Yes. I will. Take care."

She disconnects the phone and stares at me.

"What are you doing here?" she asks.

"You weren't answering your phone."

Pen's hair is scraped up in a messy bun. Her face is makeup-free. She's wearing leggings and a sloppy sweater.

"I was working. My phone is on silent as it's been blowing up all afternoon ever since the story broke." She steps aside and ushers me in. "The press got wind of me leaving the country and then someone leaked about Kris and I. It's been bedlam."

"I wanted to check you were okay."

"I'm fine. There's no keeping this woman down," she says, walking in front of me towards the kitchen. "Drink?"

"Coffee, please," I say, following behind her and sensing everything about her is *far from fine*.

She looks like she's lost weight, not that she had any weight to lose.

"One coffee, coming up."

Her voice is a little too chirpy.

She puts on the coffee machine, heading straight for the cupboard, dragging out two cups, almost dropping one as she goes.

"Enough," I say, capturing her arms and relieving her of the cups. "Sit down. I'll make *you* a coffee."

"I'm fine, honestly," she says. "I've been working."

"You're not fine, so stop saying you are. You're wired to hell. I recognise the signs."

"You don't know me," she says, flopping down into a seat. "Don't pretend you do."

I turn, hands on my hips.

"I know you better than you think I do," I tell her. "When did you last sleep? Eat?"

It's then I notice the dark circles under her eyes.

"As I said. I've been working."

"Twenty-four-seven?"

Pen shrugs. "I've slept."

"What? When you've crashed?" I huff. "What happened, Pen?"

She drops her head into her hands, her fingers in her hair. As if remembering it's screwed up, she sits up and pulls out the hairband, allowing it to cascade down her back before scooping it up and returning it to another messy bun.

"Why are you here?" she asks, slumping back in her kitchen chair.

I watch her closely as the coffee machine gurgles behind me.

"I heard about you and Kris. I wanted to check on you."

"Well, you've done that." She holds her arms wide. "Look. I'm in one piece."

I growl.

Stubborn woman.

She screws up her nose and plays with a speck of invisible flint on her leggings.

"Why are you really here, Elijah?"

Her tone is matter-of-fact, but her face displays a protective filter. One I recognise.

"Why?" I pinch the bridge of my nose and count to ten. "Why the bloody hell does everyone keep asking me why?" I say. "You're my friend. You helped me out, and now your engagement is over. I care about you, Pen. I wanted to check you're okay."

"Don't worry, Kris and my breakup had nothing to do with you," she says, although something in her tone makes me think she's lying.

I move towards her.

"The last time we spoke, you were about to get married, looking forward to starting a family. Now I hear your engagement is history and you expect me to accept *you're fine* with it?"

Pen avoids my gaze, her arms folding over her chest.

I move towards her and crouch down in front of her.

"I only found out this evening. I came straight here."

When I told Kat it hurt, I meant it. It physically hurts to think of her in pain. I want Pen to be happy. What she wanted with Kris does not differ from what Leah and my brother wanted. What Caleb and April now have.

I've had a front-row seat to *crushed dreams* so I know they're not something you just bounce back from. Working with my therapist, I'm not sure I ever did. Instead, I became withdrawn and cynical.

"Why are you *really* here, Elijah?"

Her voice sounds so soft and small, not something I recognise and I hate it.

"Kat says you've been back a few weeks."

"I have. I've been trying to get my life back on track. You know me and my plans. I needed to reconfigure my lists," she says, trying to keep her voice light and neutral.

"Pen..."

She holds up a hand.

"Don't," she mumbles, her voice catching. "You said before if there was anything you could do for me?"

"That still stands, anything. You just have to ask," I say, without missing a beat.

If there is something I can do to set her life back on track. Even if it means speaking to Kris, I'll do it.

"I need you to leave. Walk away. Let me get on with my life."

I let out a groan and drop my chin to my chest. My forehead resting on her knees.

"Anything but that," I say, unable to keep the pain from my voice. I raise my head, my eyes clashing with hers. "That's probably the only thing I can't do."

Pen opens her mouth to speak.

"Please don't ask me to walk away," I beg.

A tear tracks its way down her cheek.

"I—"

Her eyes lock on my mouth and before I can stop myself, I take her head in my hands and draw her lips to mine.

CHAPTER 40

PEN

When Elijah's lips touch mine, it's like a crescendo of fireworks being set off in my head and throughout my body. His tongue brushes my lips, and I open for him willingly, allowing him to deepen our kiss. My body temperature rises as I fall against him. I suck in a breath as he pulls me from my chair and into his lap on the floor.

My hands circle his neck and clasp his head, deepening our kiss. Our lips duel as we taste each other for the first time. My back arches, melding my curves into his hard frame, years of allowing my imagination free rein, have nothing on the real thing. Kissing Elijah Frazer for the first time is not only mind-blowing, it has the potential to be soul-destroying.

It takes all my willpower to pull myself out of his grasp and move away from his tempting lips and hard body. I crawl out of his lap and shimmy across the floor until my back hits one of the kitchen cupboards, putting some much-needed distance between us.

"Pen?"

His tone is questioning. Almost pleading.

I hold up a hand as I try to catch my breath, my heartbeat thundering in my ears.

I take comfort in the fact my breathing is not the only one laboured. Elijah seems to be struggling too.

I drop my head to my knees, closing my eyes as I wrap my arms around my legs.

I stay still despite feeling him move to sit next to me. No part of him touches me, but my body is filled with an awareness I never thought possible. Every nerve ending fires as my womb contracts with unmet desire.

We sit in silence as I try to gather my thoughts.

"That was not what I expected," I say eventually.

He wraps an arm around my shoulder, pulling me into his side. His head resting against mine.

"I'm sorry," he says quietly, although I'm not sure what for.

"Are you?" I say, looking up, our faces millimetres apart. "Are you sorry?"

His brow furrows as if he's trying to work out the correct answer.

I bite my lip, his eyes track the movement. My heart rate picks up again.

"No," he says quietly. "Are you?"

I shake my head, my stomach somersaulting as his lips break into a smile.

"Good," he says, one hand coming up and cupping my chin, his thumb caressing my cheek. "I've wanted to do that for a long time."

I suck in a breath.

He continues, his eyes scouring my face.

"I haven't been able to get you out of my head since you left..."

I close my eyes, my breath catching in my throat.

"I'm supposed to be concentrating on Lottie, on my company, but you've got me tied up in knots, Penelope Dawson. You're the only thing I can think about."

"Elijah," I all but croak.

"If you really want me to leave. I will," he says, pushing himself up.

I press the palm of my hand against his chest, holding him in place.

He freezes.

"After that kiss?" I say. "You walk out that door, and I'll rugby tackle you to the floor."

I look up into sparkling dark brown eyes.

"Sounds tempting, just to see you try."

He drops back down, his legs outstretched along the kitchen floor.

He leans over, gripping my waist as he positions me until I'm straddling his thighs.

Our faces are now level.

He grips my ass, pulling me forward until my pussy comes into contact with his very hard, very swollen cock.

We both groan at the sensation.

"Feel what you are doing to me?"

He moans, his eyes closing for a second, his skin flushed. When he opens his eyes, his pupils are dilated and shiny.

I take his face in my hands, slamming my lips to his.

Electric shock waves travel throughout my body, and I grind my over-sensitised body down on his cock, backwards and forwards, wanting to release some of the pressure building.

"Fuck, Pen," Elijah pants before pulling my lips back to his, his kiss even more demanding than before.

My throbbing core is on fire. I clutch his shoulders, his own grip tightening. I've never felt this intense level of need before.

"I don't have any protection on me," Elijah says, dragging his lips from mine.

I can hear the sorrow and disappointment in his voice.

I jump up and head to my medical cupboard. I grab a brand new box of condoms, ripping it open as I return to where Elijah is now standing.

I drop them on the floor as he grabs me around the waist and hauls me against him.

"Fuck, Pen," Elijah says, pulling back his dark eyes questioning. "Are we really doing this?"

I part my legs as his hands move to my ass. I wrap them around his waist as he lifts me up, his hardness once again pressed against my pulsing core, reminding me this is two-way.

"I have no idea what we're doing," I admit with a small chuckle, drinking in his beautiful face and flushed skin. "But I know I need this. That I need you, Elijah. Right here, right now. I want to ride you, feel you in my body until we both can't speak."

He closes his eyes, a rumble coming from deep in his chest. My core contracts sharply at the primal sound.

"Are you sure?" he asks, opening his eyes.

It's like he's staring into my soul.

"Never been more sure of anything," I tell him honestly.

I don't think I've ever felt such desperation. I need his strength, his body. I want to forget all the shit that is my life, and somehow, I know Elijah will be the one to help me do that.

"Don't say I didn't warn you."

"Do your worst."

His mouth slams against mine, taking all I have to give. He spins me around, placing my ass on the cold granite surface of the island. My hot pussy clenches even through the thin material of my leggings. Our hands are everywhere, pulling at clothes, wanting to touch bare skin. I pull his t-shirt over his head, exposing the wall of muscle that has been seared into my brain since I saw him in the gym. I run my hands over the defined planes, loving how the muscles contract under my fingers.

Elijah slides his hands into the back of my leggings, expertly sliding them down over my hips, his mouth never leaving mine. I don't think I've ever been kissed with such intensity. Ever felt so wanton.

I draw his bottom lip into my mouth and suck, his hips thrust forward against my now exposed and swollen core.

"I don't think I can go slow," Elijah says, tearing his mouth from mine as he whispers his truth against my cheek.

"Then don't," I say, pulling back and holding his face in my hands. "I want you buried in me. I need to feel you, all of you," I say.

The look in his eyes steals my breath and I almost orgasm there and then.

As if sensing my need, Elijah's hand moves between my thighs. I'm on a knife's edge, my core spasming, weeping as it begs to be filled. I want to be stretched, to have someone finally take control of my out-of-control life. His groan rumbles through his chest as his fingers glide through my wet and swollen flesh. He deepens his kiss as his fingers tease my clit, but not quite making it to where my body is begging for his intrusion.

I tear my lips from his, my body screaming, my breath panting.

"Elijah, stop fucking teasing me."

He chuckles, his mouth now against my neck before his fingers find my entrance. I suck in a breath as he slides first one, then a second finger in deep. My muscles contract sharply.

"Is that what you want, beautiful?" he asks, as he twists his fingers, curling them against my front wall.

"Oh God."

I sigh, my back arching, my legs spreading wider, wanting more. His face is so close I almost can't focus. He curls his fingers again, and I let out a deep moan.

"Yes, just that. Oh, bloody hell. I'm going to implode."

I pant as Elijah's fingers continue to explore my body. One hand deep in my pussy, the other skimming my skin. The man has magical hands. He lowers his mouth to my breast, sucking down one of my nipples, tormenting it with his teeth, every suck sending shards of desire south, making me clench around his fingers.

Elijah tuts, withdrawing his lips. His mouth moves to the spot beneath my ear, teasing the sensitive flesh before moving up and nipping my earlobe.

"I need you inside me. Please, Elijah," I beg. "I want to feel you as I come around your cock."

It's his turn to moan.

I rotate my hips against his hand.

"All good things come to those who wait," he whispers against my lips before kissing his way across my cheek. "You're going to come when I tell you to," he says, his breath teasing my ear.

I moan. "I'm close," I tell him.

"Not until I say, Pen. Do you understand?"

I nod, emitting another moan, only this time in frustration. I rotate my hips, I like this game. Elijah's fingers continue their wicked onslaught, and I stretch my thighs wider, my hips now moving of their own accord against his hand. His thumb grazes my clit, ruthlessly tormenting my bud of nerves. I bite my lips to prevent myself from falling into the abyss.

I grip his shoulders, my nails digging into his skin. His jean-clad hips thrust forward. I'm not the only one affected.

I snake a hand lower, coming into contact with the front of Elijah's jeans. His cock straining against the harsh material. I press against him, but he pulls back, clicking his tongue.

"If you want this, then you need to do as I say."

I've never been one to hand over control anywhere, but here and now, I find I want this. Want this with Elijah. It's what I need, crave. I want someone else to take charge.

I lean back on my hands, watching the man standing between my legs, his fingers buried in my pussy, his eyes watching as his fingers dive in and out, glistening in the light.

He looks up, his eyes lock on mine, before slowly travelling back down my body. My clothes are gone. I'm exposed to his gaze, but the look in his eyes burns its way over my skin.

He curls his fingers again, and I spread my legs wider.

"Elijah!" I yell.

My desire drips down his hand, my body desperate, getting itself ready.

When he adds a third finger, the burn has me dropping my head back, my hips taking on a life of their own as I ride his hand. I don't think I've ever felt this full. The pressure deep inside my core builds as my hips undulate against him. I look up to find Elijah watching me. I drop my gaze to where his fingers are moving in and out of my swollen lips, twisting and turning, my hips pumping.

"Beautiful," Elijah moans. "Look at how well you take my fingers. Wait until you're riding my cock."

He twists his fingers until his thumb finds my clit once more. The pressure building and building.

"Come for me, Pen," he says. "Now."

Elijah pulls my body against him as my orgasm hits. My head drops back once more as my body shatters around him, my muscles pulsing and spasming, gripping his invading fingers, milking them hard.

Elijah grunts but continues to work me until I'm begging him to stop, gripping his wrist, my body too sensitive to take any more.

He withdraws his fingers tenderly, the sudden emptiness overwhelming.

He pulls me against his chest, a hand smoothing my hair.

"I need you," I say, my voice husky, almost unrecognisable.

Elijah bends down and scoops up the abandoned box of condoms from the floor, tearing it open, spraying the foils everywhere in his haste.

"They were magically added to this week's shopping list," I say unnecessarily as I watch him.

He quirks a brow.

"Mum," I add.

"I would say, remind me to thank her, but I think I'll forgo that politeness," he says, tearing open the foil packaging.

I laugh, but it dies in my throat as he moves back towards me. His eyes full of desire and promise.

I sit forward and unzip his jeans, pushing them and his boxers down. He kicks them off, returning to stand before me. My gaze travels down his body, taking in his taut, defined muscles, his Adonis belt showing his dedication to his fitness.

His cock.

"Oh, boy!" I say, making him chuckle.

Elijah's body is a masterpiece. He stands still, his cock twitching under my scrutiny as I drink him in. My eyes meet his, my tongue snaking out to moisten my lips.

"I'm all yours," he says as I drop my gaze once more.

My mouth waters at the sight of him, his swollen cock, hard and weeping in the light. It twitches under my gaze.

It's my turn to moan as I wrap my fingers around him.

"Don't," he says through gritted teeth. "I won't last, and I certainly don't want to be coming all over your sideboard. I want that pleasure to be deep inside you."

I reluctantly let him go, taking the open condom from his hands and sheathing him.

He scoops his hands under my ass and pulls me forward.

I let out a squeal, and he laughs.

He smiles as his gaze locks on mine.

"I have wanted this for so long."

His words steal my breath, melting something deep in my chest.

He can't mean it.

It's something you say in the heat of the moment.

I spread my thighs once more, my body and desire taking over. His height makes sideboard sex perfect.

"Come here," I say, sliding my ass to the edge of the counter. I take him in my hand, eliciting another groan from him as I line him up with my entrance.

I place his tip against my opening, and Elijah freezes.

I wrap my legs around his hips and press forward.

"Pen," he hisses as he breaches my entrance, sinking into my body. His size stretches me, but my previous orgasm and his fingers have eased the way as we come together in the most intimate way possible.

He presses forward, pulling me towards him, his hands clasping my ass. He pauses, allowing my body time to accustom to his size, before sinking deeper.

I bite my lip, Elijah's tongue teasing it from between my teeth before sinking into my mouth. By the time he's fully seated, we're both panting.

When our eyes meet, his expression takes my breath away.

I lift my hand and cup his cheek the way he did mine earlier.

"Elijah," I whisper.

He leans forward, his lips closing over mine.

"God, Pen," he whispers against me. "You've no idea—"

Our kiss deepens as he begins to move. I squeal and laugh as he pulls me up off the side and into his chest, his hands and arms supporting me.

I wrap my arms around his neck and draw him close. Our tongues duel. The pressure deep in my body begins to build once more as he touches places deep inside, places I never imagined existed.

I lock my ankles behind his waist, our tongues and teeth clashing as our desire skyrockets. He moves me up and down his cock, his muscles bulging as he takes my weight as if it's nothing.

Lifting me, his mouth closes over my nipple, and I bury my hands in his hair, holding him close, before dropping back down.

He returns me to the side, the cold of the granite making my heated core clench. Elijah hisses as my muscles squeeze around him.

"I want to feel you come all over my cock."

"Your wish is my desire," I say, shuddering at the sheer desire in his voice.

When his fingers find my clit, my hands move to his shoulders, my muscles tighten, my body taking on a life of its own as I ride him hard, sliding up and down his rock-hard cock, the pressure building once more until I can't hold it any longer. I yell in part pain, part frustration.

"Come for me," Elijah demands, and my body does exactly that.

My muscles clamp around him hard, milking him over and over as he rides my orgasm, sliding in and out until I feel his body jerk, his orgasm filling the condom. The only thing between us.

I sit up, my legs and arms still wrapped around him. I bury my face in his neck, trying to catch my breath as I run my hands over the silky smooth flesh of his back. He stands upright and pulls me flush against him, his breathing as ragged as mine.

"I..." he starts to say.

I press my cheek more firmly against his shoulder, my nose buried against his throat.

I'm not sure how long we stay like that, but eventually, Elijah pulls back, clasping the end of the condom as he withdraws.

When he remains silent, I look up and into his face, unsure what I'm going to find.

Does he think this was a mistake?

What I see there makes my shoulders relax at the gentle smile playing on his lips.

"Well, that was unexpected," he says.

His words make me grin.

"You could say that," I reply, laying a hand against his naked chest, just above his heart, my other sliding up over his shoulder.

I should be embarrassed. I'm sitting on the side in my kitchen, my body coming down from two of the strongest orgasms I've ever experienced, having handed control to someone who has been a friend on and off for years.

Should I be surprised Elijah likes to take control?

I smile to myself.

"What?" he asks, his head tilting.

"I need a shower."

I slide forward, untangling our bodies and dropping my feet to the floor.

"Do you want me to go?" Elijah asks, his voice no longer as commanding as it was during sex.

I look up into his face and see the same level of uncertainty that's raging through my mind.

"Or you could stay," I say, before my brain can engage.

Finding I'm tired of all the unsaid things between us.

I leave the words hanging.

Elijah's eyes lock on mine, the question clear.

"I'd like that," he says, his eyes twinkling.

"You could join me in the shower," I say, as I give him a cheeky look over my shoulder as I turn towards the door to the kitchen.

Elijah quirks a brow when my lip disappears under my teeth.

"Maybe I can help clean up the mess I made."

His eyes darken as they travel south to the stickiness of our session and where my desire coats my thighs.

I nod and quirk my brow.

"It would be the polite thing to do after all," he says, taking a step towards me. "And my parents raised me to be a gentleman."

I can't keep the smirk from my face. I'm not sure Franny and Robert had this in mind when teaching manners to their children, but who am I to complain?

Without a backward glance, I take off up the stairs. I make it to my bedroom door before Elijah catches me and scoops me up around the waist. He hauls me against him, his lips once again finding my neck.

I relax into his touch.

Ooh, it's going to be a fun night.

CHAPTER 41

ELIJAH

My mind stirs as my body regains consciousness. My stomach muscles clench, my hips rising off the mattress.

I lavish in the feeling, my eyes closed as a warm mouth and tongue continue their exploration of my rock-hard cock.

I slide my hand under the covers, finding the head of the woman who's turned my life upside down in a matter of hours.

The covers move with her head. She takes me deep, her throat muscles squeezing my cock as she swallows around me.

"Fuck, Pen," I hiss.

Only to feel that same mouth chuckle.

"Don't laugh with your mouth full," I say, regretting my words immediately when she pauses. "Please, don't stop," I moan, my hand tightening in her hair.

As if on demand, she draws me back into her mouth, her tongue flicking the underside of my tip until I swear I see stars. She sucks gently, her lips and soft mouth moving up and down. My eyes roll back in my head, and I know I will not last long. Who would have thought Pen had such a wicked mouth?

When her hand gently massages my balls, I know I'm done for.

"Pen, I'm going to come," I groan, trying to pull away.

I'm unsure whether she's going to want me coming down her throat.

Pen doesn't move. If anything, she steps it up a gear, her pace increasing, until I'm writhing on the bed.

I yell. My hips thrust up off the mattress as my muscles lock. My cock jerks, spurting jets of cum into her warm, welcoming mouth. My body shudders as my orgasm subsides.

Pen's tongue and mouth continue their torment as she drinks me down and cleans me up.

I collapse back on the bed, surprised I've anything left. After our first session, we moved upstairs. Had sex in the shower, before ordering a takeaway. After our meal, we ate ice cream, or should I say we ate ice cream off each other, and with Pen straddling my thighs, my cock buried deep in her pussy.

"Morning," Pen says, appearing from under the covers, dropping a kiss on my chest as she works her way back up the bed.

"Hum, I could get used to that," I say, sliding my hands under her armpits and pulling her on top of me, my mouth locking onto hers. I can taste myself on her lips. The same way she tasted herself on mine multiple times yesterday.

"That was quite the wake-up call," I say, my hand brushing her hair from her face, sweeping it back and behind her ear.

"I'm an early riser. And I find myself totally refreshed.

You, sir, definitely recharged my batteries last night," Pen says, placing her hands on top of one another on my chest before resting her chin on top of them.

"No longer tired?" I ask, amazed as we only got a few hours of sleep.

"Different tired," she admits, stretching like a cat.

I roll until she's trapped beneath me, her wrists trapped above her head in one of my hands.

"You're insatiable, Ms Dawson," I say as she grins up at me.

Our noses touch, and her eyes darken.

She wriggles, spreading her legs until she can wrap them once more around my waist. She rubs her wet centre against my cock, which hardens against her pussy almost instantly.

"Looks like I'm not the only one who's insatiable," she smirks.

"Did sucking me off get you hot and needy?" I ask, pressing the edge of my cock against her swollen lips.

She moans as my cock slips through her desire, sliding from her entrance to her clit.

"It did," she pants.

I love how unabashed Pen is. She knows what she wants and is happy to let me do it to her. I press forward again, tormenting her clit.

She moans and tries to capture my mouth with hers, but I pull back.

She rubs herself up and down my cock, coating me with her desire. I continue to harden against her, amazed I'm ready to go again so soon. I want nothing more than to pull back and drive my unsheathed cock into her body until we are both screaming.

I pause.

What?

I've never wanted to go bareback. Even after Lottie was born, I never had unprotected sex with Darra. I never wanted another child. It became clear we were a disaster from the outset. But what was done was done, and I needed to make the most of it. But I wasn't willing to bring another child into the world, not that she wanted one.

Before I can think further, I lean over and grab another condom, pulling it on before thrusting deep into Pen. Her body arches as I invade her body once more. She must be sore as we haven't stopped, but I find her pulling me close, her hips rising to meet mine, her little pants telling me she wants more.

"Hard and fast," she cries desperately against my mouth. "I need you hard and fast."

"As the lady desires," I say, rolling us so she's on top.

Pen sits astride me, her body rising and falling. I watch my cock slide in and out as she lifts herself up before dropping herself back down.

"Beautiful," I say. "Take what you need."

My hands cover her pert breasts, moulding and rolling them in my enormous hands. I tweak her nipples in the way I know she likes.

I sit up, taking one in my mouth, rolling the hardened point with my teeth and tongue.

Pen's head drops back as she rocks, using my pubic bone to stimulate her clit. It's not long before I can feel her muscles clenching around me. She moans and shudders.

"Come for me, let go," I say as her body pulses.

I let my own orgasm loose before we both crash in a heap, her on top of me. I wrap my arms around her, cradling her to my chest, kissing the top of her head.

We remain in that position for a while, neither of us saying anything. My cock softens and Pen carefully extracts herself, disposing of yet another condom.

I lie with my hands behind my head, my naked body exposed. The duvet is long gone. We're past any form of modesty. Pen has a beautiful body, and I enjoy the sight.

She gets up and makes her way to the bathroom before returning.

She sits on the side of the bed, and my heart stutters at the look on her face.

"I need to go into the office," she says, turning away.

"Pen?"

I sit up and gently turn her to face me. Her eyes stare at the bed until I catch her face in my hands, making her look at me. After last night and this morning, there'll be no barriers between us. I'm sick of poor communication, and if she thinks after what we've shared, I'm walking out of here without a backward glance, she's mistaken.

She shakes her head in my hands, and I hold her still until her eyes lock on mine.

"Talk to me," I say.

Her mouth twists, her bottom lip disappearing between her teeth.

She sighs.

"I understand why April snuck out of Caleb's room," Pen says, her eyes once again dodging mine.

My chest tightens at her words.

"Why?"

Pen shrugs. "It's the morning after and awkward conversation time."

I sit up. "Does it need to be?"

Her eyes flick to mine, full of surprise.

"What else would it be?"

I pull her next to me. She comes willingly, which I see as positive.

"There are two options. You can say, thank you Elijah, for

all those wonderful orgasms. I'll take it from here." I pause, watching her lips twitch.

"Or?"

"Or I can say, Penelope Dawson, can I interest you in future orgasms, and will you have dinner with me tonight?"

A pink tinge spreads over Pen's cheeks, and her eyes darken.

I watch her bite her lip again, moving it with my thumb.

"Is that what you want? You said you didn't want to get into a relationship, that your time was concentrating on Lottie."

I'm surprised at how unsure her voice sounds. Pen is usually so confident.

"After last night and this morning. Do you really need to ask me that? Christ, Pen. I've just had the best sex of my life, and you're asking me if I want more? If I had my choice, you would not be going into the office. You'd be staying here with me for the indefinite future. As for Lottie, my daughter will always come first. She has to. But I selfishly can't walk away from you."

She stares at me wide-eyed for a moment.

"Best sex, huh?" she says, her cheeks darkening under my gaze.

"By far." I capture her face in my hands. "Being with you has blown my mind, as I always knew it would," I tell her truthfully.

Not that I've had much sex over the past few years. Darra and I haven't slept together since I found out Lottie wasn't mine. I've had a couple of sexual partners, but affairs are complicated. I didn't need anyone getting attached. I had Lottie to think about. Meeting someone else would have meant losing her, as divorcing Darra would have meant exactly that. It would not have been fair to anyone.

"Me too," she says with a shy smile.

I'm surprised when she holds my gaze, highlighting the truth of her words.

"So, does this mean I can take you out to dinner?"

A smile spreads over her face.

"I'd love that," she says.

"Good. I'll pick you up after work." Pen scoots off the bed. "Oh, and Pen, bring an overnight bag."

CHAPTER 42

PEN

I enter the office with a spring in my step. Multiple orgasms will do that to a girl, or so I've just found out. I don't think my libido has ever been as high. The moment we touched, it was as if Elijah unlocked something inside me, and my body has yet to recover. I'm pulsing with desire. If Elijah was to walk in now, I'd climb him like a tree and ride him until we're both puddles of goo on the floor.

I smile widely.

I've read articles on mind-blowing sex, but having never experienced it, thought it was one of those things that sells magazines.

With Elijah, it was like we couldn't get enough of each other. I wanted to try every position I've ever thought about. My body came alive with the simplest of touches. It was like craving chocolate when you know you shouldn't. I wanted to plaster my body against his toned muscles, feel my skin against his. The thought alone leaves me hot and wet.

Lust took over last night. I was desperate for his body, mind, and soul.

"Wow, you're glowing," Danika says, her eyes wide as I enter my office.

Danika has been with Dawson Tech since its conception.

"It's a great morning," I say, shooting her a bright smile.

"Clearly," she chuckles. "It's good to have you back. I wasn't sure when to expect you."

"I thought I should show my ugly mug," I say, throwing my bag onto the sofa in the corner of the room, before making my way to my desk.

Danika was one of the few people who knew I was back, and that my engagement to Kris had ended. We've been in constant contact over the phone. I warned her the press would call as soon as the story broke, but I trusted her to handle it. The rest of my staff are loyal and have shut down any gossip.

"How's the prototype going?"

I grin.

Danika knows I can't resist keeping my hand in. I'm not *a sit in my ivory tower* boss. I'm more *hands on, get down and dirty* with the team.

"I sent the outline across yesterday afternoon," I say, dropping into my chair and spinning around.

It feels good to be back where I belong.

"I know," she says, grinning at me. "The team are loving it. It's been the talk of the office. I don't think I've seen them this eager since—ever."

She pulls out her tablet before handing over the office chat.

I smile at some of the comments that are being left.

"Not as much as I've had in creating it," I tell her.

Danika shakes her head. "You seem to have found your mojo."

I nod in agreement. "I think I have."

She grins. "Pen Dawson is back. It's good to see," she tells me, putting her tablet down and pulling me up and in for a hug. "I was worried we'd lost you for a while."

I know what she's referring to. When I accepted Kris's offer, I went all in. Handing things over, switching my focus from my current life to what I saw as my future life. Planning for a family, taking a step back, and handing over the reins. It's why the past few weeks have been about me resetting, getting my head screwed back on. I'm an all-or-nothing girl. When I make a decision, I'm all in. Even if it's not for the best.

I now see the path I was heading down with Kris would have been great but not fulfilling. I was opening an office in the US, but it would never have been the same. Now I've been with Elijah. It's clear what Kris meant and why he sent me back. We *are* friends but nothing more and now I have tasted the forbidden fruit, I'll struggle to go back to plain apples. In the morning's light, my heart breaks for him. If he had a fraction of what I had with Elijah last night, with Annie, I'm not sure how he's survived without her.

My heart stops, and I draw in a breath.

"Are you all right?"

I plaster a fake smile on my face, making Danika frown.

"I'm fine, honestly. I just had a thought about the game," I lie.

Danika stares at me but doesn't call me out. One reason we're friends.

"Well, I'll leave you to it."

She grabs her things.

"We'll grab a coffee later," I call after her as she heads out the door.

She spins with a wide grin.

"Definitely."

I walk to the glass window of my corner office and look down over the bustling city beneath me.

I press my thumb and forefinger onto the bridge of my nose.

Kris and I were friends. Elijah and I are friends. But sex with Elijah was nothing like with Kris. With Kris it was satisfying, but with Elijah, my knees turn to jelly just thinking about how it felt to be with him.

But there were no promises, no potential future. He's asked me for more, and there's no way I can turn him down. His recent escape from a loveless marriage and his past sacrifices to meet family expectations have left their mark. He's already given up so much of himself. Not that Robert or Franny ever asked that of him or any of their children. But for Elijah, being the oldest, I know he always held back some of himself for fear of fucking up and letting everyone down.

While me, I *am* the fuck up, always have been. My illegal past means there's no actual future for us. I promised Robert all those years ago when he saved my ass from jail time, that I would stay away from Elijah's business. And I have no intention of breaking that promise. I won't destroy him, not when it's the only thing he walked out of his marriage with.

A long-term relationship with Elijah is out of the question. Not that he's asked me. We talked about more sex and that I can definitely be on board with. Anything more, however, is impossible. My past has once again seen to that. Elijah wants to concentrate on Lottie, and I understand that. His beautiful little girl has been through such a lot in her lifetime. I may not have had a father in my life. Mine having abandoned my mum before I was born, but Lottie has two parents who have struggled to be in the same room as one another for most of her life. Why they didn't divorce years ago, have continued to torture each other, I'll never know. But I understand Elijah wants to make that right.

I rest my forehead against the glass. Friends with benefits works. The world knows we're friends and have been for years. I'm photographed with Gabriel and Kat regularly. Being seen eating with Elijah will be no different. As for settling down and starting a family. Now I've tasted Elijah Frazer. There's no way I can look elsewhere, not until we've extinguished the fire that's raging between us.

As for my picket fence dream and a brood of children, I think fate has other plans for me. Darra and Elijah had no more children, and with a grown-up daughter, I can't imagine he would want to start again. Not that I've asked him. One night of passion does not equal - *Will you father my babies?* When Kris sent me back, I accepted that, at least for now. Children are not part of my immediate future, and I must come to terms with that, if I want to be with Elijah. And of that, I'm in no doubt.

CHAPTER 43

ELIJAH

As promised, I knock on Pen's office door at six o'clock. She throws it open and invites me in. I close it behind me before grabbing her hand and spinning her around, pinning her against the wall. Our lips and tongues clash, her response telling me exactly how pleased she is to see me.

"I've been wanting to do that all day," I mutter close to her lips, unable to keep the grin off my face.

To say she's had me distracted is an understatement.

"I've been wanting you to," she admits, her hand coming up and playing with the material of my shirt, our lower bodies pressed tightly together. "I've been having quite a few flashbacks. Not sure whether my brain is making it up or whether it really happened. But it's left me hot and wet."

She practically purrs the last words, and I'm instantly hard.

I press my cock against her, showing her exactly how affected I am, before moaning against her mouth.

"I think I need to check you're telling me the truth," I say.

I slide my hand down and find the button of her trousers,

flicking it open before lowering the zipper. I slide my hand into her panties and through the wet, swollen folds of her pussy.

I take her ear lobe between my teeth and bite down gently, being careful with the metal she wears in each lobe. Her hips press into mine.

I groan against her ear as my fingers begin to explore and spread the evidence of her desire.

"God, Pen," I say.

She parts her legs and closes her eyes in ecstasy as I find and tease her entrance and clit with my fingers.

She moans quietly and grips my shirt.

"You weren't lying," I say, gliding my fingers backwards and forwards over her swollen flesh.

She drops her head back with a thump against the wall.

"Fuck," she mumbles, spreading her legs wider, allowing me better access.

I slide my finger into her weeping body. It goes in easily and I curl it forward against that magical and so responsive spot.

I slam my mouth down on Pen's, swallowing her moan before withdrawing my fingers.

I pull them away, bringing them to my lips.

I suck down, drinking in her flavour.

Her eyes darken further as she watches me lick my fingers clean.

When I'm done, I zip her back up and redo her button.

"We may need a re-run. Put your mind at rest. I'd hate to disappoint. Maybe if there's something you want to try."

I watch her throat bob at my words, her tongue snaking out to moisten her lips.

I swallow. My body now uncomfortably hard. We're going to need to get out of here, or I'm going to have Pen bent over her desk as I take her from behind.

The thought has me biting down on a groan as my eyes wander to her desk.

Her eyes follow mine.

"You need feeding first," I say. "When did you last eat?"

I want to smile at the frown now marring her brow, but fucking her in the office is not something I want to start. The memory would mean I never got another moment of work done in my life. I can feel her disappointment, so I cup her cheeks and drop a kiss on her nose.

"Patience. All good things come to those who wait. And I promise, it will be worth the wait." I smirk. "We both need some energy for what I have in store."

Her eyes widen, and I grin. She shoots a look of longing at her desk before waggling her eyebrows at me.

"No," I say, "Let's get out of here. I want to make you scream, and I'm not sure you want the rest of your team to know what I'm doing to you."

She moans before slamming her lips once more against mine.

When we finally break apart, I say, "I've booked us a table at Marco's."

She places a hand on my chest and looks up at me with her large brown eyes.

"Do they offer takeaway?"

My fingers flex around her ass, and she groans.

"We can order from the car," I say, grabbing her handbag off her desk, suddenly filled with a desperate need to get out of here. "Need anything else?"

Pen shakes her head, laughing. I don't think I've seen Pen look so carefree or mischievous. At least, not since...I don't let my mind return there.

My lips smash down on hers one last time as I take her hand in mine, interlocking our fingers. It's not early, so when

I pull her from her office, the floor is mainly empty. Only Danika, Pen's PA, is sitting at her desk.

"Have a good night," I say as I pull Pen past her.

"You too," Danika calls after us as we move towards the elevator.

I can hear the amusement in her voice.

When the lift door finally closes, I pull Pen into my arms.

"I think Dani just got the answer she's been looking for all day," Pen says, giggling, her cheeks glowing.

I raise my eyebrows.

Pen smacks my chest. "I blame you," she says, trying to sound stern. "What are you doing to me? I'm acting like a teenager. I've got sex on the brain…I've never had sex on the brain!"

I drop a kiss on her nose.

"Me too," I say, grinning and pulling her hard against me so she can feel *just how much* she's on my brain. "I propose we relive our teenage years and have lots and lots of sex."

Pen throws back her head and laughs.

"I like your thinking, Mr Frazer. You're on!"

CHAPTER 44

PEN

The past two weeks have been crazy. Elijah and I have spent every waking moment together, sneaking around like two lust-filled teenagers.

It's like I've reverted to my teenage years, or at least the teenage years I should have lived. When instead of being free and easy, I was an angry, rebellious teen with an enormous chip on my shoulder. I pushed everyone away. It was Mum and me against the world in my eyes. It was only when I met The Frazer family my barriers began to crumble. Franny, Robert, Elijah, and his siblings took my prickly exterior and chipped away at it bit by bit until it came crashing down, revealing the real me. And while I was there, vulnerable, they didn't take advantage. Instead, they built me up, showed me all I could be. Something I embraced with both hands.

It's been hard to watch Elijah over the years and be unable to do anything to help him. But in the past two weeks, I have seen a difference. Elijah is different. It's like he's untethered the man I first knew all those years ago. The one who had the whole world ahead of him. A man whose glass was always half full and looked on the bright side of everything.

"Go and pack a bag," Elijah says as I walk through my front door.

"Lovely to see you too," I say, walking up to him and wrapping my arms around his neck.

He drops a kiss on my nose, and I frown. I pull back. That was not what I was expecting.

Last night, he walked in, and we had sex on the stairs. It's a good thing my mother didn't let herself in. She'd have got quite a shock had she been faced with Elijah's naked ass. Toned and gorgeous though it is.

"Pack a bag. No distractions. I'm taking you away for the weekend."

I lean back in his arms and stare up at him.

"Isn't that risky? People might see us."

The sneaking around has been fun. Added to the excitement, making us act like teenagers trying not to be caught by their parents. But in reality, it's more serious. He's come out of a marriage, and I've got a broken engagement under my belt. Although neither is related. The press, with our known history, would have a field day, and neither of us is ready for that.

I have too much respect for Kris to drag him into this, especially when he and Elijah are competitors. The last thing he needs is for me to be photographed with another man two weeks before our wedding was due to take place. It would be completely tasteless.

For now, Elijah and I need to keep our relationship on the down low, even from Elijah's family. I swore my mother to secrecy after she caught Elijah in the kitchen in his boxers. With Lottie out of the country and with Darra, it is even more important.

"It's all taken care of," he says, grinning. He taps the end of my nose. "Trust me."

It's strange. We may have only just reconnected, but it's like we've never been apart. I know it can't be the same in my heart; we're different people now, but that feeling I always had around Elijah is still there. The one where I trust him implicitly and know he will keep me safe. Not something I ever allowed myself to feel around anyone else, apart from Kris.

"I'm trusting you," I say, scowling, although it soon gives way to a grin. My stomach bubbles with the thought of what's to come. A weekend away, just the two of us.

I pull out of his arms and race upstairs, stopping abruptly on the landing.

"What do I need?" I shout, only to have strong arms snake around my waist. "Ahh," I squeal.

"Sorry, but I forgot something," he says, spinning me in his arms, his mouth closing over mine.

The kiss takes my breath away. When Elijah pulls away, my body is feverish, my pussy throbbing—she's become insatiable since she first had Elijah's cock!

"Just warming you up," Elijah says, his hands cupping my ass.

I resist the urge to rub myself against him, so instead, I pull back and put my hands on my hips.

"You didn't answer my question."

"Xander's island, so bring swimwear and shorts. No one will spot us." He waggles his brows. "Or you can go skinny dipping, whatever takes your fancy."

I love this new and mischievous Elijah.

The thought of skinny dipping has me breaking out in a hot sweat. Not something I've wanted to try before, but then the thought of Elijah—shit, I need to get my thoughts in gear.

I turn and head towards my wardrobe.

"We'll take the plane down and then a speedboat across from Xander's private jetty."

"I can't believe you managed to get him to agree to let us use it."

Xander's Island is supposed to be out-of-this-world. The waiting list is long and exclusive. He's very particular about who he lets stay there. He may be a close friend of Caleb's but to have availability at this short notice.

"It's who you know."

Elijah chuckles.

I relax, unable to keep the smile from my face.

"A whole weekend away?"

The twinkle in his eye lets me know exactly where his mind has gone. My nerves tingle with anticipation.

"An entire weekend. But only if you get your ass in gear. If not, we'll miss our flight slot."

We make it to the Frazer plane. Claudia is waiting to greet us.

"Lovely to see you again, Claudia."

"You too, Ms Dawson."

"Pen," I correct her. I hate formality. Everyone in my office is on a first-name basis. I ask for respect. I don't demand it. Calling me by my surname does not command respect. It simply makes me feel old.

"What can I get you to drink?"

"Champagne?" Elijah drops in.

I nod.

Why not? We're going away for the weekend, just the two of us.

"Certainly. I'll get it now," Claudia says before leaving us.

Elijah and I take our seats, his hand finding mine, interlocking our fingers.

"I can't believe you organised this," I say, my heart racing as if I'm going on my first holiday ever. "What on earth did you say to Xander? Did you tell him about us?"

"No. I simply said I wanted to get away, he was more than happy to oblige," he says, before turning to stare at me. "I want to spend time with you, just the two of us. Lottie comes back next week."

He doesn't say it, but I know things will change.

He has a daughter who lives with him. I know Lottie well. I'm her godmother, after all. I've been helping with her homework for years, but what will she think about her dad and I being together. Elijah and I haven't discussed it yet, but in reality, her parents have only just got divorced, and I'm not sure how she'll take it if she finds out about us. Teenagers and parental relationships are a big *ew*, and ours is more complex than most.

I squeeze his fingers, letting him know I understand, and I do. Lottie will always come first.

Elijah and I are friends. We just need to enjoy each other while and when we can. Leave the future to sort itself out.

"Next Saturday?" I ask.

"Yes, her flights have been confirmed."

"So we have a week. Then we can slow things down," I say, trying to keep my voice matter of fact.

"It's not what I want," he tells me truthfully.

"I know. You like the sex," I say, shoulder-bumping him, trying to lighten the mood. "We'll make it work. I'm not ready to give up on all these orgasms yet."

Elijah frowns, but Claudia reappears with our champagne before he can say whatever he was about to say. She pours us both a glass.

She leaves instantly, and I clink my glass to Elijah's.

"To a fun and a wonderful sex-filled weekend," I say, grinning.

"It will definitely be that."

CHAPTER 45

ELIJAH

Xander's island is beautiful.

The house, its surroundings, and the fact it's totally private. It's patrolled by a full-time security team that ensures all guests are protected and a team of staff who are well-paid and have all signed NDAs.

"Oh, Elijah, this is amazing."

Pen sighs, as we walk hand in hand along the shoreline, the evening sun warming our skin.

"It really is," I say, my eyes never leaving the woman in front of me. I can't believe how different I feel in the short time we've been together.

Pen makes me feel like a new man. My heart rate picks up when we're together. I'm smiling a lot more, the world seems lighter, brighter. Everyone has noticed and is questioning what has changed. I remember a time when my life was always like this. The time before. It's like I've jumped back in time fifteen years. But I haven't. I have responsibilities now, and Pen does too. I own a business, have a daughter. People who rely on me.

I now understand why Pen walked away from our business venture; her illegal activities would have made starting up our business impossible. Hindsight is a wonderful thing. Looking back, I see it was probably for the best. After the past few weeks, being with her, working alongside her day in, day out, unable to touch her would have been torture. I would never have been unfaithful to Darra, but wanting someone is a problem when you're with someone else. Maybe fate knew this and made Pen leave, saving us both a lot of heartache.

Oh hell, I sound like my mother!

Pen runs towards the waves, splashing through the surf. Her face alight.

My breath halts at the sight, and I wonder how Kristophe could let this amazing woman go? His loss, my gain.

Pen turns to me, her face glowing, and I charge forward, sweeping her into my arms and swinging her around. She squeals, and I silence her with my mouth.

As always, she melts against me, her legs wrapping around my waist, her tongue teasing the seam of my lips as it demands entry.

"I'm so happy."

She pulls back and looks down at me, her legs wrapped around my waist.

"Me too," I say.

Our foreheads touch, and we stay there for a moment, enjoying the sound of the waves gently breaking on the shore.

Pen drops her legs, and I lower her until she stands in the surf.

She takes my hand in hers and interlinks our fingers, bringing them to her lips.

"I can't believe we're here," I say, looking down at her.

She smiles. "I shall send a thank you to Kris," she tells me.

I frown. "What?"

What has Kris got to do with this?

Pen's hand comes up, and she smoothes away the wrinkle I know has appeared between my brows.

"Kris refused to marry me after I went back. He told me I deserved to be happy."

Pen tries to walk on, but I pull her to a halt and take her other hand in mine, making her look at me.

"Didn't he make you happy?" I ask.

Ashamed at the spark of joy beginning to spread through my chest.

She gives a small smile.

"He did, but I think we both realised we weren't marrying for love."

I incline my head but say nothing.

"We reached that point in our lives where we wanted to settle down, start a family. That old adage. I love him as a friend, and I respect him greatly, but I wasn't *in love* with him."

My heart stalls as she mentions starting a family. How had I forgotten that is what Pen wants?

As if reading my mind, Pen places a hand over my heart.

"Don't panic. I'm not expecting a marriage proposal or a sperm donation."

She grins at my expression.

"When I left the US, I knew I was saying goodbye to that part of my future. I'm just happy enjoying what we have now."

A heaviness settles in my body.

She wanted those things with Kristophe, but not with me? I close my eyes as my stomach clenches hard. When I open them again, Pen is staring at me, her sparkle waning.

"Come on, let's get some food," she says before I can open my mouth.

"Good plan. I asked the chef to make your favourite."

This time, when she smiles, she's back to old Pen, and I wonder whether I imagined it.

"My favourite?"

"The perfect tuna melt."

* * *

PEN TAKES A BITE, her eyes closing as she lets out a low moan.

"O.M.G.," she says. "This is…"

She doesn't finish her sentence as she takes another bite.

The chef has produced a culinary delight. Or at least in Pen's eyes.

I take a bite of my own. The melted cheese enhances the flavour of the tuna and toasted panini. I have to admit it is delicious.

"I can't believe you're finally eating a tuna melt," Pen says, grinning.

"Fine, I'll admit it is delicious, although not something I would usually eat."

Although I am not as strict with my diet as I was when Pen originally knew me. Then, it was all measured out and calculated. I even knew the exact carb and fat count on the takeaways we ordered.

It's my turn to laugh when the chef brings in a selection of grilled fish and vegetables.

"I wasn't going to force you to eat my favourite," Pen says, leaning over and gripping my hand. "But I really appreciate the sentiment."

Pen snags my panini from my plate while I load up on the fish and vegetables.

"Lottie messaged me," Pen says eventually as we're finishing up the pavlova the chef prepared.

"Did she?"

Somehow it doesn't surprise me. My daughter loves Pen,

always has done from being a little girl. It always surprised me that Darra was so free to let Pen near our daughter when she'd always envied her.

"She did. She told me she was sorry my engagement ended, and she hoped she could stay with me when she gets back for a girls' weekend."

I raise an eyebrow.

"What? She's nearly fifteen. Is it surprising?" Pen says. "I *am* a super cool godmother."

"That you are," I admit truthfully. "Thank you for always being there for her."

Pen's hand snakes across the table and squeezes mine.

"It's been a pleasure. She's an amazing young woman. She's a lot like her father."

I freeze at her words, and Pen's hand tightens on mine.

Only Gabriel and Leah know the whole truth. I haven't wanted it to affect my family's relationship with my daughter. Not that I think it would, but—she's my daughter, even if not by blood.

"There's something I need to tell you," I say.

Pen's brows furrow.

"About Darra and me."

"Elijah, I know you and Darra had issues. You don't need to explain," she says.

"I wish it was only that." I look across at her before turning away and running a hand through my hair. I inhale before turning back, my eyes locking with Pens.

"I married Darra because I didn't want to be *that* man."

Pen moves her chair closer and rests a hand on my bicep. The muscles flex under her fingers. It's always the same when she touches me.

"You married her because she was pregnant. You would never have done what my father did and walk away from your child. That's not who you are." She smiles as she grips my arm once more. "Whatever happened in your marriage, you will always have Lottie. She's the best of both of you."

I let out a sharp bark, making Pen jump.

"That's what I thought. That I was doing the right thing. I could never turn my back on my child. Darra knew that."

I lock eyes with Pen and see as realisation dawns.

"Lottie isn't my daughter, Pen. At least not biologically."

CHAPTER 46

PEN

I stare at Elijah, wondering if I heard him correctly. I remain silent and let him speak.

"That Christmas, Darra expected me to propose. I told her I didn't love her, that I wanted to concentrate on my swimming and our business, and I ended our relationship."

The blood freezes in my veins, the hairs on my arms standing up.

"Darra played me. I'd always been super careful with contraception, but as she pointed out, it's never one hundred per cent."

I put a hand to my mouth as my stomach roils, and I swallow against the obstruction in my throat.

"But you had a DNA test," I say. "Jaxson told me."

I'd always questioned in the back of my mind, Darra's convenient pregnancy, but I'd never been able to prove it.

"A friend of her father's switched out the DNA sample or simply paid him to lie. But it was forged, that much I do know."

A trickle of sweat runs down my back.

"If you aren't Lottie's biological father, who is?"

Elijah shrugs.

"I don't know, and I don't particularly care." He covers my hand on his arm with his. "The moment she was placed in my arms, she became my daughter. And now she finally is. As part of our divorce settlement, Darra allowed me to adopt her. Lottie is now officially my child."

I suck in a breath. This is one bombshell I would never have guessed. Elijah loves Lottie, always has.

"When did you find out?"

Elijah gets up from the table and clasps my hand, leading me to the sofa. He pulls me down to sit next to him.

He interlinks our fingers, almost as if drawing my strength. I squeeze his hand, holding it tight in mine, encouraging him to continue.

"It was after Lottie and Darra were in the car accident."

I close my eyes for a second.

Fuck, I remember that night well. That was years ago. He's known all this time?

"Darra was out with friends. She'd been drinking and wrapped the car around a tree. Lottie had received a head injury, and they thought she may need surgery. They tested my blood to see if I was a match should she need a transfusion."

The picture unfolds in front of me. Elijah waiting to see if his daughter needs surgery. His wife already in surgery, having her leg rebuilt.

"The doctor came out. I'll never forget. He took me to one side and asked if I knew." Elijah's matter-of-fact tone is not something I'm used to. "I asked him what he was talking about."

"And it was then he told you?"

Elijah's eyes are unfocused as he relives the moment.

I squeeze his fingers, his eyes clearing as he looks at me.

"He was incredibly kind. I was in shock. I asked him not

to mention it to any of the other members of my family. I lied. I told him I knew but hoped I'd be a match. He knew I was lying, but let it go."

"What did Darra say when you confronted her?"

He lets out a harsh laugh.

"Told me I needed to forget I ever knew. If I didn't, then she'd take Lottie, and I'd never see her again."

"Could she have done that?"

He nods, pressing his palm to his mouth before letting it drop.

"I didn't have a claim to Lottie, not a biological one. If Darra, as her mother, decided not to let me in her life..." He pauses, and my stomach clenches. "I couldn't lose my daughter, Pen." He all but whispers. "And there were other threats."

I can only imagine. Darra has no scruples.

I move closer, turning our joined hands so our forearms are now touching. Elijah's is double the width of mine. I'm beginning to understand his obsession with the gym. This happened years ago. Lottie was five or six at the time of the accident. Nearly ten years of being held to ransom. Having the one thing, you love more than anything in the world, used against you. If I hated Darra before…

He looks down at where our arms are touching.

"So that's what I did. I continued on, although I never touched her again. We were together in name only. Keeping up appearances for the sake of our families. I threw myself into work, and she…well, I think everyone knows what Darra has been doing."

"So you really have no clue who Lottie's biological father is?"

Elijah shakes his head.

"I think it's someone who was there that Christmas. The dates tied up, but I don't want to think that one of my friends could have betrayed me." He sighs. "By the time I found out

Lottie was mine, I wasn't giving her up, whatever the cost. I don't care who her biological father is. They haven't been in her life, weren't there for her birthdays, or when she grazed her knee. I taught her how to ride her first bike, showed her how to swim. Knowing Darra, they may not even have known. She may have simply used them as a sperm donor."

My stomach threatens to expel my dinner at the thought.

I knew Darra was single-minded. When she set her mind on something or someone, in this case, there was no stopping her. There was a time when I felt sorry for her. One night, she and I had our one and only heart-to-heart. I thought she was finally accepting me, allowing me into the group. She told me about her relationship with her dad. How he controlled their family with an iron fist. How she feared him. I don't think she meant to expose as much as she did. The next day, I told her I was there for her if she ever needed to talk. She looked at me with pure venom in her eyes. After that, her vendetta towards me took on a whole new level. Not that I ever told Elijah or the others. She relished telling me she was the one who paid the guy to sleep with me and spread rumours. He apologised to me after Elijah and the others spoke to him. Admitted to running up enormous debts while at uni, and when he was offered money he couldn't turn it down. He told me it hadn't been a hardship, that he really liked me…

Heat floods my body, and I clench my jaw. That was a pain I locked away, a lesson I learned about keeping my feelings and personal life close to my chest. Should I have said something then? I knew Darra was obsessed with Elijah, but to trap him in a lie. I can see now it wasn't love. It was a single-minded determination that she wanted him and was going to have him no matter the cost. Would I have believed she could get herself pregnant and pass the child off as his? Until now, no. I would not have thought even she would stoop that low, but—she hated me, blamed me for Elijah turning his back on her. She told me as much that Christmas. That our business venture was driving a wedge between them.

The time Elijah is talking about, we all spent the post-Christmas week together. The Frazer household had been a party hub.

I think back.

Was Darra paying attention to anyone other than Elijah?

He and I spent a lot of time together, locked in his father's office. We'd started planning for the future. We were caught up in our own excitement. Robert and Francesca had just agreed to back us, if we put together a proper business plan. They promised to help us set up a potential investors meeting. My stomach flutters at the memory. I remember the camaraderie we shared that holiday, one that had continued into the next term, had led to us getting closer. It was at that time I realised I'd fallen hopelessly in love with him. Darra's bombshell detonated in the March, and life changed forever.

I lean forward and wrap my arms around Elijah, resting my head above his heart.

He engulfs me in his arms, his hand rubbing soothing circles on my back.

"Does Lottie know?" I ask, pulling back and looking up at him.

"She overheard Darra and I arguing. She ran to Gabriel and Leah. They're the only two other people who know."

I look up, wondering why she didn't come to me. As if sensing my question, he smiles sadly.

"You were out of the country. I checked your place first when she disappeared."

"You haven't told the rest of your family? Your Mum?"

I sit up and stare at him.

He averts his gaze, and I cup his chin in my hands until his eyes meet mine.

"Do you think your family would love her any less?"

His chin dips to his chest, his posture slumped.

"Elijah Frazer. Your family is the most accepting family I've ever met."

He grimaces, and it's then I see the truth.

"But you know that," I say, as realisation dawns. "You were protecting Darra."

He nods.

"Why?" I stare at him open-mouthed.

After everything.

He pulls back and stares at me.

"It was bad enough, I knew. Imagine if the rest of them found out. They would've wanted to protect me. I might have lost Lottie because they wouldn't stay out of it. It wasn't a risk I was willing to take."

My heart breaks for the man before me.

"So you shouldered this knowledge alone. Oh, Elijah."

I wrap my arms around his neck and pull his lips to mine. He comes easily and sinks into our kiss, deepening it until we're both breathless.

"I'm sorry, Pen," he says. "I messed up everything."

"Never be sorry. Thank you for confiding in me. And no one is going to hear the truth from me. But I think now the divorce has gone through, you need to tell your family."

I don't add that it will help them to understand the distance you put between you all.

Instead, I straddle him and let him know everything is going to be okay.

CHAPTER 47

ELIJAH

A weekend away is what we both needed. Time to reconnect without worrying about the rest of the world. I admit, it's been a long time since I felt this free and relaxed. But then, Pen has that effect on me. Even when we were working together on projects, she had her lists but took life in her stride.

I look down at the woman sleeping, wrapped in my arms. I close my eyes and wonder how I'm going to broach the subject of Pen and me with Lottie? She's due home tomorrow. Pen says she's happy to continue in secret, but I realise I'm not. I have too much respect for her. I won't treat her like my dirty little secret.

"Dad…I'm home."

A voice breaks through the early morning silence.

My bedroom door hits the wall with a bang, pulling Pen out of my arms and her deep slumber.

"Oh. My. God. What the…"

Lottie's shrieks fill the room as Pen sits bolt upright, the sheet dropping from her torso, exposing her naked breasts to the room.

I sit up in a semi-daze as Pen clocks my cheek with her elbow as she scrambles to cover herself.

"Oh. My. God." Lottie shrieks again as Pen finally draws the sheet up and around herself. "Aunty Pen?"

The sound of horror in my daughter's voice brings me upright, and I watch on as Pen and my daughter stare at each other across the room.

"Lottie?" I say, pinching the bridge of my nose to stem the headache I know is going to hit. "What are you doing here, darling? You aren't supposed to be home until tomorrow."

"Clearly," she says, raising her eyebrows and placing her hands on her hips. "I can see you *weren't* expecting me."

Pen sits next to me, clutching the duvet to her chest.

"Hey, Lottie," she says, her voice husky from sleep.

"Don't hey Lottie, me, Aunty Pen," my daughter says.

Her fourteen-year-old sass coming out.

"I will not ask what you're doing in my dad's bed…naked. Ew!" She shakes her head and pulls a face. "Aunty Pen? Dad, really."

Her eyes flick between us, and I can see the pain in her gaze.

"I'm going to put the kettle on. Maybe you two can put some clothes on," she says, turning on her heel.

I watch my daughter flounce out of the room.

I run a hand down my face.

Pen drops her head to her bent knees and groans.

"She hates me," she says, hiding her face.

"She doesn't. Lottie loves you like a mother. You're her favourite person. It will probably be me she can't forgive."

"I may have been—past tense. That was before she thought about me having sex with her dad."

Pen turns her head and looks at me, her cheek now resting on her knees.

It's my turn to groan. Even I know no teenager wants to think about their parent *doing that*.

"I better go. Leave you to talk to her."

Pen jumps out of bed and begins pulling on her clothes. When she's dressed, she leans over the bed and drops a kiss on my lips.

"Call me later."

"So, you're leaving me to handle this?" I say.

"It's probably for the best."

"Chicken," I say, making her smile.

"Totally. Call me if you need me."

Pen makes a speedy exit.

I get up slowly, taking my time to pull on my clothes as I try to decide what I'm going to say to Lottie.

When I come out of the bedroom, I pull up short.

Pen is sitting at the island, drinking coffee with Lottie.

"I can't believe you were going to sneak out. Aunty Pen, that's a real dick move."

"Language, Lottie," Pen says, making my daughter roll her eyes.

"You were really going to let Dad fumble his way through, telling me you two are an item? Now that's just cruel."

I can just make out the smirk on my daughter's face.

I bite my lip to stop myself from laughing. I cough, letting them know I've arrived.

"Fumble?" I say when Lottie looks up.

"I'm not sure what you're smirking about, Dad. I at least expected you to act like responsible adults and face me together. Instead, I catch Aunty Pen trying to sneak out the front door and then you skulking in the background."

"I wasn't skulking. I was putting on some clothes."

Lottie holds up a hand and turns her head away, her expression one of sucking on a lemon.

"Stop," Lottie says, waving her hands in the air. "T.M.I. Way too much information."

"Pen was going to give us time to talk," I say, stepping closer and pulling up a stool opposite the two women in my life.

"If she and you are an item, then don't you think she should be here for *that talk?*" Lottie says, pushing a mug of coffee across the countertop towards me.

She's clearly not *that* mad.

I look at Pen, who's staring at Lottie. She turns to me and shrugs.

"She has a point," I say to Pen.

"Okay, so I shouldn't have tried to sneak out," Pen admits to Lottie. "My bad."

"That was very teenager-ish of you," Lottie says.

"What would you know about sneaking out?"

"Dad, I'm fourteen, nearly fifteen, not four. I listen to the conversations that go on with my friends, most of who have older brothers and sisters. Claire's Mum found Teddy's girlfriend hiding in the wardrobe when she came home."

I groan. I don't want to know about Teddy's girlfriend hiding in a cupboard or that my daughter knows why she was probably there.

"I don't need to hear this."

I run a hand through my hair.

Lottie turns to me.

"Drink your coffee. You'll feel better."

"Who's the parent here?" I ask, making her once again roll her eyes. "It's good to have you home, munchkin," I say, standing up and moving towards her, holding out my arms.

Lottie grins and jumps down off the stool before coming around the island and into my arms. I wrap her in a bear hug.

"I've missed you," I say, breathing in her scent. One that is now distinctly more grown up as she's wearing perfume.

"Dad, you're crushing me," she groans.

"I've missed you. I'm allowed to crush you," I tell her.

"I've missed you too," she says, my heart melting.

I pull back and grip her upper arms, holding her away so I can look at her properly.

"How was Italy?" I ask, finding her in one piece.

"Italy was amazing. The art school was fantastic. I have so much to show you. They taught me this really cool technique. I think you'll love it."

Art is our thing.

Lottie starts off at one hundred miles an hour. Condensing her three-month trip and all she's learned into a five-minute summary. I know these are just the highlights, and there will be more to come. We have all the time in the world now she's back.

"I can't wait," I tell her.

"Mum's shipping my artwork once it's fully dry. Then I can use it for my exams. My art teacher says I'm good."

"You are. And I look forward to seeing it."

I look over my daughter's head at Pen, who's sat watching us.

As if suddenly remembering Pen is here, Lottie looks up at me.

"Are you and Aunty Pen an item now?"

My gaze darts to Pen.

Fuck.

We haven't really discussed what we are. Friends with benefits isn't something a parent wants to admit to their young, impressionable daughter.

"It's complicated."

It's Pen who comes to my rescue.

Lottie turns to face her.

"What's complicated?"

"I've just come out of an engagement. Kris and I were due

to get married in two weeks. Your parents haven't been divorced that long. Your dad and I've been friends for a long time—but just friends," she adds quickly. "It could be complicated if it got out."

"So you're keeping it quiet?" Lottie says. "Like Tina and Gerry when they started dating. Gerry was with Julie before Tina, and he didn't want to hurt her feelings."

"Exactly like that," Pen says. "The press would not be kind."

"Is Dad the reason you and Kris split up?"

"No," Pen and I say together.

"Just asking. And don't worry, I'm happy to keep your secret," Lottie says, shrugging.

Pen and my eyes clash.

What?

"It doesn't bother you?" I ask slowly.

"No," she says, picking up her drink. "Why should it? I know Aunty Pen. She likes me, I like her. Plus, she's super cool. It's not like I have to get used to a complete stranger being around. Not like Sadie. Her Dad divorced her Mum, and his girlfriend moved in two weeks later. She'd never even met her before. It was hell."

I choke on my coffee, making Pen laugh.

"And Lottie's right, I *am* super cool," Pen says, as Lottie fist bumps her. "But Lottie, it's really important that this remains quiet. I'm sorry to ask this of you."

"It's cool, I'm cool. Honestly Dad. I'm happy if you're happy. I must say I'm a little shocked it's Aunty Pen...I thought she had more taste," Lottie says, her face breaking into a grin, followed by a squeal, as I pull her into a headlock and ruffle her hair.

When I let her go, her laughter echoes around the room as she looks at us both.

"All I ask you is to keep the PDAs to a minimum. No

kissing or sex when I'm around. Ew!" Her wrinkled nose lets us know all we need to know.

"Done deal," we both say quickly.

The thought of my teenage daughter hearing me having sex is not something I want to contemplate. Back to sneaking around like naughty teenagers. Pen shoots me a sly glance, and I have a sneaky impression that her mind has gone in the same direction.

CHAPTER 48

PEN

My intercom chimes.
"Danika?" I say.
"Lottie's here to see you."
I smile. "Send her in."

I get up and walk to the door, throwing it open as my goddaughter makes her way towards me. It's been a week since she returned and when she said she didn't mind about her father and me, it appears she meant it.

"Hey, this is a lovely surprise."

She looks at me and grins.

I usher her into my room and close the door.

"Homework, advice, or just a can't-stay-away from my favourite godmother trip?"

Lottie laughs, and the sound warms my heart. She's been doing that a lot more easily lately.

"My art work has arrived, and I wanted to know if you would come and see it," she tells me.

"Absolutely, count me in."

Her smile widens.

There's a knock at the door, and Danika enters carrying two steaming mugs of coffee.

"Coffee?" I say to Lottie

She raises an eyebrow in much the same way Elijah does. Okay, they may not be genetically linked, but bloody hell, they are father and daughter.

"I'm almost fifteen and spent the past three months in Italy."

As if that explains it all.

"Not to mention, every one of your uncles and aunts is a coffee addict," I say smiling.

I thank Danika and take the coffee, leading Lottie over to the sofas in the corner of the room. The whole office ethos is casual. I find it helps with creativity. We have lounge areas, beanbags, and a games room with old and new style games. The main office is open plan, but there are also break-out rooms should anyone want to focus. So far, this approach has made me a very wealthy woman.

"Your offices are much cooler than Dad's," she says, taking a sip of her coffee.

She flinches slightly, but I say nothing.

"Of course they are," I say. "Although designing games and developing hardware allows us to be a little less stiff. Your dad has to give his clients the right professional atmosphere when they visit."

Lottie nods. "I know, but it's still not as fun."

"Well, as you know, you're welcome here anytime."

Lottie looks down at the coffee mug in her hand, her forehead wrinkling.

I pause, knowing her artwork and loving my office is not the reason for her visit.

"Aunty Pen?"

"Yes, Lottie."

She looks up, and I watch as she bites the inside of her cheek.

"You know you can talk to me," I say.

She nods and puts her coffee down on the table in front of us before letting her eyes meet mine.

"You knew Mum and Dad when they were at uni."

It's more of a statement than a question.

"I did. Your dad and I were on the same course."

Lottie goes silent.

"Hey, what's on your mind?"

I place a hand on her forearm. Lottie looks at me, and I'm surprised at the anguish I see in her eyes.

"Come on, you can talk to me."

She always has before, especially when things were bad between her mum and dad. I was that much further removed than any of her aunts and uncles.

She inhales, pushing her hair out of her face as her eyes lock on mine.

"Do you know who my bio dad is?"

I stop sharply, a knot forming in my stomach.

"No. I don't," I say, squeezing her arm where my hand is still resting.

"Dad has told you, though?" she presses.

"Only recently," I admit.

Fuck, I'm treading on dangerous ground.

"Have you spoken to your mum, your dad?"

She shakes her head. "I tried to speak to Mum while I was in Italy."

Lottie wraps her arms around her waist.

"Mum said Dad is now my dad. He officially adopted me as part of their divorce settlement. She said I need to forget what I overheard. But is it really surprising I want to know where I come from? Dad will always be my dad and Mum my mum, but—"

Shit. Bloody hell Darra.

This is not something I can be involved in. This is between Elijah, Darra and Lottie. Elijah will skin me alive, and the last thing I need to do is get on Darra's bad side. It's not that I know any more than anyone else.

"Maybe Mum slept around behind Dad's back and doesn't know. That's why she palmed me off on Dad."

Fuck, that is the last thing Lottie needs to think!

Bloody Darra. Does she not realise Lottie's growing up? Of course, she has questions.

I put my arm around Lottie's shoulder and pull her into my side.

"Have you spoken to your dad?"

"I can't do that. It would hurt him. He'll think he's not enough."

She bites her lip, her eyes filling with unshed tears.

"Not if you explain to him. Your dad is a very pragmatic man," I say, although I understand her predicament.

But shit, this is putting me in an awkward position.

We sit in silence for a moment.

"Is it wrong I want to know where I came from?" she asks eventually. "Don't you ever wonder about your dad?"

I suddenly realise why I'm getting these questions.

I pull back and turn towards Lottie, taking her shoulders in both my hands.

"Knowing your bio dad is not necessarily all it's cracked up to be. Take it from someone who knows," I say, knowing I sound cynical, but I want Lottie to realise there are often two sides to a story. "I'm going to let you into a little secret. Nobody knows this. Only Danika."

Lottie sits up straight, inclining her head.

"Not even my dad?"

I shake my head.

"Why does only Danika know?"

"Because she's my friend as well as my PA and was here the day it happened."

I let go of Lottie's shoulders and we slump back on the sofa, facing one another.

"I met my bio dad."

"You did? When?"

"About twelve years ago," I admit. "Even my mum doesn't know this. Like you, I didn't want to hurt her, but I think maybe I should tell her."

"I promise not to say anything," Lottie says, grown up beyond her years.

But years of being surrounded by adults will do that.

"Thank you. But I think it's time I told her, anyway."

"So you met your dad?" Lottie prompts.

"I did. It was just after I made Woman of The Year. Dawson Technologies had taken off. I'd made my first million. I was an up-and-coming star, according to the newspapers."

"So what happened?" Lottie asks, leaning forward slightly.

"My dad turned up at my offices," I say. "I knew who he was. Mum told me when I was younger that they wanted different things. What she really meant was he didn't want a child. He had plans, and they didn't involve a child or baby-mummy cramping his life."

"What did you do?"

"I didn't want to make a scene, so I invited him into my office. I wanted to see what he had to say for himself. Part of me was inquisitive. And like you, I wanted to meet the man who helped create me."

"You get it then?"

"I do. More than you know."

I refuse to lie to her. But I hope my punchline will help her see. Finding out isn't all it's cracked up to be.

"Why do I feel there's a *but* coming?" Lottie asks.

I smile sadly.

"What did your father say?" she presses.

"He introduced himself. Told me he read about me in the newspaper and was proud of me. Told me I had two younger brothers. He said he was a computer programmer, had gone out into the world and made something of himself, and that I must have got my skills from him."

Lottie rolls her eyes, and I chuckle.

"My thoughts exactly," I say. "Anyway, we drank coffee and ate some biscuits. Then I asked him why he'd never tried to contact me before."

"What did he say?"

"He spluttered a lot." I smile and raise an eyebrow at the memory. "He then told me he hadn't been ready to have a child when mum had announced she was pregnant."

Lottie's mouth drops open. "What did you say?"

"I asked him whether he thought Mum had been ready to be a single parent."

I pick up my coffee and take a sip.

"What did he say?" Lottie asks.

"He spluttered a lot more."

"Have you seen him since?"

I shake my head and give her a small smile. "No."

Lottie stares at me, and I shrug.

"Do you think I should leave it?" she asks.

I squeeze her arm. "I understand you have questions. That's natural."

She wrinkles her nose.

"My advice is to speak to your mum again," I say, praying this time Darra is more forthcoming with her daughter. "But Lottie, remember a parent is the person who is there for you, who loves you. April will tell you that. Although Sarah's come back into her life, her relationship with Di and Julian hasn't changed."

"All I know is I was conceived during the Christmas holidays. When you were all at Granny and Grandpa's. Were there any other men hanging around?"

"No, there were only us. The usual suspects."

"It sounds like you used to have fun together."

"We did. So much fun. Until those holidays at uni, it was always just Mum and me. Your grandmother knew my mum worked long hours, so she gave me somewhere to go. It's how your Aunty Kat and Uncle Gabriel became such good friends of mine."

"Were you in love with Dad when you were at university together?" Lottie asks, her eyes watching me more closely than I'd like.

Damn, this girl is perceptive!

I stare at her, weighing up the odds, deciding I'm never going to lie to Lottie.

"I'm going to decline to answer that. Your father and my relationship was complicated. All I will say is we were best friends, and nothing ever happened between us."

"But you loved him," she says, her voice tinged with a hint of sadness. "Well, I'm glad you and Dad are together now. I haven't seen him smile so much in a long time. I don't think... ever. He and Mum just made each other unhappy."

"Grown-up relationships are complicated."

"It seems like grown-ups like to make them complicated," Lottie says.

I sigh and smile. "You might be right."

CHAPTER 49

ELIJAH

I watch Pen and Lottie prepare breakfast from the doorway, a sense of peace running through my body.

"Dad, what do you want on your pancakes?" Lottie asks as I enter the kitchen to find a stack of American pancakes piled high on the side.

"Wow, who else is coming for breakfast?" I ask, pulling out a stool and sitting down.

Pen looks up, her cheeks flushed. "I misjudged the quantities," she says, making me smirk. "Mrs Transmere gave me the recipe, and I thought I'd need to double it. I should have remembered American portions."

My stomach sinks as I realise who Mrs Transmere is—Kristophe's cook.

Something in my expression must give me away because Pen comes around the counter and wraps her arms around my waist.

"She made the best pancakes. I wanted to share the recipe with Lottie."

I squeeze her hand, letting her know it's all right. I know I shouldn't be jealous of Kristophe, but I can't help it. She said when we were away, he sent her back to me, but in doing so, she appears to have given up on everything she wanted in life. Reverting back to the *old Pen* before Kristophe. All work, although this time a lot more play.

I watch her and Lottie together. How easy and quick to smile Lottie is these days. Pen shows Lottie how to make pancake characters using the batter. She's a natural. Proven not only with Lottie but little Callum. How can she simply switch off her desire to get married and start a family? I can't and don't believe for one second it's possible, even if Pen believes she has.

Last weekend should have been her wedding day. She should be on her honeymoon now, making babies. Instead, she went to dinner with Lottie and me, followed by the cinema, as though it was no big deal. It's like she's pushed aside her dreams, assuming I don't want those things too.

We need to talk, but it's still early days. A marriage proposal, and baby talk I know is inappropriate one month into our relationship, but I just worry she'll regret all she gave up when Kristophe sent her back and begin to resent what we have.

"Are you going to eat one or simply stare at them?" Pen asks with her hands on her hips.

"They look delicious," I say, snagging a couple and moving them across to a plate.

Lottie stands with her hands on her hips.

"You didn't answer my question, Dad. What do you want?"

I stop my fork midway to my mouth.

Shit, I was miles away.

Lottie rolls her eyes again. This is becoming part of her teenage MO.

"Really, Dad, you need to listen. What toppings do you want on your pancakes?"

"What are my options, chef?" I ask, giving her my full attention.

She grins. "There's fresh fruit, maple syrup, bacon, lemon, sugar, ice cream, cream."

She continues to reel off the list she's memorised.

"Bacon?" I ask

"Savoury pancakes," she says, almost rolling her eyes.

"I think I'll go with the fruit."

"Excellent choice," Pen whispers next to my ear, her breath sending shivers of awareness straight to my cock. I shift uncomfortably in my seat, and Pen smirks.

Lottie turns away, opening the large fridge door. I pull Pen forward and drop a kiss on her lips, releasing her as soon as Lottie turns back around.

"Oh, pl-ease," she says, tutting.

"Sorry," I say, making Pen laugh.

I'm passed the fruit, which I pile onto the pancakes. When I take a mouthful, I groan.

"These are delicious."

Pen shoots me a *told-you-so* look, and Lottie looks pleased.

"What are you ladies doing today?" I ask.

I know Pen mentioned going shopping.

"We're going to look for outfits for Granny's birthday party."

Pen and I haven't discussed what we're doing this year. Our relationship is still officially a secret. As she was due to be on her honeymoon, she was not going to attend this years party. Now, we're going to need to be very careful, especially around my eagle-eyed siblings.

"That sounds like fun," I say.

"You're welcome to join us," Pen says.

I notice her biting her lip and wonder if she thinks she's overstepping. I hate to tell her Lottie has returned from Italy with more than enough dresses for this coming weekend and several others. This is more about my daughter wanting to build a new relationship with her, and I will not stand in her way.

Lottie and I are a pair. It's as important Lottie is as comfortable with Pen and my relationship as I am, especially if we hope to have any future together.

My skin tingles at the thought.

A future.

I realise, I'm less freaked out by the thought than I assumed I'd be. Instead, I feel lighter.

"I'll leave the shopping for you. Granny has actually summoned me. She wants to go over a few things before the weekend."

Pen shoots me a look, and I shrug.

We finish the pancakes, stashing some in a box for later. They really did make a mountain.

When Lottie runs off to get ready, I pull Pen into my arms.

"Don't worry," I say, kissing the tip of her nose. "Mum always has last-minute requests before the Frazer Foundation weekend."

"I just..."

"You just what? My mother loves you. Sometimes, I wonder whether she loves you more than me. She is certainly not going to freak out if she realises we're together."

"But—"

"No buts. I mean it. Stop overthinking things. We've been discrete. Everything will be fine."

She nods and I drop another kiss on her lips. We need to find some alone time. We haven't been together since the morning Lottie returned, taking her feelings and request into account. But I'm now craving her with every breath.

"I'll see you later," I say, letting her go as Lottie re-enters the room.

"Later," she says, her eyes filled with a desire matching my own.

CHAPTER 50

ELIJAH

Mum is waiting for me when I arrive at The Foyer and Reading Room at Claridge's. Afternoon tea is one of her favourite pastimes these days.

"I've already ordered," Mum says as I take a seat opposite her.

"Thank you."

She nods to the waitress, letting them know they're free to serve.

"I do like it here," she says, looking around.

I follow her gaze and understand. The original art déco mirrors, striking Chihuly sculpture, and gentle piano music adds to the ambience.

Mum pauses as our waitress arrives with our platter of finger sandwiches, scones, pastries, and tea. We wait while she pours the tea, thanking her as she leaves. I look up to find my mother scowling at me.

"What is it?" I ask, with a sinking dread, I know what's coming.

"When are you and Penelope going to go public?" she

says, lifting her bone china teacup to her mouth and staring at me over the top.

I freeze, making her chuckle.

"You didn't think I'd find out? That you and Lottie have been spending your days at Pen's, that she's been staying at yours."

"We haven't been keeping it a secret, per se," I say defensively, looking around and seeing who might overhear. Everyone around us is absorbed in their own conversations.

She raises an eyebrow, making me smile.

"No? So Kat knows? Gabriel? Caleb?"

I squirm under her scrutiny.

"No, they don't know," I tell her. "Bloody hell, I'm beginning to see how my siblings felt."

"Language," she says, and it's my turn to scowl.

"I'm thirty-seven," I tell her, but find myself shrinking under her scrutiny.

"Oh, no, you don't. You've got away lightly," she says, smirking. "Besides, Pen is family—she's not someone you mess with."

I lean forward and whisper, "You think I don't know that?"

I sit back and run a hand through my hair, picking up my teacup and taking a swig. The hot liquid burns my throat but gives me clarity. I meet my mother's gaze.

"I care about her, Mum. But it's complicated. There's Lottie, Kris—"

"Complicated, *shmomplicated*. Why does it have to be we make things complicated? Where there's a will, there's a way."

"It's still early days."

Mum looks at me and laughs, the sound one of pure delight.

"Early days?" She chuckles to herself. "You two have been

dancing around each other since the moment you met. Eighteen years. Early days, indeed! You were made for each other. Always were. If other forces hadn't intervened, things would have been different. You and Pen would have been together."

My mum's words hit me in the chest.

"What do you mean?"

My heart sinks. I thought I'd hidden those feelings, locked them away.

As if sensing my unease, she reaches forward and pats my hand. "I'm your mother, Elijah. But anyone with eyes in their head, who knew you two, could see it. Darra knew it. You understood one another on a level that is not usual." She smiles at me. "I have to admit when you first brought Pen home, she was a little *left field*. Her makeup, her piercings, but watching you together, the way your friendship developed."

I laugh at the memory, thinking back to Pen's white foundation, her array of piercings, and her dyed black hair. Her all-black wardrobe made her look like an extra from the Addams Family.

"But it wasn't long before I realised she was special," Mum continues.

I look over. "She was and is special," I agree.

I sink into the chair.

"All I'm saying is. You and Pen. You need to give each other a chance. That woman has loved you for so long."

I turn my head sharply to look at my mother.

What the?

"Don't look at me like that. She has loved you and supported you. When she announced her engagement to Kristophe, I must admit I was surprised, as was Louise. Especially with your divorce going through."

Ahh, our relationship mole. Louise and Mum have become close friends over the years.

"I've never…"

"Oh, Eli. The heart wants what the heart wants. I think you know that better than most."

"I tried to fight it. It's why I stayed away from her."

"I know. I've watched you both battle your feelings. Neither one of you letting them surface."

"I was a bad husband."

"No. You did what you thought was right, even when it was wrong. You and Darra hurt one another, but that young woman was determined to have you, whatever the cost or at least her father was. I think she realised forcing what isn't there never works, however much you might will it." She sighs. "But you're past that now. Neither one of you is too old to find future happiness."

We sit in silence for a while, my chest clenching. I've made such a mess of my life.

"What if I don't? I don't want to damage Lottie any further. She's been through enough. As for Pen, she doesn't want to go public because she doesn't want to hurt Kristophe. But she also doesn't want it to overshadow our relationship."

"You both need to trust yourselves. I've given both of your brothers the same advice and it's seen them happy."

"They aren't me."

Mum chuckles again. "If you're thinking of Lottie, stop. My granddaughter already loves Pen, so it's not like she'll need much convincing. Have you told her?"

I look away.

"Tell me I'm mistaken."

"No, Lottie appears to be thrilled Pen and I are together. So much so they've gone dress shopping for your birthday weekend."

One can only describe the look on her face as smug.

"As I thought. As for you and your brothers. You're all

individuals. Even the twins differ greatly from one another. But as I told them, let the universe put you on the path you need to be on. Listen and watch. As for Lottie, I've no fears there, and neither should you. I've never seen a girl love someone as much as that young lady loves her godmother, and I know the feeling is mutual."

Mum looks at me. She must see something in my expression. I've never discussed Pen being made Lottie's godmother.

"It was your father," she tells me. "He made it clear Pen was to be Lottie's godmother."

A sad smile passes over my mother's lips.

"What?" I say.

This is news to me. Darra had simply said she wanted our uni friends to be our godparents, but I think there's more to this story. When I go to open my mouth, she holds up her hand.

"Some things are better left in the past."

A sudden realisation hit.

"Did Dad have something to do with Pen walking away from our business venture?"

Mum raises her eyes to mine, her gaze firm.

"Leave the past in the past, Elijah. It's better for everyone. I'm sure you've uncovered a lot about Pen recently."

I nod.

"Then all you need to know is he protected you both."

I want to ask more, my stomach churning. Why the hell had my father been involved with Pen and her hacking? Is that what Mum means?

As if sensing my turmoil, she leans closer.

"Let it go. And Elijah. Her father's happiness is all Lottie needs. Remember, lead by example, showing her what love looks like. True love will be more powerful than anything else." She pauses. "And since she's been back, she's smiling from ear to ear, which tells me a lot."

I frown, making her laugh.

"Social media, Elijah. I'm not a fossil."

I shake my head, wondering if she'll ever not surprise me.

She's right, Lottie is much happier, but I wondered if that was a dream.

My mum's spiritualist outlook is something I've ignored. But maybe, just maybe, there's hope for me—for us.

"I know Pen always comes to the Frazer Foundation weekend. But this year, invite her as your guest."

"I told you, she doesn't want us to go public yet," I admit. The hollow feeling in my stomach returns. "She should be on her honeymoon. She's trying to be respectful."

Mum taps her lips. "But that's not all. That's not what is worrying you."

Damn her.

"No." I sigh. "I wonder if she regrets splitting up with Kristophe. Pen had her future planned out. Now those plans are in the toilet, and she's reshaping her future."

"And you can't be part of that reshaping? Have you talked to her?"

"I still question everything."

"That makes me happy because it means you care. But Elijah, relationships are not just built on great sex, although it helps. They're also built on trust and communication. Speak to Pen, tell her your fears. You'll probably find you have the same ones."

When I stay silent, she rolls her eyes, and I know she's thinking life's too short.

"As for my birthday weekend. Pen was supposed to be on her honeymoon, however, she's always attended the Frazer Foundation Day, so you can invite her. How you both act in public is up to you. Kat will be back from her business trip so you can fill your sister in. I suspect Gabriel and Caleb have already taken out bets on you two." Mum grins, a sly smirk forming. "Hopefully, your sister won't castrate you. She's very protective of Pen."

"Ha ha, very funny."

"She was there for Pen, and Pen for her. Those two are as close as sisters."

"I'm her brother," I say, feeling a little put out, but I can't deny the strength of their bond. "Why are my family siding with my girlfriend?"

I pause, while Mum's grin widens, and it's then I realise what I've said.

"There's hope for you yet, Elijah," she says. "Now, let's eat these sandwiches and pastries before they go stale. I'm starving."

CHAPTER 51

PEN

Elijah, Lottie, and I enter the Frazer family home. I'm always transported back in time whenever I come here, to that first weekend when Franny took me aside and welcomed me, despite me being like a fish out of water.

"I've put you and Elijah in separate rooms," she says, winking. "I know you're trying to keep your relationship quiet. However, you're next door to one another, and there's a connecting door."

I choke at her words, Elijah patting me on the back.

"Come now. I may be getting older, but I still remember what it's like," she adds.

I turn and hug her.

"It's why I love you so much. You never cease to amaze or surprise me. Happy birthday, Franny."

Elijah rolls his eyes as his mum and I embrace.

Franny turns to Lottie, who's watching us.

"There's a surprise I think you'll like in the snug. Why don't you come with me," Franny says, linking arms with her granddaughter, who's now taller than she is.

"What, Granny?"

Elijah takes my hand, and we follow behind the two, not needing to hide our relationship while it's just us.

Franny opens the door, and a little squeak occurs.

A pen has been set up in the centre of the room, where a small golden rust puppy is busy fighting with a rope toy.

"Granny!" Lottie says, letting go of her grandmother's arm and running forward. She turns to face her.

Franny grins. "Get in. She needs some attention, someone to play with."

Elijah looks at his mum in amazement. "A puppy. Really?"

Franny shrugs. "Well, I'm here all alone, apart from an army of staff. I decided I quite fancied some company. My grandchildren will all love a puppy, so it's the perfect way to blackmail you all into spending more time here."

I chuckle at her logic, and Franny shoots me a wink.

"What is she called?" I say, moving towards the pen.

"Well, I thought Lottie might like to help name her. Callum is a little young yet."

Lottie, is already on her knees, cuddling the furry pup.

"She's a Vizsla," Franny says. "One of our neighbours' bitches had a litter and was looking to home the last one."

As if this explains everything.

I can sense Elijah's disbelief at his mother. I know she always refused to let them have dogs growing up.

"Do the others know?" Elijah asks.

"No, I thought I'd surprise them," Franny says, and there's no missing the mischievous glint in her eyes.

"Well, it will definitely be a surprise," Elijah says drily.

I link my arm through his and give it a squeeze, earning myself a sexy smile.

"Come on," I say. "Let's leave Lottie and your mum to decide on a name."

I take Elijah's hand and lead him from the room.

We make our way upstairs and to our bedrooms.

"I can't believe she's got a dog. No strike that a puppy!"

I laugh and pull him around to face me.

"A puppy, Lottie's not going to be able to drag herself away from for quite a while."

I watch as dawning crosses his features, his hands going to my hips, pulling me against him.

My hands slide up his chest and around his neck, my fingers playing with the short hair at his nape.

"You make a very good point, Ms Dawson," he says, a slow smile gracing his lips as they descend towards mine.

He licks along the seam of my mouth, making me groan. It's been too long.

"I've missed you," he tells me, deepening our kiss, his hands travelling up into my hair and angling my mouth, his tongue tangling with mine.

He walks us backwards towards the door, his hand twisting the lock, sealing us in.

I smile at the move.

"Does this mean you're hoping to have your wicked way with me?" I ask cheekily.

"Oh, most definitely. I have blue balls, thanks to my daughter."

I moan as my desire skyrockets. All that pent-up desire. My fingers tingle with the need to touch this man. I'm already wet, my core pulsing with need. I moan as his lips move to my neck, finding that sensitive spot that leaves me weak at the knees.

I cradle his head as his lips nip and suck.

"I've missed this," I whisper into the air.

"Then I need to rectify that. I can't leave you wanting."

Before I know what he's about to do, Elijah scoops me up in his arms and deposits me on the edge of the bed.

He drops to his knees in front of me, and I watch his tongue snake out and lick his lips. His hands slide up my thighs and move my skirt up and out of the way.

I bite my lip, knowing Elijah is going to find me wet and ready. Just being around the man puts me in the mood, and I want his cock deep inside me. These past two weeks have been a lesson in restraint.

Elijah's eyes don't leave mine as his fingers play with the lacy edge of my panties.

I bite down on my lip to suppress the moan that threatens to escape, as he pulls the material to one side, exposing my heated flesh to his gaze and the cool air of the room.

"Beautiful," he says, dropping his head forward and out of sight, my skirt obscuring the view. My head drops back as his tongue sweeps from my opening to my clit.

"Elijah," I hiss as he drops light kisses on the area. My desire leaks out of me, readying me.

"All good things," he says, taking my clit between his lips and sucking gently.

My hips all but leap from the bed as desire shoots straight to my core.

"Ahh," I croak as he continues to suck my swollen flesh, his finger moving to my opening, playing with the hole that begs to be filled.

My hands move to his head, grasping it to me, not wanting the sensation to end.

He sinks a finger into my body, my hips taking on a life of their own as they move in time with his movements and mouth.

When he curls his finger into my wall, I shudder, the sensation almost too much. He repeats the movement over and over until I'm writhing beneath his hands. I hold his head with one hand and raise the other to my mouth. Biting down on it to prevent myself from crying out.

Tears spring to my eyes as I'm overwhelmed with the feelings he's provoking in me.

"Elijah," I choke.

"Come for me, Pen," he demands.

He inserts a second finger, pumping in and out as my body detonates around his digits.

My body shudders, my walls contracting hard.

"Fuck," Elijah says.

His tongue now slowly lapping at my clit as I come down from my high, my shudders slowing.

I lie back and stare at the ceiling, my body spent. My legs shake, my womb still giving off tiny convulsions. I close my eyes.

The bed dips next to me.

I open my eyes and stare at the man who is turning my world upside down.

His thumb comes up and wipes my cheek, coming away glistening.

I swipe at my eyes, surprised to find them damp.

"Did I hurt you, Pen?" he asks, his voice filled with concern.

"No, it definitely wasn't pain, unless you call, wringing every ounce of emotion out of me. Geez, Elijah, I don't even want to know where you learned that."

His cheeks darken.

I tilt my head, and he chuckles.

I reach up and pull him down, my mouth finding his, tasting myself on his lips. I push him onto his back, straddling him, my knees on either side of his waist, my skirt hitched up.

Elijah groans as he thrusts himself up against my core.

"I need you," he says.

I slide my hand between us, undoing his jeans and helping push them down his hips, along with his boxers.

"Shit, condom," he hisses as I cradle him between the lips of my pussy.

"I've been tested. I'm clean," I tell him.

"Me too," he says.

"I'm also on the pill," I admit.

Although I was due to come off it after the wedding, glad now I hadn't jumped the gun. A pregnancy now will not be ideal.

"Are you sure?" Elijah asks, his hips tipping as he rocks himself between my legs, coating himself in my juices.

"Absolutely."

I lift up, taking Elijah in my hand.

"Stop. I want to see you," he says.

I bite my lip and scoot backwards until I'm standing. I unzip my skirt and drop it to the floor, along with my soaking panties. I pull off my top and unclip my bra, letting my breasts fall free. They're not large, but the way Elijah looks at them...

I stifle a moan as he sits up and shrugs out of his t-shirt and jeans until he, like me, is naked.

"Come here," he says, lying back, allowing me to climb up his body.

I resettle above his throbbing cock.

"I need you," I say. "My body wants you deep inside, stretching me. I want to feel your cum coating my insides."

It's Elijah's turn to moan. He takes himself in his hand and I lift up, allowing him to align himself.

I feel him breach my entrance, my body stretching to accommodate his size. I press down, and we both exhale as I sink on to him.

"Pen," he hisses as he bottoms out.

I can't pull my gaze away. I move, slowly lifting myself up and down. His hands grip my hips as he helps control my movements. He sits up, taking one of my nipples into his mouth, sucking and nipping. My hands grasp his head as our bodies continue their frantic dance. I feel the pressure once again building in my core as my clit rubs against his pubic bone.

"I'm going to come," I hiss, pulling his head away from my breast and locking my mouth on his, our kiss desperate.

"Then come for me. Milk my cock. I want to feel your muscles with nothing between us."

His words have me exploding. I didn't think my orgasms could get any more intense.

"Fuck!" Elijah swells inside me, my muscles clamping down hard.

He thrusts frantically, sliding in and out, extending my orgasm until he himself shudders, his movements becoming more frantic. I feel his cock jerk deep inside me, his body releasing itself into me.

I freeze, our mouths and tongues still battling until Elijah drops back, pulling me with him onto his chest. Our bodies still joined.

"Wow," he says, brushing my hair from my face as my cheek rests against his chest.

"Wow indeed," I say, unable to move. My limbs have turned to jelly.

A car door slams outside, and I can hear Gabriel and Leah being welcomed by Franny and Lottie.

"Shit," I say, dragging myself upright.

Elijah clamps his arms around me, pulling me back down, tucking me into his side.

"You're not going anywhere," he tells me, dropping a kiss on the top of my head, his arms wrapping around me.

"Okay," I say, snuggling back down. I'm not sure I could move right now, even if I wanted to.

I rest my head on his chest and listen to his heartbeat.

My fingers tingle with the need to touch him, and I

smooth them over his skin. Something shifts within my chest as I feel Elijah's and my cum coating my thighs. I've never had unprotected sex before, so the messy aftermath is not something I'm used to. My breath quickens at the sensation. This affectionate Elijah is something I could get used to.

CHAPTER 52

ELIJAH

By the time Pen and I shower and make it back downstairs, everyone is congregating in the drawing room.

Lottie is still on the floor with the puppy, teaching it to respond to their name and sit for treats.

"Dad, Pen," she calls when Pen and I enter the room, the joy on her face immeasurable. "We've named the puppy," she says as I make my way over to my daughter.

"What did you decide?"

"Diana," Lottie says, causing me to frown.

"Ah, Diana Prince, aka Wonder Woman," Pen says, trying to rescue me from my ignorance. "A great choice."

"I'm clearly missing something," I say, looking between the two of them.

Lottie grins.

"Aunty Pen is a big superhero fan. You should know that. Especially female superheroes. Diana Prince is Wonder Woman. A strong, kick-ass woman."

The penny drops. Of course, Pen loves superheroes. It's

the reason she writes such amazing video games. Her characters are relatable and strong. Both male and female.

"Good choice of name, then I would say," I say, turning to my daughter. "As a Vizsla, she'll also be super fast, just like Wonder Woman."

Pen steps back, my mouth close to her ear.

"I learn something new every day," I whisper. "Do you like cosplay?"

My words send a shiver down her spine, and I chuckle. The thought of Pen in a Wonder Woman outfit has me hard as a rock. Not what I need with my daughter in the room.

"There everyone is."

Pen and I spring apart as Caleb enters.

"Ah, Mum's new little terror," he says, his eyes locked on the floor and the puppy, who is currently trying to climb all over Lottie. When he finally looks up, he rolls his eyes at me before dropping to the floor and joining in the chaos, clearly distracted by the small fur ball rolling around. I understand his thoughts as we were told puppies were a no-no growing up.

"Whatever possessed her?" he asks, trying to remove his sleeve from the puppy's teeth.

April appears in the doorway and follows Caleb to the floor, rescuing her husband by scooping up the puppy and holding it in front of her face.

"Oh my goodness, you're adorable."

Pen joins them on the floor, dropping next to Lottie.

"Pen," April says, leaning forward and pulling her in for a quick hug. "It's great to see you."

It amazes me how Pen has always had this effect on people, especially my family. They all love her. But then, what's not to love? She's one of the most genuine and kind people I've ever met.

"Good to see you too," she says honestly. "How was your honeymoon?"

Twinkling, love-filled eyes turn to Caleb, who returns her stare with one of his own. My chest constricts. I couldn't be happier for them both, yet I also recognise envy, knowing I never once looked at Darra that way or vice versa.

I turn to find Pen watching me. I shoot her a smile, but her eyes are serious.

I sit on the sofa and watch as the others play with the puppy, listening as April and Caleb tell us all about their trip. They visited Australia, Bali, Singapore, Thailand and spent their last week in a water villa in the Maldives, soaking up some sunshine.

"It was amazing," April says breathlessly, her gaze once again moving to Caleb.

Pen smiles, clearly happy for them both, but I wonder. This was about to be her life, despite what she says about Kris and their relationship.

There's no doubt, however, about April and Caleb's love for one another. It shines like a beacon. And that's saying something when I'm known for my cynical outlook on love.

"Did I hear Gabriel and Leah?" Pen asks.

"You did. Leah is sorting out Callum's dinner. Gabriel is dropping their bags upstairs," Caleb says, his eyes turning sombre. "I'm sorry about your engagement ending, Pen."

Pen looks at him and shrugs. "It wasn't meant to be," she tells my brother. "Kris and I didn't have what you and April have."

She doesn't say anymore, and April's hand comes over and squeezes hers.

Caleb gets up off the carpet, placing a kiss on April's lips as he goes.

"Well, it's lovely to have you here. Kris's loss is our gain," he says, running a hand down her cheek.

"Don't jinx it," I say, scooping up a puppy.

I catch Pen watching, her eyes softening as a flush darkens her cheeks.

"I think this little one needs some rest. Come on, Lottie, let's get Diana settled back in her crate. Mum says she's been crate-trained. You can play with her later when she wakes up."

Lottie takes the puppy from my arms and follows me from the room. The sudden need to pull Pen into my arms and claim her in front of my family more than I can resist.

Lottie and I return the pup to her crate and wait while she settles. It doesn't take long, all the stimulation has worn her out.

"It's okay, Dad, no one is going to guess about you and Aunty Pen. Not that I think they'll worry. Everyone loves her."

"I know, but Pen is worried about what people will think, and I respect that."

"But family won't care, they'll just want her to be happy," Lottie says.

"I know, you're right."

Mum said as much to me when we met up.

"Aunty Pen is very lucky. I hope I meet someone like you when I'm older," Lottie says, making my breath catch.

Lottie grins as she links her arm through mine, and we head back to the others.

"So, you and Elijah?" Caleb says as we re-enter the room

"What?" Pen stares at my brother, her mouth open, before her eyes clash with mine.

"Sorry, Pen, he means you're speaking again," April says, as Pen's shoulders drop.

"I was right, then?" Gabriel says from behind me.

"What do you mean, right?" Pen asks.

"That you and my brother have finally got your act together?"

"No," Pen all but yelps.

I want to laugh. She's being anything but convincing. She has guilt written all over her face, but then, is that because I know? Being cornered by the Frazer brood requires navigation, not that Pen hasn't had years of experience.

"Leave the poor woman alone," Leah says, coming to her rescue, a squiggling Callum in her arms.

"Ant Pen," he says, wriggling even harder until Leah puts him down.

Callum staggers across the floor before falling into Pen's lap, his arms looping around her neck.

"Hey, gorgeous boy, have you come to rescue me?" she asks him.

He scrunches up his little nose.

"Scue you," he says, giving her a toothy grin.

She pulls him close, her eyes closing as she inhales his baby scent. Something tugs in my chest. Pen is wonderful with children. I push the thought to one side for later.

"Did you have a good dinner?" she asks him.

"Pasta shapes," he grins at her as she wipes a tiny smear of tomato sauce from his cheek.

"My favourite," she admits to him, and I think back to the spaghetti hoops she would eat directly from the tin when she was busy studying. It used to turn my stomach, but she loved them.

Callum turns to his mum, and Leah grins.

"Not tonight, sunshine. Aunty Pen is eating with the grownups. Maybe tomorrow she can have pasta shapes with you."

He returns his attention to Pen, his hands going to her cheeks. It's clear my nephew has developed quite a bond, which is not surprising because of her relationship with Gabriel.

Lottie moves past me and further into the room, giving April and Leah a hug before turning to her uncles. Pen's eyes capture mine as I take in the toddler, who is snuggled in her lap.

"Puppies and toddlers. Your charm is showing," I say to Pen.

"You're just jealous," she says, cuddling Callum.

I smile and walk towards her. It looks like Pen is holding her breath.

What are you doing?

"Unc Lije," Callum says, squirming in her arms, trying to get to me.

I can't resist shooting her a smirk before scooping him up and throwing him in the air.

"Hey, sport," I say, as Callum squeals in delight.

"More," Callum cries, and everyone's eyes are on me as I play with my tiny nephew.

"What have I missed?"

It's Kat's voice that draws everyone's attention this time.

"Kat," Pen says, manoeuvring around friends and furniture to reach her, pulling her in for a hug.

"I've missed you too. How are you doing?" Kat says, her eyes filled with concern.

I watch Pen's throat bob as she looks at Kat. I know Pen has been torn about telling her about us, but it's not something she wanted to divulge while my sister was overseas.

My mind wonders back to Mum's comment about Kat castrating me.

"I'm doing okay," Pen says. "I've lots to tell you."

Kat inclines her head, her eyes flicking to me, her expression questioning. A glint of understanding passes through her eyes. She's always been incredibly perceptive. It seems to run in the family.

"We clearly have a lot of catching up to do," she says, linking her arm through Pen's and leading her back into the room.

"Well, you can do that over dinner," Franny says, entering behind them and taking in her family gathered together.

"Where's Harper?" Caleb asks.

"I'm here," she says, stepping into the room behind Kat.

The room falls silent.

"Wow, Harps, you look amazing," Pen says, breaking the silence and earning herself a grin.

"I thought I'd go for a change," she says, giving us all a twirl.

The transformation is stark.

Her usual brightly coloured hair has been replaced by subtle highlights. Instead of harsh lines and garish colours, her makeup is now natural and elegant. Even her clothes, have been toned down, although they still hold an air of Harper. You can't remove the entire persona.

"Wow, little sis," Caleb says, stepping forward and pulling her in for a hug. "This is what uni does to you?"

"I wanted to fit in. Old Harper stood out a little too much for my liking. This was easier. No one is accusing me of using my family money or name to get ahead."

She turns to Pen. "Using Mum's surname was genius."

She pats her arm. "I'm glad."

Harper looks up, her eyes locking with mine. "Hey, big bro. What do you think?"

"You look good, little sis," I say, earning myself a grin and a small curtsy.

I've probably been the hardest on Harper about her looks and rebellion. But having been there and watched Pen try to navigate that world, although successfully, I haven't wanted that for my baby sis. Not when I know it has stemmed from the pain of losing our father.

"Perfect, everyone is happy," Mum says, clapping her hands. "Now it's time to eat."

Dinner is a typical Frazer affair. Siblings talking over one another, catching up. Kat is quiet. She looks tired. But then it's always the same. She spends two months travelling to the different hotels, showing her face, speaking to the workforce. Offering the personal management touch. It's the same thing our father and grandfather did. It's why each hotel has a family suite, also why staff retention is at a record high.

Since Pen returned, I know they've spoken briefly on the telephone, but nothing in-depth, although I can sense my sister's questions bubbling beneath the surface. The glances she's shooting my way adding to it. With April away on her honeymoon, Leah also called Pen on separate occasions to check in and make sure she was okay. Watching Pen with my sisters and sisters-in-law, it's clear how much these women love her.

Mum has seated Pen between Kat and Leah, away from me. I think it's more her respecting Pen's wishes than mine.

At the end of the meal, Caleb stands up. "Mum, I know everyone here would like to wish you the happiest of birthdays."

Mum smiles as we all cheer. When the noise dies down, Gabriel takes to his feet, clinking the side of his glass with his knife.

"Leah and I have an announcement."

All eyes turn to Leah. One hand goes to her stomach, while the other is clasped in Gabriel's.

"Really?" Mum's choked voice says.

"It's actually a double announcement."

Gabriel and Leah both grin at each other. "

"Twins?" Mum all but shrieks. "When?"

"I'm sixteen weeks," Leah says, her smile bright. "So it's going to be a very busy Christmas."

Mum gets up and rushes around the table, pulling Leah into a bear hug.

"That's the best birthday present," she says, her eyes glistening as she cups Leah's cheeks, dropping kisses on each one before moving to do the same to Gabriel.

Gabriel wraps his arm around her shoulder and gives her a squeeze. We all know how hard this time is for her. She misses Dad every day but more so this weekend. This news is priceless. My eyes meet Gabriel's over her head and I understand now why he waited to share the news.

"Are they identical?" Kat asks.

"We don't know yet. They have separate placentas, so it's a fifty-fifty chance," Gabriel says.

Another set in the family. I wonder if they'll be as mischievous as the first pair.

My eyes find Pen. She's pulled Leah in for a hug and is saying something to her I can't quite hear. Leah smiles.

"That's wonderful news. I'm so happy for you," Pen says as she pulls away.

Caleb stands up and drags his twin in for a hug.

"I'm so happy for you both. If they are identical, I hope they aren't as cheeky as we were," he laughs.

"Speak for yourself. I was the quiet one," Gabriel says drily.

Caleb laughs. "Okay, that's very true. I hope they are more like you. At least until they're older and wiser."

Caleb gave my parents a run for their money. He was always into something when he was younger. Mum said she needed eyes in the back of her head. And when she didn't, Kat and I were placed on duty.

"On a very boring note, April and I also have something to announce too." A gasp goes up, and he shakes his head with a grin. "No, we're not pregnant, at least not yet. We have, however, had an offer accepted on the old Lofton property."

He shoots his wife a look filled with love, one she returns openly.

The Lofton property borders the family home. Caleb and April are about to become Mum's neighbours. Mum squeaks again and grabs them both.

"This is turning out to be the best birthday," she says.

I knew April was the one for him the moment she came into his life, and I wasn't wrong. There was something about her, the way he spoke her name. I always thought myself cynical, and that Caleb was the same, but with April, it just felt right. Maybe I was more open when she came on the scene than I was with Leah. Lucky for me, Leah has an enormous heart and has forgiven me.

Gabriel looks at Caleb and grins.

Caleb grins back. "We're buying a house. Moving out of the penthouse to prepare ourselves."

Gabriel slaps Caleb on the back. "It won't be long then, brother."

Caleb grins, his eyes once again returning to April with a wink. "Hopefully not."

I sit back and watch my two brothers embrace again, their grins so wide, their joy palpable. This is everything I ever wanted for them. It's why I tried so hard to protect them from the fallout of Darra and my relationship, not that I succeeded. This is what family looks like.

I look over and find Pen watching me. I give her a smile.

April and Leah get up, breaking the moment as everyone talks at a hundred miles an hour.

Mum sits back in her chair and grins from ear to ear, before getting up and hugging everyone.

Pen and I move around the table, embracing the happy

couples. It's only when Pen stops in front of me. I find my arms sliding around her waist, pulling her back against me.

She looks up, wide-eyed but doesn't move away.

"As it seems to be the night of announcements. Pen and I have one, too," I say. "We're seeing one another."

The four stop in their tracks and turn to face us.

Caleb holds out his hand to Gabriel.

"I win," he says, earning himself a scowl.

April and Leah look at their husbands in horror.

"What?" they both say, shrugging and shooting their wives a look of complete innocence.

"That's great news," April says, stepping forward and giving Pen a hug, shooting me a grin. "Pleased for you, big man."

Leah steps forward. "I knew it," she says against Pen's ear as Pen squeezes her back.

"We're keeping it under the radar at the moment," Pen says, and they all nod in agreement.

"Finally seen sense, big brother?" Gabriel says, clapping me on the shoulder.

I frown at him and shoot a look in Lottie's direction, making Gabriel look sheepish.

Lottie just shrugs and goes back to playing with Callum. It's not like Pen, and my relationship is news to her. She's taken it completely in her stride.

Lottie looks up at us all and shakes her head.

"I thought you two were on the down low," she says. "You're the worst secret keepers."

I hold up my hands, realising Lottie was too busy with Callum to have heard the other news. "Your aunt and uncle just announced they're having a baby."

Lottie's eyes widen, and it's her turn to squeal. She runs forward, hugging April and Leah in turn.

"I take it Lottie's onboard," Gabriel says quietly next to us.

Pen turns and smiles at him. "I'm her cool godmother."

"Except when I find you naked and in bed with my dad," Lottie says, making everyone turn to face us.

Pen's cheeks darken instantly, and she drops her gaze. She looks cute. I pull her back against my chest.

"That only happened because you arrived home a day early."

Lottie laughs. "I think it's a good thing I did."

"Quite something when your teenage daughter is teasing you," Caleb says. "Wait until Lottie—"

"Don't say it!" everyone shouts simultaneously.

I send my brother a warning look that he seems to find hilarious.

"Well, with all this excitement, I think it's time we vacate and move to play Monopoly," Mum says, motioning for everyone to move to the other room.

Gabriel scoops up Callum from his highchair.

"I'll take Callum, and we can watch a movie," Lottie says. "Congratulations again."

She takes Callum from her uncle and leaves us behind. I watch her go. She's getting so grown up.

Pen has not joined the family for a game of Monopoly for years. I hope she knows what she's letting herself in for. It's still as crazy and competitive as always.

"Pen, how long and how did it happen?" Leah says.

I eavesdrop on their conversation, wanting, no, needing to know what she tells them.

Pen laughs at the barrage of questions.

"Brother, are you even paying attention?" Gabriel asks, throwing a cushion at my head.

I scowl in his direction, more interested in Pen and her conversation.

"It just sort of happened," she says honestly. "Elijah came around and—what more can I say?"

"Well, seeing Lottie caught you in bed together, I take it things are a little more than friends," April laughs.

"Don't, you'll make me blush," Pen's hands go to her cheeks.

April and Leah laugh. "Remember, we're married to Frazer men," they both say, looking at one another and laughing.

"Hard to resist," April says.

"Incredibly. When a Frazer man sets his heart on a woman, there's no stopping them."

I splutter, but my sisters-in-law aren't wrong. When we give our hearts, we give them in their entirety. I now understand my mother and father.

My heart stalls when I hear Pen's next words.

"Elijah and I are having some fun."

Is that what she thinks?

I know I don't have any rights to her. She's only just come out of an engagement.

I try to focus on the game in front of me.

But when I look up, Pen's watching me. She smiles, and I smile back.

Whatever this is, we need to take it slowly and enjoy the moment.

After we pack up, I make my way over to the women.

"Who won?"

"Kat."

Kat appears at my side, grinning. I'm pleased to see my sister looking more alive. That's what beating your siblings does within the Frazer household.

"I'm off to bed," she says. "I'll catch up with you in the morning," she adds pointedly at Pen.

"I'll look forward to it. Want to run?" Pen asks.

"Absolutely."

Kat turns on her heel and leaves us.

I hold out my hand, and Pen clasps it.

"Bedtime," I say, smirking as she stifles a yawn.

"I thought you would never finish."

"I couldn't just roll over," I tell her, knowing she's fully aware of the competitive streak my siblings and I have.

We make our way upstairs and find Lottie and Callum asleep on one bed. Toy Story playing in the background.

Gabriel retrieves Callum while I scoop Lottie into my arms and carry her to her bedroom. Mum has always made sure Lottie had her own room in the house. I lay her down on the bed and cover her with the duvet. Stepping back, I look down at my daughter. Pen rests her hand on my shoulder. I turn to the woman who's crashed back into my life.

"She's growing up so fast," I say.

"She is, but she loves you with all her heart."

I know Pen's right. Lottie and I have a strong bond. But I look at my little girl and see the woman she's becoming. She's getting bigger before my eyes. In a couple of weeks, she'll be fifteen. Darra has asked for her to spend the weekend with her in Italy. I have yet to ask Lottie what she wants to do. I know Darra is missing our daughter.

I lean down and drop a kiss on her forehead as we make our way outside.

"Stay with me tonight," I say, turning and pulling Pen into my arms. "It's not like they don't know about us."

Pen quirks an eyebrow. "Was this your plan all along?"

I feign innocence, but I'm glad my family knows. That they're happy, or at least ninety per cent of them are.

Kat has already told Pen she'll be having words with her tomorrow before the party. She wants to know how I finally won her over.

"I'll stay with you," Pen says as I interlink our fingers and lead her to my room.

When we get inside, I close the door, dropping a kiss on

her nose before moving to her neck and the spot just above her collarbone that has her shivering. Pen moans and desire shoot straight to my cock, and I'm instantly hard. Memories of her coming apart on my tongue and fingers fuel the fire. It's like I'm permanently in *horny mode* whenever Pen is near. Not that she's any different. My hand finds its way under her dress. Wet and ready, her body desperate for my cock.

She locks her arms around my neck, and we give in.

CHAPTER 53

PEN

Kat's waiting for me in the kitchen, and I'm pleased I packed my running clothes.

Elijah's still in bed, post-coital, after I woke him with my lips tormenting his cock. The feel of him coming into my mouth has left me wanting more, but I promised my friend and I will not renege on her, for her hot and sexy sibling. Therefore, this run is exactly what I need.

"You've dragged yourself away from my brother?" Kat says, leaning against the kitchen side, her eyes sparkling. She looks more refreshed this morning.

"Did you think I wouldn't be able to?" I ask as we push our way out of the back door and onto the gravel pathway.

"Debatable," she chuckles. "Woodland or road?"

"Woodland, there are going to be a lot of delivery vans heading this way, according to Leah."

Leah has been helping organise the yearly fundraiser since she and Gabriel first got together. I think Franny used it to snare her into the family. She's always had a knack for knowing what is best for her children.

"Okay, let's go," Kat says, taking off with a laugh.

We jog in silence for a while.

"How's work going?" I ask as we hit the trees, entering their coverage.

"Good." she sighs. "I just need to get a couple of the developments back on track."

"Issues?"

"You could say that. The architect—" she lets out a sigh. "Let's just say his credentials didn't match the man."

I know what that means for the project. Wasted time, effort, as well as potential resources.

"What are you going to do?"

"I need someone to replace him. Someone I can trust who bloody knows what they're talking about."

I don't want to point out the obvious. Jaxson Lockwood would be perfect. Not only does he work regularly with Caleb, but is also a family friend, having gone to uni with both Elijah and myself, but most importantly, he's one of the most sought-after architects in the world. His eco-stance and environmental developments are first-class. He's won more awards than I think even he can keep track of.

"Don't say it," Kat says, stopping, one hand resting against a nearby tree. She sucks in air as she tries to catch her breath.

"You're out of shape," I say, continuing to jog on the spot.

"Try living in hotels for two months. The gym is fine, but long hours and restaurant food. I just want a home-cooked meal. Running machines are different to the great outdoors. Part from my visit to see you. That's all it's been."

I know what she means. I hate being away from home. It's been fun cooking with Lottie and Elijah.

"So, if you're not going to ask Jaxson, what are you going to do?"

Kat shoots me a look to kill, and I laugh.

"No way is that man going anywhere near my project."

For all the years of our friendship, I've never understood

what happened between them. To me, Jaxson has always been a standup friend. Has always had my back. But Kat's dislike for him is deep-rooted and is one topic we agree to disagree on. So, wherever possible, we keep him out of our discussions.

After graduation, Jaxson left for an internship in the US, but their relationship had already soured by then. For years, I thought Kat fancied Jax. She was always watching him with Elijah when she thought no one was looking. But then she got together with Zach, our other friend, and I assumed I was mistaken.

She pushes off the tree and begins running again.

"Don't you think you're cutting your nose off to spite your face?"

She growls, sounding very similar to her brother.

"I'm just saying. Can't you delegate the project to someone else? Then you'll have nothing to do with him personally."

She turns and faces me, running on the spot.

"Can you imagine the board? They'd have a field day with that. It would play right into their misogynistic hands. The old fossils," she fumes.

"But aren't they questioning why Jaxson is not being appointed?"

Kat doesn't answer. Instead, she turns and continues running.

"I dragged you out here to talk about you and my brother," she says, signalling this conversation is over. "Not Lockwood."

"What do you want to know?" I tell her, running up alongside her.

"Everything," she says. "Although keep it PG, I really don't need to know about my brother's performance in bed."

I laugh and fill her in on everything that's happened.

We're still laughing when we burst back into the kitchen. Kat draws up short.

"Kat, Pen," Jaxson's smooth voice comes from across the room, where he's nursing a mug of coffee.

Kat ignores him, turning to me. "I'm going to grab a shower. I'll see you later."

I move to the fridge but watch Jaxson's eyes as they follow Kat. I grab a bottle of chilled water from the shelf and pull off the top before taking a deep swallow.

I move toward Jax, who's still staring at the empty doorway.

"Hey, stranger," I say, placing a kiss on his cheek. "I'd give you a hug, but—"

He holds up his hands, his attention now on me.

"That's okay. It's the thought that counts," he says, smiling.

"Exactly."

He inclines his head. "I hear you and Elijah..."

"Bloody hell, news travels fast, and it's supposed to be on the down low."

He chuckles. "Like you, I'm family. Fran couldn't help herself. Plus, I couldn't be happier. It's about time you two sorted out your shit."

"Another reason I didn't want everyone knowing."

"What? Worried you two won't work out."

It's my turn to incline my head.

"Jax—"

"Hey, I was there, remember?"

"I know, and I'm not sure how I would have survived it without you in my life."

"I kept your confidence. Even though Elijah was my best friend." He gives my arm a squeeze. "I really am happy for you both. You deserve the time to see where this relationship can go."

I turn to look at the door where my friend has gone.

"She needs you."

His lips purse, his eyes hardening.

"Not going to happen," he says in a very unlike Jax way.

"Look, I don't know what happened between you two. She's as tight-lipped as you are, but she needs you now. Or at least your expertise."

He shakes his head.

"I've tried Pen. Really, I have, but Kat hates me. It's safer for everyone involved to let us be."

I nod, knowing I can't push any more.

Elijah takes that moment to enter the kitchen. He walks up behind me and circles my waist.

"I'm sweaty," I say, grimacing.

Instead of moving away, he grins and pulls me closer.

Jax raises an eyebrow at Elijah before bursting out laughing.

"You're a goner, my friend."

I sense Elijah's grin before he drops a kiss on my neck. His loss of inhibitions in front of our friends and family causes something to shift within my chest.

Jax winks and I realise.

He's not the only one.

CHAPTER 54

ELIJAH

Pen snuggles into my side as we watch reruns of *The Office*.

"Your mum called me this morning," Pen says. "Apparently, the fundraiser raised more this year than ever before."

I chuckle. "Nothing, of course, to do with The Foundation's *poster girl's* offering all those additional internships," I reply, dropping a kiss on her head.

"Or the fact you then copied me and added some of your own."

"Ah, I couldn't be outdone by my girlfriend."

Pen freezes in my arms, her head tilting so she can look me in the eyes. "Girlfriend, huh?" she says, her eyes twinkling as she stares at me.

I drop my lips to hers, my heart rate settling back to a normal rhythm.

"Well, if I was to give us a name," I say.

Pen chuckles. "There are many names we could use to describe us, but girlfriend, I can get on board with."

"Pleased to hear it, Ms Dawson."

I take her lips with mine, deepening our kiss. She melts into my body. We fit together perfectly, and I can't get enough of her.

"I love my daughter, but I'm glad we have the next week together."

It's been hard with Lottie around to find time for us. She's accepted Pen and I are together, but we've been careful not to overstep. The last thing either of us want is for her to feel like she's in the way, or gross her out.

But the thought of a week where I can have Pen in my arms and back in my bed whenever we want, has my breath quickening and my skin tingling at the thought of her not holding back as she comes around my cock.

"Did she get to Dani's?" Pen asks, bringing me back down to earth.

"She did. She messaged me to say she's arrived and Dani's dad is taking them to the airport in the morning. I'm not sure why I couldn't have taken her, but I'm trying my hardest to let her have some independence."

I was disappointed when Lottie told me what she arranged. I wanted to see her off before she went to visit her mother for her birthday.

"She's growing up fast. Don't take it personally. I know Dani's parents live close to the airport. It's more like the girls will be up all night chatting and want a lie in."

I pull Pen back against me. It helps to have a woman's perspective. Especially one who knows my daughter so well.

"Pen, did my father know about your hacking?"

Pen freezes in my arms.

"What? Why?" she asks. "That's a strange thing to ask me."

I sense her trying to make her body relax, but her initial response tells me all I need to know.

She pulls away and sits up.

I turn to face her.

"Not really. I was thinking about how well you know Lottie, and it reminded me of something Mum said the other day."

Pen drops her chin to her chest.

"What did she say?"

"That he was protecting us both."

"She shouldn't have said anything," she says quietly.

"Why? Because he was involved?"

I hold my voice steady, as Pen's breathing increases.

"God, No. Your dad helped me. *Shit,*" she says, running a hand down her face. "Look, I made a promise a long time ago to never discuss this with you. Please, Elijah, don't make me break that promise."

I know how much Pen loved my father. The feeling was mutual. He had a lot of respect for her, too. She brought Gabriel out of his shell. Is super intelligent, has an excellent business brain for someone so young, or so he kept telling me and everyone else who would listen.

"Okay, I won't push. But Pen. If Dad helped you, I'm glad. I'm certainly not angry."

Pen looks at me as if weighing up my words.

I hold open my arms and draw her back into my side.

Dad was definitely involved, and I wish I could thank him for helping her.

I drop a kiss on her head, and she swivels, looking up at me. Her hand cups my cheek.

"All you need to know is he did what was best for both of us."

I lower my mouth to hers and she opens for me instantly.

She pushes back and stands up.

I watch as she removes her clothes, one item at a time. Her eyes never leaving mine. When she's finally naked before me, she straddles my hips, her legs spread wide over their breadth. Her lips find my neck, licking and sucking. I move my head to one side, allowing her access to the sensitive skin, my cock swelling between us.

Her hands slide under my t-shirt, and I pull it over my head. She works her way down my chest, her lips creating their own roadmap. When she draws one of my nipples into her mouth, my hips jerk.

She chuckles and continues to torment the other, rolling it between her finger and thumb.

"I think we need to lose the trousers."

Her hands go to my belt, and she makes quick work of the button and zipper. I lift my hips, allowing her to slide them down along with my boxers.

"Beautiful," she says, taking my cock in her hand and stroking it firmly. I drop my head back and watch as she lowers her mouth, her tongue teasing my slit. Pre-cum leaks out onto her tongue and she swallows it down.

"Pen, I will not last," I say, dragging her off and up my body until her breasts are pressed against my chest.

"Is that so?" she says, her slick entrance finding my cock, riding it between her lips, she coats me in her juices, preparing us both.

She pulls up, my cock standing between us. She positions herself above me perfectly.

Her gaze locks on mine as she presses down, my cock breaching her entrance. She holds my gaze as I fill her up, her muscles contracting around me as I sink deeper and deeper into her silky depths.

"Fuck, Pen, I don't think I'll ever tire of this feeling. You're perfect."

She gives me a shy smile and rolls her hips. Her eyes open as she locks her lips on mine.

"I'm going to ride you until we're both too tired to move," she whispers.

I moan into her mouth.

"I need you and want you, Pen, more than I ever thought physically possible," I say, pulling her more firmly against me, wanting to crawl into her skin.

It's Pen's turn to moan, her hips moving more frantically.

I become lightheaded as something shifts within my chest, something that tells me I'm never going to be the same.

My hands move to her hips as she glides up and down my cock. The only sound echoing around the room is the carnal sound of our bodies coming together.

I bite her bottom lip, sucking it into my mouth, eliciting a groan that causes her pussy to contract around me. I love how sensitive she is. How much I crave her.

She speeds up, her clit pressing against my pubic bone as she rolls her hips. I move my hand between us, my thumb finding her swollen bud of nerves.

She bites her lip, her head falling back as she rides me hard and fast. I pinch her clit as I know she likes.

"Now," I say, watching as she shatters above me, her chest and cheeks flushed as her pussy strangles my cock.

I thrust several times more, before following her over the edge, loving the feel of my cum coating her insides, of her sensitive flesh swallowing mine.

I roll us sideways onto the sofa, our bodies still joined, our legs entangled.

"I…" I pause, the words sticking on my tongue.

My chest constricts. I've only ever uttered those words to Lottie and my family.

I place my forehead against hers. I close my eyes and draw in a breath.

When I open them, Pen is smiling up at me. A dazzling

smile that sinks deep into my chest, locking itself in place, filling my heart with hope. I pull back and look down at her.

Pen places a finger on my lips.

I draw in a shuddering breath as I wrap my hand around the back of her neck, and pull her forward, my mouth finding hers, sealing our love with yet another kiss.

CHAPTER 55

ELIJAH

The phone rings next to the bed, and I roll over with a groan.

Pen and I sealed our love all over the apartment last night, finally falling into bed in the early hours.

"Elijah," I say, answering.

"Where the *fuck* is my daughter, you bastard?" Darra screams down the phone.

I sit up, running a hand down my face, forcing my eyes to open.

When I finally do, I realise it's midday.

"Has her plane been delayed?"

Pen rolls over next to me and opens her eyes. She's now awake. She shoots me a questioning glance and I shrug.

"I'm not a fucking imbecile, Elijah. The plane landed. Lottie and her friend were no-where to be seen."

My temperature drops and an uncontrollable shudder sweeps through my body.

"What do you mean, they weren't on the plane? That's not possible. She stayed at Dani's house last night. Her dad was dropping them at the airport."

What the hell? Has there been an accident? Fuck!

I pull my phone away from my ear to see if there are any missed messages.

Nothing.

I run a hand through my hair. Pen sits up next to me. Her face shows the same concern raging through my body. She can hear Darra without her being on speaker.

Pen picks up her phone and shows me as she dials Lottie's number.

It goes straight to voicemail.

When she tries again, the same thing happens.

Pen jumps out of bed, grabbing the dressing gown I bought her when she first stayed over, wrapping it around herself. There's no time to appreciate the beauty of her naked body this morning.

She grabs my laptop and logs in, pulling up the location software I placed on everyone's phone years ago.

Lottie's phone last pinged at the airport five hours ago. Then it goes dead.

Fuck, did someone kidnap her?

I squeeze my eyes shut, my breath coming in quick, shallow bursts.

Pen looks up, coming towards me. She takes my phone and puts it on mute, placing it on the bed next to us. Pen's hand lands on my arm and she squeezes, trying to offer me comfort, but for the first time, I want to shake it off. This is my daughter, and she's missing.

Instead, Pen ignores me, taking my face in her hands as she forces my gaze to hers.

"You need to breathe," she says. "We're going to find her, but you need to focus. Think Elijah. You're Lottie's best chance."

Her words snap me out of my haze. I draw in several shuddering breaths, listening to Pen's voice as she talks me through some controlled breathing.

She's right, panic won't help Lottie. I need to use logic, reasoning.

"Elijah, you bastard." Darra's voice comes over the line again. "Are you still there?"

"When was the last time you spoke to Lottie?" I ask, putting the phone on speaker so Pen can hear what is being said while she's busy tapping away on my computer.

"Her tracker's been disabled," Pen whispers, her wide eyes meeting mine.

"Disabled? Impossible. They give off a signal even when the phone is switched off."

Pen spins her laptop around so I can see DISABLED in bold letters, next to Lottie's tracker number.

Fuck!

Darra, unaware I'm talking to Pen, hisses down the phone.

"No *shit* Sherlock. I thought you were the security expert. Even I could tell you that."

"Don't be such a bitch, Darra. You think I'm not concerned? I'm trying to work out what's going on."

"I'm boarding a plane and will be at Heathrow in two and a half hours. You better have Mason or someone there to pick me up."

Before I can say anything, she hangs up.

I throw back the covers and get up.

Pen remains quiet. All I hear is her fingers tapping on the keys.

I head into the bathroom and splash water on my face. I avoid looking in the mirror, not sure I want to see the person staring back at me.

Why the hell did I listen to Lottie? I should have taken her to the airport, seen her on the plane myself.

Lottie assured me Dani's dad was going to do it. That

she's fifteen, I need to let her be a grownup. After the company espionage, I should have realised Lottie could be a target. What if whoever was in charge of the operation to sabotage my company has come back for revenge? It's not like we ever caught them. Peter Levon is still refusing to give up the person who hired him.

Fuck, I should have had a security detail added to her.
Dani.

She was supposed to go to Italy with Lottie. Darra just said neither girl arrived.

I grab a towel and head back into the bedroom, scooping up my phone and searching for Dani's father's number. The girls have been friends for years. I've even played golf with her dad.

"Elijah," he says, answering within a couple of rings, music playing in the background.

"Sorry to bother you, Huw, but is Lottie with you?" I say, choking down the rising panic that's threatening.

"No," he says, chuckling. "We're in Mexico. A family holiday."

What, Mexico? Did I misunderstand Lottie?

My stomach sinks. "Dani is with you?"

"Yes," his voice sounds confused. "Elijah, is everything all right? Is Lottie okay?"

I pinch the bridge of my nose. "I don't know. Lottie is missing." I exhale loudly, my voice catching as I say the words aloud. "She said she was with you, and now—"

"She's what?" I can almost picture the man sitting upright. "What do you mean? When? How?"

"She was due to go to Italy for her birthday. She told me Dani was going with her, that she was staying with you last night, that you were taking them to the airport."

"Hold on," he says. His voice gets quieter. "Dani. Can you come here?"

I hear him talk to his daughter.

"Dani, if you know something. This is important."

I hold my breath, hoping she can shed some light. If Lottie's confided in anyone, it'll be her. My muscles twitch and my heart pounds drowning out everything else.

What is going on? Surely Lottie knew Dani was going to Mexico with her parents.

My heart beats rapidly in my chest as I struggle to draw air into my lungs.

Pen appears behind me, her hands running up and down my back, soothing.

"Breathe," she says quietly. "We'll find her."

I turn my head and stare at the woman offering me her support.

How can she know?

I can hear Huw talking to his daughter, but struggle to make out Dani's words.

"Elijah?" Huw's voice comes back over the phone.

"Here," I say.

"Dani said something about Lottie looking for her birth father. I'm sorry, man, I thought you were Lottie's dad. I don't know whether that helps or sheds any more light on the situation."

I swallow hard, bile burning the back of my throat.

"Thanks Huw. If you can keep that information quiet. I'll explain everything when you get back. Does Dani know any more?"

The line goes quiet again, and I can hear Huw and Dani talking in the background.

"Sorry Elijah, apparently, we left before the DNA test results came back."

DNA tests? What the hell are you up to, Lottie?

I turn to Pen, who's gone as white as a sheet next to me.

"Thank you," I say. "Can I call again if I need to speak to Dani?"

"Of course. Good luck. If I find out any more, I'll call. Let me know when you find her."

I turn to Pen, who's dropped onto the side of the bed, her head in her hands.

"What do you know?" I say, my voice cold, my chest pounding, hoping she's going to say nothing, but I know she isn't.

Pen looks up, her eyes pained.

"Lottie came to me a few weeks ago and asked me if I knew who her biological father was."

I suck in a breath, a vice like grip taking hold of my chest.

"And you didn't think to tell me? What the hell, Pen? You didn't think I should know my daughter was questioning who her biological father is?"

Pen sits up, her face a mask. "Don't turn this around on me. She spoke to me, we talked. I told her she needed to speak to you or Darra."

"But you just had to be the *cool* godmother and keep her confidence."

"That's not fair, and you know it. She tried talking to Darra over the summer and she shut her down. If you want to blame anyone, blame the woman you married."

She gets up and slams into the bathroom, the door banging loudly behind her.

She opens the door again and looks out.

"I've called the police. They'll be arriving shortly. I wasn't taking any chances."

Then she closes the door once more.

I drop onto the bed, my elbows resting on my legs as I try to get enough oxygen into my lungs. I look at the closed door, unable to speak past the lump in my throat. Running my hands through my hair, I tug hard at the roots.

Fuck, fuck, fuck!
Bloody Darra.
I'm so stupid. I should have expected this!

Pen slams back out of the bathroom five minutes later, showered and changed.

"Before you point the finger, I told Lottie she needed to speak to her mother again, or to you. She told me she didn't want to upset you. That you might think you weren't enough. She's a young woman, of course she's going to have questions. Maybe I should have said something. I now wish I had, but hindsight is a wonderful thing," Pen says, her arms folded over her chest, but I can hear the desperation and panic in her voice.

"Why did she come to you?"

My heart sinks as I read her expression.

"As I said, she asked Darra over the summer and she wouldn't answer her. Told her you were her dad now and she should forget about it. Lottie also knows I had an absent father. She asked if I'd ever been tempted to meet him," she says, dropping herself onto the bed next to me.

"What did you tell her?"

"I told her the truth. I met him and it wasn't all it was cracked up to be. That just because you carry someone's DNA doesn't mean they're someone you want in your life."

I turn to face Pen.

"You met your dad? I didn't know," I say slowly.

We talked about it at uni. Pen was always blasé about her dad, but I felt there was more to it. Had to be.

She shrugs, and I suddenly feel the chasm the years between us has formed.

"Why would you? Even Mum doesn't know." She pauses. "Look, I was hoping Lottie was going to do the grown-up thing and speak to you."

"She's fifteen," I say.

"Exactly. She's fifteen. She'd be classed as a woman in some cultures. She's not a little girl anymore."

"From the woman with so much experience in raising children."

I know I've said too much by the look on her face. Taking out my frustration on Pen is not something I should do, but Lottie's my daughter. Not Pen's. She should have told me!

Pen looks at me, her voice quiet, monotone.

"I may not be a mother, no. I haven't been that blessed. But I was once a fifteen-year-old girl, one who didn't have a conventional upbringing, spent a lot of the time on the outside looking in. Lottie may have had a mother and a father, but her life has been far from conventional, and what she found out… before you sling mud and your frustration in my direction, maybe you need to take a good hard look in the mirror. Both you and Darra."

"Pen—"

"Don't. I'm going to make us both something to eat before the police arrive."

She walks to the bedroom door without looking back.

Fuck!

But I can't worry about Pen's hurt feelings. I have to think about my daughter, about finding Lottie.

I pick up my phone and begin calling around.

Everyone agrees to meet at my apartment within the hour.

I get dressed.

CHAPTER 56

PEN

It takes all my willpower not to slam the bedroom door. I know and understand Elijah is panicking. I am too. Lottie is missing, God only knows where.

I lean against the wall outside the room and close my eyes, inhaling deeply, trying to calm my racing heart. I hate conflict, but I will not be used as a scapegoat for the *bitch* he married. The years of having to put up with her snide comments and bitchiness are well and truly over.

I head into the kitchen and flick on the coffee machine.

"Where are you, baby girl?" I say to the air as I make my way to Lottie's bedroom.

The silence inside is deafening.

Why the hell didn't I mention our conversation to Elijah? If I had... maybe...

No point in thinking *what-ifs*. It's now a case of tracking her down and we will. Heaven only knows what she's got herself involved in. Has she actually worked out who her biological father is?

I move to her desk and look through her drawers.

Like her father, Lottie is organised, and her drawers are neat and tidy. Everything has a place. I pick up a stack of papers and flick through them. Homework, some sketches.

I stand in the centre of the room and look around.

Shit, come on, Lottie, give me a clue.

I move to her bed and drop to the floor, checking underneath it. Again, nothing.

What teenage girl doesn't stuff her dirty clothes under her bed? Lottie Frazer, you need corrupting.

I can hear her chuckling at my comments.

I shuffle across the floor on my knees, moving to her bedside drawer.

A couple of steamy romance novels whose titles I recognise. A few photographs of her and her friends, a notebook. I flick through the pages, but again, nothing. A few story ideas, but no big reveal.

I stand, placing my hands on my hips.

If I was a teenage girl, where would I hide my secrets?

I come up blank. Mine were always locked in private files on my computer.

I look back at the desk. Lottie's laptop is missing. I presume she has it with her.

Damn!

I move to her ensuite.

Nothing, not even her bin has anything in it. Chrissy must have emptied it.

Damn.

Elijah appears behind me.

"What are you doing?"

I turn and look at him. His face echoing the strain I know he's feeling. He looks like he's aged ten years. The stress lines around his eyes and mouth are deep.

"I'm looking for clues. If Lottie has found out who her

biological father is, I was hoping she may have left evidence. Instead, I find my goddaughter is a neat freak."

"She isn't normally," Elijah says.

"Then why is her room so tidy?"

"Probably because she hasn't been back long enough to turn it into its usual tip."

I move to her desk drawers and open them, showing him the neat and organised space.

He frowns.

"All her draws are like this. Is there a space where she might not have cleared up after herself?"

I'm realising my goddaughter is a smart cookie. She's cleared up so no one could stumble across her plans.

"No," Elijah says, rubbing his forehead.

"Where's her artwork? She was going to show it to me. We just never got time."

Elijah freezes.

I incline my head.

"Where's her artwork, Eli?"

He turns on his heel, and I follow behind him. He leads me upstairs, pausing outside a door with a security keypad.

A lot of security for a storeroom.

He turns to me and opens and closes his mouth.

"Pen, look. What I said earlier—"

I hold up a hand. "Let's just concentrate on finding Lottie. She's all that matters right now."

Without another word, he enters a code and pushes the door open.

It's the smell that hits me first. Oil paint and turps.

Canvases line two walls. Not just a single canvas but hundreds.

"Holy shit," I say, moving further into the room. "Are these all Lottie's?"

I turn to face Elijah, who's stood awkwardly in the doorway.

"No," he says, running a hand through his hair, his eyes not quite meeting mine. "Most of them are mine."

If he came over and shoved me, I could not be more surprised.

"Yours? I…"

I turn around and move towards the wall. There must be hundreds of paintings stacked up. Not just doodles but amazing paintings.

I spin to face him. "But—I."

"Remember that little paint-by-numbers set you bought me?"

My jaw drops.

"These are a little more than paint-by-numbers, Eli," I say, turning back to the paintings lining the walls.

These are good, I mean really good. Elijah is an artist and a talented one. Somehow, I'm less surprised than I should be.

He chuckles. "Just a little."

"Well, don't think you're getting away with this," I say to him. "I need to know more, but now we need to concentrate on finding Lottie."

"Her paintings are over here," he says, moving towards the corner where there's a separate setup. "She prefers watercolours."

I stare at the artwork. Lottie, like her dad, clearly has a talent for art. No wonder she went to art school over the summer. This needs to be nurtured. I think back to the stick painting of Lottie's I still have on my refrigerator.

"She's good," I say.

I may not be an artist myself, but I am an art aesthete.

"She is." I can hear the pride in his voice.

I move to the desk, nowhere near as neat as her bedroom.

This time, the bin under the table is full. I pull it out and place it on the table bench.

Bingo

I stare at the contents in front of me.

"No way," I mumble. "You clever girl."

Lottie is smarter than I realised. A sense of pride sits in my chest, although I'm going to strangle her for what she's doing to her dad.

"What?" Elijah joins me.

In the bin are seven wine glasses. Each holding a sticker. Jaxson, Zach, Quentin, Xander, Marcus, Tristan, Dad.

The little minx. No wonder she was so keen to help with the clearing up. My mind darts back to how she was happy to return everyone's used glasses to the kitchen at the end of the night.

If I wasn't currently so mad at my goddaughter, I'd be impressed with her resourcefulness.

Elijah looks at me.

"She's run DNA tests?"

"At least we know what she's doing and potentially where she's gone," I tell him, although I notice he's gone slightly green around the gills.

Not surprising.

It's one thing to know your daughter isn't biologically yours, but another thing to find out one of your friends potentially knew and did the dirty with your ex.

I turn to Elijah and squeeze his arm.

"A positive. If she's found one of these men is her biological father, at least we know she's not in any danger."

No one on her list would hurt a hair on her head. They're all like family. The question now is, which one carries her DNA, and did they know it?

Elijah and I rummage through the rest of the papers but find no sign of the test results.

The doorbell goes, snapping us out of our trance.

We head back downstairs.

Elijah heads to the door, looking back as he reaches it.

"Pen, what you saw upstairs..."

"Your secret is safe," I tell him. "It's not like I don't carry a tonne of my own."

Elijah nods and opens the door.

Caleb and Gabriel enter together.

"We left April and Leah at home, just in case Lottie shows up there. We've promised to keep them informed."

Elijah nods. "Thank you," he says. "Good thinking, especially after last time."

It's Gabriel who nods while Caleb looks between his two brothers. He shoots me a glance, which I acknowledge. He nods but doesn't press, clearly knowing all will be revealed shortly.

The door goes again, and Kat enters.

"Harper is going to stay at uni in case Lottie shows up there. Mum is also going to stay at home. I've spoken to the concierge at my apartment. If Lottie shows up, the staff have me on speed dial, and someone will stay with her until we get there."

Elijah nods and motions for everyone to sit down. I open his laptop and call the two absent Frazer members. Both answer on the second ring.

"Any news?" Franny says, her usual pitch elevated.

"Nothing yet. However, we have some news."

"Has she been kidnapped?" Harper says, her voice shaking. "Please tell me she hasn't been kidnapped."

There is no mistaking the panic in Harper's voice.

"No, nothing like that. Or at least we haven't received a ransom note," I say, stepping in for Elijah.

I look at him, his face has gone white, his hands shaking. Gabriel moves next to him and grasps his shoulders.

"Come on. You've got this," he says, giving him a quick shake. "No one is going to care. They love you and Lottie. That will never change."

Elijah nods, although his spark is extinguished.

"Elijah?" I say, turning to him. I swallow when he looks at me with dead eyes.

"Pen, what the hell is going on?" Caleb says.

I look at Elijah once more, but he has sunk to the sofa.

"We think Lottie is trying to track down her biological father," I say.

"Her what?!" Caleb blurts out

His eyes flash between me and Elijah.

There's a silent pause before the room erupts, everyone talking over each other. I look up to see Franny looking on. She stares at me.

Oh fuck, she's known all along?

"Enough!" I shout over the noise. "This is not helping."

Everyone stops, their gazes moving to Elijah.

"There's a list of people she tested," he says. "We think she…"

His voice trails off.

"Who?" Caleb asks, stepping forward. "Who has she tested? I don't understand?"

"Everyone who was there that Christmas and New Year. It looks like one of those names is positive."

Caleb looks confused until the realisation dawns. I watch his throat bob as he swallows.

"You mean?" he says, his tanned skin having gone deadly pale.

He looks at me, and I nod.

"Can you call them, ask them if Lottie is with them? No blame, we just need to know she's safe."

He nods, knowing exactly who I mean.

He leaves the room, his phone in hand.

I turn and find Elijah staring at his mother on the screen.

"You don't seem surprised, Mum," he says, his voice devoid of all emotion.

She shakes her head sadly. "No."

"How long have you known?"

"I had my suspicions from the beginning. They were confirmed when you found out."

"And you didn't think to say anything?"

"What was the point? Lottie is your daughter, my granddaughter. I've never cared about biology. She is ours, always has been and always will be."

Elijah's face hardens. "You don't think me knowing would have helped?"

"No, you would have felt you needed to leave Darra if I'd said anything. Your pride would have kicked in, and Darra would have taken Lottie. That was not a risk your father or I would take."

My eyes well at Franny's words, knowing she means every syllable. She practically adopted me as a daughter. Invited me into her family. She tried the same with Darra, although she never appreciated what she was being offered. I wonder now whether it was guilt, knowing that Lottie wasn't theirs, that kept Darra from accepting their love.

I turn to find Kat staring at the floor, not saying a word. She looks up as if sensing my gaze. Her eyes are filled with the level of pain I've only ever seen when her father died.

I shake my head, but her eyes tell me I'm wrong. It becomes crystal clear where her dislike for Jaxson stems.

Does she think it's him?

Surely she can't believe that about him?

No way.

Out of everyone, Jaxson would never have done that to Elijah. He would have cut off his right arm for his friend. He certainly wouldn't have slept with his girlfriend. He didn't even like Darra. And he definitely wouldn't have let her trap Elijah into marriage if he knew.

Jax was as horrified as I was when Elijah proposed. My mind and body rebel against the thought.

But then, was it all a ruse? Do you ever really know anyone?

CHAPTER 57

ELIJAH

The police arrive and take my statement. They ask how long she's been missing.

Fuck!

I admit I haven't seen her for over twenty-four hours, thinking my fifteen-year-old was staying with her best friend, who I didn't realise was actually holidaying in Mexico. Talk about a bad father! I didn't even know where my daughter was. Hadn't thought to check.

Has she ever done anything like this before?
How was she after your divorce?
Are you in a new relationship?
How does your daughter feel about Ms Dawson?
Do you have any idea where she might be?
Fuck, fuck, fuck!

The secret I've held for ten years is about to be exposed. Charlotte Frazer isn't my daughter, at least not biologically. The great Elijah Frazer was cuckolded by a friend and his wife.

My stomach churns, my muscles ache.

Why the hell didn't you talk to me, Lottie? Where the hell are you, munchkin?

My apartment becomes a hive of activity. The phones are tapped in case it does turn out to be a kidnapping. Another wave of nausea hits me as the officer in charge explains they can't take any chances when my bank balance is as high as it is.

I know in my heart, though, this isn't that. All evidence points to Lottie tracking down her mother's lover. Her *real* Dad. My heart fractures all over again, the same way it did when I first found out all those years ago.

Pen comes up and places a hand on my back. I turn my head and look at her.

"How are you holding up?"

Typical Pen, no platitudes of everything will be alright, especially after the way I spoke to her this morning.

"Pen, I—"

"Don't," she says, cupping my cheek. "We'll find her. She's going to be okay."

"That's not what I meant. This morning—"

"I get it. I should have said something. I'm sorry. But I'm warning you, I'll not be your or anyone else's scapegoat. But know, I love you. We'll discuss this later after we get her back."

She presses her lips to my cheek, and I wrap my arms around her, pulling her close and breathing in her scent to ground me. She's always been so strong. It's not surprising my daughter turns to her. I couldn't ask for a better role model.

She pulls my head down to rest on her shoulder.

"Everyone is here for you," she whispers next to my ear. "Mason called. Darra has landed and is on her way here. You're not alone, Elijah. You need to remember that. Lean on us."

I stand up and run a hand down my face.

"I'm going to get showered and freshen up."

I'm still in the clothes I pulled on after Darra's initial call.

Pen nods and cradles my cheek. She says nothing, but that one touch conveys her love and support as no words can.

She squeezes my hand before heading back to the living area for now, the new control room.

I stand under the shower and let the jets of water hit me from all angles. I throw back my head to hide my tears of despair and desperation in the fast-flowing water until I'm left gasping for breath. I drop my head and shoulders forward, pressing my hands against the shower wall, gulping down air as I struggle to get my emotions under control. I can't fall apart. I won't.

What I would give to hit the pool and swim until my legs and arms don't function or paint until my hand cramps. Anything I can lose myself in.

I switch off the water and stand, hands against the wall, letting the water run down my body until goosebumps form on my skin. I wipe my eyes with the back of my hand before pulling a towel off the rack and rubbing myself down. I avoid looking in the mirror, not wanting to see the broken man before me.

I pull on a set of clean clothes, going through the motions. My chest feels empty.

It's not like I don't get why Lottie wanted to know this piece of information. I just wish she'd spoken to me about it. Not to her mum, not to Pen. But maybe she knew I couldn't help. After all, I would never have married her mother if I'd known the child she was carrying wasn't mine. Lottie would never have been my daughter.

A sinking feeling hits my stomach.

Caleb has spoken to four of the names on her list. Lottie is not with any of his friends, and I can see the relief on his face. My brother and his friends had reputations as *players*, but sleeping with older women, his brother's girlfriend? I think even Caleb was wondering. Not that we were much older. Six years.

But that leaves only two names. Both men I considered my best friends.

The doorbell chimes.

Time for battle.

I make my way into the living area as Darra swans into the room. Her eyes are red and swollen, although her make-up is otherwise perfect. Even her lipstick is intact.

"Where's my daughter?" she says loudly, her eyes clashing with mine.

"Mrs Frazer," one of the police officers says, coming up to her. "If you'd like to come with me. I'll be happy to fill you in on what we know so far."

"Who?" I say, my voice cracking slightly. I cough, needing to clear the blockage that's formed. "Who Darra? Who did you sleep with? Who *is* Lottie's father?"

Darra's colour drains visibly, even under all her makeup. She straightens her spine, her shoulders back. A stance I recognise when she's about to go into battle.

"What? What do you mean?" she says, looking around her, eyes wide.

When her gaze meets mine, she scowls.

"You're her father," she lies, dabbing at her eyes, fluttering them at one of the police officers.

I pinch the bridge of my nose.

"Everyone here knows, and we don't have…time for this."

I thrust my clenched fists deep into my pockets. I'm not and never have been, a violent man, but right now, I want to strangle my ex-wife for all her games.

"I'm talking about Lottie's biological father. It will save us a lot of time if you just tell us who you slept with. Lottie has run a DNA test on everyone who was there that week. She's found something out. Our best bet in tracking her down is if we know who to contact."

She folds in on herself and drops onto the sofa. A nearby police officer guides her, but I'm out of patience.

"Cut the crap, Darra. I know she asked you over the summer, and you stone-walled our daughter. I've never wanted to know, but now is the time for you to come clean. Who the hell did you *fuck* that week?"

"Mr Frazer, please."

I shoot the officer in question a look that has him stepping back.

My siblings and the police officers in the room all turn and stare at Darra expectantly.

"Mrs Frazer, please. If you have information that can help us find your daughter, I would suggest you share it with us."

Darra looks at me, the fight gone out of her eyes. Her indiscretion is out of the bag. Her dupe is now known. She can no longer act the victim.

The poor wife of a workaholic, someone who turned their back on her for his career.

I know what's been said about me, about our relationship. I let it lie to protect our daughter, but I'm tired of taking the blame.

"Mrs Frazer?"

Darra snaps out of her trance and looks at the officer. Her eyes move to my sister. Is that guilt? No.

Oh shit!

I take a step towards Kat, who's currently in a staring match with my ex.

The doorbell chimes.

Pen makes her way past me to the door.

"Lottie, thank god," I hear her say.

I'm in motion before I realise it.

Lottie looks at me, her eyes filled with tears as she takes in my appearance.

"I'm so sorry, Dad," she says, throwing herself against me. "Please forgive me."

I wrap her in my arms, her tiny body almost disappearing in my size.

I look up to find the last person I expect to see standing behind her.

We stare at each other.

"You better come in," I say.

CHAPTER 58

ELIJAH

*E*veryone is silent as we walk back into the main hub.

"Lottie."

Her name is called in relief. She remains tucked under my shoulder, her arm locked around my waist, head down.

"Lottie? Darling," Darra says.

"Mum?" Lottie says, her head coming up. "What are you doing here?"

"You expect me to ignore the fact you didn't arrive on the plane you were supposed to?" Darra says, her voice actually catching. "I know you think I'm the world's worst mother, but—"

"I don't think you're the world's worst mother," she replies. "I sent you a message telling you I was staying here for my birthday," Lottie says, looking around her and realising the living area of the apartment is full of police officers and family members. "You didn't get it?"

"Clearly," Darra says.

Lottie pulls her phone out of her coat pocket and holds up the message to her mother.

"Mr Frazer?"

I turn to the officer in question.

"As Miss Frazer has returned?"

"Yes, please," I say.

We need no more of our dirty laundry aired in public.

"If you need a statement, I can bring her to the station later."

He nods and motions for his colleagues to clear up and move out.

Everyone remains silent until they leave.

Pen steps forward and lets them out. I can hear her talking in the corridor by the door. Knowing Pen, she'll find out what happens next. Always organised, forward-thinking.

"Hey, button," Caleb comes up and gives Lottie a hug. "You had us scared."

"I know, I'm sorry, Uncle Caleb. I should have checked my message was received."

She turns and looks at the man standing silently inside the door, his hands deep in his pockets.

I've ignored his presence until now. Not wanting to think about what this means. To me, to my family.

Darra looks past me. I didn't think she could go any paler, but I was wrong.

Everyone's eyes follow her gaze.

"What the—" Gabriel hisses.

His eyes go to my sister sitting silently on the sofa, her eyes cold and hard, locked on the man in the doorway. The only outward signs she's affected is the tightness of her expression and the rapid rise and fall of her chest.

"Zach?"

Caleb's voice is incredulous as he says his name, breaking the spell.

Caleb's eyes flick between Zach and my sister. Their relationship may have been over for the past three years, but they were together on and off for twelve. Casually at first, but they lived together for seven of those years.

Darra gets up and moves towards Zach. She touches his arm, but he shrugs her off.

"No," is all he says.

She looks taken aback by his rebuke.

I would laugh at her expression if it wasn't for the severity of the situation.

His eyes meet mine. They're filled with acceptance but also an underlying strength.

Lottie's eyes move between everyone. A sadness fills them. I give her a squeeze, my arm still around her shoulder.

She looks up at me. "I'm sorry, Dad," she says. "I didn't mean for this to happen."

I turn her to face me, cupping her face.

"Listen to me. You have every right to know who your biological father is. I just wish you'd spoken to me. You scared me, princess. You going missing—"

She throws herself forward and into my arms. Her heaving sobs, heavy against my heart.

I move us towards the sofa and sit down, pulling her onto my knee and cradling her against my chest as I did when she was a little girl. Whatever happens, she'll always be my little girl. No one can take away our past.

I whisper soothing words until her tears subside.

Pen appears with a box of tissues. Handing them to Lottie, offering her a reassuring smile. I take her hand and give it a gentle squeeze in thanks.

"Didn't take you long," Darra hisses. "I should have guessed."

The venom in her tone is unmistakable. Pen freezes but ignores her, instead offering Lottie another smile.

"You just couldn't wait. As soon as I was out of the equation, you moved yourself in. You always wanted what wasn't yours."

Pen straightens and turns towards Darra.

"Elijah doesn't belong to anyone. He's an amazing man and father," Pen says.

"He's a broken workaholic. Good luck to you. You're welcome to my sloppy seconds," she spits.

Pen bites her lip, her eyes flicking to mine. I let her know it's okay. Pen likes to fight her own battles, and somehow, I think this has been a long time coming.

"By all accounts, you broke your relationship, not Elijah. Why did you ever think a marriage based on a lie was going to work?"

Darra straightens her shoulders.

"It wasn't supposed to be a lie. If it hadn't been for you, Lottie would have been Elijah's biological daughter, but he spurned me, broke our engagement."

Eyes turn to me.

"We were never engaged," I point out.

"Only because of her," Darra hisses. "He told me he couldn't marry me, didn't love me. But it was because he wanted you." She points a manicured finger at Pen. "The freak from a single-parent family." Darra shakes her head, staring at Pen. "How could he want you when he had me?"

Pen shakes her head, her expression sad.

"So you decided you'd take him, anyway."

"It was that or be made homeless. Daddy dearest, you see, decided it was a Frazer he wanted as a son-in-law. No one else was good enough for his princess. He sent me to that university with strict instructions. I was to leave with a ring on my finger. If not, I was making my own way in the world."

Pen looks green as she absorbs Darra's words. She looks at me, but this is nothing new. I already knew the *why* she trapped me. It came out years ago when I confronted her.

"I wanted to marry her," Zach says suddenly, stepping forward, his eyes locked on mine. "I went to see her dad when I found out about the baby." He shakes his head sadly. "As Darra said, I wasn't good enough. He threatened Dad. He'd just moved jobs, told me he'd set him up, that he had the power to do it. Showed me footage of... I couldn't."

He drops his gaze. Zach is the eldest of five. His siblings, like Harper, were much younger than him. If his dad had lost his job...

His eyes fly to Lottie. "Then he told me if I interfered and warned you, there'd be no baby."

Pen draws in a sharp breath.

Fuck. I always knew my father-in-law was a bastard, but I didn't realise he threatened the life of his unborn grandchild.

Lottie buries her head in my chest, and I'm not sure she needs to hear any more. None of this is her fault. How she came into the world, she shoulders no blame. She's the innocent party in all this. I kiss her head and tilt her chin until she's looking at me.

"I told you once before. You may not carry my blood, but you will *always* be the daughter of my heart. Wherever you come from, however, you came into this world. You will always be mine. I love you, Lottie Frazer, and I will always be here for you, no matter what."

Her arms fly around my neck, and she squeezes me tightly.

"I love you too, Dad."

"Always."

Darra hisses and I shoot her a look that has her drawing herself upright.

"Zach is her father," she says. "He was my lover for years even after you threw me aside."

Zach's hands go to the side of his head, pressing hard. His gaze darts to my sister, who's sat still. Her eyes glazed.

Pen shoots me a worried glance.

"I never threw you aside. You lied to me. Until that point, I tried to be a good husband, make our marriage work."

Darra laughs. "Is that what you call it? You never wanted me. You wanted her. It was always her. Pen this, Pen that! Does she even know you paid your lecturer to make her your partner?"

She points a perfectly manicured nail at Pen, her mouth twisting in malice.

My gaze moves to Pen's, and she shrugs. "I knew. I met Mr Dunn a few years ago, he confessed all. I must admit, I was flattered."

Pen winks at me, and Darra screeches and stamps her foot.

"With me, you went through the motions. What did she have that I didn't?"

"She cared about me, about my well-being," I say softly. My eyes not leaving Pen's.

Darra turns to Zach, her hand grazing his chest.

"Zach was there for me. He didn't spend all his time locked in an office or with our child. He was there for *me*."

"While I was building a future for us," I spit, tired of the same old story. Darra wanted to party, live what she deemed *the life of a billionaire's wife*.

Zach steps away from Darra, clearly not wanting to get caught up in her theatrics.

When she reaches for him, he stops her.

"No, I'm not Lottie's father. You took that option away when you refused to stand up to your dad. I would have given you the world, but it wasn't enough. Lottie should have been mine, but she isn't and never will be. Elijah is her dad. I'm only glad my best friend was the one to raise her, and I've watched him love her with every ounce of his being, even after he found out. You have used too many people, Darra.

Both you and your family. Enough is enough. Own what you did. I beg you for your daughter's sake."

I choke.

Best friend?

He slept with my girlfriend or my newly ex. I'm not sure I want to know which way around it was. He then stood by and let Darra dupe me into thinking his baby was mine. Not much of a *best* friend.

My eyes flip to my sister, who is sitting stoically. Her face is a mask, shielding the turmoil she must be feeling. Shit, this is not just about me anymore. I never wanted this for my sister, and I wanted none of my family caught up in my mess. I've spent years trying to protect them.

"What was I?" Kat says quietly. Her eyes never leaving Zach's face. "If you continued your affair with Darra, why did you need me?"

He turns to face her, his chin dipping to his chest, his body becoming unnaturally still.

"Kat," he says, the apology in his tone.

"You were sleeping with her while you were living with me? You lied to me. You deceived me."

A dark redness sweeps up his neck and across his face. A sheen of sweat breaks out on his forehead and upper lip.

"Kat," he says again, although his voice is quieter this time. "I—"

"You were convenient. Enabled him to stay near Lottie," Darra says, her tone gleeful. "He should be thanking you."

Zach's face crumples. He cares about my sister. I know he does.

"You're as frigid as your brother. Is it surprising he looked elsewhere?"

Zach spins on Darra.

"Shut up. Enough of your toxic lies."

I stand up and pass Lottie to Pen, stalking towards Darra.

"Get out."

Darra looks up at me, her face filled with hatred, but there's also a hint of fear.

Caleb grabs my arm, not that I would touch her. He should know that. But I need her gone.

"Don't give her the satisfaction," he hisses, stepping in front of me, his hands on my chest.

He nods at me before turning around.

"Get your toxic ass out of my brother's apartment."

Darra sends Caleb a look of contempt.

"Do as he says," I hiss. "Before I return us to court and remove everything I agreed to. Believe me, I have more than enough evidence to do it."

Darra stares up at me over Caleb's shoulder.

"Lottie, you're coming back with me," she says, looking around us at Lottie, who's curled in on herself on the sofa.

Lottie jumps up and wraps her arms around Pen, shaking her head.

"No, no, no. I'm sorry. Don't make me leave," she pleads, her voice coming out in heart-wrenching sobs.

"She doesn't have to go anywhere with you," I tell her. "I'm now legally her father. Your threats no longer stand. If you know what's good for you. You'll turn around and leave. Now."

She looks at me, weighing up, if I mean it. Whatever she sees in my expression has her turning on her heel.

"Zach?" she shrieks as she makes her way to the door.

Zach says nothing, his eyes still locked on my sister. When he doesn't move, Darra harrumphs and storms out, the front door slamming shut behind her.

Gabriel and Caleb drop to their knees by Kat, but she stands up and shrugs them off. Instead, she walks to Lottie, taking my daughter's face gently in her hands. She drops a kiss on her cheek.

"I'm sorry, Aunty Kat," Lottie says, a fresh set of tears running freely down her cheeks.

Kat smiles at her sadly.

"You, my darling girl, have nothing to be sorry for. I'm sorry you got caught up in the games of adults. All you need to know is we all love you unconditionally. Whoever your father and mother are, you're Lottie Brooke Frazer, and you always will be. I need to leave right now, but I want you to know that has nothing to do with you. I love you, sweet girl."

Lottie lets go of Pen and hugs her aunt. "I love you too, Aunty Kat."

"I need to go," she tells Lottie as she pulls away. "But we will all get through this. Call me if you need me."

Lottie nods.

Pen's hand comes up and grips Kat's arm, sending her a silent message.

Kat's eyes meet Pen's.

"I need time," she says, earning herself another acknowledgment.

Kat hugs each one of us in turn, making her way to the door.

She passes Zach, who grabs her arm. She pauses, her eyes going to where his hand is encircling her bicep. She looks up and whatever he sees has him dropping his hand.

"We need to talk," he says quietly.

"We do," she says, her eyes now looking ahead. "But not now."

He dips his chin in acknowledgement, and then she's gone.

Harper and Mum disconnect.

"I'm going after Kat," Gabriel says, earning himself a nod from Caleb and Pen.

Caleb follows our brother out, not even acknowledging Zach.

Everything I tried to protect my family from has not just exploded, but it's taken out half the block with it.

Zach stands with his hands in his pockets, his eyes on our daughter.

"Lottie, if you ever want to talk, you know where to find me."

He, too, turns and leaves without a backward glance.

My ears ring in the silence.

CHAPTER 59

PEN

The aftermath of the grand reveal has had far-reaching consequences, and I feel like I'm caught in the middle.

I sit at my kitchen table and rest my head on my hands.

"I don't know what to do," I say.

"All you can do is be there for them," Mum says, rubbing a soothing hand down my back.

I've been staying with Lottie and Elijah, Lottie having begged me not to leave. It's been a little awkward, as Elijah and I still haven't discussed his meltdown or how hurtful that was. As a result, it's sat like an elephant in the room.

Today, I've taken a mental health day and called in sick. Danika told me she'd cover for me, and I know she will. So here I am, trying to make sense of the chaos. I want to fix what I fear may be irreparably broken between the people I love.

"How is Lottie coping?"

To Mum, Lottie is the unwilling victim in all this. She never liked Darra, not only because she was the reason my heart broke, but because Darra always looked down her nose at the little people. Surprising when her own father made his millions through hard work alone. Started out by selling his wares on a market stall in the East End, no better than anyone else.

I sigh.

"Lottie keeps apologising to her father. Elijah keeps trying to reassure her she was well within her rights. I'm there telling them, they love each other and everything will be okay, they just need to give it time." I press my thumbs into my eye sockets, trying to ease the constant pain that's taken up residence behind my eyes.

"But she's not a child, and she's certainly not stupid. She heard the ramifications, listened to her mother spew her toxic hate."

Mum wraps her arms around my head, pulling it into her stomach, rocking me.

"Give it time. There were a lot of secrets uncovered. Painful secrets. Time will heal these wounds, but it will not happen overnight. Kat, Elijah, Darra, Zach, even you. Every single one of you has been affected."

I've tried not to think about what she said in terms of my involvement or Elijah's feelings. The past is the past, and I wish more than anything it had stayed there. Why did Darra have to sleep with one of Elijah's friends? Why could it not have been a stranger?

"I called Kat," I say, looking up at Mum through blurred eyes. My friend's pain is suffocating. "She's hurting, and I don't know what to say or do."

She shakes her head. "There's nothing you can do. All you can do is wait and be there for her when the time is right. Kat's had a shock. But she's strong. She'll work through it in her own time. When she's ready, she'll come to you. All you can do is let her know you'll be there, whatever time of day or night."

I know she's right. Zach and Kat may no longer be a couple, but to have found out about his betrayal like she did, and with Darra, of all people. Kat fought her instincts when she saw what Darra had been doing to Elijah over the years. Zach knew that, as he was privy to her thoughts because they were living together. To have been betrayed in this way by the man who was supposed to love her, support her, a man she trusted. I could string him up myself for what he's done to my friend, to both my friends.

"And Elijah?"

I shake my head.

"It's like something has finally snapped inside him. He's always been so strong. Whatever life has thrown at him, he's tackled head-on. The end of his swimming career, Darra's pregnancy, their marriage, his father's death. Even after finding out Lottie was not his daughter, the man has rolled with every proverbial punch. Now..." I bite my lip and swallow against the lump in my throat. "He kisses me, makes love to me, but it's like a part of him has withdrawn. He gets up for work, goes into the office, does a day's work, and comes home. We have dinner and watch TV, but it's not the same. I'm not sure if it's because Lottie spoke to me and I said nothing or if it's more than that. He tells me everything's fine, but it's not."

"Oh, hun. It's only been two weeks." She pulls me back against her, her lips kissing the top of my head. "I will not say everything will be alright. I can't guarantee that. All I will say is, you and Elijah, you've had to overcome so much more than most. You've found your way back to each other. Hopefully, this is a blip. All you can do is be there for him and Lottie. Help them navigate these new waters. And if it gets too much, you can always come home."

"When did you become so wise?"

She grins. "The day I gave birth to a smart-mouthed

genius child who would keep me on my toes but show me what love really is."

I wrap my arms around her waist. "And I wouldn't have it any other way. I love you, Mum."

And then I tell her about my father coming to see me.

She takes my hand and sits down, holding them in her lap.

"I know," she says, smiling. "I probably should have told you."

"Told me what?"

"After you kicked him out of your office." I can't miss the twinkle in her eye. "He came to see me, wanted me to intervene."

I choke on the air I inhale. "He what?"

Mum giggles, a sound I haven't heard for a while. It makes her sound young and mischievous.

"I told him *I'd* raised you to be a strong, independent woman, and if you wanted nothing to do with the deadbeat loser who had donated his sperm for your conception, that was up to you."

"You didn't!" I stare at her open-mouthed. "Good for you." I grin. "I'm sorry now, I didn't tell you."

"I have to admit it was a shock seeing him after all those years. I did, however, wonder what I ever saw in him. He was so cool at school, two years older, handsome. All my friends were jealous that he wanted me. But that afternoon, when he turned up in an ill-fitting suit, whinging about how you'd asked him to leave... Instead of finding him attractive, I simply thought, *how dare you?* I realised my life, and yours, was so much better without him in it. You were the best gift to ever come out of that man. "

"It's been quite the journey," I say, thinking back to my life growing up. Glad I've been able to make her life easier.

"It has. But life is filled with ups and downs. It's how we

deal with them that counts. You have to decide now whether Elijah Frazer is worth fighting for. Whether your life is better served with him in it or not. It's not just about what he wants."

I know what I want. But whether what is currently broken can be neatly fixed, I don't know.

The cracks are getting wider, and Elijah seems to have shut me out.

But is he worth fighting for?

Hell, yes.

CHAPTER 60

ELIJAH

Time has stood still. My head and body feel like I've been on the fast spin cycle, my thoughts tumbling and churning.

Concern for Lottie, and now Kat, trying to make sense of my life and how I've ended up where I am. Wondering what the hell I did to deserve this?

My phone rings, and Gabriel's name pops up.

"Hey," I say, connecting the call.

"Elijah, how are you? Caleb is here with me."

"Hey," Caleb's voice comes over the phone. "We just wanted to check in and see how you're doing?"

What he really means is, he's called into Gabriel's office on the way to work, and they're sitting drinking coffee.

I sigh. I'm tired of telling everyone life is okay when it's not. I can imagine them staring at each other as the sound comes over the phone.

"Have you spoken to Mum?" Gabriel asks.

My stomach tightens. "No," I say, more sharply than I probably should.

"No judgement from us. What she and Dad did was wrong. We've told her as much. She knows that."

"I'm not ready to go there yet," I admit.

Her knowing about Lottie and not telling me.

Part of me understands her logic. It was, after all, the same as mine, but for years, I've carried the weight of that knowledge alone and been forced to navigate Darra's blackmail by myself.

"How's Lottie doing?" Caleb asks.

"She's devastated. Blames herself, thinks she's ruined everyone's life, however much I tell her the *sins of the father*, although in this case, her mother. This could have been avoided if Darra was honest with her, with me."

"Her tenacity makes it hard to believe she isn't a Frazer. Did you ever get to the bottom of how she disabled her tracker?" he asks before adding. "It shows that environmental factors are as important as biological ones."

He should know. April was raised in the foster system. Her foster parents have had an enormous impact on her life.

"She bought a cheap signal jammer. I'll be updating all our trackers shortly," I say. If I didn't have scientific proof to the contrary, I would have sworn Lottie was mine.

"Is Pen still with you?" Gabriel asks, and I know he already knows the answer.

He and Pen are close. My little brother used to find every opportunity to spend time with her. Initially, I thought he had a boyhood crush until I realised it was Pen's brain he was enjoying. She challenged him, made him question what he knew.

"She is. Lottie begged her to stay. She's been trying to reassure her, this isn't her fault."

"How did she take Darra's revelation?"

I pinch the bridge of my nose.

"We haven't discussed it."

"What do you mean? That was quite the bombshell. Surely, she's had something to say about it."

I don't want to admit to my outburst the morning Lottie went missing or that things have not been the same since. I've apologised, told her I was angry and out of line, looking for someone to blame, but that's not an excuse, and I know it. I said some incredibly hurtful things, when all Pen's ever done is the best for Lottie, for my family, and I threw that in her face.

"Elijah?"

"I fucked up, okay?" I say.

"What the hell did you do now?" Gabriel hisses. His protective streak coming out.

"Lottie told Pen about wanting to find out about her biological father. That she had spoken to Darra, who had shut her down."

"And she didn't tell you?" Caleb intercedes.

"No. And I said some *things*," I admit.

"Have you apologised?" Caleb asks.

"Of course I have. It's just everything is different. I feel like we're all walking on eggshells, and I just don't know how to make it right."

"Pen loves you," Gabriel says quietly. "If you've apologised then she'll be okay with that. She's not a teenager. But Elijah, how are you? I mean, really? This is a lot. Maybe, and I say just maybe, Pen and Lottie are all picking up on your confusion, your uncertainty."

Silence descends as I take in his words.

"I don't know how I'm supposed to feel," I admit.

My best friend and my girlfriend duped me into marriage, knowing I loved someone else. Lied to me and my family for years. That same friend moved in with my innocent sister, only to continue screwing my ex-wife. The whole thing is a damn train wreck.

"I don't know what I want anymore. Everything I've spent my life doing, building up, seems tainted."

"It sounds like you're having a midlife crisis," Caleb says.

"I'm not that bloody old."

"It's not about age. Something has happened that's forced you to reevaluate your life. You need to look at what you have, and decide what you want to fight for, what's worth expending energy on. If Pen is part of that, then fight for her. If she's not, then you need to let her go," Caleb says.

"When did you get so wise?"

"You won't like it, but I've been listening to Mum."

The thought of letting Pen go makes me sick to my stomach. The simple thought of her not being in my life makes my heart ache.

"I can't let her go," I admit quietly.

"Then what's holding you back?" Gabriel asks.

I look around myself. I'm not in the office today. I couldn't face it.

"Think about what Caleb has said. For the first time, I agree with my twin," Gabriel says, followed by an *ouch*.

"We'll leave you, but remember, we're only a phone call away."

"Thank you," I say as we end the call.

I get up and move to the kitchen. Zach has written me a long letter. I opened it but put it straight in the drawer. I'm not yet ready to forgive or forget, and I'm not sure I ever will be. If it had only been me affected, maybe, but he drew my sister into it. That I'm not sure I'll ever be able to forgive. Right now, I want to wallow in my anger, in the betrayal. For too many years, I've put other people's feelings first, above my own. Not anymore. He knew about the ruse. He knew I was in love with Pen, yet he kept it to himself.

My doorbell chimes, and I make my way to the door.

"Logan, come in," I say, stepping back.

"Hey, cousin. It's good to see you. Caleb and April have a good honeymoon?"

"They did."

Logan is a Frazer, the eldest son of Dad's younger brother. He's a couple of years younger than me, but growing up, we were close, until Darra.

He follows me into the living area.

"Your call was cryptic. To say I'm intrigued is an understatement," he says, walking deeper into the apartment.

"You kept it to yourself?"

"As requested. What's with all the cloak and dagger?"

"I want to show you something, and I need you to be honest."

My hand goes to the back of my neck, rubbing the skin, my stomach churning the same way it would before a swim meet.

"You know me." He grins. "I've made my fortune, being brutally honest."

I chuckle. It's the reason I called him. Logan Frazer is renowned for his brutal honesty. His articles in some of the world's leading magazines and newspapers attest to that. He knows his stuff, and as such is highly respected in his field. It's why he's here.

The past week has led to a lot of soul-searching. My brothers are right. Something does need to change. I don't want my future to look like my past. I don't want to be a corporate slave, I want to explore other possibilities, and this is the first step.

"Lead the way," Logan says.

We climb the stairs, butterflies roll in my stomach, and my mouth goes dry as we reach my studio door.

"Discretion."

He raises an eyebrow as if I need to state the obvious.

"Okay," I say, closing my eyes and pushing open the door to allow him to enter.

CHAPTER 61

PEN

I walk into the apartment to raised voices.

"Lottie, you need to speak to your mother," Elijah says, his voice getting louder.

It's been a month, and I know Darra's been blowing up his phone. Leaving messages everywhere, threatening to go to the press and let them know he's keeping their daughter hostage. She's even tried to call me, but I've blocked her number for now.

This is an argument that's been going on for days. Both of them are as stubborn as one another.

"No, I won't speak to her. How can you say that after everything she's said and done? I don't care if I never speak to her again."

Lottie's eyes fill with tears, her hands on her hips as she faces her father.

She sees me enter.

"Aunty Pen, tell him."

I hold up my hand. "Lottie, this is between you and your dad."

"How can you say that, Aunty Pen? She broke you two up,

kept you and Dad apart with her lies. She's a selfish bitch, and I hate her."

"Lottie! Do not call your mother that," Elijah shouts.

"Why not? It's true. She and Grandpa. I hate them."

Shit.

I hoped she hadn't picked up on that part of the argument.

"Your dad and I were never together, Lottie. We were very good friends, but that was as far as our relationship went."

"But you wanted it to be more. No one is surprised you're together. Even Granny is happy."

I shake my head. "The past is the past. It wasn't our time."

The words taste chalky, coming out of my mouth.

Is now our time? I really don't know.

I'm still struggling to understand how Darra played everyone so much. For years, she had two men dancing to her tune, but for different reasons. I'd be happy for Lottie to never speak to her toxic and manipulative mother ever again. But that's not what Lottie needs. Lottie needs to find peace with her mum, whatever that looks like. Darra is her mother, and whether she likes it or not, she needs to hear her out. Whatever she then decides must be her choice.

"Well, you can't make me," she says, turning around and storming into her bedroom, the door rattling on its hinges as she slams it shut.

Elijah turns and storms into the living room, raking a hand through his hair.

"Bloody hell," he seethes.

I move up behind him and wrap my arms around his waist. He stops, spins in my arms, and pulls me against him, his head resting on top of mine.

"I'm sorry you came home to that," he says.

"Give her time," I say, looking up, our mouths mere

millimetres apart. "Whatever she needs. If she's going to be receptive, she needs to be ready to listen to Darra's side of the story. If not, it could make things worse."

"I know," he sighs. "It's just I've had Darra calling her solicitor. I'm tired, Pen."

"Lottie is a strong, independent young woman. She has the right to make up her own mind, and Darra needs to accept that. She had her chance to answer her questions in the summer and didn't. She has to live with that. When the time is right, Lottie will come around. Until then..."

"For someone with no children, you have an amazing insight," he says.

A full three-sixty from the morning, Lottie went missing.

My stomach clenches at his words, but I force a smile.

"I was raised by a young, single mum. Life was not all roses."

He drops his forehead to mine.

"I didn't mean it. I will keep apologising. You've been one of the best things in my daughter's life. She wouldn't be as rounded if you hadn't stepped in when Darra and I were making a mess of it. You're one of the reasons she's strong and independent. You are an amazing role model."

My throat clogs at his words.

"I love you, Pen. I'm glad you're here with me. With us."

I raise my hand and cup his cheek, the butterflies finally settling.

"I wouldn't want to be anywhere else. I love you, too. I have for longer than I can remember. We can get through this together. But Elijah, you're shutting me out, and that's not something I can cope with."

"I'm trying, but old habits die hard. I want to be better. I like who I am around you. I'm looking at making changes. Please don't give up on me."

"Never, if that's what you truly want. But you need to be honest."

"I'll try my best. And when I'm reverting back, I give you full permission to kick my sorry ass from here to kingdom come."

I chuckle until his lips cover mine, his tongue teasing the seam. My hands snake up around his neck, pulling him closer.

We both groan as my phone rings.

Our foreheads touch again before I pull away, instantly missing the warmth of his embrace.

"Pen," I say.

"Is Elijah with you?"

"Kat," I say, flicking the phone away from my ear and putting her on speaker. "I've put you on speaker. What's going on?"

"Elijah, why the hell haven't you been answering your phone?" Kat seethes down the phone.

"It's in the bedroom. What's up?"

"We have an incident."

"What do you mean?"

"I mean, someone has hacked into the hotel's systems and has basically blown up my booking system, ordering everything."

"That's not possible. The firewall is secure." Elijah shoots me a look, and I shrug, confused, but I decide to step in. The siblings don't need to be arguing. This is about damage control.

"What do you know, Kat?" I say, holding up my hand when Elijah goes to open his mouth.

"I have the perpetrator on camera. One of the cleaning staff logged on to the hotel system using one of our terminals."

"Do you have him in custody?"

"No. We have a good picture. His credentials are fake."

Elijah blanches. His team run background checks on all the family's employees.

"Send the picture across. I'll see what our facial recognition software can find."

"Already done."

"Are you reinstalling the backups?"

"Yes. Thank goodness it's only affected this hotel as far as I'm aware. We're going to have to try to follow a paper, email trail, and hope we don't miss anything or anyone."

"I'll head over to your office and see what I can salvage. Leave Elijah with the investigative stuff."

"Thanks Pen. I'll tell the guys to expect you."

I turn to Elijah, who's already pulling up the hotel security footage.

"Oh fuck," I say, taking in the man's face, who stares directly at the camera.

"You know him?"

I nod. "But he's a ghost. A hacker for hire."

He's also supposed to be on our team.

"You know who he is?"

"I do," I admit, not wanting to lie to Elijah but knowing I can't give him any more information.

What the hell?

I recognised his coding style from the code inserted into the Frazer Security code, but to have hit the Frazer Hotel chain as well...

Something is definitely going on.

"You go, see if you can help Kat reinstall the backups. Ensure nothing else is amiss."

I step forward and into Elijah's arms, our lips meeting.

Elijah pulls back and cups my cheek. His eyes stare into mine.

"Take care. I love you."

I smile up at him.

"I love you too. Watch out. Someone is out for you. This cannot be a coincidence."

I call a taxi and make my way to the Frazer Hotel Kat mentioned.

My phone rings, Caller ID unknown.

"Tailor?" a man says.

"What the hell are you doing?"

"Saving your bacon and probably several hours of work."

"I got your message. *Subtle!*" I add with an influx of sarcasm.

Seeing his face staring back at me was not something I expected. Not when we're supposed to be on the same team. We've also been trained to remain undetected. He was taking a big risk.

"Mind telling me what the fuck is going on and how you're involved?"

"I was trying to prevent a disaster without tipping my hand. I thought the email delay was quite genius." His smug tone makes me want to hit someone. "A thanks for the heads up, would be nice."

"You always were a *little prick*, Needle."

He chuckles. "Not very original."

"I wasn't trying to be. I'm stating a fact."

"Look, I knew you'd handle the code issue. It's your level of expertise, after all. I couldn't give myself away. I'm deep undercover, you know that. Seamstress would not have thanked me for blowing years of prep. Not when I'm this close."

I know he's right, and I appreciate what he's done. But thank you is not something one says in our line of work. The connotations are too high. Owing someone.

"What the hell have you found yourself caught up in?" I ask, suddenly concerned he's putting himself in danger.

We might not be friends, but he is good at his job, and our country needs people like him to provide the intelligence to keep the rest of us safe.

"Okay, now I know you're involved. Who is behind it? Which organisation?"

"That's the thing, I don't know. I keep hitting a brick wall. We followed a lead, but it went nowhere."

"What do you mean?"

"I intercepted a message. Something about *teaching that young whippersnapper his place*. He was told to stand down, but it was clear he ignored them. Told them he'd see him finished the same way he did his father."

My stomach drops, and I swallow the acid that hits the back of my mouth.

"Tailor? You still there?"

"I am," I choke, trying to breathe past the lump in my throat. I switch on my gadget to prevent anyone from listening, including the driver.

"Does that mean something to you?"

"Robert Frazer died in a car accident seven years ago. It was reported as an accident, but it wasn't. He was run off the road."

There's silence on the other end of the phone.

"You think this could be linked?"

"I don't know. When you intercepted the message, did you get anything else?"

"I tracked the IP address, but it made little sense. It's a stately home. The guy who lives there is a fossil. I just assumed it had been routed. When the team investigated, he didn't have the equipment, and there was a full browser history. There was no sign of any foul play."

I squeeze my temple points, trying to stem the headache forming.

"And the name of the fossil?" I ask, already guessing the answer.

"Sir Leonard Crawley."

"That cantankerous old bastard."

Needle draws in a breath. "I take it you know him?"

"The man tried to use his position to threaten a friend of mine last year. Elijah stepped in," I tell him, wanting him to know what he stepped into. "He has a nasty reputation for making unwanted advances."

Needle sucks in a breath.

"He also doesn't pay his bills. I warned him I didn't work for free. Which gave me the perfect opportunity to call."

He can't risk exposing himself undercover, not when he's spent years positioning himself. Genius. By letting us find out about the sting on Elijah's company and work it out ourselves, he covered his back, just made his mole look incompetent.

"There's a flash drive under the second desk of the hotel library. It will reverse the virus and reinstall what it deleted if the backups aren't sufficient. Save you some time."

"I'll retrieve it when I get there."

He chuckles again. "You're welcome."

"I'm out of the game."

"You'll be missed. You're one of the best."

"Anything else?"

"Take care. If this guy is behind this, he's not working alone. He knows how to cover his tracks. As I said, they came up empty-handed when the team went in. All I'm saying is, be careful."

"I will," I say, my brain now firing wildly, trying to link together what I've learned.

"Before I go, just so you're aware, it's outside my remit, but I caught wind of it. I don't know what he has planned. But someone is going after the youngest Frazer."

My heart sinks. "Lottie?"

"No, Harper Frazer. There's chatter but no details."

"Shit," I hiss.

Harper is finally getting her life together after her father's death. The last thing she needs is to be derailed by some old man with a vendetta.

"Thank you, Needle."

"There she goes," he chuckles. "Don't worry, I'll only come calling if it's a life-or-death emergency."

"Make sure it is."

He ends the call as I pull up to the hotel.

Kat is waiting at the entrance.

"It's okay. I can fix this," I say. "We just need to take a detour to the library."

Kat frowns but leads the way.

When we arrive, I feel around under the desk, smiling as I pull out the flash drive. I look up at the camera in the corner, knowing Needle will be watching. It's what we do. When I said he was a ghost, I wasn't lying. I was, when I was working with him.

"What's that?" Kat asks.

"The vaccine," I say. "I want to check it first, but it should reverse the virus."

She stares at me.

"I don't want to know, do I?"

I shake my head. "No, you definitely don't."

CHAPTER 62

ELIJAH

Pen returns a while later and I sense immediately something is wrong. I've been pacing the floor after her call.

"We need to apprehend him," I say.

"No, we don't. I promise he knows no more than we do," I say. Needle is a first-class prick, but I'm not going to mess up his cover. "He gave us all he knows."

"What the hell do these people want with Harper?" I ask, running a hand through my hair.

"That's what we need to find out. I know it's hard, but we need to be sensible. If we go in all guns blazing, we could make this worse," Pen says, squeezing my arm. "Tell me what happened last year?"

"Not a lot. I made it clear to him that if he or any of his cronies went near April, there would be consequences."

"What did you threaten him with?" Pen raises an eyebrow.

"A few skeletons he thought he'd hidden. I made him aware he wasn't above the law, whatever his title, I'd hand my findings over to the police."

The dossier I collated made me sick. The number of women who filed complaints of abuse over the years. Women who, like April, had worked at various clubs around the city. Complaints that magically disappeared as they were paid off or covered up. I'd even found hospital records of accidents Mrs Crawley had suffered over the years. The woman was either incredibly clumsy or, more likely, someone else was involved. Then there's his son's fiancé. She disappeared, and although I could find no wrongdoings, something did not feel right. I read the other girls' statements after she disappeared. The man is a nasty piece of work. But then, after hearing him threaten April, I already knew that. However, having illegally obtained the documents, after I submitted them to the police, all they could do was file them and issue him a warning. However, his reputation was damaged.

"The police officer in charge may have had her hands tied, but she made a public statement by issuing the warning at his Gentleman's Club. She told me she hates men like him who use their power and privilege to control and hurt," I tell Pen.

"So do I. I'll make a call. See what can be done. Do you still have copies of the files?"

I rub the back of my neck. "I didn't exactly gain the information legally. It's why the police couldn't use them."

Pen grins. "Are they official documents?"

I nod, as most of them were.

"Then have no fear. The people I know will deal with that side of things."

"I really don't want to know, do I?"

She shakes her head. "It's in my past. But when the people I love are threatened, I'll use every tool in my arsenal to protect them. If he or whoever he works with is going after Harper next, then I'm going to stop him, bring him down. No one hurts what is ours."

She knows I will fight for my family. That's never been in question. To know she will stand beside me... My pulse races as I stare at her. The determination in her eyes floors me. She means every word. I've always known Pen cares about my family, but going into battle for them? She already stated helping me might open a can of worms for her. What will it mean for her if she helps Harper?

"I love you," I say, pulling her into my arms, knowing I will do everything in my power to protect her too.

She grins up at me and presses her lips to mine.

"Not as much as I love you. Now stop distracting me and get me those files. I need to make some phone calls."

I step back and head to my office. I pick up the phone and make a call of my own.

"Mum," I say. "We may have an issue."

"Please to hear from you too. I heard about the hotel. Kat told me it's under control, thanks to Pen."

"There may be more."

She moans. "Do we know where all this is coming from? Are they related?"

"Crawley," I say.

Silence descends on the other end of the phone.

"That old bastard. Never knew why your dad allowed him anywhere near this family."

"Was it a case of keeping your enemies closer?"

"I'm thinking it was. There was a lot more to your father than—"

She cuts off.

"I'm not a child, Mum," I say.

She sighs. "I know, but the past is done. Your father, gone. There's no point dredging it up when he's not here to answer any questions."

"True."

"What have you uncovered?"

"Apparently he's going after Harper."

Mum sucks in a breath. "Why?"

"We don't know. Maybe because the rest of his plan has failed. She's the baby of the family. The most vulnerable."

"Do you know what he plans?"

"No."

"Call Quentin. He may have heard something on the grapevine. If he has, I would have thought he'd have said something, but he may not know to look."

"I will. And don't worry. We'll sort this."

"I know you will. I have every faith in you." There is another pause. "Elijah, I'm sorry I didn't say anything. I honestly thought it was for the best. When you said nothing, I thought maybe you wanted to ignore it. When things between you and Darra got worse…I made a mistake, and I'll take that with me to the end of my days."

"Mum, I love you. I understand why you kept it quiet. But it was hard having to carry that knowledge alone. But you're right. If I'd known you knew, I would've questioned whether I should've done more. I may have lost Lottie altogether."

"I know," she says quietly. "We will talk about this some more later."

"We will."

I disconnect the call, open my laptop, and my hidden directory. I scour my files until I spot the one I'm looking for.

"Okay, Pen, let's see what your friends can do," I mutter.

CHAPTER 63

ELIJAH

When Pen enters the office, I drop the file directly to her machine. She hits a few more buttons.

"And now we wait," she says.

I pull her into my lap, and her arms wrap around my neck.

"We'll find out what he's up to," Pen promises.

"I hope so. Harper's had enough to deal with in her young life. I know I've been hard on her, but that's what big brothers are for."

Pen chuckles. "I'm not sure Harper would see it that way. But she loves you. Family supports one another."

My phone rings. Quentin's number flashes up.

"I need to take this," I say.

Pen moves off my lap to perch on the side of my desk.

"Quentin," I say. "I've got you on speaker. Pen's here too."

"Hi, Pen," he says. "What can I do for you? Your message was a little cryptic."

I fill him in and hear him moan.

"What is it with that man?" he hisses. "I've not heard

anything on the grapevine, but then I've not been looking. I have the family name flagged in case a story comes in, but he may know that. Our friendship is not exactly a secret. Give me a couple of hours, and I'll see what I can find out."

"Thanks Quentin. I'll owe you one."

"No worries. We'll speak soon."

He hangs up, and I stand up, moving towards Pen.

She grins up at me. "Your desk?"

"Why not? It will help me the next time I'm working late."

Pen's arms wrap around my neck, and she pulls me down. Our lips touch as her phone rings.

Our foreheads meet and Pen chuckles.

"Sorry, looks like we're wanted."

Pen answers her phone.

"We're bringing him in."

"We'll be right there."

Pen clicks off and drops off the table.

"Time to go. Let's see what the old bastard has to say for himself."

* * *

It's unorthodox, but they let me stand behind the mirror and watch as the officers questions Sir Leonard Crawley.

He sits there smugly. He doesn't even try to deny what he's done, but according to Pen's source, the man is bankrupt. Has been cut off from those who he previously classed as friends. As for associates, he's not giving anything away. It's beginning to look like what started out as a vendetta against me may have become a way to replenish his depleted cash. Selling access to the highest bidder through my firewall.

His lawyer is doing his best to keep him quiet, but it's like he wants the world to know what he's done. It's like he thinks he's untouchable.

"Do you know who I am? I am Sir Leonard Crawley. Twelfth Earl of—"

"Sir, I don't care who you are. There are allegations of espionage being laid out against you."

Crawley sits back and crosses his arms over his chest.

"I think it's you who doesn't understand, lad. They couldn't make the charges stick before. What makes you think you're any smarter than the last one who tried?"

He chuckles to himself like it's all a game.

The pompous old git really doesn't have a clue. Mum wonders why my brothers and sisters have so many issues with people of *our own* class. This is why. They don't live in the real world. Don't care about those around them.

Pen and Kat are shown into the room. Pen having gone to meet Kat at the entrance.

"No denial. It's like he's been waiting to be caught. He thinks he's above the law. It's sickening," I say, a sense of unease settling in my stomach.

"And you can tell Elijah Frazer, karma's a bitch. He threatened to ruin my reputation and my name. For what? That little whore his brother was fucking." The venom in his tone is clear. "Just like his father. He wasn't any more successful in bringing me down. He should take heed."

I suck in a breath. My father died in an accident. A tragic accident. A hit-and-run driver ran him off the road. They eventually caught the guy, only to find he was four times over the legal limit.

The police officer who's with us turns to me. I see the question in his eyes.

"He threatened my sister-in-law last year. I provided a dossier on him. Everything I uncovered in his seedy past."

"I'd like a copy, if you have one. There are several incidents that have his name attached to them. Including the disappearance of a girl his son was seeing." The officer says.

My blood runs cold.

"I'll have it sent over, again. But I have to warn you. I didn't get these legally. I probably shouldn't be saying that to an officer of the law, but it's why your colleagues couldn't use them before."

Pen steps forward. "Call this number," she says.

The officer takes the paper she's holding out and nods.

We turn and look into the room and watch as Crawley becomes more and more irate. It's like he wants to be heard, but isn't being given the recognition he wants.

His face grows puce with the vitriol he's spouting. The two officers with him try to calm him down but to no avail. His lawyer tries to halt proceedings. Take a break to speak to his client.

We watch in horror as Crawley freezes, his eyes wide and mouth open. His hand goes to his chest.

"Tell them it's not over," he hisses. "Tell him and that little spy of his—"

He cuts off, his eyes rolling back in his head as he slumps forward onto the table.

The officers in the room dive into action. One hits the emergency bell, alarms going off. The other pulls Crawley onto the floor and begins administering CPR.

The officer next to us calls for an ambulance, as Kat, Pen and I watch helplessly as they try to resuscitate Sir Leonard. An ambulance crew arrives in record time, but after twenty minutes they call time.

We all look at each other.

"*Shit.*"

CHAPTER 64

PEN

News Reports describe Sir Crawley's death as *a tragic loss to society. The death of a true gentleman.*

The reason for his presence at the police station is swept under the carpet by the powers that be. According to them he was assisting police with their enquiries, and probably the reason, his wife could not wait to assist the officers sent to deliver the news of her husband's tragic death. She was apparently more than forthcoming in showing them his hidden office.

A woman scorned and all that. After suffering years of beatings and infidelity, she got her own back.

The Seamstress has been on the telephone. She gave me the heads up about several up-and-coming arrests. His den was an Aladdin's cave of evidence for several cold cases. It looked like Crawley liked to keep trophies. Tapes of blackmail and extortion.

Three days after Sir Leonard's untimely death, the body of his son's fiancée, Simone Asher was found, perfectly preserved in a freezer in one of the estate outbuildings. This was the saddest discovery. She'd been strangled.

I give April a hug. She knew Simone, they worked together for a time.

"We all really hoped she'd just left," April says, turning to Caleb, whose arms come around her. "She was like me. She didn't have any family."

Caleb drops a kiss on April's temple.

"I've taken care of it," he says. "Her funeral is all in hand."

Elijah's phone rings.

"It's Quentin," he says.

Answering and putting the phone on speaker.

"Quentin, I'm here with Pen, Caleb, and April."

"April, I'm sorry about Simone," he says. "Unfortunately, I have further bad news."

Elijah pinches the bridge of his nose.

"I know what he's done."

My breath catches. If we were hoping the death of Crawley was the end, then we were wrong.

"Tell us," Caleb says, his voice monotone.

"I'm sorry, Caleb. They've released a sex tape."

My stomach drops, and Elijah's colour disappears.

"What the fuck?" Caleb says. "Are these tapes real? Surely, Harper wouldn't be that stupid. I know she went off the rails for a while, but—"

"I've tried to stop them from being published, but the gutter press are like a dog with a bone. Young heiress caught in a scandal. They don't give a shit. It's all about selling papers."

"She's twenty-four years old. Why would he try to ruin her?" Elijah asks.

"Who knows what slight he felt justified this? It may have been another way to make money. He will have sold these tapes for a lot. You need to get Harper to safety. If this story hits and she's on campus."

Quentin doesn't need to say anymore.

"I need Harper Frazer picked up and taken to safety," I say into my phone.

"A lot of favours you're asking, for someone who's out."

"Don't bullshit me," I hiss. My endless patience has now been stretched to its limit. "She's an innocent victim in all this."

There's silence on the other end of the phone.

"I'll let that one go, Tailor. Someone is already on their way to pick her up. They'll take her to her mother's."

I pinch my temples. "Thank you."

"You're welcome. Remember, Robert was my friend too."

"You found something?"

"Of course. The evidence Robert had gathered. It looks like he found out about some of Crawley's links to organised crime."

A sob catches in my throat, but I choke it down. Elijah shoots me a questioning look, but I wave it away, giving him a forced smile. It's up to The Seamstress and the people upstairs, whether the Frazers ever know the truth, that's not up to me.

I end the call.

"They're picking Harper up now. Let her know it's safe to go with our men."

Elijah leaves the room to call Harper. I sink down onto the sofa.

Caleb and April are quiet.

"Why Harper?"

I shake my head. "She's the baby of the family, the one you'll fight to protect. Why not go after her? If you want to hurt someone."

"This is all my fault. If Elijah hadn't stepped in—"

Caleb takes his wife in his arms. "Don't you dare. None of this is on you. If Crawley got what he wanted, you may have ended up like Simone."

April shudders. I doubt Simone will be the only body uncovered.

"We'll sort this out." Although at the moment, I don't know how. Not even my computer skills can work faster than the internet and reposting.

We may prove the tapes are doctored, but in the short term, it won't matter. There are people out there who love nothing more than to see the mighty brought to their knees. Whatever good the Frasers do, this will be a juicy scandal and there'll be those who lap it up, irrespective of whether it's true or not. Harper's reputation will be in tatters.

I run to the toilet and empty the contents of my stomach, finally giving way to the tears I've been suppressing since first hearing Crawley's words of hate.

CHAPTER 65

PEN

Two days later, experts have proven the sex tapes were doctored, but it doesn't matter. The damage is done. The press and broadcasters are having a field day, dragging up Harper's rebellious years in the time after her father's death.

The family is in crisis mode. Press are camped outside every office, The Foundation headquarters, and even April's dance studio. They're like vultures preying on a caucus.

Harper is asked to withdraw from her course, the principal's citing she's sorry, but the unwanted press attention is not good for the university's reputation. Going under her mother's maiden name and even with her new look, with her face plastered all over the papers and TV screens her anonymity no longer held up against the investigative journalists.

I don't think I've ever seen Elijah so furious, but Harper simply said she couldn't go back anyway, so it wasn't worth him causing himself an aneurism.

Harper is currently hiding at my house with my mother. The Frazer home and all her siblings are under siege.

"What now?" she says, coming into the kitchen. "I can't exactly hide away for the rest of my life."

"No, I agree. But you can stay under the radar until it's blown over. Your Mum and Elijah are working on taking the papers who published and distributed the material to court. Taking down all copies once they have been distributed—it takes time."

I don't want to add, it will be impossible. We remove one and it pops up on another three sites almost instantly. People may know it's not Harper, but it isn't preventing them from watching it, and it's her innocent face they're seeing.

"I made it onto daytime TV," she says, although there's a catch in her voice.

"I know."

I walk up and wrap my arms around her. The women had sat and gossiped about the tapes and what had been released. We can't sue as they were clever in making sure they pointed out the videos were fake, but it didn't stop their character assassination of an innocent young woman.

She wraps her arms around me.

"I was trying to get my life sorted out."

"I know," I say, squeezing her tightly, as if holding her will make it all disappear. "We'll get you back on track."

She looks up at me and shakes her head.

"I don't see how. I was incognito at uni. Now everyone knows who I am, and what's worse they all think they know what I look like naked. Not great for me, even if the uni says they'll allow me back. I'll have them all staring and watching, speculating...you know the saying *no smoke without fire*."

My doorbell goes.

"Wait here," I say, looking at the monitor on the wall. "It's okay, it's my mother."

Unsure why she doesn't simply use her key.

"Mum?" I say, throwing open the door.

Mum walks past me and into the hallway, unlocking and opening the internal garage door.

Franny steps out.

She wraps me in a hug. "Thank you for looking after my baby."

"Mum, what are you doing here?" Harper says, appearing behind me.

Franny lets go of me and holds her arms out to Harper, who instantly bursts into tears. She throws herself at her mother, her bravado of the past few days finally crumbling. Franny rocks her and we leave them with some space.

Mum and I enter the kitchen.

"Before you ask, I drove into a multi-storey car park. Franny jumped into the boot of my car. We made sure she wasn't followed."

I stare at the pair of them before chuckling.

"Very spy thriller of you," I say, earning myself a grin.

"I like to try." Her expression becomes serious. "Franny needed to see Harper. She has a plan to get her out of the country for a while."

"How?" I ask.

I know if Harper takes a commercial flight, she'll be spotted. If she takes the family plane, they'll simply track the flight path, and the vultures will be waiting for her. The story may not have been picked up abroad, but it doesn't mean it won't be if she is seen to be making a run for it.

Harper and Franny enter the kitchen. Harper's eyes are bloodshot. She gives me a weak smile.

"Hey, you needed to let it out," I tell her, running my thumb over her tear-stained cheek.

She nods, her eyes filled with so much despair. If Crawley wasn't already dead, I'd want to kill him myself.

"What's the plan?" I ask.

Knowing Franny, she will have dotted the *i*'s and crossed her *t*'s.

"My friend owns a fashion house in New York. She's offered Harper a place to escape. Continue her studies as an apprentice. She'll have to go under an alias, but the company is large enough that she should be able to disappear, at least until things blow over. I've been assured the story is but a side issue in the US. The Frazer Hotels are popular, but as a family, we don't warrant the same headlines there."

"And you trust this friend?"

"Completely," Franny says. "We go way back."

"How are you going to get her to the US?"

"The plane can take her."

"They can track the flight plan."

Her face drops.

"Let me see what I can do. Kris may be able to help. He's due over in a couple of days to meet with Elijah."

Although Elijah is very sketchy about why.

Franny and Mum frown. "You're still in contact?"

"Absolutely. Kris is my friend and always will be. Before you ask, Elijah is well aware. He is the reason Kris is coming."

The two older women look sceptical.

"He's also the reason I'm with Elijah," I admit, hoping Kris doesn't mind me sharing this nugget of info. "He sent me back, told me to follow my heart."

Harper grins for the first time in days. "I love that. That's *so* romantic."

Franny looks at me and smiles. "Remind me to thank the man. And there's no judgement here. Good friends are important, and if he's willing to help, he might just be the perfect solution."

CHAPTER 66

ELIJAH

"Are you sure?"

"Absolutely," I say, looking up from the draft document in front of me.

I meet his gaze.

"Does Pen know?"

I tilt my head. "Not yet."

"May I ask why?"

"You can, but I'm not sure I owe you an explanation."

He sits back, his arms crossed over his chest.

"I care about her. You know that."

My shoulders tense at his words. My heart rate increasing.

I stand up and move to the window, staring out over the city.

"I know," I say.

It wasn't that long ago the guy was going to marry her. They were going to settle down, start a family. If it wasn't for Crawley and his vendetta against me and my family, Pen would forever have been lost to me.

"Then, before I decide, I'll ask again. Why haven't you told her?"

I turn to face the man at the table.

"She knows you are meeting with me. She just doesn't know why, not unless you've told her."

He looks at me and smiles. "I haven't said a word."

"Then I could ask you the same question. Why haven't you said anything?"

"Intrigue."

"So my offer intrigues you?"

"I wouldn't be here if it didn't."

We stare at each other for a moment, each weighing the other and their words.

I sigh.

I lean back against the window. My arms are by my side, resting on the windowsill.

"You want to know why? Because I'm not doing this just for her. I'm doing this for me—for us. If anything, the past couple of months have taught me that I want and need to stop being a slave to all this and the past. I want a fresh start."

I sweep my arms forward.

He smiles, surprising me with a short nod.

"I get that," Kristophe says. "You're lucky to have her. Pen's a wonderful woman."

It's my turn to smile.

"She is. It's why I want to give her everything she's ever wanted and was stolen from her, from us." I run a hand through my hair and swallow against the bitter taste in my mouth. "I nearly lost her. I'm not prepared to risk that again."

"You did, but Pen's heart won out and I would never stand in her way. She would kill me for saying this, but I was only ever the consolation prize. She wanted to settle down, and I took advantage of that. Not something I'm proud of, but it aligned with my own desires and timeline. When I realised she was still in love with you." His gaze loses focus, as if he's caught in a memory. He looks up and gives a sad smile, his gaze catching mine once more. "I knew that kind of love. It's not something I was going to deny her if you felt the same." His smile widens, and even as a man, I can see why Pen was with him. "And from where I'm sitting, it's clear you do. But mark my words. If you hurt her, I'll be back. She deserves better than the way you've treated her." He sighs. "But the heart wants what the heart wants."

My adrenaline spikes and I bite my tongue.

She's mine.

I hate the fact she nearly married him. That he's held her in his arms, made love to her. Was going to start a family with her.

But I also know he's right and I won't deny it.

"She does deserve better, but I can promise you this. You'll never get another chance with her. I'm going to be there for her for the rest of her life, or as long as she wants me. Give her everything her heart desires."

Kristophe smiles. This time it reaches his eyes. "But giving up your life's work? It's not something Pen would expect. Are you expecting her to do the same?"

My laugh is genuine this time. "Ask Pen to give up coding? Her life's work? No. That would be like asking her to cut off her arms. I'll never ask her to give up anything. I simply want to offer her more of myself."

"What are you going to do? I know I don't know you very well, but I can't imagine you playing the role of house-husband."

"I have something in the pipeline," I say, but chuckle when I'm thrown a questioning look. "Not something I can share just yet."

"Fair enough. And Todd? He's capable of running the London office?"

"More than capable. He's been with me from the beginning. He was at university with Pen and I. Pen recommended him when she walked away from the company. He's been involved in every decision, sits on The Board. Has the respect of the workforce."

Kristophe stands up, his hand outstretched. "I've looked over the figures and forecasts. You run a tight ship."

"Did you expect anything else?"

"If I'm honest, no."

"So we potentially have a deal?" I ask, holding my breath.

"As long as the legal team is happy, then I am. I've wanted to expand into Europe."

It's the reason I approached Kristophe first. I asked Todd, but he didn't want that financial burden, however he has shares in the company, and I've agreed a deal where he takes over my role when I step down. It's a win-win.

"Todd is waiting for you downstairs," I tell Kristophe, clasping his hand in mine. His handshake is strong.

"Your sister," he says, moving to the door. "I've arranged for a makeup artist to go to Pen's. She'll change Harpers' appearance. Once she's on my jet, she'll be safe, I promise you. The plane will then refuel and head to New York. I have a stewardess uniform she can wear to disembark, and a car will be waiting to transport her to her destination."

"Won't an unplanned flight and extra crew member look suspicious?"

He smiles. "Don't worry. One of my stewardesses is remaining in the UK to visit family. Harper will take her spot on the flight if anyone checks. As for New York. The plane is set to pick up members of my family. I sent them there for a shopping expedition. There'll be no questions asked as it's bringing them home."

"I don't know how to thank you," I say honestly.

"You don't have to thank me, just make sure you take care of Pen. Her happiness is all I'm interested in."

"You have my word."

Kristophe turns and leaves the room. I look around. Frazer Cyber Security has been my life for the past fifteen years, built from the ashes of my old life and a broken friendship.

Now it's time to say goodbye, rinse off the bad memories, embark on a new adventure.

No ghosts as I step into the future.

CHAPTER 67

PEN

Kris enters with his friend in tow.

"Hey," I say, moving forward and kissing him on both cheeks.

"Hey yourself," he says, his smile warm and comforting, reminding me why we're friends.

He takes my forearms and holds me away from him.

"You look well—" he says. "Happy."

It's my turn to grin.

"I am. You can say I told you so if you want to," I say, knowing my grin must look like that of The Cheshire Cat.

"What me?"

I roll my eyes, enjoying the easy banter of a strong friendship. I wondered if it would be awkward, but it isn't. We've reverted to B.E. Before Engagement.

Mum comes out of the kitchen.

"Kris," she says, coming forward.

Kris stoops and kisses her cheek.

"Lovely to see you again, Louise."

"You too. Thank you for helping, Harper."

Harper appears in the doorway behind us.

"Yes, thank you," she says, stepping forward, her hand held out. "I'm Harper Frazer."

"Pleased to meet you, Harper. This is Tash. She's here to help transform you."

Harper smiles at the woman next to Kris.

"Shall we get started?" Tash says.

Harper nods and holds out her arm, leading her upstairs to where she's been staying.

"Let's get some tea on," Mum says, and I watch Kris grimace.

"That will be a coffee, Mum," I say, smirking at him.

"Of course," she says, chuckling to herself. "Come on. I've also been baking. I have fresh scones just out of the oven."

"Perfect," Kris says.

"So, how was your mystery meeting?"

"Interesting," he says. "That's all I'm going to say."

I harrumph. I know his meeting was with Elijah, even if neither man has told me why. To say I'm intrigued is an understatement, but if Elijah has said nothing, he has his reasons. I just need to be patient.

Having Harper stay here has meant he's stayed away. We've spoken on the phone, but his whole family has kept their distance. As our relationship is not public knowledge yet, they have no reason to suspect I'm harbouring the youngest Frazer.

We enter the kitchen. Mum has laid out quite the spread. Finger sandwiches, pastries. The perfect afternoon tea.

"This looks amazing, Louise," Kris says, taking his usual spot at the island.

It seems strange having him back in my space, even if it has only been a couple of months. So much has changed. My whole world has changed in that time.

Kris helps himself to food, Mum keeps up polite conversation. After a while, she looks at me.

"I'm going to see if Harper and Tash want anything," she says, making a sharp exit.

Kris chuckles.

"She never was subtle."

"No, that's my mum," I say, my elbows on the side, my chin resting on my hand.

"When are you and Elijah planning on going public?" he asks, taking another bite of scone, the jam and cream oozing over the edge.

"I don't know. We haven't discussed it. There's no rush."

"I hope you're not holding back because of me."

I smile.

"It's not been discussed, but also, I don't want any baggage. Talks of infidelity, rumours of affairs. There are pictures of us all together at Caleb's wedding."

He shakes his head. "You need to stop worrying about what everyone thinks. This is about you and him. What you have together. The rest of the world be damned."

"But what about you? You won't remain unaffected."

"No, but I'm in my forties. I'm a big boy. A few intrusive journalists are not going to ruin my day. I want you to be happy, Pen. And I can see that Elijah makes you that."

"He does. Thank you for making me face it."

"Isn't that what friends are for?"

"True friends," I say.

"Know I will always be there for you. Whatever you should need."

"The same goes for you, too."

"Does he know?"

I look up, my eyes clashing with his.

What the?

"Know?"

He raises an eyebrow.

"How?" I ask.

"You have the same glow Annie had. How far along?"

"I don't know. I've only just missed my period. I haven't even done a test yet."

"I may be wrong. If I'm not, congratulations."

My hand goes to my mouth, and the sickness I've been holding in for the past couple of days rears its head.

I run to the bathroom, emptying my stomach into the toilet bowl.

I lean against the sink and stare at my reflection in the mirror.

I swill my mouth out and spit the water into the sink, scraping my hair back.

Fuck! Could Kris be right?

I make my way back into the kitchen.

Kris looks at me, his eyes full of concern.

"Pen?"

"Don't," I say, my throat tightening, a sharp pain sparking in my chest.

This can't be happening. Not when we were so close. Why has life done this to us?

Kris gets up and pushes my head between my knees.

"Breathe," he says. "That's it. In for four, pause, now out for four. Slowly."

I concentrate on the sound of his voice.

When my breathing finally regulates, I sit up.

"Want to explain why the woman who was so desperate for a child of her own has just had a panic attack when she thinks she might be pregnant by a man she clearly loves and who clearly loves her?"

I pinch the bridge of my nose.

"It's complicated."

"Not really. A child is a gift, Pen."

"I know, and I am happy. Please believe me. It's a shock, not one I was expecting. I imagined we'd have more time.

We've barely found each other. This is not something we've discussed. We've hardly discussed anything." I shudder. "Oh, hell."

Mum takes that moment to reenter the room. I shoot Kris a warning look, which he acknowledges with a smile.

"Everything all right?" Mum asks, her gaze flicking between us.

"Fine," I say, patting her arm. "Probably something I ate earlier clearly hasn't agreed with me."

She walks up and places a hand against my forehead. "You do feel a little clammy. Maybe you should go and lie down."

"I'll be fine," I say. "I can lie down when everyone has gone."

Harper appears at that moment. I only recognise her because of the clothes she's wearing. Tash has done a remarkable job reshaping her nose and cheekbones.

"Wow," I say, making her laugh. "No one, and I mean *no one*, is going to recognise you. Especially with that honey blond wig."

"Tash has done an amazing job," Harper says, breathing a sigh of eager relief.

"Are you ready to go?" Kris says, standing up.

Harper switches her gaze to him, her chin goes up, her shoulders back.

That's my girl.

"Absolutely. Thank you again."

He smiles. "My pleasure."

Mum and I walk everyone into the garage, where Kris's UK driver has been waiting patiently.

Kris hugs me. "Take care of yourself."

I smile at him. "I will."

Harper is next. "Look after my big brother," she says.

I grin. "I will, if he'll let me."

"Oh, he'll let you. I never remember him being as free and easy as he is when he's with you."

"Thank you. Take care of yourself, Harper. You have the phone I gave you. It's a secure line. All your family members have one, so you can talk without the risk of anyone tapping into it. If you need us, we are here."

"You're amazing. Thank you for everything."

She wraps her arms around me once more, squeezing tight.

"Now get in before I cry," I tell her.

"Oh no," she laughs. "It was bad enough this morning with Mum and Kat."

"Exactly," I say, her outline blurring.

I blink rapidly, brushing a tear off her cheek. "Take care."

She turns and climbs into the car.

Kris pulls me in for a hug. "Look after yourself."

"You too."

My emotions rise to the surface as I shut the door behind them, closing Harper and Kris in together.

I hit the button to open the garage door and watch the car back out.

My hand goes up, even though the blacked-out windows prevent me from looking in.

"It won't be forever. Just until all this drama blows over," Mum says, running a hand down my back, the same way she used to when I was a child.

"I know, but of all the Frazers for him to go after in this way. Why her?" I say as the car disappears out of sight. I hit the button and wait for the door to close.

I follow Mum back into the kitchen.

"So is Kris right? Are you pregnant?"

I stop and stare at her.

"What?"

She shrugs. "I heard the tail end of your conversation."

I drop my ass onto the stool I vacated when Harper left.

"I don't know. My period is late. But I've been taking my pill. I haven't been ill or sick."

My mind goes back to me being sick at Caleb's, but I would have already been pregnant at that point.

"Why do you look so worried?"

I look up and raise an eyebrow.

"Oh, I don't know. The last woman Elijah was in a relationship with got pregnant and he was forced to marry her. Maybe I don't want history repeating itself."

"Is the child Elijah's?"

"Haha, very funny. Of course, if it exists, it's Elijah's. What do you take me for?"

"Then I'm not sure what the problem is?"

"Did you listen to a word I just said?"

"Every single one. But I still don't see a problem."

I stare at her, trying to work out what's going through her mind.

She shrugs. "It's not like Elijah has proposed. Even if he does, you don't have to accept." I open my mouth, but she holds up a hand. "Hear me out. Elijah is a grown ass man. He married Darra because he was young and did what he thought was best for everyone. He is no longer young and naïve. He also loves you. That is clear for everyone to see."

She steps closer and takes both my hands in hers, rubbing her thumbs over the backs soothingly.

"Elijah loves you. If it had been you who came to him fifteen years ago and said you were pregnant, he would have happily married you. The problem was not the pregnancy. It was the woman. He never loved Darra. He may have thought he did, at one point. But I think it was more ease. She was there, and she met his needs. She and her father wove a web of deceit and then she sprung the trap."

"But what if he doesn't want any more children? It's not

like we've had that discussion. We've barely been together three months."

My voice rises as I voice my growing panic.

Mum lets go of my hands and cups my cheeks.

"Elijah knows why you were marrying Kris. He knows what you want. I can't see him not wanting to make you happy."

"But I want his happiness."

"Oh, Pen, happiness…and I'm talking lasting happiness is give and take. It is a two-way street. Neither party can give up their heart's desire without serious consequences."

She must read something in my expression, because she gives me her best *Mum* look.

"Before you completely despair, speak to Elijah. He might surprise you. And if you only think he's doing something because it's the right thing, tell him you won't marry him until after the baby is born."

CHAPTER 68

ELIJAH

Harper calls me on our safe line to say she's on Kristophe's plane.

My phone pings again as she sends a picture on the group chat. I inhale, not recognising my baby sister. I'll hand it to Kristophe, he's been a tremendous help in getting her to safety and I feel better knowing he's there, especially now she's heading to a new life, albeit temporarily, until we can close down what's going on here.

My stomach churns at the thought of her being alone in another country. But Kristophe has reassured me. He'll be there to help, day or night. He has a vast network all over the country.

My buzzer rings and my heart picks up.

It's been too long. I throw open the door and pull Pen into my arms.

"I've missed you," I say.

My mouth closes on hers as I pull her into the apartment, slamming the door closed behind her.

She kisses me back with the same enthusiasm, a gentle

groan escaping against my lips as I pull her hard against me, letting her know exactly how much.

Her hand slides under my t-shirt, my muscles contracting sharply as she rakes her nails gently against my skin.

I pull my top over my head, walking her backwards and into the main living room.

Pen freezes. "What about Lottie?" she asks, pulling away.

"Really? I'm seducing you, and all you can think about is my daughter?"

She drops her head against my chest and groans. "You know what I mean."

I laugh. "I do. Lottie is spending the night with Dani. Girl stuff apparently. Not something I would understand."

I grimace, making Pen laugh. "She's growing up. Just wait until she meets a boy."

"Please, don't remind me," I groan, before pulling her back into my arms. "But, the positive, it does mean we have the apartment to ourselves for the whole night."

Pen gives me a smouldering look and I pull her back against me, our lips tangling as our hands work frantically to remove unwanted layers of clothing.

When our skin is finally bared, Pen spins and grips the back of my sofa, looking at me over her shoulder.

I grin and step forward, dropping to my knees.

"What?" she protests.

"I need to taste you," I tell her, closing my mouth over her centre before dragging my tongue from her clit to her opening. She's ready and wet. I tease her with my tongue, playing with her sensitive flesh. My tongue dipping in and out of her entrance. I hold her hips steady as I use my tongue and mouth to drive her higher. When she comes apart, I jump to my feet, lining myself up with her convulsing entrance, before sliding home. The walls of her pussy clamp around me as I slide in and out, picking up speed. She moans loudly as I drive forward, before withdrawing, her muscles clenching hard against my cock.

"You feel amazing," I say, dropping a kiss between her shoulder blades, my hand coming around and covering her breast, tweaking and pinching her nipples, the way I've found she likes. Pen stands up, her back against my front. I bend my knees slightly, but her height allows for me to continue driving in and out of her.

"Oh," she squeaks, her hands coming up and around my neck, pulling me down until my lips find the sensitive spot just above her shoulder.

"I'm going to come again," she says breathlessly, her amazement clear.

"Then let go," I say, clamping my lips onto her neck and sucking.

Her body trembles, her muscles locking. I speed up my own movements, pumping in and out, my own orgasm building. I drop my hand to her clit, to continue her orgasm until she is writhing and groaning. I pump in a few more times, her muscles driving me over the edge. I feel my cum spurt into her warmth, a feeling of contentment I've never experienced before overwhelming me.

"Marry me," I say against her skin, unable to stop the words.

Pen turns her head with such force I have to pull back to prevent her from head butting me.

"What did you just say?"

"I said. Penelope Dawson. Will you marry me?"

Pen stares at me wide eyed. Her top lip caught between her teeth. When it pings out, I notice the mirth in her eyes. "Elijah Frazer, are you really asking me to marry you with your cock buried deep in my pussy and your cum running down my leg?"

"I suppose I am," I tell her with a shrug. Withdrawing from her body and scooping her up into my arms. Pen lets out a laugh and wraps her arms around my neck.

I carry her through my bedroom and into the shower, before taking my time to clean her up. I finally wrap her in a large fluffy bath sheet, my towel knotted at my waist.

CHAPTER 69

PEN

"Marry me," Elijah says again, pulling me into his arms when we finally get out of the shower and get dressed.

I grin up at him. "Don't you think it's a little soon. Lust is one thing, but how do you know you're still going to want me—"

He stares at me wide-eyed, his arms snaking around my waist, pulling me against his chest, as my pulse picks up.

"God, Pen. Want you? I've wanted you for longer than I can remember. Forced myself to suppress those feelings, knowing I could never have you."

He looks at the ceiling before his eyes meet mine, the truth of what he's saying shining out.

"I've sat by and watched you date other men, knowing I had no right to my jealousy, or to you. In the beginning, I didn't understand what it was, but then as we got closer. After you nearly drowned and then my accident. It was like a weight around my neck." I watch his throat bob. "When you got engaged to Kristophe…I can't explain it."

His voice catches and I can see the anguish in his face.

He drops his forehead to mine.

"Do you know I was going to ask you out the day Darra told me she was pregnant?"

I freeze. My muscles cramping as I stare at him, a pain forming in the back of my throat.

"It wasn't my imagination," I whisper.

His outline blurs through my unshed tears.

"No, my love. Even then, you were all I could think about. But then, when Darra told me she was pregnant, I suppressed those feelings. I had created another human being, it was no longer about what I wanted. They had to take priority."

I sob and Elijah pulls my head against his chest, smoothing my hair, kissing my hair.

"I'm so sorry I hurt you. I wasn't sure you felt the same way. When you told me you were happy for me and Darra, I was gutted. I thought it was all one way, and I'd misread the situation."

"Jax never told you?"

"Told me what?"

"I went out that night and got incredibly drunk. I called him, and he collected me. Sat with me all night while I threw up. Made me drink some bloody awful concoction the following morning."

"He never said a word," Elijah admits. "And that would be his magic hangover cure. Tastes like shit, but is surprisingly effective."

"He's a good friend."

"He is. You were the only other person apart from Jax who didn't care about my last name. Treated me like any other pain in your ass."

I chuckle as a tear runs down my cheek.

Elijah catches it with his thumb.

"Don't cry," he whispers. "It's breaking my heart."

"I thought I was crazy, that I'd misread our friendship. I felt like such a fool."

"Why?" he asks.

"Because why would someone like you, tall, dark, handsome, intelligent, and wealthy, ever look at or want someone like me?"

It's his turn to stare wide-eyed at me.

"Why on earth would you think that? You were perfect for me. You are perfect." Elijah shakes his head. "If anything, you've always been too good for me. You're smart, beautiful, driven. Everyone you meet loves you."

"But you had Darra. She was the perfect girlfriend, she looked and acted the part. Everyone said so."

"Well, everyone was wrong. *Acted* being the operative word. Darra was all about my name. She even admitted as much before she announced she was pregnant. She wanted us to be the perfect power couple. Love never came into it for her." He sighs. "You saw my mum and dad. Love is what we were raised to believe in."

He drops his lips to mine, showing me in a single kiss the truth in his words, and something inside me thaws, a new warmth spreading throughout my body.

"I love you, Penelope Dawson. I've waited a long time for you. Please say you'll marry me."

"But we've barely spoken outside of work for the past fifteen years. It's been all business," I point out.

"And you think that's been easy? I built a wall. Initially, because it wasn't fair to either you or Darra. I wanted to give my marriage a chance. See if I could make something of it. But it takes two, and then when I found out about Lottie. It all seemed so pointless."

He pauses, his face twisting in pain.

"After that, Darra and my relationship soured. I still wasn't free. She held Lottie over me at every turn. However much I wanted to reconnect, I couldn't turn my back on my child or the secret I was being forced to keep. Reconnecting would have hurt more than I could bear. You were so successful. My family loved you. I was jealous of my brothers and sisters who got to spend time with you."

I raise a hand and cup his cheek, letting him know I understand.

"I wouldn't have expected you to. I love Lottie, and I'm sorry she was used against you. You're an amazing father."

"I had no idea you saw me as anything other than a friend. Not that I could have done anything. I would never have asked anything of you when I couldn't give you one hundred per cent of myself."

"So you built a fortress around yourself. Wanted to keep your troubles away from those around you," I say, realising the full scale of what he's been through.

Knowing the impact his disastrous relationship has had on the twins alone. Luckily, they met women who were worth fighting for, who broke down their barriers.

"I hate to say it, but you weren't very successful."

"I realise that now. At the time, I thought I was protecting those I love."

I look into his eyes and see the truth in his words. I lean in and gently place a kiss on his lips.

"You know, those who love you would have helped. A problem shared is a problem halved."

"I know. Only at that time, I felt trapped. I couldn't see a way out. Didn't think anyone would understand."

I get it. When you're in the thick of things, it's often hard to navigate a path through it, especially when you're isolated.

"I spoke to Mum. I know she said nothing for the same reason I didn't. It would have made the whole situation more complicated."

"I get that. But you also need to understand anyone who

loves you would have never judged you. They would have supported you."

"Maybe not. But I was my own judge and jury. But I'm older now. I don't care what anyone says or thinks. I love you. I want to spend the rest of my life with you. Have and raise a family with you, if that's what you want?"

The uncertainty in his voice steals my breath, and I choke on the air I've inhaled.

"You want more children?" I squeak.

He grins. "With you, I want a football team."

"But I assumed." I pause when he raises a brow. "Well, when you didn't have any more children after Lottie, I just assumed."

"It's dangerous to assume. You, of all people, should know that," he says, a small smile playing around his lips. "The truth is, I didn't want any more children with Darra. We didn't love one another, and I didn't want to bring any more children into a loveless marriage."

"Oh," I say, my heart rate picking up. Is it possible? "I…"

I realise how stupid I was to assume. But what will he think? My hand goes to my still-flat stomach.

Elijah watches my movement. His eyes sparkle as he drops to his knees. He places a kiss where my hand is.

"I would love nothing more than to watch you grow big with my child in here. To have you, the mother of my child, hopefully, children."

I bite my lip as yet another tear escapes and makes its way down my cheek. My hormones are already in overdrive.

"About that," I say. "We may have already passed go and collected our two hundred pounds," I say. "I'm late."

Elijah rocks back on his heels and stares up at me. "Are you serious?"

"I'm late and have been suffering some sickness. I put it

down to stress, but I did a test before coming over here and—"

"You're pregnant?"

I nod my head, not sure how he's going to take it.

"I'm not expecting anything from you," I say quickly, my hand cupping his cheek. "I don't expect you to marry me, you got trapped into one marriage. I refuse to do that to you."

Elijah is off the floor and sweeping me into his arms, swinging me around.

"You think I'm going to let you get away with not marrying me? Have you listened to a word I've just said? I love you, woman, more than I have ever loved anyone. I can't imagine life without you, and now you tell me you're pregnant. It looks like fate is stepping in once more and telling us we have to make a go of it."

I throw my head back and laugh. My tears are free-flowing now.

"I have to warn you. I seem to be prone to tears at the moment."

Elijah grins. "Then I'll have to work extra hard at putting a smile on your face."

"Oh, you do that, Mr Frazer."

His mouth slams down on mine, our tongues tangling as I sink into his body.

"I love you, Elijah Frazer, and I would be honoured to be your wife."

"Thank goodness."

I pull back, my hands resting on his shoulders.

"What about Lottie?" I ask.

"What *about* Lottie? You think she'll have a problem with us?" He takes my head in his hands. "She'll be thrilled. She asked me the other day if I was going to propose, if we might have babies. She loves her cousins. I had to all but drag her away from Leah and Gabriel's after Callum was born."

"It's just..."

"What?"

"I love her like a daughter. I don't ever want her to think that isn't the case."

My heart is still breaking for Lottie and all she's been through.

"And that's the other reason things will be fine. Lottie loves you, too. You have the strongest of bonds. One thing I'm learning, especially after everything that's gone on recently, is communication is important. You and Lottie already have that."

"About work," I say.

"The choice is yours. You can work or not work. I have something I was going to discuss with you. It was finalised today, but in all the excitement—"

Elijah pauses, and I incline my head.

"I'm selling Frazer Cyber Security," he says.

I stare at him for a moment. "Wow, that's not what I was expecting you to say."

"I want to change my life. Not in a midlife crisis kind of way, but I've realised life is too short."

He leads me to the sofa, and we sit down.

"Darra was right when she said she was married to a workaholic. I have been. It's been my crutch for too many years, a distraction from my day-to-day life. Since you've come back into my life, I've realised I don't want to be locked in an office from six AM until midnight, be on call twenty-four seven, three hundred and sixty-five days a year. I want to start enjoying life again, the way I did when I was swimming."

"But you were always so animated about Frazer Cyber Security in the beginning," I say, confused by what he's saying.

"I was when I was about to be working with my best

friend, but after she was forced to bail on me." He shoots me a wink. "That same company became a means to an end. A way to support a wife and child. Yes, I've been successful, but I'm a driven man. I can't do anything by halves. That's just who I am."

"What do you plan to do? I take it you do have a plan."

I know Elijah too well. He's not a man to sit around and twiddle his thumbs. He'd be bored in five minutes.

"I want to paint," he tells me. "Come with me."

It's then I remember the room he showed me when Lottie went missing. We haven't had a chance with everything else that's gone on to revisit the little nugget I knew nothing about. Elijah, The artist.

Elijah gets up and drops a quick kiss on my lips before taking my hand and pulling me after him. We make our way upstairs and towards his art studio. He presses on the keypad until the door unlocks.

As with the first time we entered, I'm hit with the smell of oil paint and turps.

The next is the light. The room has floor-to-ceiling windows, letting in an enormous amount of natural light. Not something I'd really taken in the last time I was in here.

I walk forward and stare at the picture on the easel. A half-finished painting of me.

"Elijah, it's…"

"This is my other passion… besides you."

"But Kat, Gabriel, no one has ever said anything."

"That's because they don't know."

"How do they not know? You're incredibly talented. Anyone with half an eye can see that."

"Only my mother knows, and Lottie, and now you and my cousin, Logan. I invited him around to see what he thought."

"And?"

"He wants to exhibit my work, represent me. Already has some potential buyers for a few of the pieces."

My jaw drops.

"He owns galleries around the world and wants to showcase me."

"I know who Logan Frazer is. He's one of the world's foremost art dealers, come critic. Elijah, that's huge!"

"Do you remember the paint-by-numbers set you gave me when my ankle was broken?"

I spin to face him. "I gave that to you as a joke. To make you smile."

"Well, the joke turned out to be a life changer. I did that one, then ordered more. My therapist saw it as a positive. Mum enrolled me in art classes. I had a teacher come to the house twice a week during my recovery. I've never stopped from that moment on."

"You mean to tell me you've been painting for fifteen years, and no one knows... Lottie..."

He grins at me sheepishly.

"Painting is something Lottie and I do together. She might not be my biological daughter, but we share a lot of common interests. Swimming, art...not so much computers. She prefers to use her creative side."

"I support you in whatever endeavours you choose. I shall look forward to standing next to you at your first exhibition."

Elijah swings me into his arms. His voice is breathless.

"I want to marry you, raise a family, and paint. I know how much your job means to you, and this way, you'll know you can go to work, and I'll be around. Or you can stay home with me. The choice will be yours."

I suck in a breath, my heart rate increasing to almost painful levels.

"Yes, yes, yes... yes to everything. To marrying you, to

raising a family with you. A thousand yeses to you painting. You are so talented. Yes to being your partner in life, of growing old together. I'll not be repeating your initial proposal. It's a little x-rated for our future grandchildren. But I love you, Elijah Frazer, and I can't imagine life without you."

His lips touch mine, and that is the last thing we say for a while as we cement our love on his art room floor.

"What next?" Elijah says as we lie in each other's arms. "I understand you protecting Kristophe's feelings, but what about us? We've both spent so many years putting other people's feelings above our own. It's finally our time, and I don't want to wait."

"Kris doesn't care," I tell him truthfully.

"You discussed it with him?"

"He asked when he came to collect Harper. Asked when we were going public."

"What did you say?"

"I told him we hadn't discussed it."

He grins. "I'm discussing it now."

I pull back and smile. "I can see that. Whenever you're ready. I can see the headlines. Frazer Cyber Security sold to wife's ex-fiancé."

"It does have quite a good ring to it."

"I think so, too."

CHAPTER 70

ELIJAH

SEVEN MONTHS LATER

Pen sits down with a grimace.

"Shit," she mutters. "If I get any bigger, I'm going to need you to purchase haulage equipment."

I bend down and drop a kiss on her lips.

"You're beautiful. Even if you do require help to get up."

She flips my arm with the back of her hand and grins.

"Good thing you've spent all those years working out. Hauling me out of the bathtub last week... I wasn't even sure you were going to manage it."

"Hey, that's not fair. You were covered in soapsuds, and I didn't want to drop you."

Pen grins, and I drop down onto the sofa beside her, pulling her into my arms. My hand goes to her stomach, where I'm immediately greeted by a sharp movement under my hand.

"Little Frazer wants to say hi to Daddy," Pen says as the kicking continues.

I move my hand, only to have it followed. My heart melts, and my throat clogs.

"Not long now, little one," I say, untangling myself and placing a kiss where the last kick or punch came in.

Pen runs a hand through my hair as I rest my cheek against our child.

"The cake has arrived!" Lottie runs into the room, her excitement palpable. "Oh, Dad, leave my little sister or brother to rest," she says.

"I notice you changed it around this time," Pen says, grinning up at Lottie.

I look at my daughter, who winks.

"Can't be giving it away by accident," she says.

Lottie is the only one who knows the baby's sex. Pen thought it would be fun for her to be involved in the gender reveal. Although she's had help from Mum, Louise, and April in organising today's party. Lottie is the only person who knows what the cake will reveal.

I chuckle and hold out an arm, inviting her to join us. She drops down next to us, her arm stretching around me, resting on Pen's stomach.

"Hey, baby. I'm counting down the weeks," she says, her eyes sparkling.

To say Lottie is excited about the imminent birth of her sibling is an understatement. Even with the birth of Leah and Gabriel's identical twin girls, three and a half months ago, and little Callum growing up fast, she's declared this is her own sibling, one she doesn't have to give back or share. Pen laughed and told her she may not feel that way, once her baby brother or sister makes an appearance and is crying or taking her things. But she's adamant, and knowing Lottie, she's going to be an amazing big sister. Even dirty nappies don't seem to be a deterrent. She's been helping Leah with the twins to get in some practice.

"Why are you so excited? You're the only person who knows, apart from our doctor, what the cake reveals," I say, pulling her close.

"Exactly," she says, grinning up at me. "And I'm guarding it with my life. No peeking, Dad."

"As if I would."

Both she and Pen look at me as if they don't believe me.

"Hey, I'm hurt, you two."

"Ha, the man who has spent his life running checks on people," Pen says.

"That's my job."

"Is that so? How many times have you tried to get me to drop hints about whether you and Pen are having a boy or a girl?"

I shrug and grin. She has a point. She places her hands on her hips and raises an eyebrow.

"It's okay. I've locked the cake in Grandpa's old office," Lottie says. "No one is getting a preview. Not that you have much longer to wait. You really have waited until the last minute," Lottie says as Pen shifts on the sofa. I know she's struggled over the past couple of nights, trying to get comfortable.

"Need a hand?" I ask.

Pen shakes her head, her brows furrowing.

"No, it's just this ache is getting worse. My lower back."

She groans and I help to move her forward, massaging the area she's rubbing.

"How long has it been going on for?" Lottie asks.

"A couple of days, but it's definitely getting more acute. Your brother or sister is getting antsy."

"Are you sure it's not contractions? I was reading on the internet that sometimes contractions can be an ache, especially at the beginning."

I look between Pen and Lottie.

Shit.

Lottie's not kidding. I thought I was the one who had read up on everything.

"It's early," Pen says, her eyes locking on my daughter's.

"But not that early. Eight and a half months. When they've already told you you're having a big baby," Lottie kindly reminds Pen.

Pen's hand goes to her back, and she begins to rub circles again.

"Help me get up," she says. "I'm sure if I move around a bit."

Lottie and I stand in front of Pen, and each hold out a hand. She grins at us as we haul her to her feet.

"Oh crap," Pen says, looking down.

My eyes follow hers, widening at the wet patch now soaking its way through her trousers.

"Looks like I was right," Lottie says, heading for the door. "Granny," Lottie yells as she disappears before reappearing quickly.

"Don't just stand there, Dad. I'll grab Pen's bag and the baby stuff. You need to get to the hospital."

As if given an electric shock, I cradle Pen's face in my hands, my lips landing on hers.

"Hey, beautiful. You ready?"

"No." she grins. "But it's a bit late for that now."

Her hand goes to her stomach, running it lovingly over her enormous bump. When I told her, I couldn't wait to see her swollen with my child. I meant it and still mean every word.

I take her arm and lead her to the door. Lottie reappears with one of Pen's pregnancy skirts and a clean set of underwear.

"Thought you might like to change before we go," she says breathlessly.

"Lottie, I love you," Pen says, grabbing Lottie and pulling her in for a hug. "What would I do without you?"

"You'd have to deal with Dad all by yourself." She grins and shrugs. "Dad, stop standing there and help the mother of your child, my baby… oops, nearly. Get out of her wet trousers and into something more comfortable. Uncle Caleb has brought the car around and is waiting for you. He's put the bags in the boot."

I jump into action, my head spinning. This is so different from Lottie's birth. Darra had been induced. It had been calm until the contractions had really hit, but we had already been at the hospital.

Lottie and I help Pen into her skirt.

"I love you, Penelope Dawson," I say, leading her into the hallway and down the stairs, my arm wrapped around her ever-expanding waistline.

Pen breathes deeply.

"Back at you, big man. Let's do this," she says, her eyes shining. "I think you were right about the contractions, Lottie," Pen says, her white knuckles gripping the banister.

Lottie grabs her phone.

"Tell me when the next one hits."

We make it halfway down the stairs when Pen bends double.

I curse under my breath.

"Okay, let's go with the next one," Lottie says, her eyes meeting mine.

We continue making our way slowly down the stairs and across the hall when Pen is hit with another contraction.

"Er, Dad, that was barely three minutes. I think we need to speed this whole process up, or I'm not sure you're going to make it to the hospital."

Mum appears next to me.

"I'll call an ambulance."

I scoop Pen up into my arms.

"No need, Caleb is waiting. We've got this."

Mum rushes forward and opens the front door. Taking Pen's hand in hers, she smiles.

"Hey, Franny, sorry to ruin the party, but I think your grandchild wants to be a part of it."

"Same as its father. Elijah made an impromptu appearance, so it definitely runs in the family. Now get yourself to hospital, labour is enough drama for one day. A home birth… I think we can live without."

Her arm snakes around Lottie's shoulder.

"We'll follow later."

I make my way through the front door, Pen still in my arms. Caleb hops out and opens the back door.

"Your chariot awaits," he says, making Pen chuckle.

"Thank you, kind sir, but can we get a shift on?"

"At your service."

The rest of the family has followed us out of the house.

"No one touches that cake," Lottie says, "Now we wait and see."

I run back and pull her in for a hug.

"We'll see you later," I tell her.

"Dad, go! Get Aunty Pen and my baby… whatever… to the hospital."

"Still no hints?"

She grins.

"Go!"

I sprint back to the car and buckle up. It's going to be a nerve-wracking drive with the hospital fifty minutes away.

CHAPTER 71

PEN

I look down at the bundle in my arms. Tiny eyes blink up at me, and a nose and mouth scrunch as they take in the world. The pressure in my chest grows, and I draw in a ragged breath.

Elijah smooths the damp hair back from my forehead. I look up, his gaze stealing my breath. Who would have thought... it's taken us sixteen years to get here, but life couldn't be more perfect.

"You were amazing," he says, his lips meeting mine.

It's been a tough couple of hours. By the time Caleb got us to the hospital, I was already in the final stages. No time for pain relief. It was all down to listening to my midwife and pushing. And boy, did I push!

"I was, wasn't I?" I chuckle, my free hand coming up and cupping his cheek. "I love you, Elijah Frazer."

"I love you, Penelope Dawson, soon-to-be Frazer."

I scoot over on the bed, and he drops himself next to me, pulling our daughter and me into his arms.

"Whenever you're ready, I know there's someone desperate to see you both," Elijah says.

"Oh my goodness, Lottie's outside? Why didn't you say? Send her in. She needs to meet her baby sister," I say, wanting to share this moment with her.

Elijah moves to the door and opens it. He says something to whoever is outside.

Lottie appears in the doorway, her movements cautious, her eyes instantly locking on the bundle in my arms before flying to meet mine.

"Come over here," I say with a grin. "Meet your baby sister."

Lottie lets out a choked sob as she rushes to my side.

"Are you okay?" she asks, her eyes running over me.

"A little tired, but it was worth every second," I say, moving my arm to give her a better view of her baby sister.

Her eyes drop to the little bundle snuggled into my chest.

She reaches out a hand, her finger crooked, but she pauses, her eyes going to mine.

"You can touch her. Hold her if you want."

She stands up, her eyes moving to her dad.

He appears at her side, his arm sliding around her shoulder.

"She's beautiful," Lottie whispers.

"I take it the cake is pink?"

Lottie looks up and grins. "I have no idea."

We both shoot her a surprised glance. Lottie shrugs.

"I simply handed them the envelope you gave me and asked them to make a cake to match whatever was inside."

"So you didn't know?" Elijah and I say together.

"How could you resist?" Elijah asks.

Lottie looks up at him and grins.

"I didn't want to mess up and give it away. It's been more fun this way," she says. "Plus, the surprise has been amazing. Waiting with Uncle Caleb and the others, who are all outside in the waiting room, dying to meet my baby sister."

"They can wait," Elijah says, giving her shoulder another squeeze. "There will be plenty of time for them. This is our family time."

He leans down and scoops our tiny daughter into his arms. She almost disappears from sight.

"Take a seat. Your baby sister needs to meet you properly," he says.

My eyes mist over as I watch him cradle our child against his chest. As if sensing my gaze, he turns and smiles, my heart catching. I never realised it was possible to love someone else this much.

Lottie turns, almost diving into the nearby armchair. Elijah gently lowers the baby into her arms, and I watch as my soon-to-be step-daughter/goddaughter, holds her baby sister for the first time.

"Hey," she whispers, her voice catching. "I'm Lottie, your big sister and number one fan. We're going to have so much fun together. I can't wait to introduce you to the world."

I swallow against the lump forming in my throat. A tear tracks its way down my cheek. Damn these hormones. I have no doubt Lottie will be the best big sister a girl could ever want. How have I got so lucky?

Lottie looks up at me, her brows creasing as she takes in my tears.

"Are you okay?"

"I'm good. Just loving seeing you together," I tell her truthfully. "She's so lucky to have you as her big sister."

Lottie smiles shyly. "Have you decided on a name?" she asks.

"Amelia Brooke Frazer," Elijah says.

His eyes never leave his two daughters, although my hand is now tightly clasped in his.

"That was the name I chose," Lottie says, her eyes wide.

"It is, and we decided it was perfect. Another story you'll be able to share with her as she gets older," I say.

Amelia turns her head and starts to nuzzle Lottie.

"Someone's hungry, I think," Elijah says, scooping Amelia up and placing her in my arms.

I fumble with my top and watch as our daughter takes a couple of attempts to latch on. My heart melts as I look up and find my new family watching us.

"I love you guys," I say to them.

"We love you too. Always and forever."

EPILOGUE

KAT

"Ms Kathryn, welcome onboard," Claudia says.

"Thank you, Claudia. It's good to see you again."

I make my way into the family jet and place my laptop on the table. I'm glad for once, we have a bedroom, and I can hopefully finish up what I need to do, and then get some sleep. It's going to be a crazy week if I hope to get all the issues sorted in time.

"I'll leave you to it," she says. "Captain says we'll be ready for take-off in about fifteen minutes. Can I get you anything?"

I drag my water bottle out of my bag and shake it.

"I'm good."

I need to keep my wits about me. I have too much to do, however tempting several gin and tonics sound right about now.

I take my seat and strap in as the engines begin to whirl. It's a good thing I don't mind flying. This job certainly has me racking up air miles.

I lean back and close my eyes as we take to the sky. The change in pressure makes my ears pop, and my stomach sink.

As the plane rights itself, the door at the back of the cabin opens and I sit up sharply, my heart rate increasing.

I turn my head sharply.

"What the hell are you doing here?" I say, my voice sharp.

"You've refused to take my calls."

He folds his arms over his chest before dropping into the seat opposite me. "Now I have your undivided attention."

"You know it's illegal to stow away."

"I'm on the manifesto," he says. "If only you'd checked."

My hackles rise at his smug tone.

"You always did think you were clever," I hiss, staring at the man in front of me, my body tingling as the ache in my chest intensifies.

"There was a time when you liked that," he says.

"That was a lifetime ago and before I knew better."

I cringe inwardly. Everything I thought was true has turned out to be a lie.

"You've wasted your time. I've nothing to say to you," I add.

If it wasn't time-critical for me to be at my destination, I'd have the pilot turn us around. Land at the nearest airport and order him off, but I can't. Somehow, I have a sneaky suspicion he knows that.

"It's a good thing I have plenty to say to you."

ABOUT THE AUTHOR

Zoe Dod writes emotionally intense billionaire fiction, with complex characters, swoon-worthy romance and a host of plot twists that will leave you guessing until the end. Her books are written in British English.

Prior to becoming a writer, Zoe began her working life as a software development manager in The City of London. In her mid-thirties she retrained as a primary school teacher, and loved teaching children to write and tell stories. She left teaching to spend more time with her family, and it was then she uncovered her love for writing romance.

Zoe lives in The New Forest, Hampshire, England with her husband, two adult children (when they're back from uni) and her fur babies.

She loves reading and writing. When she's not doing either of those, she's on long walks in The New Forest or attending Zumba classes

Sign up for her monthly Newsletter www.zoedod.com
   You can follow Zoe on
   Instagram: @zoedod_author
   Facebook: Zoe Dod - Author
   Tik Tok: @zoedod_author

ALSO BY ZOE DOD

<u>Forgive Me Series</u>
Always You
Only You
Until You

<u>The Frazer Billionaires</u>
The Donor Billionaire (Gabriel's story)
The Playboy Billionaire (Caleb's story)
The Broken Billionaire (Elijah's story)
The Ice Queen Billionaire^ (Kat's story)
The Rebel Billionaire^ (Harper's story)

* * *

^Coming Soon